A Kyame Piddington Mesmeric Thriller

Adventures in Second Sight

Volume 2

Barry H. Wiley

eISBN 978-0-6922-5478-3

http://amazon.com/dp/B00LP287CK

ISBN 978-0692691533

ISBN 0692691537

www.creatorofmysteriousstories.com

Acknowledgements

Personnel at the Monte Carlo Casino who requested anominity, and those in the 'kitchen' who very kindly answered my questions, the first being how many zeros in the European wheel, to which they stepped aside let me look for myself. The staff at the Boston Athenaeum who quickly found and delivered my multiple requests for articles from obscure journals, while tracking down obscure books on gambling particularly the book by Sir Hiram Maxim. and whose shelves had the two books by Victor Bethel that first triggered the initial plot ideas for Kyame's second adventure.

Thank you ladies and gentlemen.

Here is wisdom. Let him that hath understanding count the number of the beast:

for it is the number of a man; and his number is

six hundred threescore and six.

Book of Revelation, Chapter XIII, Verse 18.

Lobby Bible (King James Version)

Hotel de Paris, Monaco

1896

Let him consider his system wisely:

that the numbers of the wheel total the number of a man;

six hundred threescore and six.

V. B.

Monte Carlo Roulette Systems

Friday Evening, January 10, 1896

Hotel Hermitage

Monaco

Behind the man the Dog's Head promontory, Tête de Chein, rising high above the shifting sea, was limned against a slim moon. Dressed in "climbing black" as he thought of his working clothes, he turned and looked back at the hotel wall. Third floor ... third balcony from the right. There were no night sounds, except an occasional muffled feminine laugh -- a gruff male tobacco cough.

Tonight was different from so many other nights. Tonight he did not steal for himself -- he didn't really need any more money to continue to live the life of which he had always dreamed -- in a small comfortable villa above the bustle of Cannes, above the inviting beach -- and above the ever tossing suspicious sea.

He grinned as he shook his hands to loosen his fingers, warm the blood. After tonight, there would be none of the usual problems of identifying the correct connoisseur to purchase the stones of particular distinction and notoriety that would lay hidden in his valise. Rather tonight, he shook his head, he did not really even steal -- it was more of a simple transaction.

He was performing an Imperial service for a fee of 150,000 gold Marks, a fee he had confirmed three hours earlier had been transferred into his special account in a small bank in Rome. In addition, any and all police records relating to his past work in one of the principal European countries would be expunged -- permanently. That promise was unshakable. It came directly from the crown himself.

All, he smiled, shifting his shoulders a last time, assuming a successful night.

But, had it not been for an awkward mistake four months ago, he would not even be here tonight, regardless of any fee. That mistake was sharp in his mind, in order to avoid any possibility of a repeat. He had trusted the wrong person, a misjudgment that had breached the wall of anominity he had erected with such care, and had enjoyed so many months.

Invisible in black, he moved silently through the tailored bushes and flowering shrubs to the base of the hotel wall. He recovered the short ladder he had left there in the early afternoon during a brief but hard rain shower that had driven everyone inside. It would raise him to the first ledge. From there he would find his way with "fingers and toes" -- as he had once explained to a beautiful, marvelously naïve French woman one night in Marseilles who had been easily convinced that he was a retired special intelligence agent of the French *Deuxième Bureau*, much like a dashing character from equally naïve romantic fiction.

***

He pulled himself up and over the railing of the balcony. There was some pain in his back – from too much relaxation. He grinned under his mask. True, he needed more frequent exercise, but not practice.

The moon, like a guilty accomplice, had withdrawn her light behind a cloud. A soft step, another, and he stood at the partially opened French doors. There were only the sounds of deep slumber of the man and his wife. He automatically touched his pocket to confirm the critical material was still in place after his rapid climb.

The door swung silently open. He knelt, then went to his hands and knees as he entered the room. His target was the suit coat that the Count de Dagoneti had worn earlier that day at the Monte Carlo Casino. The closet was on the other side of -- but no! -- the coat was thrown over the back of the chair at the dressing table. A gown was on the floor, silken to his touch. He smiled. They had been in a bit of a hurry. That is always best, for the first time of the evening -- then later, slower, more deliberate -- deeper.

He reached into the coat pockets one by one until he found the casino chips. He withdrew them, and replaced them with the chips from his pocket. Ten 1,000 franc new

Monte Carlo chips out; ten 1,000 franc new Monte Carlo chips in.

The transaction completed, he turned to crawl silently back to the French doors. Once on the balcony, he drew the one door back to its original partially open position. He stopped at the railing to listen. Nothing. The night itself was complete silence, complete blackness. The moon remained hidden.

He was over the railing and down the wall of the hotel to the ground in less than a minute. He left the ladder behind the bushes and moved quickly through the closely trimmed greenery. Crouching down, he reached a spreading tangerine tree where he had left a black bag hidden in its lower branches. There would be no outcry, as no apparent crime had been committed; but, as he had painfully learned over the years, *négligent difficulté entend,* carelessness meant trouble.

He quickly changed back into black evening trousers and a white double-breasted dinner jacket, straightened his black tie, brushed the soil from his custom-made Italian patent leather pumps, and, smiling in anticipation, strode down the marbled walkway toward the Jardins du Casino and then on to the Casino itself where he was known as Baldur, the Count von Trotha, a suitably modest title to explain his wealth.

Von Trotha would be welcomed at the tables by the useful elite as a cautious but successful risk-taker, and for his generosity to the needy -- needy gamblers, that is.

A satisfying night that had been -- ah, no -- unsatisfying. He had seen some exquisite jewelry on the dressing table -- had even allowed his fingers to brush lightly over it -- but had left it. Now, he wished he had taken it. It would be accounted as just another robbery of the carelessly rich on the Riviera and would not cause his client any trouble -- but, the deal had been *strict*, in, out and don't touch anything.

All right, then. He shrugged. The night was done. The tables waited.

Riveria di Ponente

San Remo, Italy

Sunday, February 2, 1896

The patient rolling surf whispered its eternal message of indifference to humankind -- and to the body it rocked gently in the sand. Washed clean by the touch of the sea, there was a large ragged wound across the man's throat. He was dressed in an unbuttoned white double-breasted dinner-jacket and black evening trousers, but his feet were bare. Both hands lay open to the sky. His shirt pocket held a five thousand franc chip from the notorious Casino that dominated the cliffs a few miles to the west

He would be rocked by the sea for yet another hour before the first morning strollers would discover his body, as the sea pulled back, retreating from the recurring foolish problems of humankind.

Secretum secretorum

Tu operans sis secretus horum.

[The secret of secrets;

Thou that workst them,

be secret in them.]

1

Shifting his burly body in his chair, President Grover Cleveland reached down, unlocked and opened the second drawer on the left in his desk. He withdrew the single paper there and, after pushing piles of documents aside, slid the deciphered cablegram across the desk to his former Attorney General, Richard Olney, and now his Secretary of State for the past eight months.

As Attorney General, Olney had put down the violent Pullman strike of 1894, an act that had made legions of new friends, as well as adding a new range of implacable enemies, but which had clearly shown that though quiet voiced, Olney was a man of relentless, even merciless will.

Gray haired with a heavy gray mustache and two years older than the President, Olney had immediately made his mark in his new position by upgrading all foreign

American diplomatic posts from Legations to Embassies, giving notice that the United States was diplomatically equal to all other countries, particularly European.

Olney noted the grim expression on his friend's large mustachioed face. Grover Cleveland's broad smile could light up a room. But now the well-lighted Oval Office seemed dark.

Cleveland had weathered politics at all levels, mayor of Buffalo, New York, then Governor of New York then President from 1885-89, and now at 59, President once again, since 1893 -- the only Democrat to be elected against a continuing flood of Republican control with his opposition gaining 100 seats in the House in the 1894 election; a very public reaction to the continuing national financial troubles of 1893.

Cleveland was publicly noted by both his critics and supporters for being average, only more so than most men. And though his political enemies persistently attacked his policies, no one ever attacked his honesty, or his willingness to listen.

Also, since July 1, 1893, with a secret shared only with his wife and with Olney, he had undergone difficult and risky surgery to remove cancer from his mouth. The recently inaugurated president had felt a roughness on the inside of his mouth, a roughness that seemed to grow. When it was confirmed as cancer, Cleveland wanted to keep the surgery absolutely secret, so it was carried out by three physicians in the main cabin of the presidential yacht, the Oneida.

Utilizing a unique cheek-retractor enabled the surgery to be done entirely inside the mouth and thus avoid any external incisions. Cleveland's entire left upper jaw was removed and replaced by a specially constructed replacement of vulcanized rubber that maintained the original contours of Cleveland's face, and, remarkably, his normal voice and pronunciation. President Cleveland addressed a special session of Congress two weeks later. No one in his audience had detected any change.

Tapping the paper, Cleveland said, "The English ambassador hand delivered that message to me half an hour ago, Olney. It is the subject of the utmost secrecy, even within the English government itself. Only the Queen and the Ambassador ..."

"And the code clerk at the British Embassy, sir," said Olney smiling. "Code clerks have mouths, too ... and sometimes grasping hands. We have had some experience with that ... from both sides."

Cleveland nodded agreement to his Secretary's clear point. "Yes, Olney ... certainly. I am assuming here a certain rigor in the English vetting of their embassy people ... but your point is acknowledged. As you see, the English Prime Minister, Lord Salisbury, is asking for our help in Southern Europe. He requests an answer from me within the week. But we have no help to give ... officially."

Cleveland pushed back from his desk, brushing his forefinger across his thin black mustache, a nervous habit as he collected his thoughts. He had a large map of Europe on a tripod against the far wall of the Oval Office which had been used in an earlier meeting. He tossed his hand toward it. "Salisbury requests we supply several intelligence agents to temporarily replace the agents that the English have recently lost. Six of them have been killed, in one way or another, in the past seven weeks. They have only one agent left operating in the area, in southern France. He's located in Monaco.

"And Salisbury has no other agents available he can send, not for at least three months … and, naturally, he wants to know why he has lost his people. He wants that information very quickly. Salisbury, as you can see in the note, is concerned that some kind of major threat is developing in southern Europe; but hasn't as yet been able to give it any shape, any details."

Receiving the cablegram back from Olney, the President dropped it back into the drawer of his desk and locked it. "Our problem is that the United States has no government vetted intelligence agents anywhere in Europe. And, except for that strange group you have assembled, Olney, your so-called Anglo-Oriental Marine Insurance Co., there is no one else I could call on. Even assuming that there is anyone in that group who could meet the need. Whatever it is. Even the British Ambassador has not been fully briefed on the specifics."

Olney stood. "I will apprise Judson Rowland immediately of a possible need. Mr. President, may I be blunt with him? I would bet my life on his integrity."

Grover Cleveland looked up into the bleak dark eyes of his Secretary of State. He had trusted difficult missions to Olney before. He nodded. "Tell him what you feel he needs and get back to me with your thoughts." As Olney walked toward the door, the President added with curt emphasis, "Sooner, my friend, sooner than later."

2

Villa de la Mirage

Nice, France

Tuesday, February 4, 1896

"Washed ashore! Where?" His broad face, with its heavily waxed Imperial mustaches, was severe and cold as he looked up from deciphering two cablegrams. A long saber scar along his right cheek bone flushed a livid pink -- a familiar warning signal to his men.

"On a beach near San Remo, Excellency. The body was discovered by a French family walking the beach."

He slammed his large hand flat on the desk, causing his nearby stemmed glass of cognac to wobble, almost tipping, then it settled back, a few drops escaping to the desktop. "You assured me, Bäcker" – stabbing his forefinger at his senior aide – "assured me that Trotha's weighted body would be disposed of far enough into the sea that it could never … *never*, damnit, was your word … never reach the shore!"

His aide, the Ritter Heinz Bäcker, shrugged nervously. "The cord, sir, the cord holding the weight had apparently been bitten in two by some shark or other creature. The strength of the tides are unpredictable ..." At the sharp wave of a hand, Bäcker went silent.

Johannes Friederich Wagner, to the public an astute, even crafty banker, a consummate womanizer, and a high-risk gambler on the tables at the Casino; however to the Kaiser, he was a senior member, a *Veertrauensmänner* – VM – a confidential man, of the new secret Imperial organization referred to only as N. A respected member of its new NIV – Fourth subsection of N, devoted to sabotage.

Wagner turned back to the cablegrams on his desk. "Trotha was a fool," he said "He had only to perform a simple service, for which I paid him handsomely, and then crawl back into his *kleine hütte* … his miniscule hovel in Cannes. He was warned … by me. But the fool spoke carelessly to an Englishwoman who, fortunately, is an Imperial friend." He examined one of the cablegrams, tossed it aside. "Call the good lady in question to confirm tonight at the tables ... and keep me informed of the Trotha developments."

The aide clicked his heels, turned sharply and left, closing the door gently, and gratefully, behind him.

Wagner pushed back from his cluttered desk. He stood at the window in his second floor office in the Galerie Charles III that looked down through the exotic gardens to the commanding white ornamental twin-cupolas of the notorious Monte Carlo Casino. He could feel his

7

blood beginning to pulse in anticipation. He smiled. Was it the woman, or the little white ball on the roulette wheel? Wagner turned back to his desk.

He would have to reinforce his mesmeric suggestion on the woman tonight.

3

Sturtevant House Hotel,

New York City

Thursday, February 6, 1896

"There is nothing in the Ten Commandments against gambling, Kyame," said J. W. Cadwell. "Only against blasphemy, betrayal ... and losing. Try it again. Your middles are smoothing out." He leaned over to turn up the wick of the brass table lamp. The winter evening was already growing dark, and after 44 years on the road as America's most successful mesmerist, Cadwell's eyes were beginning to bother him, as well as a recurrent tightness in his chest.

A tall, bearded man, his brown, but graying hair reached his shoulders, his beard now trimmed more closely than when he was younger. J. W. Cadwell had built a reputation for integrity both as a performer and as a man; and as also not someone to risk offending. His voice, various reporters had observed, could "bend audiences". His hands, however, had, when necessary, bent necks to their breaking point.

Yours truly
J. W. Cadwell

J. W. Cadwell

Kyame Piddington pushed an errant black curl back in place, riffle shuffled the cards, turned the top card face up on the deck, a three of clubs, then dealt four aces, the three of clubs never moving as each ace appeared, her finger position on the deck never changing.

"Good. Two from the bottom, one Greek, and one from the middle." Cadwell drew heavily on his cigar, his dark eyes never leaving her hands. "Now kings. Your Greek, by the way, Kyame, was superb." He shifted to another chair to watch her hands from a different angle.

A Greek was a card dealt second from the bottom.

With her long slim fingers apparently dealing from the top of the deck while actually dealing from the center, one king appeared, then a second, a third ... she cursed softly.

Three kings and a wayward queen. A queen of hearts who stared up at her with an insolent smile -- or so it seemed.

Kyame frowned. "How did I miss, J. W.? I had the kings culled in the center. Easy."

The bearded mesmerist turned the queen over and peeled away the king sticking to the back of it. "The deck is not clean, so some cards may stick together if you aren't careful. But your handling, whether shuffling blind or honest, is identical ... that is the key to all advantage playing, Kyame ... uniformity in all action. That is the inviolable rule. Along with another: control your anger. The advantage player loses all advantage when he loses his temper." He grinned, raising his coffee cup in a toast. "Your Papa would be impressed ... if he could be here."

Cadwell watched her remarkable face carefully in the lamplight. In the past weeks, even the casual mention of her brutally murdered father could cause her to tear up and lose concentration. Even with her hardened experiences gained from the age of eleven traveling with her father for five years throughout the towns and cities of the American west as The Impossible Piddingtons, a second sight act; seventeen was still too early an age to have lost both her parents: her father to murder, her mother to consumption -- and to now be alone with no family.

Cadwell and his wife, Margaret, had become her family as they could never have children, but then Margaret herself had died only three months ago after forty-nine years of marriage, and Cadwell now had to temper his own emotions.

Kyame had assured J.W. that her heart was settled, but she could still feel the sharp pain of Papa's brutal killing by the Bing On tong eight months earlier in San Francisco. Sometimes the agony stabbed her without warning. But now there was no change in her expression, only a roguish smile and glistening green eyes that could rip up the heart of any young man.

"Just like inducing a mesmeric trance, J. W. ... I need to be more careful, or I look like a silly fool," said Kyame, her jaw set. She fluttered and stretched her fingers. The two hour practice session in Cadwell's suite at the Sturtevant House was starting to tell.

"Cramps?"

When Kyame nodded, Cadwell scooped up the cards and dropped them in his jacket pocket. He glanced at the darkening window. "Almost time to meet Dr. Mar-Tan. We'd best be moving."

Their dinner meeting was not to be at the astrologer's elegant home on Doyers Street in the depths of New York's Chinatown, but at a small stylish restaurant, Scarlet House, next to an antique shop only a block from the brooding opulent four-story mansion of financier Collis Potter Huntington at the corner of 57th and Fifth Avenue.

Huntington was known as the last the Big Four, the four men who had created the Central Pacific Railroad, built the western half of the first transcontinental railroad, and who had established through their Southern Pacific Co., a virtual monopoly over all transportation in California.

It had been Huntington who had coined the expression "all the market will bear" as the SP priced the cost of shipping produce just short of the point where the farmers would give up and not plant again.

During his now infrequent visits to the West Coast, Huntington immediately became the most hated man in California; unless you had a deal to pitch.

Eight months earlier in San Francisco, Kyame had successfully placed the internationally known industrialist under a mesmeric trance.

Though Huntington was 74 at the time, Kyame recalled, always with some -- uneasiness, his large bald head, broad shoulders, his face concealed behind a stubby gray beard, but mostly his intense challenging, even menacing eyes, and, she smiled, his immediate assumed command of the entire room of wealthy men and women gathered that night at the Rosner mansion. Harry Rosner had paid for the mansion with profits from his illicit opium trading. Kyame had stopped that, and the "sharp Mr. Rosner", permanently.

But still, she had worked her mesmeric wonders with the industrialist -- "the unbridled capitalist" he was labeled -- giving him a deep sense of inner peace with her mesmerism, which he had acknowledged to the crowd, deeper than he had never experienced before. But Kyame had no desire to ever meet Collis P. Huntington again.

As they walked toward the restaurant entrance, Kyame noted the horseless carriage parked near the entrance to the Huntington mansion. In the growing darkness, the notorious contraption resembled a four-wheeled cart loaded with scrap material. Kyame had seen one for the first time only two days earlier when J.W. had picked her up at Grand Central Station. The horse of their cab had reared up in fear when the engine of the horseless cart had been started. Loud bangs, one very loud explosion, foul smelling smoke drifting across the street as other horses shied and dodged to get away from the fearful thing. Then, once two black-coated men had mounted it, the crazy thing actually had begun to move! Kyame had never seen anything like it as the thing slowly started through the traffic gathered at the Station. The carriages, omnibuses and carts immediately scattered in every direction. Finally

14

it disappeared behind its rapidly enlarging cloud of white smoke, snapping, banging, clattering into the bewildered street traffic.

"What is it for?" Kyame had asked. Their horse had settled down and with a last angry snort of defiance toward the disappearing beast had started to pull their cab again.

"It is, according to its inventors, according to the newspaper articles, the replacement for the horse," laughed J. W. "There are two now on the streets in New York. Most people simply want the police to seize the things and get them off the streets and out of sight. I, frankly, agree. There may be a replacement for the horse in the decades ahead, but that horseless carriage is not it."

Kyame had emphatically agreed.

***

As Kyame entered the restaurant, a bowing red-jacketed waiter held the polished glass door wide, Kyame observed that most of the antiques visible in the window of the shop next door were Chinese.

As she had been trained by Papa, Kyame quickly memorized all the contents of the window, then just as quickly determined how the descriptions of the objects, as painted fans, jade vases, lacquered incense boxes, and such would be "sent" by the silent codes she and Papa had worked so hard to perfect. The code had gradually become a second language for them, enabling father and daughter to

15

carry on a silent private conversation while surrounded by others.

She moved on, nodding to the waiter's gracious greetings. Kyame brushed her fingers against the crystal *bi* disc suspended from a heavy gold chain around her neck that she had worn each day since receiving it from Dr. Mar-Tan. Its presence beneath her blouse always enabled her to more sharply focus her thoughts, her powers.

Like any moments with Dr. Mar-Tan, Kyame knew it was going to be an interesting evening.

4

Guided by the gold and red liveried waiter, Kyame and J. W. Cadwell followed the young man to a private dining room.

"Your party is here, mademoiselle ... and sir." He pulled back the heavy red curtain and bowed.

As Kyame entered the room, Dr. Mar-Tan immediately rose and bowed to her. His smile grew wider as Cadwell entered. Turning to the two men at the table, who had also risen, Mar-Tan said, "May I have the esteemed honor of presenting the most remarkable young lady of my experience, Miss Kyame Piddington. Miss Piddington, this is Dr. Haroon Kahn, an old friend from the cold mountains of India; and Mr. James Dixey, an importer and the owner of the amazing shop that stands next to us ... and to which we will adjourn following our dinner."

Kyame nodded in acknowledgement and extended her hand first to Kahn, a tall, lean, gray haired and bearded man with near black but friendly eyes, and then to Dixey, blond, blue-eyed with a lethally attractive smile who stood about her own height. Each of the men bowed over her hand. Gathering her lustrous blue skirts, she sat at the chair held by Cadwell.

"And gentlemen, my most trusted friend, a master of the arcane arts, Professor J. W. Cadwell."

The men shook hands and settled in their chairs.

Kyame smiled as Dixey hesitated before reaching inside his suit jacket. "Gentlemen, please smoke as you wish." She grinned. "So long as it is not a pipe."

Dixey laughed and withdrew a cigar. "Miss Piddington, you are already near the top of my list of beautiful women whose company I have enjoyed, but with your kind understanding, you now are at the very top."

Kyame bowed her head. "My thanks, Mr. Dixey, for your kind compliment. May I ask" -- glancing quickly first at Mar-Tan, who nodded -- "how long you have been importing? The objects in your shop window are exquisite, particularly the magnificent rice patterned *bi* disk … a jade of the Han dynasty, I believe."

Dixey stopped lighting his cigar, his eyebrows raised.

Haroon Kahn frowned, his dark eyes becoming intense.

Mar-Tan, his round full features glistening in the lamps of the room, asked, "J. W., how long did Miss Piddington study the shop window of my friend?"

Cadwell exhaled, smiling, his cigar burning evenly. "About three, maybe four seconds, I'd estimate, Mar-Tan."

Mar-Tan turned to Dixey. "And, James, where in the window is that *bi* disk?"

Dixey was shaking his head. "In the back of the display, Mar Tan ... the *back* of the window. The more visually spectacular pieces are near the front, to catch the eye, as it were ... but the *bi* disk is the most valuable of the lot." He turned to Kyame. "My God, Miss Piddington, how can you do that? And with so little light in the window. I think only one small lamp was on."

Kyame laughed. "The lamp went out as we passed. But" -- as she pushed an errant black curl away from her eye -- "truly *seeing* the window was a discipline instilled by my father ... when I first became a key part of The Impossible Piddingtons.

"We would pass a window and Papa would ask me to remember the contents as we walked. Once away from the window, he would hand me a notepad on which I wrote what I recalled. Then we would return and compare my notes with the window contents. I first remembered the general layout of the window, then after more practice, I began to recall the details. By the time I left the act for art school almost three years ago, I could recall everything in a window, or in an office, usually in less than two or three seconds.

"Naturally, I keep working at it, to improve my time. It is also an important aid to my painting." Her grandmother had had a strong artistic memory that Kyame had inherited, but she held back on mentioning any further details of her family.

"Miss Piddington," said Kahn, his voice soft and deep. He leaned forward, his elbows on the table. "That is truly impressive. Dr. Mar-Tan has described The Impossible Piddingtons to Mr. Dixey and myself, an impressive story as well ... and, in its way, a most sad one. But," he paused. "Han dynasty? Are you also an expert on Chinese jade?"

Kyame shook her head. "Certainly not an expert. I have seen extraordinary jade objects at Dr. Mar-Tan's home and also at a dealer's shop in Boston ... near where I live at the present time. And naturally, I have read of Chinese history, as I have of Indian. Both are truly fascinating areas of study ... of truly fascinating peoples.

"It would seem, Dr. Kahn, that the real mysteries of the East lie in the hearts of the peoples, not in lost temples and hooded lamas as the romantic novels always suggest."

As Kahn nodded and started to respond, Mar-Tan said, "May I suggest, Miss Piddington and gentlemen, that we allow the waiters to begin their work. Perhaps, we can return to history in the course of the meal.

"James, the wine choices are yours, as always."

20

5

"A most excellent choice of port, Dixey," said Cadwell, leaning back to allow his plates to be cleared by the silent waiters. "I don't recognize the markings on the black bottle, but it has the unique richness of at least thirty years of aging in a carefully tended Portuguese cask."

James Dixey smiled. "Closer to forty years, Cadwell. From my own cellar. Thank you for your compliment. And you, Miss Piddington? It is not often I encounter a young woman who so clearly appreciates good port."

Kyame replaced her empty stemmed crystal glass on the table. "I would have guessed fifty years, Mr. Dixey. It is superb. It reflects the elegance of your window next door." She had been taught by her mother that the most effective approach to a man's mind was through recognizing his acumen and judgment -- true or not.

Dixey bowed his head to her compliment.

Mar-Tan, balancing his glass with two fingers, nodded to Kyame, "Your Chinese, Miss Piddington, may I enquire how many characters have you mastered thus far?"

"722, which means I must still keep a dictionary close at hand. My teacher, daifu Liang Changying, is most diligent, constantly honing my control of the four tones. Her patience with me has been impressive … given my own, ah ... intensity." She flashed a quick smile. "She won't allow me to slip … *even once*. Thank you, my friend, for your recommendation of her."

Mar-Tan smiled. "Daifu Liang has the same relentless curiosity I detected in you, Miss Piddington. She also is a Wood Tiger, your celestial cousin."

Khan frowned. "Chinese, Miss Piddington? That is a most difficult ambition. You have my admiration for even attempting to climb that mountain."

Kyame watched Khan as he swallowed the last of his port. As he dabbed his lips with his napkin, Kyame asked, "Your yellow *ruhmal*, Dr. Kahn. Are you a devotee of the black goddess, the daughter of stone, of Kali, of Bhowani ... of Thuggee?" She had noted the yellow scarf tucked into Kahn's wide belt when she had been introduced.

Mar-Tan's eyes went wide. Dixey was alarmed.

Cadwell simply waited. He knew Kyame too well to be uneasy.

The Thuggee, the hereditary organization of assassins, garrotters, fanatical followers of the four-armed black Hindu goddess of destruction, Kali, an order, which after almost three hundred years of existence, had been brutally suppressed over fifty years ago by the military

22

forces of the British East India Company in 1840 -- but there were always rumors of local revivals.

Kahn's eyes went cold momentarily, then he relaxed. "Miss Piddington, you amaze me with your observations and your insights." He withdrew the yellow scarf. It was weighted at one corner. Extending it across the table to her, Kyame took it in her hand. The yellow material was silken and smooth. Touching the weighted corner, she asked, "Three silver coins?"

Kahn nodded. "How, may I ask, are you so aware of Thuggee? Have you traveled in my country?"

The scarf carried multiple fragrances -- of spices, of cardamom, of saffron and clove.

"I know of Thuggee, Dr. Khan, because I encountered a Thug with my father three years ago when I was fourteen. His name was Buhram. He taught me to use the *ruhmal*, the yellow scarf of the stranglers ... and other things." She extended the scarf back to Kahn.

"Miss Piddington," Mar-Tan leaned toward her. "I share my friend Haroon's amazement. Let us adjourn to deserts and coffees in James' welcoming shop. Where, I hope, you would please tell us of your experience with Thuggee."

Dr. Haroon Kahn's smile was thin as he rose from his chair and replaced the yellow ruhmal in his belt. "Yes, Miss Piddington, how came a Thug to America?"

23

6

Holding a brass oil lamp high, James Dixey led his four visitors along a dim narrow hallway to his private sitting room at the rear of his darkened shop. As she followed the importer, holding her flowing skirts against her legs, Kyame could discern curious, interesting shapes in the shadows but said nothing.

"Please, Miss Piddington," said Dixey, holding the door for her.

As she entered, Kyame quickly scanned the richly paneled room. Its overflowing bookcases reached the ceiling on two walls, while deep teal-green leather Queen Anne chairs waited invitingly before a glowing coal fire. A young Chinese woman elegantly dressed in a red cheongsam dress embroidered with gold dragon and phoenix designs bowed to Kyame. As the servant approached from the shadows of the far corner, her open hand extended toward one of the leather chairs. "I am Meifeng, Miss Piddington. Please be seated."

With everyone settled, Meifeng returned with a gold and white porcelain coffee service, placing it on the low table around which the chairs were positioned. As she began pouring, Cadwell smiled. "A room worthy of you, Dixey. Just a few of those titles up there could keep me happily occupied for weeks."

"I quite agree," said Kyame. "Your customers must feel privileged to be here. An excellent selling tool."

Replacing his cup on its saucer, Dixey grinned. "Ah, Miss Piddington, again you go directly to the heart of a matter. Yes, I think of this as my closing room. If I do not have a sale in hand before the customer departs this room, then I have seriously, very seriously failed in assessing the situation."

Meifeng returned carrying a tray with five golden bowls filled with small pastries and candied fruit.

Kyame let her eyes roam the room as the men fell into a discussion of the unique coffee. The pastries were matchless in themselves. She had experienced coffee boiled over an outdoor fire and drunk in blistering tin cups in the hills of Colorado as well as in the finest bone china of the Palace Hotel in San Francisco. Flavor mattered, but, as Papa had always taught her, your companions were the real aroma of a good cup of coffee.

When the conversation paused, Kyame asked, "Mr. Dixey, may I examine the marvelous jade sword there, by that display of kris daggers?"

Dixey nodded. At his raised fingers, Meifeng moved immediately to bring the sword to her. "A well-chosen item, Miss Piddington," he said, his lips tight. "But for a tragedy, it would not even be here tonight. The purchaser, a valued client, the Count von Trotha, was found

25

about a week ago on the beach in San Remo, Italy, with his throat slashed. He had a five-thousand franc chip from the Monte Carlo Casino in his shirt pocket. So far, as I understand, no suspect has been arrested for his murder."

Murder. Kyame shivered even in the warmth of the fire.

She looked up as Meifeng approached. The blade of pure milk-white jade was almost two feet long, its hilt and pommel were of contrasting red jades inlaid with gold filigree. Kyame ran her fingers over the intricate carvings of two dragons in combat.

"A marvelous work, Dixey," said Cadwell. "I could not even attempt to estimate its possible value."

When Kyame remained silent, lightly stroking the sword with her fingers, Mar-Tan leaned forward. "Are you feeling your *woo shyr* spirit, Miss Piddington, of being a traveler between the worlds of the here and the not-here?" Mar-Tan had developed Kyame's horoscope during her first visit to his Chinatown home eight months previously. He had determined that she was an Earth Tiger, then startled her when he pronounced that the core of her soul was that of *tsyh ker*, the essence of an assassin. He had been proven correct a few weeks later in San Francisco when she had killed first in self-defense, and then in cold revenge for her father's brutal murder by the hatchet men of the Bing On tong.

Kyame looked up, smiling. "I was just admiring the remarkable touch of the artists. It is so different from the touch of the beautiful sword in your home, Dr. Mar-Tan. There were three carvers, at least three, who worked this miracle and they so blended their talents in this faux weapon ... remarkable." She looked across the table at Mar-Tan. "Yes, Xiansheng, my teacher, I admit touching the sword sent my thoughts roaming." She raised the sword with both hands to Meifeng

Hassan Khan watched the black-haired young woman, her green eyes so alight with intelligence, with a brilliance that was more polished steel rather than cut crystal. He replaced his cup. "The Thug, Miss Piddington ... and I appreciate your correct pronunciation, not the English distortion[1]. How came a Thug to America?"

As Meifeng refilled her cup, Kyame started her thoughts back toward Portland, Oregon, to 1894, almost three years in the past, to the last weeks in which the Impossible Piddingtons performed, the final occasions that she and Papa had joined together on a stage -- to cast the *glamorie*, to convince an audience that in entering the theatre they had crossed the enchanted boundary, and that

---

[1] The word *thug* means deceiver, from the Hindi verb *thugna*, which means to deceive. Thug is correctly pronounced Toog, slightly aspirated. From Col. Meadows Taylor, *Confessions of a Thug*, Kegan Paul, Trench & Co., London, 1839.

they were privileged to be witnessing the wonders of genuine second sight.

"I found the Thuggee to be of particular interest, Dr. Kahn, because I am interested in what and how people believe. In my smokey acting for our second sight act, working with Papa, I had to engage the beliefs of the audience in order for The Impossible Piddingtons to be of theatrical interest." She paused. "To cloud the minds of the audience with the shadow of doubt ... in order to separate them from the normal life of the streets outside the theatre. To convince those men and women in the audience that just maybe what they were experiencing in our act was not just a clever stage trick but the real thing, that it was something beyond their common understanding and experience. And ... belief is what drives all human life, is it not, gentlemen?

"Each night, in my first step onto the stage, as Papa taught, I had to believe myself that I possessed second sight. For the Thug, it seems, Dr. Kahn, that Kali is also such a compelling goddess who demands unwavering belief."

"*Kali ke Jae*, Glory to Kali." Kahn bowed his head. "I agree. The goddess can be most demanding ... and oftentimes most impatient."

"Papa and I arrived in Portland, Oregon," she continued, "after a difficult week up in Seattle. Seattle was to be our final moment on stage, the close of the act ... and then we would take the train together down to Sacramento where I would start east toward Boston and art school, while Papa would continue on to San Francisco where he had a position in a bank, Montgomery & Hill, waiting for him. We had been speculating about when the Impossible Piddingtons might perform again ..." She paused to sip her coffee. Kyame saw Cadwell's concern in his eyes, as she spoke of her father, but there was no stab of pain. Not this time. "But the audiences in Seattle had become jaded because of the number of conjurors who had recently come through the city. The large illusion shows of Harry Kellar and Herrmann the Great along with several magic and second sight acts in the local theatres. Seattle had just been *magiked* to death." She smiled. "I don't think that's a real word, but that was what we experienced. So, we needed another week or two to get our funds into the planned final condition. So, consequently, we went down to Portland, to close out the career of the Impossible Piddingtons."

Portland, Oregon

Monday November 6, 1893

Kyame sat against the main lobby wall a good distance away from the broad stairs leading up from the brass bound doors of the Nortonia Hotel on Eleventh Street, SW, in Portland. Located near the theatrical district, the Nortonia was a hotel accustomed to theatre people, though it still required upfront cash payment from any performers and their managers. Even then, Kyame would get occasional sharp questioning glances from women as they passed through the lobby to the Lady's Reception Room, the proper place for proper women to wait. But Kyame could not watch the lobby traffic from the curtained off Lady's Room; and she preferred the company of men anyway.

The air reeked of cigar and pipe smoke as the over-stuffed sofas and the rocking chairs in the lobby filled rapidly with recent morning arrivals apparently from a ship, judging from the labels on their steamer trunks. Kyame recognized theatre trunks with their faded painted promises on the sides. She and Papa had never painted "The Impossible Piddingtons" on either of the two trunks they used.

An older man, favoring his right leg, with a walking stick of polished black with a gold head-piece, the head of some animal, arrived at the top of the stairs. He paused to take a deep breath and to look around, with some intensity, then, his decision made, he continued on to the registration desk. He carried a worn brown leather satchel and was followed by a Nortonia uniformed Chinese bell-hop struggling with an obviously heavy unmarked trunk.

Curious, Kyame rose from her rocking chair to follow and to stretch her legs. Her still slowly oscillating chair was seized within seconds by a bleary-eyed traveler.

Papa should be arriving in a few minutes. He had been able to pick up a quick split-week booking for them at the Pantages Theatre a couple of blocks away because of the illnesses of two scheduled acts. Measles and whooping cough had opened the opportunity for them.

"I don't wish sickness on anyone, Daughter, but if they are going to be sick, now is certainly the right time," Papa had smiled.

"J. Casel Hosey," the man whispered, covering a cough behind his hand. "You received my message from Hong Kong?" He leaned heavily against the registration desk.

"Yes sir, we have held your room though your ship was four days late." The clerk smiled. "We always assume at least five days tardiness for any Asian ship this time of year. You are on the second floor rear, Mr. Hosey, as you requested." He nodded to the bell-boy leaning against Hosey's upright trunk, who then gripped the leather straps with both hands and began to drag the trunk toward the stairs. Turning away, Hosey slowly mounted the carpeted stairs.

Hong Kong. Kyame wanted to see Hong Kong someday. She caught sight of Papa coming through the main doors and walked toward him.

Drawing her to one side, Papa said, "We are set for tomorrow, Kyame. Three shows a day beginning at two in the afternoon for the next three days, with an option for the week following. We will need to do some quick local digging to prepare for the press demonstration here in the hotel conference room tomorrow at eleven in the morning." He put his arm around his daughter's shoulders. "I am going to miss you, Daughter ... very much." He kissed her forehead.

Kyame's eyes moistened. She would miss Papa as well, and she would miss feeling her heart pounding as she stood in the wings waiting for the curtain to open -- for their orchestral cue. No matter how often they had rehearsed their codes, practiced their silent timing, or had performed, something unexpected always happened during the performances. Papa had told her to play her hunches whenever she might feel something beyond the codes and the practiced materials. If she missed, as he had instructed her early in their partnership, it will only make The Impossible Piddingtons look more genuine. Only tricksters, con-men, and politicians ever claimed to be right all the time. They had both laughed.

She told him about the Englishman, J. Casel Hosey, and his heavy trunk. "He has an English passport and he is very nervous, always looking over his shoulder. He is from India via Hong Kong. Calcutta, I think I heard." She paused. "His hands, his right one is heavily scarred but his left is smooth."

Papa nodded. "Some of our audience for tomorrow morning is certain to include guests at the hotel, perhaps Mr. Hosey. Let's see what we can find."

Kyame nodded. She started walking toward the Lady's Reception Room where she would sit and listen to the women's gossip for an hour or two. She detoured when she saw the bellboy return to the lobby, his face angry, rubbing his wrists.

His brass nametag said Charles.

"*Ni hao*, Charles," Kyame said. "May I address you by your own name?"

The bellboy stopped, his eyes raised. "You speak correctly, Miss, I am honored. I am Chao ... so they made me Charles. How may I be of service to you?"

"You are angry, Chao, may I ask why?"

Chao's lips tightened. "That English ... fool, he treated me like a donkey," he whispered. He glanced at the registration desk where the clerk was looking for him.

"Pretend you are giving me directions, Chao. I will deal with the clerk if necessary."

Chao smiled, as he pointed, moving his arm as if directing her. "He is very nervous over the trunk, which is very heavy. He acts like it contains delicate glass, but I suspect it is something much more valuable. He asked me if any gentlemen from India had visited the hotel. He was quite concerned, though he tried to conceal that concern. He promised a gold coin if I saw such a gentleman and told him of it.

"Then he dismissed me, dismissed! without any payment. Like breaking my back for his miserable trunk was sufficient honor. But I must be going."

Kyame nodded, then extended her hand. "I may need your assistance, Chao, later. Please accept this for your valuable time."

The bellboy's eyes lit up, seeing the five dollar gold piece. "At any moment, Miss, you may call on me." He bowed to her, then walked quickly toward the clerk beckoning him.

***

Sitting in their room, Papa frowned at his daughter's suggestion. "Digging for local information is one thing, Kyame, but breaking and entering is another. We have enough rumors, gossip and local dirt for tomorrow from your listening to the ladies … and from my buying beers at the saloon down the street."

"Papa, I can be in and out of Hosey's room within less than six or seven minutes. If I find anything we can use, that would be great … if not ...," she shrugged. "The hotel door locks here are no trouble. They are the same make of triple-warded locks as in Denver and Kansas City.

You know I can do it." She reached into her pocket and withdrew a thin strip of steel with two small nibs at one end. "This pick will open every room lock in this hotel," she said, flashing her bright roguish smile.

John Piddington smiled. Yes, his amazing daughter could do it, pick most locks, see things quickly and get out. She had saved him from a jail sentence by doing just that several months earlier in Kansas. And they could use a unique bit of information to spice up the press demonstration.

"When?"

"Chao, the bellboy, told me that Hosey will be taking tea in about an hour. I will watch the second floor corridor from the back stairs. Once I see Hosey start down the main stairs, I will go to his room. Chao will come up and knock twice on the door in passing when he sees Hosey start to return. I will be out in less than a minute." She smiled a mischievous smile that her father loved to see, so like her beautiful mother -- and a smile that was impossible to resist.

***

The lock on room 207, rear, opened within a few seconds, Kyame, wearing a maid's uniform and her glossy black hair wrapped in a tight bun, was inside immediately. The uniform, a sometimes useful prop, was always kept in her trunk. Performing the mental wonders of second sight

35

sometimes needed more a physical than mystical assistance. She dropped the towels she had been carrying on a chair next to the door.

The trunk was against the far wall. Hosey's leather satchel was -- not there. Hosey must have taken it with him.

Checking the closet first, she found a torn stub from a second class train ticket from Jubbulpore to Calcutta in a suit coat pocket. The suit itself, of good quality tweed, smacked of sweat and tobacco smoke, badly needed cleaning. She would have to look at a map of India to know where Jubbulpore was.

In a pocket of another soiled suit, she found a torn swatch of yellow cloth. She left it.

The lock on the trunk was a new brass Chubb lock, notorious for being difficult to pick, as Texas Jack Vermillion, an associate of celebrated con-man Soapy Smith, had once shown her in Denver. Though he had been very friendly, Vermillion had been clearly a very dangerous unstable man whom Kyame had avoided whenever possible -- but he did like to brag about his skills with locks. But, with patience and time, the Chubb could be opened. Kyame had neither asset available at the moment, but tried her luck anyway.

She grinned.

Hosey had left the trunk unlocked! One of those unique moments that Papa had called a special gift from Hekate, the Greek goddess of magic.

Raising the lid of the trunk, her jaw dropped. Cushioned with thick blankets and wrapped in multiple layers of white silk were two golden four-armed goddesses, three full-bellied gold lota bowls, two gold and emerald ceremonial daggers, and several smaller bejeweled items that there wasn't time to inspect. Loot from a temple, it appeared, or from some rich man's mansion.

She started at the heavy steps of someone passing near the room door, steps which move -- moving away from the main stairs. Someone coming back from the hotel tea possibly. Time to run before more people were in the hallway.

***

Chao carefully stacked the woman's polished leather trunk with the other two. He looked up to glimpse the English fool carrying his valise. Hosey was starting slowly up the stairs. Too soon! He was leaving the tea early. The young Miss who had asked his help! He had taken her gold and promised his help!

"Charles ... Charles?"

Chao turned.

The woman wrapped in furs held out a ten dollar gold piece. "Please see these trunks to our room. My brother, Mr. Parsons, will be arriving in a few moments. Please direct him to the dining room. He is very tall with blonde hair."

Chao bowed over the coin. Hosey was just passing out of sight up the stairs.

*** _

Kyame closed the trunk. With the two picks required for a Chubb she quickly locked it. It was infinitely easier to lock a Chubb with picks than to pick it open. In three quick long steps she was at the door. Cracking it open an inch, there was no one in view in the hallway toward the stairway. Suddenly, a man passed down the hall toward the main stairway, moving within inches of her. She silently pressed the door shut. She waited, waited, then edged the door back open an inch.

Hosey! He was just appearing at the second floor landing. He stopped and looked back as though someone had called his name.

Kyame gathered the towels which she had carried to complete her maid's disguise and stepped quickly out into the hallway.

With her pick, she quickly locked the door of 207, then ran to the end of the corridor to the back stairs and up one floor to their room at 311 without looking back.

Looking back always proved to be a bad strategy. The instant taken to pause and look back could be the instant of observation. She pushed their unlocked door open. As she entered, Papa closed and locked the door after her.

After changing out of the maid costume and brushing out her hair, Kyame accepted the cup of steaming coffee from Papa. Sitting with Papa at their small fireplace, she explained what she had found.

Papa nodded. "If Hosey is there tomorrow, we can ring in what you have found in several ways. The yellow cloth might mean something. We'll go with that first and use the rest as the situation develops." He kissed his resourceful daughter on her cheek. "Mama would not have approved your taking the risk; but she would have been proud of your results, dear Kyame." He then began to describe what he had learned.

They could do the act without local information, but the local material elevated the act to another, more compelling level. To Kyame, the local skeletons, as Papa had sometimes referred to it, transformed the act into a more threatening mode, one which the people always remembered longer. And it gave her several tools, options to utilize in her smokey acting to truly scare them, to challenge the spectators to question, and finally, in most cases, to shake them into belief, to recognize the presence of a unique power.

***

"Bloody tricksters, these second sight people," J. Casel Hosey growled softly to the sharp-featured young woman sitting next to him. "I've seen beggars like these in theatres all over the Empire.

"You watch, Miss. You watch … I'll put'm right."

The well-dressed woman edged away, shifting her chair. When another chair became empty as a man left to respond to a message, she quickly moved to it.

The Piddington press demonstration utilized reporters from Portland, from *The Morning Oregonian, The Bee*, and from papers from three surrounding towns, as well as a young reporter, Gerald Fern, from the Portland *Business Journal*. "I need to find someone who can read the future of the railroads, if they have any," Fern had responded to the whispered query from one of the other reporters of why he was there.

John Piddington had carefully noted the names of all of the reporters present for later follow-up.

As always, dressed in one of her three special performing gowns, and blindfolded, Kyame sat on a board across two saw-horses on a raised platform to apparently ensure to the audience that isolated on the board she could not receive any secret assistance.

However, instead of making the act more difficult for Kyame, raising her higher actually allowed her to see more easily under the blindfold, down the sides of her nose

40

further out into the audience, to catch Papa's silent signaling, the positioning of his feet, at a greater distance.

As Papa gave his introductory remarks he walked slowly up the center aisle until Kyame coughed softly which would mark the point at which, seeing under the edge of the blindfold, she would lose sight of his shoes. That would be the furthest point away from her that Papa could signal.

By first signing information from two or three spectators in front, Papa could get information on spectators far in the rear while Kyame would be presenting her revelations of those at the front. Papa would then walk up the aisle to get back into her view to silently sign information on those in the rear. Working all the audience, not just a narrow group in one area, always confused reporters, along with some publicity hungry local amateur magicians, intent on grabbing newspaper space by exposing the methods of the Impossible Piddingtons.

To Papa's silent cuing as he moved about the room, Kyame had described objects from the reporter's pockets, even to describing the engraving of a mermaid inside a gold watch that the reporter from the *Business Journal* had not even opened to show to Papa.

"How can you do that?" Fern asked anxiously, to the raised murmuring of the audience. "Not even your father has seen the mermaid. How, Miss Piddington, how can you do that? Second sight means you see through your father's eyes, which is marvelous enough … but he never saw the mermaid.

"How?" he repeated.

"Sometimes, sir," said Kyame, "memories become vivid thoughts. You were thinking intently of the mermaid shortly before coming here to the hotel … were you not?" suggested Kyame helpfully.

Standing silently in the center aisle, John Piddington smiled in appreciation at how his daughter was making the connections. Not even her mother could match her now.

Gerald Fern hesitated for a moment. "My God, you're right. There was a sketch of a mermaid on the front page of the *Oregonian* this morning. It reminded me of the engraving. It's going to be the name of a new cargo ship." He fell back in his chair, his face pale. "Are you Piddingtons ...?" he struggled. "Are you the real thing? Not just another music hall act?"

"That is for you to judge, sir," Kyame responded gently, catching Papa's signal to move on to Hosey. The demonstration had gone well, but it was time to close. She had missed when Papa had signaled to miss, and had described a woman's round mirror as a pill box, but had gotten the color, deep pink, correctly.

Hosey was getting restless. Kyame had carefully glimpsed his feet from under the blindfold, their shifting

42

apparently as he glanced around him, behind him. Already edgy, he was an ideal target.

Piddington walked quietly to the far side of the room, away from Hosey. The Englishman had refused to allow him to see anything. "I'll not let you code anything to that young witch up there!" Hosey had snapped as others watched. Piddington had nodded and moved on to another member of the audience.

Kyame suddenly sat up rigidly, raising both hands as though trying to grasp something. "I can see it, but it is just beyond my reach!" She saw two of the reporters immediately turn to watch Papa, who was standing still near a far wall with his back turned to her. The reporters shrugged and turned back to Kyame.

"It's yellow, yellow ... a yellow cloth." Hosey physically started at her saying the color. "A place ... a place, somewhere in India, Jubbapore, I think." She moved her hand as though wiping something away. "No, no, it is ... Jubbulpore." She caught Hosey's feet suddenly come together as if to rise, to escape.

Perfect. Now to make him run

"Jubbulpore, a prison place," she let her voice drift higher in tone. "A prison for followers of ... *Thuggee*! Someone here in this room ... over there" -- she pointed toward Hosey -- "I feel it, somewhere on the back row.

Someone in the back row has something yellow from ... no, not from Jubbulpore, from somewhere else in India ..."

Kyame pushed herself off the board to stand "Oh Papa!" she suddenly cried out. "Papa! Something dark ... black! A fierce four-armed goddess, a Hindu goddess is standing before me, all black, all black with red bloody lips. She is angry! So angry! Something about her ... her gold!" Kyame suddenly screamed, "She ... She is ... *Kali!*"

Kyame heard scraping from chairs moving as many turned to see what might be behind them. Hosey was on his feet, clearly panicked.

Moving back within her range, Papa signaled Kyame to close.

Kyame holding her arms across her chest, caught a quick glimpse of an impeccably dressed dark-skinned man looking into the conference room. Kyame raised her hand, "A man from India is here! Here!" She tore off the blindfold. "I cannot see anything else," she cried. "I don't want to see more!" She fell into Papa's welcoming arms.

"Man from India?" Papa whispered as he held his daughter, gently guiding her to an empty chair, apparently to rest from her nervous strain.

"Just saw him ... so threw him in," she murmured, sitting with her head held in her hands, her elbows on her knees. The audience was edging away toward the doors. No one came near them. The reporters all stood a few feet away scribbling hurriedly on their notebooks, then, one by one, ran for the door.

Papa made a tight fist with his right hand, then relaxed his fingers. The sign for "solid job" that was always Kyame's greatest, sweetest reward.

***

Kyame sipped the coffee that Papa gave her as they settled in front of the cold fireplace in their room. An artist from *The Morning Oregonian* was coming within an hour to sketch Kyame for their planned story.

"There was a two-volume encyclopedia," she explained, "that a guest had left in the Lady's Reception Room. The article on India in it gave me the explanation of the goddess statues I had seen in Hosey's trunk. Kali was called the daughter of stone, the black goddess, and several other things, but I used only a little of what the article said. It seemed enough. There was a paragraph on Thuggee, mostly the practice is located around Calcutta. And the yellow scarf, the *ruhmal,* that the Thugs used for strangling a victim." She looked over the rim of her cup. "I want to go to India someday, Papa," she said. "I want to meet Kali… face to face."

The light knock at their door stopped her.

Papa opened the door to a small dark-skinned man dressed in a cream colored suit.

45

"My apologies, Mr. Piddington," he said softly, bowing, "for disturbing you and your remarkable daughter, when you must be very tired from your performance.

"My name is Buhram, sir. I am of Calcutta. May I speak privately with you?"

Buhram bowed his head slightly as Kyame stood and extended her hand when Papa introduced him. She was slightly taller than the Indian. "You are astonishing and beautiful, Miss Piddington. Your knowledge of Thuggee is beyond anything I would have expected in this ... barren country. Your respect for Kali is quite evident and beyond what I have experienced from any European."

Accepting the coffee offered by John Piddington, Buhram sat on a chair next to Kyame.

"How may we be of assistance, Mr. Buhram?" she asked. "You have come a long way."

He smiled. "I am just Buhram, Miss. No mister." He sipped, then his face grew dark and angry. "The man, Hosey, is a thief and killer. I care nothing for his life. The goddess will deal with that in her own way. I have trailed him across India from Jubbulpore to Calcutta, how you knew that I can only believe that the goddess herself told you, or she led your thoughts. I missed Hosey's ship leaving Calcutta and had to wait three days for another. I missed him again in Singapore because a storm delayed our landing. Then again in Hong Kong." He paused to sip his coffee.

"What do you seek?" asked John Piddington.

"J. Casel Hosey started, Mr. Piddington, with three trunks of valuable holy relics taken from the treasure room of Kalighat Temple in the south of Calcutta. I am of Haldar descent, sir, a *sevayet*, a serving man of the Goddess, and am second to the ruling priest of the temple. I am privileged to clean the Goddess's feet each morning in the Inner Sanctum of the temple, that worshippers may know She is cared for while in their prayers as they view her icon. The security of the temple is also my responsibility. Those relics were blessed directly by Kali herself over the past nine generations of my people. The Goddess demands their return."

"Who is Mr. Hosey?" asked Kyame.

Buhram grimaced. "He was the British district supervisor. Hosey was a friend and a direct representative of the Marquis of Lansdowne, the English Viceroy. We trusted Hosey initially, as his predecessor had proven trustworthy, but he began to demonstrate a corrupt spirit, lusting after our young women, after our gold … and finally after the very things of Kali Herself, taken from the heart of the Temple."

"The Viceregal office began to suspect something and sent auditors to the district, at which point Hosey disappeared."

"Are you a Thug, sir?" Kyame saw the tip of a yellow scarf tucked into his belt.

In a motion faster than Kyame's eyes could follow, the yellow scarf appeared at Buhram's fingertips. "Yes, Miss Piddington, I am Thug, but I have not killed ... in India. All that ended fifty years ago. But I am of a Thug family." He smiled. "My grandfather, also Buhram, is venerated throughout Thuggee for his prowess before the Goddess. He killed nine-hundred and thirty-one times, and then he stopped counting. He surely killed beyond a thousand. No other Thug ever matched him.

"Each generation still, once a Thug boy reaches twelve years of age, he is taught the techniques of the ruhmal ... that they may not be lost, that Kali's yellow scarf may be respected."

John Piddington was startled when Kyame asked, "At a proper time, will you teach me the ruhmal, Buhram?"

He first looked to John Piddington. "Sir, your daughter makes a request I must answer. How shall I answer? My religion denies knowledge of the ruhmal to women ... in my country. But I am obligated here even as you have patiently listened to me and have offered me the honor of your hospitality. You have accepted me, a dark-skinned man, as true without challenge."

"My daughter and I must read people quickly in our profession, Buhram. We have both read you as true." Piddington looked over at his daughter, her brilliant green eyes intensely alive. "And, in some places, theatre people are treated the same as dark-skinned people. If she wishes the knowledge, and you can provide it without disrespect to your goddess, then I have no objection."

Buhram nodded. "Then it will be done, Miss Piddington. But first I must retrieve the relics of Kali."

Kyame replaced her cup on the table. She smiled. "I have some ideas about that." She looked up at the knock at their door.

Buhram immediately stood. "You have visitors. I must leave, but I must as well stay in the shadows."

Piddington stood. "It is a newspaper artist to sketch my daughter."

"Wait in the bedroom, Buhram," said Kyame. "It will take only a few minutes and we can resume our discussion."

"We must be at the theatre for our first show in about an hour, Kyame," said Papa. "Perhaps, Buhram, we can reconvene here after our last show which will be at nine o'clock. Is that convenient for you? There is a door into the hallway in the bedroom."

Buhram nodded his agreement and disappeared into the bedroom as Piddington opened the door to the artist.

***

Hassan Kahn's eyes softened as Kyame paused to sip her refilled glass of port. "Remarkable, Miss Piddington. Yes, Buhram is venerated in Thuggee as no other Thug. It was his grandson, then, who taught you the ruhmal?"

Kyame nodded.

"You have been uniquely blessed by the Goddess. Did he, Miss Piddington, also introduce you to the *Ramasee*, the secret dialect of Thuggee … and, perhaps" he added softly, "to the sacrifice of *Tuponi* ... the sacrifice of the *goor*, the sacred raw yellow sugar?"

Kyame shook her head. "He spoke of the origins of Thuggee and gave me some of the words of the Ramasee to illustrate how they coded their secret meanings." She smiled. "I am quite familiar with that genre of communication. But of the Tuponi, Buhram said that was beyond what he could reveal to any woman. Nor, though he mentioned it, did he describe the use of *datura*, the poison of the thorn apple."

Kahn nodded. "You have still been uniquely blessed."

Dr. Mar-Tan had been watching her carefully over the rim of his crystal glass as she had told her story of the Thuggee. He replaced the glass on the table, and leaned toward her. "Miss Piddington, the more I learn of you, the more my initial reading of your soul seems to resonate. I would join with my friend in saying that you have been uniquely blessed."

J. W. smiled. "Kyame, we await the resolution of your story, eh, Dixey?"

Dixey nodded. His attitude toward the young woman had changed as well, as though something had been confirmed in his mind.

***

The third floor hallway was empty when Kyame and her father returned to their room from the Pantages. Their three performances had gone well, with the reporters from the morning in the front row in the first and second shows.

"Almost nine. Time for our Thug friend to arrive, Kyame," said Papa.

She nodded. A plan had been running through her mind, to draw off Hosey to allow Buhram and Papa to gain

51

access to 207 to remove Kali's objects first to their room, then to wherever Buhram wanted them.

A light knock. Kyame immediately opened the door.

***

Kyame watched Hosey as he stood at the registration desk writing out a telegram.

Chao stood obediently nearby, his hands clasped behind his back. As instructed by the black-haired young woman, he watched the British fool closely while acting subservient. He bowed as Hosey turned away to go into the dining room, then moved to block a man from using the telegram pad. "I will bring you a fresh pad to use, sir," said Chao taking the pad used by Hosey. He walked to a storage closet next to the registration desk, took a new pad while leaving the Hosey pad. The desk clerk reappeared, frowned then turned to another guest.

Kyame waited until the desk was empty of guests and the clerk had gone inside his office behind the desk. She quickly withdrew the Hosey pad from the storage closet and moved to a far corner of the lobby. The sun had just set, the gas lights were being lit along the darkened street outside.

Lightly rubbing the top sheet with one of the sticks of charcoal from her art box, the impressions of what Hosey had written began to appear:

52

Have all goods, the message said, leaving ptd eight am tomorrow stop arrive yours at noon stop gold for gold only. The telegram was signed, H.

Papa nodded. "Yes, tonight, Kyame. We cannot wait." He grinned. "Your Chinese friend supplied the spare key for 207, so we can move quickly."

Buhram shook his head. Her description of Hosey's message had clearly bothered him. "How? How can you know such things, Miss Piddington?" He was dressed as a Nortonia bellhop. He had quickly agreed when Kyame had said, "Dark-skinned uniformed men are invisible. You will be helping Papa with the trunk, so no one will notice you."

Chao had supplied his second uniform which he used when his best uniform was being cleaned. It was a loose fit on Buhram. "You will have to move the trunk twice so the uniform will be necessary." She glanced at the two fifty-pound bags of coal that Papa, after waiting for darkness, had borrowed from the storage room in the rear of the hotel that opened out onto an alley. He had picked the lock, removed the two bags, then tied one bag to the rope lowered from their window -- theatre folk were always given the rooms in the back of hotels -- that Kyame and Buhram pulled up to the room. Then the second bag. It took less than ten minutes to get the bags from the storage room to their room.

Chao knocked on 207. He heard the British fool totter to the door. "Sir," he said, when Hosey carefully

53

opened the door a couple of inches with only one frowning eye showing. "There are two telegrams for you at the registration desk. They are marked confidential, otherwise I would have been honored to bring them to you."

Hosey grunted, stepped away, then reappeared opening the door. He leaned on his black walking stick. Chao turned away toward the back stairway where Mr. Piddington and the dark man were waiting.

"Hey, Chinee, where are you going?"

"Mr. Hosey, I go to serve another guest," responded Chao, bowing.

Hosey tossed his hand and turned limping toward the main stairway. "On your way then, man."

***

Kyame saw Hosey slowly, awkwardly descend the stairs. She was wearing one of her performing gowns, of shimmering pink and gold satin. She had already drawn unwelcome attention from two men in the lobby when she appeared from the dining room. A well-dressed attractive theatre girl was always considered fair game by any traveling man, but Kyame had brushed aside their smiling insistent invitations.

She would delay Hosey to allow Papa and Buhram to move the trunk to the Piddington room, unload the temple objects, reload with the two bags of coal and return the trunk to Hosey's room. Papa would mark the floor in Hosey's room to ensure the truck was positioned exactly as Hosey had left it. Their room was in the back and one floor above. Papa had estimated fifteen minutes, twenty at the outside needed for Kyame to stall Hosey. If, he had cautioned, if he was able to pick the Chubb lock quickly. They could not expect another blessing from Hekate. Kyame assumed twenty-five minutes.

Hosey's eyes widened when he turned to encounter Kyame arrayed in gold and pink.

"I feel I must ask your forgiveness, Mr. Hosey," she said, her head cocked to one side, an eyebrow raised, "for causing you such, such discomfort yesterday. We must impress the press, as I am sure a man of your ... wide experiences would understand. How may I apologize?" Kyame watched the flame of lust flare up in his eyes.

She felt dirty even talking to the Englishman.

Hosey tapped his cane two or three times. He took a breath, a narrow smile crossing his face. "We can speak more privately, closely ... more closely in my room, Miss Piddington. May I say how that gown becomes you?" He reached out to finger the material of her billowing gold satin sleeve, then held it to draw it closer. Kyame let him draw her closer, his aura of tobacco and stale beer turned her stomach, but there was twenty minutes to go.

Chao approached.

"The Columbia lounge is empty, Mr. Hosey, if you wish a private conversation." Chao bowed as he spoke, his hand sweeping toward the door across the lobby.

Kyame began to move in that direction as Hosey eagerly took her arm, pressing up against her.

***

John Piddington sweated. Five minutes of picking and the Chubb still wouldn't open. Buhram could only stand and pray fervently to his black goddess ... while Piddington muttered words that were not prayers under his breath.

He paused, wiped his sweaty hands on his trousers. "I will get it, Buhram, but it is a most difficult lock."

"I pray only, Mr. Piddington, that Kali will give you the special patience of an assassin, of a gambler, as well as that of an old priest. She will guide your fingers ... if you allow her."

Piddington smiled. "I will gladly accept any help, Buhram. My daughter is at risk, so I will let Kali come into my fingers."

Another minute of probing the lock, then Piddington realized he had been too anxious, letting Kyame's dangerous assignment bother him too deeply. Just too anxious -- and too confident. He moved his hands away leaving the two picks in the lock, bowed his head to relax,

56

flexed his fingers, then started again. A moment -- a small movement -- then the soft click. The lock was open!

"*Kali ke Jae*! All praise to the Goddess!" sang Buhram softly, then prayed again in Hindi as Piddington opened the trunk. The gleaming gold objects were breathtaking.

***

"You are breathtaking, Miss Piddington. Kyame, what a seductive name ... if I may use that very descriptive word." His tobacco breath almost gagged her as he grinned with no attempt to conceal his raging lust.

She had allowed Hosey to sit close to her on the leather love sea -- then as she spread her skirts, she let the edges cascade across his legs. He suddenly squeezed her arm with one hand and jerked her down against his chest, throwing his other arm over her shoulders to stop her from pulling away. Kyame blocked his hand grasping for her breasts.

"Not here, sir, not here!" she demanded. "That door could open at any time!"

"Upstairs then, quickly, woman," Hosey snapped, "quickly! To my room."

***

The second coal bag was in the trunk. Piddington locked the lid down. "Now we must move, Buhram."

Buhram lifted one end, then Piddington lifted the other. The door stood open a bare inch. The Thug kicked it open as he backed through. Piddington lowered his end, reached back to pull the door closed behind him. As he picked up his end, a sharp pang stabbed at his heart. Kyame! "Quickly, Buhram, I feel my daughter in danger!"

Buhram nodded as he stepped more rapidly toward the stairway.

***

Kyame's heart sank when Hosey opened his door. She had planned to just push Hosey away and leave but it was too soon. Oh ... too soon.

"My trunk! Gone! Goddamn you, woman! You and that loathsome pa of yours are trying to steal from me!" His face a purplish mask of fury, Hosey slapped Kyame hard across her cheek and thrust her across the room. She tripped across his leather valise and fell hard, her head striking against the edge of the fireplace. Her face went numb.

For a moment Kyame couldn't think, her eyes closed against the growing pain across her face. Even with her eyes slightly out of focus, Kyame saw Hosey draw a sword from his walking stick.

"I'll cut that pretty face of yours to ribbons, you scheming slut! Then I'll cut the heart out of that pa of yours, and have my gold back!"

Hastily pulling her skirts aside, Kyame struggled to regain her feet. She snarled, "Those statues go back to Kali's temple, not to your melting pot, Hosey." She dodged as his sword slashed through her sleeve. Seeing a vase on the bedside table, in one motion she reached out and threw it at Hosey's head in one motion.

When he moved to duck away, Kyame sprang toward the fireplace to grab the poker leaning against the wall. She swept it across in front of her, knocking Hosey's sword away.

Hosey growled, swore and thrust again at her face. Kyame parried the blade away, but felt its point graze her forehead. A warm flow of blood started down, partially blocking the sight of her right eye.

When a noise at the door caused Hosey to hesitate, Kyame leaped forward to thrust the poker hard into his chest. He staggered backward, his crippled leg buckling under him. Kyame raised the poker and swung down across the side of his head tripping over her skirts and falling as Papa came through the door.

"My god, Kyame!" he shouted, dropping the trunk to throw himself on Hosey as the man reached out with the sword to chop at his daughter.

In an instant, Buhram, his faced distorted into rage, leaped into the room, snapped his yellow scarf around the throat of Hosey, his lifelong training moving his hands without his thinking. Hosey gasped.

Piddington jerked the sword from his hand, tossed it across the room.

"Kyame!"

She brushed the blood from her face as she came to her knees. "I'm all right, Papa, just a little cut." Her eyes went wide as the yellow scarf went tighter on Hosey's throat, Buhram's face strangely calm. "Buhram, Buhram, don't kill him ... don't kill him. Please."

Buhram's eyes widened as they met the green of Kyame's eyes, blood smeared across her lips. He bowed his head.

"As you have commanded ... daughter of stone."

He let the scarf drop from his hands. Hosey lay back silently, his eyes closed, but he was breathing. Blood was spreading slowly across his face from Kyame's blow with the poker.

"Quickly, we must replace the trunk and close the door. Hosey is not going to move," she said. Kyame did not want Hosey's life on Buhram's hands.

That was her responsibility.

***

Kyame replaced her crystal stemmed glass on the table. Kahn frowned, his eyes questioning.

Dixey asked, "What then, Miss Piddington?"

"Yes," joined Dr. Mar-Tan, "how did you resolve the ... the issue?"

Cadwell, who had never heard the complete story before, simply waited, pursing his lips against a sudden tightness in his chest, then it faded.

"Buhram, with Papa's help, moved the temple objects from our room to the closet in his room the floor above ours." She grinned. "I was too bloody to be seen by anyone at the time, I'm afraid.

"Two days later, Buhram booked a ship to San Francisco and then on to Hong Kong."

"But Hosey, Miss Piddington?" asked Mar-Tan. "What about Hosey?"

Kahn watched closely as the remarkable green-eyed young woman leaned forward, her elbows pivoting on her knees, her face going cold, her voice dropping in tone.

"While Papa and Buhram were busy moving the temple objects, I dragged Hosey to the window. There was a bottle of whiskey on the floor next to his bed, so I poured some whiskey over him ... to give him that right stink ...

61

and pushed him out the window. He fell two floors, hit the corner of a wagon and didn't move."

She had shuddered, watching Hosey fall as a brief wave of hate swept through her. When they had once been in a Nebraska town, Mama had warned her against letting hatred control her thinking after the son of a local minister had insulted her as "only a theatre girl, hardly above a dog". "You grant them special power over you, Kyame, if you let your hatred rise up," she had insisted. Kyame had learned that Mama had been right.

"We never saw Hosey again," she said simply.

Kahn brought his hands, his fingertips together, touched them to his lips and bowed his head. "Buhram saw the Goddess's face in yours, Miss Piddington. You have done for Her what no woman of Thuggee has, you have killed in Her name, killed, in the end, as She commanded generations ago, without blood. I stand in your debt, Miss Piddington. Buhram was right to teach you the ruhmal. The daughter of stone truly stands beside you.

"*Ultra Auroram et Gangem*", whispered Kahn, "beyond the dawn and the Ganges ... a sacred place of dreams ... a place that, I believe, Miss Piddington, is within your reach ... even now, at *this* moment.

"*Kali ke Jae!*" he said softly. "Glory to Kali."

Kyame trembled as her heart stilled as though a spell had been cast over her. She slowly let her breath out, took another. Kyame nodded to Kahn's inquiring dark eyes.

Even now.

Watching Kyame closely, James Dixey sat silently for a moment, then looked at J. W. Cadwell, and nodded. "I am even more impressed, Miss Piddington, as I am sure everyone else is. I am confident that you are the right one for the task with which Judson Rowland has been presented."

"Anglo-Oriental?" Kyame asked, leaning back into her chair, the mystic moment fading, but she was certain, that strange numinous feeling would re-emerge somewhere in the future.

She recalled her last meeting with Judson Rowland eight months ago at the San Francisco train station as she had prepared to return to Boston when he had asked if he could call on her talents again. She had answered yes, without hesitation, without condition.

Dixey smiled. "Our loose organization is everywhere, it seems. But now to the reason for this evening's gathering ...utterly fascinating as this evening has been already.

7

Thirty-seven years old, Friedrich Wilhelm Viktor Albert von Hohenzollern, His Imperial and Royal Majesty, Emperor of Germany and King of Prussia, was the second Kaiser to be named Wilhelm, his grandfather had been the first. Wilhelm also held some thirty-five other titles of royalty.

Wilhelm felt his thoughts drifting as he shifted uncomfortably in his padded leather heavily-ornamented chair at the head of the long council table surrounded by the principal ministers of his government, or more accurately, of the Imperial German Government.

Shooting pains had returned to his left ear, after almost three days of freedom, pains which ate steadily at his already short patience, forcing him to grit his teeth until he could deal with the hellish discomfort in private.

Were his former Chancellor, Prince Otto von Bismarck, still in the government, all eyes would be focused on the other end of the table. But after acceding to the throne in 1888, Wilhelm had summarily dismissed Bismarck in 1890, when the Kaiser became convinced that the Chancellor was fomenting a legislative coup d'etat.

However, Wilhelm still encountered echoes of the Iron Chancellor wherever he turned in the loose assemblage of sovereign kingdoms, errant duchies and other arrogant independent titles that was Bismarck's jigsaw Imperial German Empire. As King of Prussia he commanded the Prussian Army, but then could only press, negotiate, even cajole the titled riffraff in the other portions of the Empire to cooperate -- which often they chose not to. Even the constitution put in place in 1871 by von Bismarck was a confusing bureaucratic concoction of blurred lines and authorities which was observed whenever convenient by whichever minister was involved.

At least von Bismarck, at 81, had been finally and safely put away at his castle in Friedrichsruh.

Even the Reichstag was splintered among a changing group of political parties, some of which, Wilhelm had once smiled at the absurdity, actually qualified under Bismarck's law as "enemies of the Reich", Poles, Alsatians and others. And the only Imperial structure that was in fact a national German institution was the *Kaisermarine,* the Imperial Navy, which was itself barely seven years old.

The Kaiser glanced upward toward the life-size portrait of Frederick Wilhelm II, *Friederich der Grosse*, the Great, hanging on the far wall. Painted life-size as a heroic knight in brilliant armor, Frederick dominated the room as he had all of Europe ten decades ago; a domination that Wilhelm felt was his own divinely ordained destiny.

After all, he had been born on the 27th of January, the same day as Mozart, a connection Wilhelm felt had not been accidental as he too would change and enrich the world. He was certain that in the years ahead the world could not make a major geopolitical decision without the approval of the German Emperor.

The Crown Council meeting with its endless minutiae of this and that was dragging ever slower. He had made the important decisions, such decisions that were his Imperial prerogative, and was allowing discussion to continue on other matters, but his patience was ebbing rapidly.

Enough! Enough!

His left hand with its paralyzed fingers started to slip from the chair arm, but he quickly, below the table out of sight, and without looking down, restored the hand to its position.

His left arm, paralyzed as a result of his breech birth which had almost killed his mother, was six inches shorter than his right, but through relentless, some whispered

66

merciless, even brutal childhood supervision by his unsmiling Calvinist tutor, Dr. Georg Hinzpeter, the withered arm could never be used as an excuse by the seven year old Willy. He was never praised by Hinzpeter even when little Willy, after numerous punishing falls, finally became a confident one-handed horseman.

But then, even a seven year old Hohenzollern Prince could not accept praise from a lesser person.

Finally, the Kaiser tossed his right hand. "Enough!" he bellowed, and nodded toward Vice Admiral Hans Hugo, the Graf von Drascher. "Remain, Admiral," he ordered.

With much scrapping of chairs, the bemedaled, mustached and ornately uniformed officers and the frock-coated ministers quickly gathered their folders and papers together. Each first bowing toward the Kaiser, began striding rapidly for the high arched marble-inlaid double doors.

Count Alfred von Schlieffen, Chief of the German General Staff since 1891, monocled and elegant in his wasp-waisted dark-blue field marshal's uniform sparkling with decorations, paused at the door as though to politely allow others to precede him from the room, but rather it was to cautiously look back at von Drascher and the Kaiser just huddling together at the far corner of the long table. The Count's deeply lined face was calm, even pleasant as he nodded first to one and then a second minister as they passed, but, partially concealed behind his gray mustache, his jaw was tight. What fool plan is percolating now in the Imperial brain? Von Schlieffen would defend the Army's preeminent rights if -- if -- he flipped his left hand slightly. Whatever. The Count finally turned and left the room, hearing the great doors thud shut behind him. He would start very discrete probes into von Drascher's activities, even to have him followed. No one could anticipate the Kaiser, he sneered, his face no longer pleasant, no one could trust the Kaiser's almost hourly enthusiasms.

* * *

Waiting a moment as the others, particularly the Count von Schlieffen, walked silently away from the table, Admiral, the Count von Drascher then walked briskly from his position near the end of the council table to his place at the right of his sovereign. Always take the position at the right, the Kaiser's strong side.

His ear pains momentarily abating, the Kaiser could relax his jaw. He took a short breath to "balance himself" -- as he always thought of resisting his recurring left ear problems that had been with him for as long as he could remember.

Wilhelm felt more comfortable with von Drascher, as the gray-haired and mustached Vice Admiral was missing two fingers on his left hand from a youthful hunting accident and was losing the sight of his right eye. Wilhelm always felt a bit more comfortable in the company of human imperfection. There would be no critical comparisons that might float behind someone's eyes as occasionally occurred at court; comparisons which none, regardless of title, ever dared to express.

But von Drascher was more than loyal. The battle-hardened officer could be utterly silent and utterly ruthless as required. Wilhelm could playfully ridicule many of the titled pomposities of the court and visiting royalty, even so far as to playfully punch the short-statured King of Italy on his recent visit to Berlin; and then to openly revel in their cowering responses.

But never -- never mock the Graf von Drascher.

Vice Admiral, the Graf von Drascher withdrew a green file folder from inside a manila folder. It was a file no other senior officer or minister even knew existed, including Reich Chancellor Chlodwig zu Hohenlohe-Schillngsfurst, who had been sitting across from von Drascher at the council table.

The instant that Wilhelm nodded toward them, two black-red-and-white liveried attendants drew the great doors closed. With the final click of the latch the vast room became soundless, the admiral started, speaking slowly as his Emperor could become quickly impatient with von Drascher's rural accent.

"Your Majesty, here is the status of the four ships. They have been concealed in the Ebing shipyards as commercial shipping and will appear to be that when launched." He slid four pages from the green file across the table.

Wilhelm spread the papers with his right hand, quickly noting the summary status of each along with the date and location that the necessary armaments would be mounted -- well away from where any British agents could observe without -- experiencing lethal risk. He tapped the data on the first ship, SMS Prädator, the Predator, which was only two months from launch. The other three were three to four months behind that.

"That ship cannot fail to launch on schedule, Admiral," the Kaiser said coldly. "Other wheels are turning which cannot be stopped ... without ... without serious awkwardness to the *Kaiserreich* ... to Me." Wilhelm had always looked with deep envy on the British Royal Navy, the ability of the government of his grandmother, Queen Victoria, to project British power anywhere in the world. She had the vast wealth of the entire British Empire to draw from, while he had far more limited resources which forced carefully calculated priorities in building a High Seas Fleet. And Prussia and Germany did not have the naval customs and stalwart institutions of England. The Reich was based on deeply embedded Army traditions; therefore His Navy would have to be His personal creation from the start.

Wilhelm had barely become Emperor when the British government under Lord Salisbury's guidance as Prime Minister had passed the Naval Defence Act in 1889 with its two-power standard. Under the Act, Britain was committed to maintaining a battleship force equal to that of the next two countries (France and Russia) combined. Parliament had allocated £21.5 million over five years, equivalent to, as Wilhelm had calculated, 430 million Gold Marks (GM)! An amount beyond the Reich's capability to match, even draining funds from throughout the government.. The act had been renewed in 1894 and was still in place now, in 1896. The dreadnoughts were of the Royal Sovereign class, at 15,500 tons the finest battleship in the world.

While he would continue to build up the Imperial Navy to support the Imperial colonies and to raise Germany's world position, Wilhelm had developed another plan, one which, he was confident, would cause the government of his grandmother to pause.

Wilhelm knew two English foreign agents were watching the building of one battleship, scheduled to launch in late 1898, which should cause the British government little immediate concern.

However, at Ebing, a more isolated shipyard, the keels of the four predators had been laid seven, eight and nine months ago. They would be fast, heavily armored commercial raiders with carefully concealed armament of two 3.5 inch guns, six heavy machine-guns and four torpedo tubes, scheduled to begin launching in 1896. Their coal-fired steam-turbine engines could drive them to a flank speed of 30 knots, in smooth sea conditions for two to three hours, at the most, or risk depleting the ship's store of coal.

But they were fast enough, for long enough, for their purpose.

Two suspected British observers had been removed from the Ebing location, their bodies transported for disposal in southern France.

Even with its steadily growing production of steel and iron, the German Reich could never match the English Navy battleship for battleship, the effort would bankrupt the country; but the predators could suddenly appear in certain *necessary* locations to impose His will, to imbalance the British decision making, to force them to hesitate.

If the British Royal Navy hesitated, so would all European navies.

The Kaiser was half-English by birth, his English mother, Victoria, was the former Princess Royal, the daughter of Prince Albert and Queen Victoria. He had been Queen Victoria's first grandchild. To the barely suppressed criticism of the German court, the Empress Victoria used English tutors for her Willy's education. He had been Willy since there already too many Fritz's in the family. She also favored English physicians to deal with her son's disabilities, who had fitted the young boy with ugly appliances to try to stretch and correct his withered left arm, a regimen which had forced the boy to endure more daily pain while withdrawing further into himself and away from others his own age.

Now even in his seventh year as Emperor and King, the only daily newspaper that Wilhelm read was the London *Daily Graphic*. There were mutterings in and outside the court that the Kaiser seemed more English than Prussian; and other much quieter whisperings, that the Kaiser seemed unable to focus on any major area for long, opting to spend much of his time relaxing on the Imperial yacht, the Hohenzollern II, with its gold-plated fixtures.

The crueler rumors were driven by the Bismarck family in retaliation for the Kaiser's abrupt dismissal of the Iron Chancellor. But the inevitable court gossip was never of interest, rather it was the continuing development of the British Royal Navy that occupied Wilhelm's thoughts, dominated his priorities and those of his agents in Great Britain and elsewhere, even including two helpful if naïve Americans in New York.

But even with the renewal of the Defence Act, Britain had never actually achieved the two-country standard, even with more millions of pounds and thousands of tons of steel. But even then the Royal Navy was unmatchable.

Wilhelm resolutely guarded his *Kommandogewalt*, the absolute power over the Army and Navy that all German rulers had striven to create and protect, tempered, occasionally only by the budget limitations imposed by the Reichstag -- but there were ways around that -- which was where the Predator monies had come from.

The new battleship, the first German ship with triple screws, the 11,599 ton Seiner Majestät Schiff (SMS) Kaiser Friedrich III, was intended for the North Sea, "the German lake" as one unnamed London *Times* reporter had once written, inaccurately. Laid down in early 1895, the battleship would cost 27 million GM when finally launched. But each of the four 11 million GM predators were for deployment elsewhere, locations the Kaiser had not revealed even to von Drascher, nor, certainly, to the Imperial Navy Cabinet which was unaware of the four ships existence. All that could wait for the final assignment and training of the crews.

In two months. Then the Army would be brought into the discussion as well.

The Kaiser nodded his approvals, initialed the expenditures, and watched as the Admiral closed the arched doors behind him. The latch clicked. The Emperor of Germany and King of Prussia stood, shifted his useless left hand into the special pocket in his uniform jacket -- it was a bemedaled Field Marshal's uniform today. Wilhelm paused to closely examine *der Grosse* once again: the steady confident gaze and the resolute jaw -- the man's assured inevitability.

Destiny. Firmly setting his own jaw, but against the preliminary ear pains, Wilhelm started for a side door that led to his inner private office where instead of a chair at his personal desk, he used a stool shaped like a saddle.

A divine destiny.

In two months, three at the most, the beginning, the creation of his *Seegeltung,* his sea presence.

Wilhelm suddenly spit out a stream of curses. The ear pains suddenly exploded, stabbing at his mind. He moved faster toward the dark medicine in his desk, his stride awkward, as he compensated for his slower moving left leg.

The Kaiser bellowed more curses.

8

State Secretary of the Imperial Navy Office (RMA)

Berlin

Tuesday, February 11, 1896

Admiral Hans Hugo, the Graf von Drascher was born the second son of the Prince Eugin Hugo of Drascher-Lippe, a small principality that Chancellor Prince Otto von Bismarck had scooped up into his collection of histories and places that became, with the incorporation of Prussia, his Imperial German Empire. Drascher's father had not wanted a German Empire, had not wanted to be a part of a German Empire; he had only wanted to live peacefully in his small castle by the river Weser, respected by his people, hunt the local deer and boar, and pass on his titles to his eldest son as they had been passed down to him from across six generations of the Drascher-Lippe holdings. Hans Hugo had been sixteen when the principality vanished into Bismarck's hands. His elder brother was still a Prince, but of nothing but four impoverished and irrelevant villages clinging to the banks of the Weser. Years ago the beloved castle had fallen into terminal disrepair.

As added encouragement, Bismarck had intervened with the Diskonto Bank in Berlin to cut off Prince Eugin's funds to force the "unification" of Drascher-Lippe with the Empire. Thus in 1890, the Graf Von Drascher and his close friends had rejoiced with the best champagne when the new Kaiser had cast Bismarck out of his government, and thus Wilhelm II had earned his staunch loyalty. He had toasted the eternal glory of the Reich of the Emperor of Germany and King of Prussia, Wilhelm II.

But now the Graf von Drascher was uneasy. Fifty-two years old, twenty-nine years in the Kaiserliche Marine, promoted to Rear Admiral by Wilhelm I, the grandfather of Wilhelm II -- but in von Drascher's hidden opinion and, he knew, the very private opinions of a number of other senior officers, the German Empire did not need a High Seas Fleet, not at the expense of weakening the Army or, in trying to compete with the British Royal Navy, and, in the process, bankrupting Germany. The Kaiser was as dedicated to a High Seas Fleet as his predecessors had been to the Army, and von Drascher had supported that dedication with his own. But in the past two years, and then finally in only the past weeks with the Kaiser's first public use of the terms *Weltmacht und Weltpolitik*, world power and world dominion, had deeply shaken von Drascher and others.

What lay ahead?

German access to the oceans was geographically very limited, though improved when the 100 kilometer

Kaiser-Wilhelm Canal between the Baltic Sea and the North Sea was opened in 1889 -- at a cost of 150 million GM. But even then, there were no overseas coaling stations in place to support any High Seas Fleet operations around the world.

The push in the Foreign Office for the establishment of German colonies in Africa, the Pacific Ocean, and even in China in competition with France, Great Britain and Russia without the means of assured overseas supply, was another policy that was drawing more and deeper concern.

One evening one of von Drascher's closest friends with twenty-three years of naval experience, too far into his brandies, had leaned across the table and muttered, "Damn, my good friend, we are being gently pushed by the people in their frock coats into a crippling war."

Von Drascher and the other two senior naval officers at the table went pale. Von Drascher quickly looked around at nearby tables to see if anyone had overheard the comment. Fortunately, the beerhall had erected its customary walls of raucous noise.

When the Highest came to His throne no German naval tradition existed as there had been for the British for over a hundred years. It was the Army that was the backbone of the Reich. But Wilhelm II had publicly declared, "We have a dire need for a strong fleet." And so the German naval tradition began in 1889 with Wilhelm II, only seven years ago, when for the first time, His Highest appointed an Admiral to command the Imperial Navy, instead of an Army General as in the past.

The entire German Navy in 1896 was now four armored frigates under construction; two armored corvettes that were designed in 1892 and just launched, and four battleships of the Brandenburg class, 10,000 tons, designed in 1888. Those ships had been launched in 1892 at a cost of 15,832,000 GM each. They used compound-armor for the first time, a design originated by Harvey in the U.K., Krupp in Germany, and Simpson in America.

But the Brandenburg ships could not measure up even to the British cruisers. The five new Kaiser Friedrich III class ships could alter that situation, assuming the British did not introduce any remarkably new vessel technology, when the five finally launched in four or five years. But there was no central master plan for naval construction to ensure efficient use of Imperial funds, nor for an Imperial Naval Strategy, just "limitless fleet plans" and "countless cruisers" as a prominent member of the Reichstag had sarcastically dismissed the latest request for funds.

Drascher shrugged his shoulders in frustration, or … was it in defeat?

In 1889, in one of the first decisions in his new reign, the Kaiser had dissolved the Imperial Admiralty and split its responsibilities between a Chief of the High Command of Navy (Oberkommando), with a rank equivalent to the commanding general of the Army, who would be responsible for strategies and tactics, deployment of ships and men, along with the movement of ships in foreign waters. All administrative control was given to a State Secretary of the Imperial Navy Office (Reichs-Marine-Amt, RMA) nominally serving under the chancellor. The RMA was responsible for the construction and maintenance of all naval units. It, in turn, was split into ten departments, each designated with a code letter as: Shipyards (B), Construction (R), Nautical (K), Central (M), and General Navy (A). With their split responsibilities the groups did not talk to each other, but they *all* talked to the Kaiser.

Von Drascher had hidden the Predators in the private shipyard in Ebing. With the bureaucratic obstructions surrounding all naval decisions he had labeled them as K, Nautical.

No one, he had observed uneasily, had noticed.

He recalled a recent meeting of the RMA senior group leaders attended by the Highest. As the meeting dragged on with conflicting declarations, priorities, and issues, von Drascher, who sat in the rear of the room, could see the face of the Kaiser begin to go cold, a familiar warning sign that von Drascher had learned to dread.

Suddenly Wilhelm had stood and bellowed, "I am tired of these discussions! I simply command and that is it. To Hell with it! I am the Supreme War Lord! I do not decide. I command!" He turned and the first Grand Admiral of the Imperial German Navy stomped out of the room.

Indecision reigned.

But what about the Predators due to launch in only three or four months, with their modern technology and hidden armaments? Von Drascher pulled a rolled map of Europe from its tube and spread it out over his desk, placing books at the corners to hold the large sheet in place. Where? Where did the Kaiser propose to use the Predators? A question that he, von Drascher, had not considered before -- a question that duty had prevented him from asking, even to himself -- until now.

The North Sea? He paused. Perhaps alongside the new Kaiser Friedrich III battleships when they are launched. But why His urgency and secrecy *now*? Harass the British coast? Mein Gott! That would be national suicide. Not the Atlantic. The Predators, even with their advanced armor and fire controls, would be only mosquitoes irritating the vast British merchant shipping, insects to be destroyed by a squadron of battleships -- or heavy cruisers, more likely.

So where?

The Kaiser's urgency suggested something else. The Mediterranean -- that was it! In the confines of the Great Sea the Predators could be in their element. Hit and hide. But where? And, von Drascher pursed his lips, more importantly, *why?* What were his Kaiser's objectives? After a moment, then another, the admiral tapped the map at the only logical place, the only objective worth the risk, and softly swore as a cold chill swept down his backside.

Mein Gott! No, no, not there!

Rumors in the past several months had begun to spread softly in the halls of the government palaces, that Wilhelm II was "not quite stable" -- even, and with far greater caution, *geisteskrank*, insane. Rumors that von Drascher himself had fought to destroy as unforgivable and disloyal.

But now -- now?

He slowly lowered himself into his chair, placed his hands over his scarred face -- and wept.

9

Washington, D.C., was dark with a steady light rain brushing and searching across the windows of the President's private study on the second floor of the White House. The sun would not rise for another two hours but it wouldn't be seen in the heavy storm clouds forecasted.

Sitting forward in his leather rocking chair, wrapped in a heavy brown and red robe, Grover Cleveland handed his Secretary of State the deciphered cable from the British PM.

Your answer sir stop time is of the essence stop

Olney, in turn, handed Cleveland the telegram from Judson Rowland.

The President looked up sharply. "Seventeen! A seventeen year old girl is all America can muster to help the British?" Cleveland was stunned.

Before Cleveland could respond further, Olney said quietly, "Judson Rowland would bet his life on Kyame Piddington's abilities, my friend, and I in turn would bet mine on Rowland's judgment. Her story, if asked, will be that she is traveling to Monaco to paint the portraits of some titled people whose names she cannot reveal. She is to observe and report to Sir David Oswald Wilkinson at the British Foreign Office, and to me as often as possible, but certainly within the first week of her arriving in Monaco.

"Her communication point, according to my conversations with the British military attaché here, will be Smith's Bank in Monaco through the bank's manager, the Honorable Albert Victor Bethell. If she encounters any serious problems, and, *in her judgment*, her life becomes at risk, Miss Piddington is to return to England immediately and may, as necessary, call for assistance from any British official office, anywhere."

Cleveland nodded. "But seventeen, Olney. Does her family know?"

"Kyame Piddington has no family, Mister President."

Cleveland leaned back in the rocker, he passed his hand across his mouth, frowning. Then, "I am in the position of asking a girl who could be my own daughter to put her life at risk, an unknown risk ... even possibly a lethal risk." He slowly shook his head.

Olney waited, watching his friend struggle with the moral decision. He was confident that he knew what the result would be.

After a moment, Cleveland swung forward on the rocker, stood, and said: "Send Kyame Piddington; and, Olney, when she returns from this task, I want to meet this extraordinary young woman, privately, here.

"Notify the Prime Minister by cipher immediately." The President stopped. "But, Olney, don't tell him her age."

As Secretary Olney went down the stairs to the first floor communications office of the White House, he smiled. Rowland already had Miss Piddington positioned, waiting at the New York office at 61 Broadway of the Hamburg-America Line to take possession of her ticket for the Atlantic crossing to England on the S/S Auguste Victoria. Given the President's decision, Kyame Piddington would arrive at Southampton within six to seven days. Scotland Yard detectives would be waiting to escort her to London.

And, Olney resolved himself to spend some serious time with the remarkable Kyame Piddington when she returned.

Rowland had described the Piddington girl to Olney as a presence he never wanted coming after him.

10

S/S Auguste Victoria, Hamburg America Line

En route

Saturday, February 15, 1896

Kyame held her breath, moving faster as she walked near the ship's dining room. With the sea now calm, the effects of her first two days of raging and retching seasickness were finally fading, but the experience had still left her weakened and unsteady. She had relied on Mar-Tan's settling cure, cups of hot ginger tea, which had helped, but yesterday, encountering a particularly heavy sea had reversed all her progress and had driven her back to retching again and again into the toilet until she finally fell to her knees slumped against the wall, devoid of any energy. But now, the most vicious symptoms seem to have abated; but like relentless assassins, still lurked in the shadows close by.

A British gentleman in expensive tweeds, seeing her walking with her hand against the wall and noting her pallor, had stopped to cleverly suggest Lord Nelson's seasickness cure. At least the tweedy gentleman had thought it clever. The famous naval hero of Trafalgar had been notorious for his persistent seasickness, and when asked for his cure by a reporter had explained, "Sitting under a tree". The wide toothy grin of the Britisher had been sickening to her, and she pushed on by him to get out on deck and into the bracing sea air. Just being away from everyone, to suffer in private was all she needed to start getting things under control.

Kyame had experienced some wild stagecoach rides when she and Papa were going from one small town to another across Oklahoma, Texas, Kansas, Nebraska and Colorado as the Impossible Piddingtons, which made the ship's movements seem gentle in comparison, but it was the ship's relentless rolling and the shifting of the floor along with the sight of the endless surging sea through the port holes that had so completely thrown off her bearings, and had mercilessly churned her guts. Much as Judson Rowland in San Francisco had once described his latest bout of seasickness, arriving from Hawai'i. But, at least in the stagecoach, the surrounding countryside was stationary and gave a solid reference point.

But even then, even with her improving condition, the insistent clinging odor of breakfast pork sausages that Kyame caught as she walked by the dining room almost unraveled all her progress in one step.

Holding her breath, Kyame strode more rapidly.

***

Holding her hat securely with both hands, Kyame returned inside, the cold winds slammed the doors solidly closed behind her. Kyame approached the double brass-bound glass and oak doors of the ship's card room for a place to sit and rest before resuming her exploration of the Auguste Victoria first class deck. Seeing her approach, a member of the ship's crew held the door for her. A senior member apparently, based on his gold-braided uniform and white visored cap.

"Good morning, Miss," he said, raising his white cap and bowing slightly. "I trust you found breakfast satisfactory."

Breakfast...?

Kyame swallowed hard as she felt her stomach churn at the renewed memory of sizzling pork.

"It was fine," she managed, to close off the discussion. She nodded as she passed by him into the room, a layer of cigar and pipe smoke drifting across the room like a curious though benign, or perhaps a mischievous spirit.

The first-class card room of the German ocean liner, Auguste Victoria, was spacious with three large circular polished mahogany tables along one wall, inlaid with mother-of-pearl in the shape of hearts, diamonds, clubs and spades. Six hexagonally shaped green-baize covered tables ran down the center. Arranged along the far wall were green and red leather wing chairs with two black velvet upholstered couches at each corner.

Each table had a low hanging Tiffany stained-glass shade with a crystal oil lamp which illuminated only the playing surface. Even with lunch still two hours away, three of the hexagonal tables were active with poker and whist players, some laughing while others loudly damned their luck.

Kyame stood for a moment to watch the nearest circular table, then stepped away so as not to appear to be too interested in the cards they held. Experience in saloons, and in elegant hotel card rooms had taught her not to appear to be too interested in any of the games. That invited the wrong kind of attention and suspicion. But, in turning away, Kyame caught the move of the black bearded, elegantly dressed gentleman in a well-tailored dark gray sack suit, as he smoothly dealt a Greek to his ally across the table from him, along with another card from the middle of the deck.

Kyame recognized that she had caught the dealer's moves because she was at an unexpected and thus an unprotected angle from the dealer's range of vision. Face-on, to the other players, the cold dealing would have been undetectable.

She recognized the dealer as the man who had introduced himself to her as E.S. Andrews, president of the Brandon Commerce Co. of Chicago, when they had awkwardly brushed shoulders climbing the main staircase to the first class staterooms on the first day while the liner was still moored at the New York City dock.

After politely apologizing for the encounter, Andrews, who had stood an inch or two shorter than Kyame, had hurriedly explained that he was traveling to London to establish a new company office; too quickly and too smoothly for it to be the truth, Kyame had concluded.

And his eyes.

Kyame instantly recognized the malevolent cunning embedded in Andrews' probing blue eyes when he had looked at, when he had instantly apprised her -- so like the eyes of the successful -- of the still living gamblers she and Papa had encountered in their travels, in the boarding houses, hotel lobbies, rail cars, and saloons. And backstage, where some had come where they, like some others, had considered her a theatre girl, as simply a thing whose time they wanted to buy for a five-dollar gold coin, and sometimes less. Kyame shuddered when she had approached her stateroom door. E.S. Andrews was not a man she wanted to know.

Judson Rowland had insisted she travel first class, as it would be a "more interesting hunting ground" and physically safer, more secure than the lower tiers. Anglo-Oriental Marine Insurance always travels first class, he had laughed, especially when Mr. Cleveland was paying the bills.

The other three men around the poker table with Andrews were collecting and arranging the cards they had called for after their initial ante had been thrown on the table. Kyame noted Andrews' ally -- acts too casual, he must be the one -- dressed in a tight fitting satin vested blue suit, brushed a finger across his thin gray mustache. There was no change in Andrews' expression.

Normally, the lead gambler would want his ally at his left to negate any cuts before the plug man dealt. Possibly the left hand chair was already occupied when the play had started.

Ladies were not generally expected or welcomed to join the gambling games, as Kyame was quietly instructed by the ship's Purser, who had opened the door for her. "The presence of a lady would restrict the abilities of the gentlemen to fully express themselves", he whispered to her when she had moved away from the Andrews game. "The card room is reserved after dinner for, ah, quieter games as bridge in which ladies are certainly welcome."

A well-stocked polished mahogany bar was at the far end as waiters in trim blue-and-white uniforms moved rapidly among the tables, their trays balanced at the tips of their fingers. A large rectangular beveled mirror was centered behind the bar. Portraits framed in heavy gold of the German countryside and seacoast lined two of the walls, while a large formal portrait of Kaiser Wilhelm II in an ostentatious white military uniform with the elaborately gowned Empress Auguste Victoria beside him, was centered on one wall.

"Does the ship get a cut of the stakes ... a rake-off?" Kyame whispered in return.

The Purser, G.E.W. Jellicoe, his brass name-tag revealed, raised his eyebrows in shock, his lips tightened. He vigorously shook his head. "Rake-off!" he gasped. His eyes widened at her use of such an expression, his whisper coarse. "Why ... why of course not, Miss. The games are of individual challenges of risk ... of gentlemen matching wits and strategies ... and resources. The Auguste Victoria desires no say in the games' conduct, except, naturally, to ensure their honesty. We have never experienced any instance of cheating on this ship in its four years of crossing the Atlantic." His smile became arrogant. "And, as a further precaution, Miss, the only cards allowed to be used in the card room are the ship's own cards made exclusively for the Hamburg-America Line in Germany ... and available only onboard after the ship has left port."

Kyame nodded and smiled, as Andrews palmed a card from his fanned hand, smoothly replacing it with a card from his sleeve, probably using a mechanical hold-out strapped to his arm. There were other less risky but more demanding methods. They were methods that required hours of intense practice. The round of betting continued. The gold coins and paper currency in the middle of the table grew steadily.

Her opinion of Andrews as a player went down a bit, as Kyame had learned that the top advantage men never used a mechanical contrivance. A one-armed, though remarkably handsome gambler, who was called Le Renard, the Fox, had instructed her over lunch with Papa at a hotel in Julesburg, Colorado, "Mechanicals are cumbersome, unnecessary, and a constant menace to a an advantage player's reputation. Only a player of uncertain confidence would consider using holdouts and other mechanicals."

"May I then watch, sir," said Kyame, smiling, "from a suitable distance that would not restrict the gentlemen's freedom? Matching odds with decisions is an interesting insight to a gentleman's ... character ... is it not?"

G. E. W. Jellicoe nodded with a graceful sweep of his hand toward the black velvet couch well away from any of the tables, as he beckoned to a waiter. A well-dressed older lady was seated in a green wing chair against the far wall, sewing, and seemed to be mumbling something, talking to herself. As Kyame unbuttoned her coat, her fingers touched her loaded over-under derringer. Laying the coat beside her, she spread and straightened her skirts that had been blown into disarray in the sea winds and settled back into the velvet couch. The weighted yellow scarf of Kali was in her skirt pocket.

Kyame noted that seated at the far table with three other men, a partially bald man wearing pince-nez glasses in a white-vested pinstripe suit occasionally glanced over at the woman on the couch.

Kyame ordered Darjeeling tea when the white-jacketed waiter arrived, who then vanished only to return barely five minutes later with a tray of a white and blue porcelain pot, cup and saucer, a pot of warm milk, a bowl of sugar, a pitcher of hot water and a plate of tea cookies with HAP embossed on them. As the waiter poured, Kyame glanced over at the nearby table.

"Species of a left-handed goat!" One of the players at the Andrews table suddenly cursed, his face flushed, slamming his cards down on the table, as each of the players were revealing their hands. "I would have sworn ..." He noticed Kyame and abruptly smothered his curses, gritting his teeth.

Andrews' partner, smiling, leaned over the table to scoop up the mound of coins and bills, as Andrews himself shook his head at his bad luck, tossing his cards haphazardly on the table. He withdrew a cigar from a vest pocket, drew it under his nose to inhale its fragrance. He glanced over at Kyame, then back to the table.

Kyame, in an automatic reaction, touched the loaded 41-caliber derringer in her skirt pocket, the same weapon she had used twice with lethal effect in San Francisco eight months earlier.

Andrews' quick glance had been filled with intense suspicion.

"A well-played hand, sir," Andrews said, his voice a controlled melodious tenor, to the blue suited winner, who nodded his acknowledgement. The cards were being gathered up by the player to the left of Andrews in preparation for dealing the next hand.

A handsome haul, Kyame thought, but she couldn't quickly estimate the value as the currency was principally British and French, with apparently some German and American mixed in. She was still converting the various exchange rates. One English pound, 1£, was worth about $4.85, so the pot seemed worth at least $250, probably more.

It didn't make sense for plug-men to score too much too soon on a voyage, J.W. had instructed, when they had been once discussing cheating strategies in his hotel room. That could squelch the flow of cash, and potentially draw too much early attention. Any cheaters on board a ship would most likely work two-pluck-two or even, possibly, three-pluck-one, in teams of two or three, to ensure steady winnings but not always by the same player. No competent professional would work an ocean liner without a reliable ally. Working without an ally was for locations where the advantage gambler had a ready escape route available if things became uneasy, like, J. W. had suggested, on a train.

Cadwell had then told her a story of a pair of Irish cheaters who had posed as an elderly and harmless couple, he a retired accountant and she a former schoolmistress. They were never suspected until a member of the crew of the British liner on which they had been traveling discovered a deck of marked cards stuffed behind the piano while cleaning the card room. A Frenchman, who had won big, was brought before the first mate and charged with cheating.

"The couple, working their system with their cards, had won steadily above average amounts, but they had never won enough at any one time to draw any attention," Cadwell had explained. "Their downfall came when, after resuming their youthful personae, they were overheard laughing about the fate of the Frenchman, whose remarkable luck at the tables had been genuine, but whose luck before the first mate had been abominable. The cheaters hadn't noticed the chief engineer of the British ship sitting with his wife behind them."

She and the mesmerist had laughed over their coffee at the time. Then J.W. had added, "You must have the patience of an old priest ... or better, that of a hungry assassin to successfully cheat ... to be able to recognize 'the moment', that exact instant in time when a hidden move can be safely accomplished."

Kyame had no interest in actually cheating, she simply wanted to be able to do it if she ever had to, and, even more, she wanted to be able to detect it, much like the challenge of figuring out a magician's tricks.

And, it was fun to make the cards do unexpected things. So long as, she had frowned, a roguish queen didn't stick to a lazy king.

***

Relaxing on the couch and spreading her dark blue skirts, Kyame smiled up at the Purser who then turned and left the card room. She leaned back deeper into the black velvet couch to sip and to continue to casually observe the games, particularly the cheaters at the game near the doors. The ship was almost three days out from New York bound for Southampton, England, where in four more days or so, depending on the track of a forecasted storm, there would be someone from Scotland Yard to meet her at the pier to escort her to London, to the Foreign Office ... and then to ... where?

Sipping the marvelously fragrant Darjeeling, and watching now the husband-wife team working their system at the further table, she reflected on a comment an elderly gambler had made to her in Denver in her travels with Papa, a comment with which J. W. Cadwell had been in full agreement. The gambler's handling of the deck had been undetectable -- even after he had showed Kyame his blind shuffle and blind cut. Undetectable.

The gambler had enjoyed her amazement. "There is but one pleasure greater than winning, Miss, and that is, in making the hazard." The gambler had also warned her that: "Winnings from the table are 'pretty money', and would always be spent as freely as water. Understand," he added, "casino managers liked to see big winners; their apparent success always drew more players eager to match the success … and, at the end of the day, the casino would take all the money plus profits back anyway."

Then he had grinned, a toothless grin as he had pawned his teeth for a sandwich and a bottle of rye. "Manipulation, in the end, is better than speculation. But," he had emphasized, tapping hard on the table, "always, Miss, realize that even when you detect a plug-man's move, know that there may, and probably will be moves that you didn't pick up. Those are the moves that will do you in … always, always do you in if you get overconfident." He spread out his scarred fingers on the table. Four of the fingers of his right hand were missing their fingertips, apparently chopped off by quick-eyed card players. "Your hands, Miss, are far too delicate for this treatment for exercising poor judgment."

Kyame recalled the chill that went down her back seeing his ragged fingers. Papa had commented later that the old gambler's lesson was one to remember even away from the card table.

***

In his elegant closing room and leaning back from the low table with its golden china, James Dixey's countenance had changed, hardening, as he had drawn a paper from inside his jacket.

"Our evening has been remarkable, Miss Piddington, but this is the basic motive for our gathering. This telegram is from Judson Rowland, whom you know well.

"The British Prime Minister, Lord Salisbury, has asked President Cleveland for help in the south of France. All but one of the British intelligence agents in that area have been killed. The PM is worried that something is developing but has no data on which to take action. Thus he has asked the President if he can reposition some American agents temporarily until the British Foreign Office can identify and transfer some replacements from other colonial areas.

"Your role would be to gain understanding of the deaths of the agents as quickly as possible, communicate that to the local contact of the Foreign Office … and return to the United States on the first available ship." Dixey paused to sip his port. "Secretary Olney asked Mr. Rowland for recommendations as America … and everything we discuss in this room must be strictly confidential as, gentlemen, you all recognize … America has no government agents in Europe at this time.

"Judson wants," James Dixey had leaned toward Kyame, "he wants to recommend you, Miss Piddington, but not, naturally, without first gaining your approval. In addition to a regular passport, you would also be issued a diplomatic passport to be used as you might deem necessary."

Dixey paused as each of the men watched her.

After a moment, Kyame said, "I don't speak French and have never been in Europe, Mr. Dixey. Surely, America has more resources available ... than just ... me?" Her cocked half-smile brought smiles to the faces of each of the men. She glanced over at J. W. Cadwell, her eyebrow raised in query.

The mesmerist drew heavily on his cigar, then breathed out the smoke slowly. "I would trust you to handle this situation, Kyame, before I would trust anyone else. Your Papa, I believe, would be honored by your meeting this urgent need of the President."

Yes, Kyame could almost feel Papa's presence in this room of books and jade, his smile of reassurance, of confidence, as he had done so many times as they had waited back-stage. "Now," he would whisper just as they would walk onto the stage, "now, dear Daughter, we scare them."

Kyame nodded to Dixey. "If I can help, Mr. Dixey, I will do my best."

Dixey had extended his hand to her which she had grasped.

Dr. Mar-Tan closed his eyes for a moment, then looked up and over at Kyame. "I would agree, Miss Piddington, with my good friend, the mesmerist. Your spirit of *tsyh ker*, of the essence of an assassin ... you truly are the Shadow of the Tiger, young miss. You have a name to be feared."

Haroon Kahn nodded, his lips tight. "I have no doubt, Miss Piddington," he said, "as you carry Her yellow ruhmal that Kali Herself will walk beside you."

***

Kyame rose to return to her stateroom, her stomach settled and calm. She didn't notice Andrews carefully studying her as she left the card room, his deep frown and his sharp glance toward his partner.

There was to be magic tonight after the dinner according to a handout left in each first class cabin.

Magic and Mystery

in the tradition of

The Great

Jean Eugene Robert-Houdin

To be presented

by

M. Pierre André Reymond

Paris, France

To immediately follow desert

11

The Imperial Yacht: SMY Hohenzollern II

Transiting the Kaiser Canal to the North Sea

Saturday, February 15, 1896

Dressed in his favorite uniform, that of a British Admiral of the Fleet, a rank granted him by his grandmother, Queen Victoria, with his lifeless left hand inserted into its special pocket, Kaiser Wilhelm II sipped his coffee, another sip, then replaced the cup on its saucer, turned the page, to page 138, of the American Captain Alfred Thayer Mahan's *The Influence of Sea Power_on History*, published six years ago in 1890, a book which Wilhelm had ordered mandatory reading by all of his naval officers. A book of which he had first written in a telegram sent in May, 1894, to his childhood friend, the American journalist, Poultney Bigelow, with whom he had once played cowboys and Indians:

"I am just now not reading, but devouring Captain Mahan's book and am trying to learn it by heart. It is a first class work and classical in all points. It is on board all my ships and constantly quoted by my Captains and officers."

The yacht library was silent, lighted with brilliant sunlight through the large porthole windows with books and manuscripts filling shelves reaching the ceiling on three walls. A large white rug with the yellow, black and red symbol of the Kaiser woven in its center spread across the entire room, stopping only a foot short of the bookcases and of the yellow and black marble hearth. Mahan was propped up on the reading table, held securely against the gentle rolling of the 400 foot long yacht by a set of steel braces. Page 138 was already heavily underlined in his customary blue, particularly the sentence about half-way down the page. He put down the cup, then picked up the blue pencil and underlined the sentence once again.

It is not the taking of individual ships or convoys, be they few or many, that strikes down the money power of a nation; it is the possession of that overbearing power on the sea which drives the enemy's flag from it, or allows it to appear only as a fugitive; and which by controlling the great common, closes the highways by which commerce moves to and from the enemy's shores. This overbearing power can only be exercised by great navies...

Great Navies! Wilhelm clenched his right fist, bringing it down softly on the table again and again.

Mein Gott, great navies!

But the crucial foundation of great navies was, according to Mahan, the battleship -- not the commerce raiders, armored cruisers and torpedo boats of the

Kaiserliche Marine, the Imperial Navy. It was a motley collection of vessels that had created a jumble, an embarrassing chaotic mess of the 1893 Naval Exercises. Too many ships, too damn many *kinds of ships*, too many old ships, faulty tactics, and too much, too much undisciplined disagreement among his flag officers.

Germany had an aging fleet without a rudder ... *oder sogar ein verwechselt Kompass*, or even a confounded compass, for that matter, the Kaiser snarled to himself.

Weltmacht ist Seemacht – world power is sea power. Wilhelm dropped the blue pencil to sip more black coffee. His jaw began to tighten as he reflected on the past three days in Berlin at the end of which he had to escape to his yacht to keep his sanity.

The execrable -- no -- the obstinate Reichstag committee on Naval Affairs had voted to reduce spending on his Hochseeflotte, his High Seas Fleet, in favor of leaving more funds to the Army Committee for the purchase of a hundred pieces of 7.7 centimeter field artillery along with the horses and carriages to drag them about. *Mere feld Kanonen!* More field canons! A thousand more pieces of artillery would not make Germany a world power! Only battleships and heavy cruisers could defend the eight overseas colonies of Imperial Germany against the grasping English and French!

Too many cruisers the Committee had privately complained, thirty-six! When they, also privately, would only consider four! And, perhaps, not even fund those when it came to a public vote.

Wilhelm's jaw tightened further. There were, by God, other ways, other avenues he had --

"Your Majesty," the pleasant voice said, "you promised me a tour about the deck of your magnificent yacht this beautiful morning."

Wilhelm breathed deeply, sucking down his frustration with Reichstag politics and the clumsy actions of his Naval officers to look up into the startling blue eyes of the enchanting Countess Natalia Mergasova, a relation of some kind of the Russian Ambassador in Berlin. Yes, last night at dinner he had promised a promenade to the extraordinarily attractive young woman, dressed now in deep blue accented by shimmering gold. He smiled, dropped his blue pencil, and rose to bow and kiss her delicate fingers.

"Of course, Countess," said Wilhelm. "It is my pleasure."

***

The original Imperial Yacht (Staatsyacht), SM Hohenzollern, used by Wilhelm's predecessors had been only a paddlewheel steamship that had become hopelessly outdated. Wilhelm had dismissed the vessel to the ship-breakers in favor of a new innovative design, more reflective of modern German engineering prowess.

However, with funds limited by the Reichstag, the Hohenzollern II had to be designed for dual usage: as the Kaiser's Imperial yacht in peacetime, and as an armed sloop (mounted with eleven guns) during wartime.

With its twin screws and 9,558 total shaft horsepower, the yacht could cruise 785 nautical miles at 20 knots or 1,565 nautical miles at 14 knots, with a top speed of 21.5 knots.

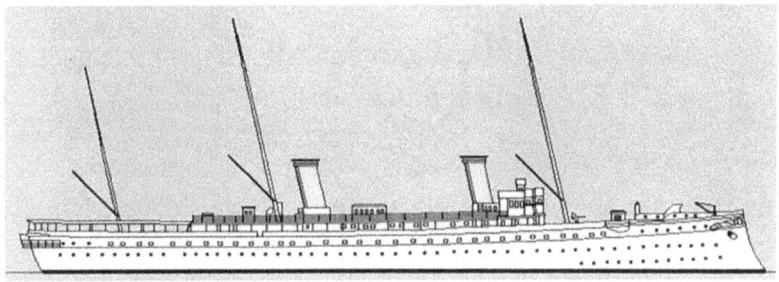

SM Hohenzollern II

The Kaiser had suggested converting two or three of the unused staterooms to coal storage to even further extend the ship's range at top speed, a suggestion not yet implemented. With a crew of over 300 men, some of whom were always armed, and always escorted by a light cruiser, the Kaiser's safety was never at risk. Responding to government reports extolling the tight cost controls used in building the yacht, a reporter, no longer employed, had pointed out that the value of just the gold plating on the railings of the Hohenzollern II was equivalent to over six years of income of a skilled craftsman at the Krupp Works. The story appeared only once.

"Magnificent, Your Majesty, your ship is almost threatening in its size and speed. It takes my breath away." The countess's hands fluttered in her attempt to express her awe. "How fast are we going now?"

Wilhelm turned to his aide, a Lieutenant, who was following them at a discrete distance.

"Presently 18 knots, Your Majesty. Our range at that speed is 872 nautical miles, sir."

The Countess was clearly impressed, her remarkable eyes went wide. "Why … why Your Majesty, we could just … just go to Norway today." She tossed her hand as though it would be nothing. "With no trouble at all."

The Kaiser was elated and nodded his agreement. He planned a Norwegian trip later in the Spring followed by one to Italy in the Fall if the Foreign Ministry thought it useful -- or he would just go if he chose.

"Such foreign voyages are extensions of the peaceful diplomacy of Imperial Germany," said the Kaiser. "No rational government seeks war, Countess, certainly I do not. Making strong alliances, as with your own nation, with my cousin, Czar Nicholas II, would help ensure the peace of the coming decades. My Foreign Minister will be exploring such alliances in the weeks ahead ... with my full support."

Then he shrugged. "Yet, in Great Britain there have been a steady number of trash novels and fairy stories published over the past many months predicting war between my grandmother and me, even an invasion of southeastern England by Germany. I have even read one of them by a man named Le Queux. It was as silly a tale as any I read as a child.

"Prime Minister Salisbury's government, according to my ambassador, is even considering establishing a Secret Service Bureau to track down and arrest all my spies." He laughed. "The English books and magazine stories suggest I have 5,000 spies in Great Britain." Wilhelm laughed again, and wished that were true.

"But how many, sir, do you have?" Countess Natasha asked, her head cocked coquettishly. "Surely the British have spies in Germany."

He nodded, but not as many now as the English had two months ago when he had issued his blunt order: "Put out all the British eyes!" His Reich Chancellor Prince Hohenlohe had paled, but his Chief of Counterintelligence had smiled. Relations with Great Britain were steadily fraying since the Kaiser's personal intrusion into England's actions in the Transvaal in South Africa. And -- but that was for later, without the presence of the beautiful Countess.

As their promenade led them toward the stern, the Kaiser pointed out the SMS Geier, a new light cruiser launched less than two years ago, running about a half-mile behind the yacht in the canal.

"If you promise not to tell, Countess, I have seven secret agents in Great Britain."

Natasha held up her right hand in mock pledge and grinned. "I will never tell, Your Majesty, even to the Czar himself."

Wilhelm found the young Countess beguiling with her unbounded enthusiasm for experiencing exotic locations. There weren't, it seemed, enough words to describe the pyramids of Egypt and the glories of ancient times, which was a topic Wilhelm himself had always intended to pursue. But it was her adventures at the roulette wheels at Monte Carlo that most captured his interest.

With the winds strengthening, they stopped to re-enter the library for tea as the Countess Natasha began to describe the system she used to challenge the Bank at Monte Carlo.

***

Glancing at the deciphered cablegram, Sir Septimus Browne raised his eyebrows. "One young woman is all the Americans can spare us?" He tossed aside the worn copy of *Answers* that he had been reading, its cover emblazoned with the latest scare story by William Le Queux, "The

Great War in England in 1897", in which the invading enemy forces are a coalition of the French and Russians. The banker grimaced as he rose from the desk. "I can only hope then that this Miss Piddington is the second coming of Joan of Arc.

"I leave for the South of France tomorrow, Thomson," he said over his shoulder. "Please so inform Lord Salisbury, if he should have any final instructions for me." He grasped his ebony cane and limped to the door. If not Joan d'Arc, then a healthy guardian angel would do.

Great Britain and Imperial Germany, he mused as he closed the door, were like two locomotives on the same track going toward each other under full steam. Colonel William Swaine, the British military attaché, had described, in diplomatic cipher, his last audience with the Kaiser in Berlin as "heated", and described the German Emperor as "bursting with pathological excitement". Even the two senior German diplomats present had seemed shaken by their ruler's violent words. Swaine finished by saying that had it been anyone other than the Kaiser, that he would have drawn his sword to squelch the insulting onslaught.

First to Berlin for four to five days to get more understanding, then south to Monaco to meet with Muffin and V.B., and return to the Prime Minister.

Now, this Piddington woman from America, an America which had been threatening England with war over Venezuela only about five or six weeks ago. Browne frowned and limped faster.

The American would be another piece on the great chessboard. A resourceful queen, he hoped, or perhaps only a knight with limited moves.

***

Wilhelm sipped his tea as he enjoyed the glorious Natasha describing the opulent gambling rooms of Monte Carlo. There seemed to be an inadequate number of adjectives available to her in three languages as she struggled with German, French and Russian to bring the excitement of extravagantly dressed crowds, the titled and wealthy from all Europe to life for the Kaiser's close attention -- and finally, the play itself, to challenge the Bank, the intoxicating thrill of seeing the little white ball bounce on its random way around the whirling wheel.

She laughed. "An English aristocratic lady explained to me after she had won 42,000 francs on just four consecutive coups, that she looked on her winnings as mere loans from the Bank at a usurious rates of interest, as the Bank takes all the money back in the end anyway … and then some extra." She laughed again. "But," she confided, "I kept most of my winnings with a system taught me by a most solicitous English baron."

At the rise of the Kaiser's eyebrow at the mention of a system, she asked, "May I have the honor of describing my system, Your Majesty?"

Wilhelm nodded to her and then to the approaching servant carrying a silver wine service to replace the morning tea.

"Baron Ellesmere explained that I could practice his system using a shuffled deck of cards as all the successful roulette systems are based on even odds."

At Wilhelm's finger-snap, a servant immediately produced a deck of playing cards emblazoned with the Imperial coat-of-arms. At the Kaiser's direction, the servant shuffled the cards three times and placed the deck before the Countess and withdrew.

"The Baron's system is not infallible, naturally," said the Countess, then leaned closer. "But," she whispered, "it never failed me over my six days at the wheel." Leaning back, she continued. "You wait for the first coup to set your color." The Countess turned over the top card, the two of Spades.

"Black," she said.

After several minutes of turning cards, describing her bets and her fluttering fingers, the Kaiser nodded when she asked if she had been clear in how the Baron's system worked.

113

Then Natasha looked up at Wilhelm, cards spread out in front of her. "If my system works, then the card I turn over will now be red. I will bet 100GM" -- she put down a banknote -- "will you," she said, grinning, "will you, Your Majesty, bet against me?"

The Kaiser relaxed, his earlier angry frustrations of the morning had faded in the aura of the seductive irresponsibility of the beaming Countess. He withdrew a banknote from his pocket and, without noting the amount, dropped it on the table.

"And the card is?" he enquired gently, an eyebrow raised.

The Countess reached for the deck, stopped, then turned her hand up, withdrew, and waited for the Kaiser to turn the card.

He bowed his head in acknowledgment, reached out and turned over ... the Queen of Diamonds.

The Countess clapped joyously, then swept up the banknotes, noting that the Kaiser's banknote was for 1,000GM.

The Kaiser leaned back laughing, enjoying the young Countess's triumph.

Yes, he would like to go over the Baron's system again, to fully understand -- and perhaps personally put it to the test in Monte Carlo -- incognito naturally. Winning a few hundred thousand francs at the expense of Prince Albert of Monaco could be a useful diversion from other concerns.

Perhaps next week in Monaco? And before other events interfered.

12

S/S Auguste Victoria

En route

Dr. Markus von Müller dropped his newspaper, *Allgemeine Zeitung*, on the table next to his glass of champagne. Another Hamburg America liner making for New York from Southampton had transferred the latest European newspapers for first class passengers as the two ships had passed within hailing distance at sunup. Removing his pince-nez glasses, he sharply tapped the newspaper with them as he turned to his wife, Lora, sitting next to him, the other two chairs at their designated dining table still empty. "*Törichten unsinn!*" he growled. "Foolish nonsense!" The first-class dining room of the Auguste Victoria was filling rapidly. An attractive couple in evening dress passing their table had looked over at his sharp remark, then walked on.

"Wie kommt es dazu?" Lora responded in her customary soft voice and gentle Bavarian accent. "How so?" She was always ready to support her husband's opinions on any subject. Thus had their twenty-two year marriage been an almost consistently happy one, even with occasional stresses from business risks and investments. Her principal role was running the house and the kitchen, and their three maids, and aiding in her husband's activities. Their only despair had been that they could not have children. Once the doctor had pronounced his verdict, Markus had drawn her more closely into his work to help her deal with her agony. She had responded well. Lora looked up as the Purser in formal evening uniform approached their table, escorting a tall, very attractive black-haired young woman dressed in a flowing gown of vivid dark-green and gold.

Speaking in English, he said, "Please excuse me, Dr. and Mrs. von Müller. May I have the honor of introducing Miss Kyame Piddington of the United States, who will be sharing this table for the balance of our crossing."

His face a wide smile, Dr. von Müller immediately rose, extended his hand, and said in careful English, "You are most welcome, Miss Piddington."

As she settled into her chair, and acknowledging Mrs. von Müller's gentle welcome, Kyame asked, "I noted, Dr. von Müller, that you were most upset by something in that newspaper. May I ... may I ask what that was?" She leaned back to allow a waiter in white and blue livery to arrange her place setting and deliver a crystal flute of champagne.

"Prost!" declared von Müller, gallantly raising his glass, to which Kyame raised her glass to touch the ringing crystal glasses of the doctor and his wife. After a long sip, von Müller said, "Ah, yes, you are most observant, Miss Piddington. Do you know the name, Sigmund Freud?"

Kyame shook her head and sipped again.

"He is a relentless self-promoter ... a cocaine-intoxicated Jew from Vienna", as if that explained everything. "Freud has been claiming that he has discovered new ways to probe how the human mind works, but with little clinical evidence to support his extravagant claims." Von Müller sipped again, pursing his lips in pleasure. "And now," he tapped the newspaper with his finger. "Now this Freud" -- his voice turning sarcastic -- "has decided that the words already commonly used to describe human mental conditions are not good enough, so he is now calling his collection of fairy tales ... *psychoanalyse*! Psychoanalysis! Yet another word for absurdity!"

Lora reached over to tap her husband's arm. "Dear, dear, too much. Our beautiful table-mate is not so involved as you."

Kyame smiled. The doctor's face had flushed red, but he nodded and sat back, draining the last of his champagne. A waiter immediately appeared to refill his glass.

"I must apologize, Miss Piddington. I am only a humble veterinarian who treats the hunting dogs from the estates surrounding our village in Bavaria, south of

München, er, Munich ... not a stylish Viennese neurologist filled with drug-induced mental aberrations." He smiled. "You travel to England, Miss Piddington? We are returning home, to Schwangau near the great castle of Neuschwanstein is being built. You must come ... see our castles."

Kyame waited as the first dishes of the evening meal were being placed before them. The evening menu had been distributed to each cabin for selections earlier in the afternoon. This would be Kyame's first formal meal after recovering from her sea-sickness. When her stomach remained calm as she read the menu, Kyame had decided it was time to rejoin society. She had selected the roast beef with mashed potatoes, which seemed the safest for her first meal; while the doctor and his wife had selected the stuffed pork chops with sliced cinnamon apples.

"I was thinking, Doctor, with your clinical specialty, that, perhaps, following Dr. Freud, you should announce to the newspapers that you are an expert in canineanalysis."

Von Müller and his wife erupted in laughter that immediately brought shushes for quiet from adjacent tables. Von Müller muttered some apologies, but continued to chuckle.

"Delightful, my dear Miss Piddington, just delightful," said Lora.

Kyame smiled and said, "I am Kyame to my friends. And I am sure I would be enchanted by your castles."

Acknowledging her suggestion, the three went to their Christian names as they began their dinner, with the doctor still chuckling. He would, he said, on his return home, have business cards printed for his friends and clients announcing his new modern profession.

As Kyame picked up her fork and knife to assault her dinner, she felt a sharp prickling down her back. She shuddered. Someone was watching her. She glanced over her shoulder, caught a glimpse of a man in evening dress suddenly look away. Kyame turned back to her food.

"Ist something wrong, Kyame?" asked Lora, frowning.

Smiling, Kyame shook her head. "No, not at all, Lora. Just a sudden chill." As she cut her meat, Kyame knew she had seen that man walking the halls of first class, but then he had been dressed as a liveried servant. A uniform can render a person almost invisible to casual observation. She had utilized that fact herself on more than one occasion.

A ship's detective, perhaps, like those hotel detectives who roamed the halls that she had encountered while traveling with Papa. As theatre people, she and Papa were always watched by suspicious detectives. But why here … and why now, at dinner?

***

As they began to spoon the desert, date and walnut steamed sponge pudding, Lora returned to Freud. "My close cousin, Alfred von Tirpitz, a senior officer in the Imperial Navy, a Rear Admiral ... he is now Commander of the East Asia Squadron based in Hong Kong ... agreed with my Markus that Dr. Freud ist ... geisteskrank?" She turned to von Müller for help.

"Insane," he suggested.

"Yes, insane. Alfred said he had enough serious developments facing the Imperial Navy not to waste time on such drivel as Freud, who belonged in a madhouse anyway." She leaned toward Kyame and whispered conspiratorially, "Alfred has the ear of the All Highest, Kaiser Wilhelm II, you know."

Sitting back, Lora continued, "Alfred also told me before he left for Hong Kong, that he has been closely studying the book of one of your American naval officers, a Captain Mahan, which even the Kaiser himself has been reading."

Kyame smiled as Lora again invoked her cousin's name, obviously very proud of the rank and social status of her Alfred.

121

Lora was a bit overweight but she must have been a beauty when she and Markus had been married, but perhaps too many pork chops. Kyame tightened her lips. That was an unfair thought. If she were to sketch Lora, she would remove about ten pounds from her -- Kyame noted Lora's frown.

"I'm sorry, Lora. I am an artist. I was sketching you in my mind. I apologize if I have made you uncomfortable."

Her frown vanished. Lora immediately brightened. "Do you paint?"

"Yes. I am traveling to the south of France to fill commissions to paint some titled clients." Her first use of her cover story. "But I cannot mention their names, I'm afraid."

"Kyame," said Markus, "would you sketch my Lora? I would, naturally, pay any usual fee."

Kyame waved her hand. "No fee, not for friends. I will deliver a sketch at tomorrow's dinner."

Lora's mouth dropped. "Tomorrow? But would I not have to sit for some hours for the drawing?"

Kyame shook her head. "No, Lora. I paint and draw from memory. That makes it more convenient for both of us." She smiled as Markus' eyebrows rose.

"From memory!" he remarked. "Most impressive, my dear! We will look forward to tomorrow at dinner."

"And I will look for Captain Mahan's book in the ship's library," said Kyame. "I have an interest in naval history and, if your esteemed cousin describes it as important, then I am certain Captain Mahan is worth reading with care."

Lora sat back, her bowl of pudding already empty, smiling happily at Kyame's response.

Judson Rowland had mentioned to Kyame before her departure that Germany, under the Kaiser's insistent direction, was aggressively and very publicly striving to expand the Imperial Navy. He suggested that Germany's naval focus might provide an insight to what may lay ahead for her. So, Kyame resolved, she would find the Mahan book and read it, though she wasn't sure how much of it she would understand.

The waiters had cleared the tables of the desert plates, placing bottles of cognac and of port with crystal stemmed glasses on each table, along with a silver coffee service with white and blue porcelain china.

Pouring coffee for Lora, Markus, at Kyame's nod, then poured port for her, and cognac for himself. The port was good, Kyame reflected, but did not match marvelous brew which James Dixey had served in his closing room.

After a few minutes, Kyame looked up as a small bell was rung. A four piece ensemble of piano, two violins and a cello were taking their places at the back of the dance floor. A young woman in a short black satin skirt and ruffled white blouse with billowing sleeves positioned a table at the center of the open floor, then placed a chromed candelabrum on it, and quickly withdrew. The table was like the magic tables Kyame had seen many times in her second sight travels, a tripod base with a single chromed shaft supporting a black velvet table-top encircled with a gold embroidered black velvet fringe hanging down.

Clearly, it was time for magic.

"My Lords, ladies and gentlemen," announced Purser Jellicoe, resplendent in formal naval evening dress of gold braid, boiled white shirt with high wing collar, black tie and tight black waistcoat with satin highlights. Then, nodding to the large circular Captain's table in the center of the room, "Captain Wörmann and guests." Turning back to the other diners, "I trust your dinner was satisfactory." A small scattering of applause brought a gracious smile to G.E.W.'s lips, which Kyame thought was too practiced. She did not applaud, though her beef and potatoes had certainly been good, but far more importantly, they had stayed down.

"To bring you this evening," he continued, "from Paris, magic and mystery in the manner and style of the late great Robert-Houdin. May I have the honor of presenting ... Monsieur Pierre André Reymond."

Jellicoe turned with a sweep of his left hand, as a smiling young dark-haired man in evening dress walked briskly to the center near the table. He bowed to the polite applause, then raised both hands, his fingers rippling gracefully to emphasize both his hands were utterly empty. As Reymond scanned his audience, his gaze hovered momentarily on Kyame, then moved on.

Kyame smiled as their eyes met.

The ensemble began playing something familiar, which Kyame couldn't identify, as the conjuror stepped toward the audience raised one hand as though pointing at something -- at his slight jab of his finger, a fluttering white dove appeared!

The audience gasped in surprise. Kyame was stunned. The bird production was beyond anything she had ever seen. It was as though Reymond had pointed at a specific spot in the air and drew the bird from its invisible hiding place. Marvelous!

The bird settled on Reymond's extended finger to strong applause. He turned, allowing the bird to hop to an arm of the chrome candelabrum, where, after shifting itself once or twice, it settled, gently cooing.

Reymond stepped toward the Captain's Table and found a second bird hiding in the air near the shoulder of the Captain, which brought an immediate grin to the

125

Captain's face, and even louder applause. That bird also hopped onto the second arm of the candelabrum.

The magician walked to the other side of the floor and, looking about as though searching for something lost, he found a third dove that had been apparently hovering behind the elaborate hair arrangement of an elderly lady who screamed in surprise which raised quiet laughter across the audience.

Kyame had watched from back stage as many birds were produced by magicians on the same theatre bill as the Impossible Piddingtons, even once a large belligerent raven that had eyed the audience like his next meal, but nothing as purely magical as Reymond.

Marvelous!

The three white doves shifted about on the arms of the candelabrum when Reymond grasped it and raised it up as though to prove that all the birds were there. A large white and blue striped foulard appeared in his other hand as Reymond walked toward the Captain's Table.

With a simple flip of his hand the silken cloth spread and settled lightly onto the birds, concealing them and the candelabrum, the light from behind Reymond cast shadows of the birds and their support against the cloth, as the accompanying ensemble had raised the beat, style and volume of their playing.

Reymond bowed to the Captain, then tossed the foulard into the air.

The three doves had vanished!

Kyame's jaw dropped in amazement. Utterly unexpected! She had thought the short-gowned assistant would bring out a box or something into which the magician would place the birds, *and then* vanish them, like all the other magicians she had seen -- but this! Stunning! She enthusiastically joined the rousing applause of the audience, as did the von Müller's.

This was magic!

But, sadly, the magic did not continue for long, as Reymond dropped a billiard ball he was manipulating which rolled under the Captain's table. After a few moments, one of the men seated at the table retrieved the ball and returned it to the conjuror. Reymond's face was flushed with embarrassment as he completed his routine to uneasy silence.

"Magic can be an unpredictable art," he said in English with smile and a quick Gallic shrug. The audience remained silent, but that girl in green had a marvelous coquettish half-smile, as if she understood his situation.

A few moments later Reymond gracefully showed a beautifully finished and decorated box to be completely empty. As he tapped the box one last time to emphasize its emptiness, the secret load of colorful silks suddenly released unexpectedly, the silks fluttering across the floor.

Kyame cringed at Reymond's misfortune, with memories of a few of her own fiascoes rushing quickly across her memory. Magic and second sight were certainly unpredictable arts, as Kyame would certainly agree. She noted that the expression on the Captain's face was no longer friendly.

His final rushed routine of remarkable card manipulations were superb in Kyame's opinion, and brought the audience back alive with occasional gasps of surprise.

His show ended with Pierre André Reymond's final graceful bow to the audience's polite applause, and even though the Captain was not applauding, the Frenchman's eyes sought once again for the remarkable black-haired young woman dressed in green sitting near the back of the room. She was turned, speaking with the man, von Müller, next to her at the table. He would remember her...

Turning back from von Müller's comment, Kyame smiled happily. Even with his problems, Pierre André Reymond was truly magic.

13

Kyame started running happily up the dirt road as the white and green house appeared just over the ridge. It was their Ohio house where the three of them had lived while Papa had worked at the bank in town, in Warren, before second sight and the Impossible Piddingtons. The wide welcoming front porch that almost encircled the house -- with its large porch swing that squeaked when all three, she and Mama and Papa, would sit on it, reading books and magazines together, and sometimes singing together in the evening when the weather was warm.

She would never complain about that squeak again, as she ran toward the steps. The second step Papa had repaired once when it had come loose, causing Mama to drop some groceries. Reaching the front door, she noted the door stood open an inch or two, pushed it open and rushed in.

The front room was silent. Kyame walked toward the back of the house, toward the kitchen, "the real living room" Mama always called it. But it was silent and empty, too.

Kyame went to the ice-box and pulled the door open. There was always a pleasant surprise ... but the ice-box was empty ... and wasn't even cold. She opened the ice chest to check the block of ice that Papa would bring in the back door, held with ice tongs. He would then swing the 25-pound cake of ice up into the ice chest. Mama would take whatever scraps of ice were left from the previous block and make iced chocolate milk. But there was no ice in the ice chest -- and no ice scraps left.

Kyame turned to look around the kitchen, everything so friendly and familiar. Nothing. No sounds, no crumbs from baking, no -- then she realized -- it was the dust. Dust covered everything, the counter, the table, the chairs.

Mama would never …

Suddenly Kyame was awake! A great wave of fear washed through her as she frantically look about the room. She couldn't think of where she was. Sitting upright, her heart pounding, after a few seconds Kyame connected. She was on a ship. But more than that, Kyame realized, realized that she was utterly alone. Mama and Papa had seemed so close, always just around the corner in that house, but there had been no one there, no one at all.

Only all-encompassing <u>emptiness</u>.

What was she doing here, what was she going to do? Could she do it? Her hands were shaking with fear. Couldn't she just run away – run from everything? Kyame threw the blankets aside, pulled on her robe, wrapping it tightly and walked out into her small sitting room. She walked over to a port-hole, pulled back the curtain. A fading moon sent brief glimmers across the dark waves that steadily, relentlessly washed past the ship.

Kyame took a deep breath – then another one. It had been months since a dream like the house-dream had caught her by surprise, had momentarily shaken her self-confidence to its core. In the past, in the weeks right after Papa's death, he and Mama had appeared in some way in the dream, reassuring her, but this time they weren't there. She was the only one walking through that silent house.

It was just her, only her -- now.

As Kyame walked across her dimly lit sitting room to the tea service, she brushed her fingers across the crystal *bi* disc that hung between her breasts, her thoughts settling at its touch. The carafe of hot water was still hot, heated electrically. Kyame spooned out what had become her favorite morning tea on the ship, a blend of Assam and Ceylonese teas that seemed to make her blood flow faster.

As she set the three-minute timer, a shock of doubt froze her. Could she really? Irritated, Kyame shook the question away. Too many people were depending on her, whatever may lay ahead. The fragrance of the brewing tea lifted her spirits. As she had promised Papa so many times, standing in the wings: "Tonight, Papa, I will scare them down to their shoes!"

Kyame sipped, swallowed, smiled, then laughed. Taking the plate of teas cookies with her she walked to the

Queen Anne chair near a port-hole. Yes, she grinned, right down to their darn shoes! She leaned into the chair and found herself reflecting, reflecting on the three silver antique coins in her pocket.

***

In her visits with Dr. Mar-Tan at his breathtaking home on Doyers Street in the depth of New York's Chinatown, and when they would meet at restaurants in New York, they had often discussed various techniques for divination as astrology, the Tarot, palm reading, other techniques of sortilege, and the I Ching. Kyame had expressed doubt, polite doubt as she respected Mar-Tan as a valued friend and his perceptive wisdom, but doubt nevertheless regarding any form of divination.

Kyame doubted that divination of any kind was possible. After all, how could colorful symbols in a deck of cards, or the roll of dice, or the far off stars, have any impact on the actual life of a human being?

Kyame acknowledged that she and Papa had used a divinational theme sometimes when working with small crowds or with reporters one-on-one, but that was to give their presentation a clear focus, not to actually try to tell the future.

Mar-Tan had laughed. "I would not expect anything else from a mind as practical, wise and creative as yours, Miss Piddington. And, I deeply accept your kind regard."

Then he had leaned across the table, they were at Delmonico's, and dropped three ancient brass Chinese coins before her. "The I Ching, honored inquirer, however is something you should consider ... not to 'tell the future'. I agree that line can only be crossed with the greatest caution ... but to suggest a focus for the day that may lay ahead of you ... rather to fore-tell, to clarify options." He picked up the coins. "These I have used for many years, but any three coins are suitable, but it is always best to use the same three in your excursions in the *Book of Changes*, so that they may take on some aspect of your person."

Kyame moved her plates to one side. "I am ready, my teacher."

Over the next half hour, Mar-Tan first cupped the coins between his hands for a moment, fixing his question in his mind, then dropped the three coins onto the table. He noted their configuration, explaining how the trigrams and hexagrams of the I Ching were constructed, from the bottom up, and once constructed how they were to be interpreted.

"Your question, Miss Piddington, should always be as specific as you can make it."

The results were suggestive, fore-telling, but not strictly divinatory; more Kyame came to feel, more for a guide for meditation, for reflection. She began to drop the coins as Mar-Tan instructed. They had to finally stop when two waiters stood solemnly at their table with strained patience waiting to clear the table.

***

Now Kyame took three coins from her skirt pocket that she kept wrapped in her yellow ruhmal. They were three silver Indian coins with strikingly different images on opposite sides. Pushing her tea cup and saucer aside, she first cupped the coins, fixed her question, then dropped the coins, noted the configuration, then dropped them again, and again, and … until her hexagram was assembled from the bottom up in her mind. It was *Ku*, number 18, the lower, inner trigram meant wind, while the outward, upper trigram meant mountain, which when combined into a hexagram meant: Before you can go forward you will have to fix that which has gone bad. Be patient before you strike, but when you strike you must be as lean and sharp as a surgeon's knife.

Ku also was the name of a venom-based poison used for Chinese witchcraft.

Her question was: What waits for me as I cross the water, the ocean … and the Channel?

She had committed the 64 I Ching hexagrams and readings to memory. Kyame only considered the hexagram for the present; she never transformed the present hexagram into a future one. Those readings were always too vague, and, to her anyway, never rang true.

134

So, now what has gone bad that needs fixing? The British agent situation seemed an obvious answer; after all, that was why she was where she was, on the ship crossing to England and then on to France. Or was there more? And what strike like a scalpel would she need?

Kyame collected the silver coins, wrapped them in the yellow scarf and slipped them back into her pocket. She leaned back, closed her eyes, and let *Ku* wander her mind.

14

S/S Auguste Victoria

En Route

Captain Mahan wrote a heavy book: 557 pages with a number of fold-out maps. And it was the tenth edition in the six years since it was first published. Clearly it was a book of some serious importance.

The librarian's eyebrows went up when Kyame placed the book in front of her. "Naval strategy seems a bit of a strange interest for a young woman as you, Miss Piddington … even for an American," said Agnes Herwig, as she wrote the date and Kyame's stateroom number in her library log. Herwig was dressed in a ship's short jacket and high-collared white blouse with a long skirt in matching deep blue. Her glistening blonde hair was wrapped in a tight bun, which emphasized her pale blue eyes and her perfect symmetrical face as though it had been molded from white marble, to match her underlying chilling presence.

"I'm interested in naval history, Miss Herwig, and this book was recommended by friends, so an ocean voyage seemed the right time."

Miss Herwig nodded and, with both hands, lifted the book up to her. Her eyes followed the young American woman out the door. The American was the first passenger in the last three Atlantic crossings to check out Captain Mahan's book ... and the first woman, ever. Agnes, of course, had read the tome as soon as she had learned of the Kaiser's interest in it. It had been a struggle as she had found the book to be weighty endless dull commentaries on naval strategies over the past many decades, even centuries. So why the Piddington woman?

***

Kyame's jaw was set in anger as she walked down the corridor toward her stateroom with Mahan under her arm, the front cover concealed next to her body.

Stupid! Stupid and careless!

As J. W. had instructed her when handling cards, to do something out of expected character only drew unnecessary attention, even suspicion -- perhaps harmless, but still unnecessary, *unnecessary*!

The German librarian, Kyame had learned, was a notorious gossip and would surely say something to someone about her. She should have waited for Agnes Herwig's absence during lunch when an indifferent ship's clerk would sit-in to cover the library desk.

Kyame had been conceited in her carelessness. She was accustomed to the company of unique men as Dr. Mar-

Tan, as well as the medium, Maze Edwards, and J.W., of course, and others, who understood her background, experiences, and hidden capabilities, and so she had not thought differently when getting the Mahan book.

In her conceit, she had momentarily forgotten why she was on the damned ship!

Her face flushed red; Kyame bit her lip in anger. Hopefully only an instructive mistake -- instructive and not a serious one.

***

As Kyame approached her stateroom door, E.S. Andrews passed, walking rapidly the other direction. He nodded perfunctorily to her as he passed; she nodded in acknowledgement. He was obviously angry and very much in a hurry.

Her door pushed partially open, Kyame glanced back following Andrews for a moment down the corridor, saw him knock once, then thrust the door of a stateroom open, kicking the door closed after him.

She noted that the door was one door away from a ship's bulletin board. She would check the number, then perhaps learn whose room it was. It could be useful to put a name on Andrews' partner whose reddened face she had glimpsed as the door was slammed shut.

The partner's card handling had not been as practiced, as natural as Andrews', at least in the brief time Kyame had observed before leaving the card room. The partner had exhibited the tendency of some inexperienced magicians she had watched who would do a "get-ready" move, as Papa had called it, just before they executed a difficult sleight with card -- a hunching of their shoulders, or a sudden look away as though that would draw away or misdirect the observers, but actually drew more attention. Such an action was also called a tell, a visual mark in the proceedings that something, whatever it was, had just happened. Almost invariably the get-ready was just before the magician executed the shift, or pass, when the top and bottom portions of the deck would be reversed, a move gamblers sometimes used to negate an honest cut.

After some work, her own shift had met J.W.'s approval, but also his firm admonition never to use it except when doing a harmless card trick.

Doing a shift -- which required just a brief moment longer holding and concealing the deck than would be natural -- that short delay in the midst of a money game might be just enough to trigger mistrust in some players, such that they would leave the table rather than run the risk of facing an experienced advantage player.

As J.W. had explained, "Suspicious players don't wait to discover the precise action; they simply retire to a less misty atmosphere."

Even when they would sometimes practice back stage in front of a full-length mirror, Kyame noted that the awkward magician would still do a get-ready, sort of ingraining the movement. None of the professional gamblers she had met ever hesitated in their card moves, and neither did she, something her practice sessions with J.W. had embedded in her -- along with his gentle but insistent admonitions. She would then stop, and start over until every move blended into a single motion.

***

Kyame stopped a maid in front of stateroom number A223. After looking up and down the corridor, she said, hesitantly, "May I ask ... I met the gentleman whose stateroom that is ... ah, last evening. He was most kind, but in the noise of the crowd I could not clearly hear his name when we were introduced. Could you tell me his name?" She shyly cocked her head. "You understand, I'm sure. He *was* most attentive ... and I am a bit embarrassed."

The black and yellow uniformed maid, Inge, her brass tag said, grinned, and nodded. "Of course, Fraulein Piddington ... his name is W. E. Sanders, he is an American mining engineer from Chicago, I believe I heard. He plays a great deal of Patience, or Solitaire as I think you Americans call it. I always find decks of the ship's cards spread on his table."

Kyame leaned closer to whisper, "You won't say anything to Mr. Sanders or to anyone will you?", as she pressed a five-dollar gold piece into Inge's hand.

The maid giggled and nodded as the attractive black-haired girl walked away. Of course, she would tell no one. Perhaps the American girl would pay again for other information regarding Mr. Sander -- like the long knife in a special pocket of his suitcase, the small revolver under his pillow -- but then she had discovered in her two years of crossings that many travelers carried weapons. But she had no idea what that strange contraption was that she had found at the bottom of a dresser drawer with two leather straps. Maybe some bizarre American erotic activity? As she had overheard from some comments by ship's officers, Americans generally were unpredictable. All of which insight was based on Inge's customary methodical first inspection of the passengers' staterooms in her corridor, including Miss Piddington's.

***

Now that she had her extended eyes and ears in place, Kyame knew, as she walked toward the morning tea room in the Ladies' Saloon, more information from Inge was probably there for the -- paying. She grinned as she walked. The Saloon was the most elegant room she had ever experienced. Even, she felt, a king's castle could not match the mirrors, large gild-framed oil paintings, hangings of luxurious silk and damask, the adjoining more sedate music room with a glistening black grand piano and porcelain candelabras, and the view through a wall made almost entirely of glass. The Saloon was set forward on the promenade deck with a clear view over the bow of the ship and with fresh sea air flowing through ducts in the ceiling throughout the room. She had glimpsed Lora von Müller moving about the room, but chose not to engage her.

Kyame shook her head. The Saloon was almost too much, almost suffocating in its richness. She turned and left.

***

The Frenchman smiled and nodded his appreciation when the black-haired girl looked up at him and with an opened hand beckoned him to the deck chair next to her. She seemed unaffected even in the brisk winds.

The magician would help block the stiff sea breeze blowing down the deck, she thought, and, Kyame admitted to herself, Pierre André Reymond was quite, well, quite attractive.

Kyame smiled, a little more warmly than usual, then blushed at her boldness. "I am Kyame Piddington, Monsieur. I greatly enjoyed your show last night," she said, closing her book with a finger keeping her place. She had left Mahan in her cabin as something that might draw unwanted attention, along with her now five pages of notes hidden in the ship's German-English Bible in the shelf over her bed. The heart of Mahan seemed to be given on page iii, the first page of his Preface, where the author observed that "sea power was not synonymous with naval power", an insight Kyame had never encountered before. Other notes followed quickly and she was only up to page 55. Captain Mahan was a smooth and confident writer, and a surprisingly enjoyable one.

She chose the Bible because Papa had pointed out that the one place that was generally not touched in the boarding houses in which they had stayed during their travels were the personal Bibles of the travelers.

Wrapped in a heavy green woolen coat with a silver silk scarf tied around her hat and chin which kept her hat in place, Kyame had taken another intriguing book with her to the sun deck, though there was little enough sun.

***

"A most remarkable new volume from the English writer, Mr. H. G. Wells, Miss Piddington", a ship's clerk, J. Baader, according to his name-tag, had said, as he handed her the small slim book, his English almost unaccented. "I understand that Mr. Wells wrote seven drafts that required almost seven years in order to complete the work to his satisfaction. *The Time_Machine: an Invention* received very enthusiastic reviews in all the London papers, and the German journals as well when the novel first appeared in translation June of last year. The Time-Traveller is certain to be the most ... ah, unusual literary character of the year."

Only a few pages into the story, Kyame could readily agree with the substitute librarian's high assessment of Wells' work; but seven years work for only one hundred-fifty-two pages? Remarkable. But it did have the uncanny feel of Edgar Allan Poe, that uncomfortable magic.

***

"You are most kind, Mademoiselle Piddington," said Reymond as he settled into the chair. "The show did not go so well as I had intended. The Captain was not pleased with my fumbling."

A waiter arrived with Kyame's tea, took Reymond's order and disappeared.

"But small things always happen," said Kyame, "only a dropped ball, a Jap Box that released too soon, I've seen much worse things happen in magic acts. Once a duck that was to be produced got loose and the performer had to chase it all over the theater." She grinned and laughed. "The audience was so excited and laughing, that the magician included the escaped duck in his program from then on." Kyame sipped the hot strong Assam blend which seemed the ideal antidote to the chill winds.

"Jap Box? Ducks? You know of conjuring and magic apparatus?"

Kyame bit her lip. Again! Too much! "Yes, I know several American magicians ... and some of their secrets."

She smiled. "But not all. Your dove production was superb. I have no idea how you might have done that. It was effective enough to be real ... real magic."

Reymond grinned with pleasure. Beautiful and understanding. Marvelous! Then he frowned. "Now, Mademoiselle, you are most kind and supportive. But, I fear, the Captain is not so ... so generous. I was to perform again tonight, a different routine with some mindreading, but Captain Wörmann has said it is to be a musical program, not magic. And there are very few evenings left before Southampton. Perhaps only one or two depending on the storm track.

"I need the Captain's recommendation to be able to perform on other Hamburg-America liners. I was hired only conditionally for this crossing. Our Captain does not have the highest regard for Frenchmen. There are very few magicians performing on the principal Atlantic crossings and I thought ..." His Gallic shrug spoke eloquently.

Kyame sipped again. Would it be too far out of character to -- then she had an idea. "What if you identified a team of cheaters working the ship's card room? Would not the Captain be more disposed ... more positive toward you, Monsieur Reymond? According to the purser, Mr. Jellicoe, there has never been any cheating discovered in the four years the Auguste Victoria has been in service, yet I observed cheating even while Mr. Jellicoe was speaking to me." She continued, "I don't believe they have discovered cheating because they don't want to look."

Her intense green eyes were compelling. To know such a woman; but card cheating? "You observed cheating?" How did this young woman know of card cheating?

"At least two Americans, Mr. Andrews and Mr. Sanders, are working as a team playing poker, and may collude in other games as well. They act, like most such teams, as though they do not know each other. Andrews is clearly the best plug-man of the two. Mr. Sanders is a bit ... gawky in his card handling, though they do cross-fire at times.

"There is also another team, an older man and woman, that also seem to be working the room, but I have directly observed the cheating of Andrews and his ally.

"So, Monsieur Sorcier, my suggestion is that you reveal to the Captain that there are cheaters on his ship, demonstrate some of their moves, and then identify them." She quickly added: "I need not be any part of that, and would not want to be." Was she outside of expectation again -- talking of card moves to a magician? She pursed her lips. Or was she just looking at a way to help out a man who was of -- well, of interest?

Pierre Reymond was silent. Who was this young woman, really? "How, if I may ask, Mad ...?"

"My name is Kyame." She hid her smile behind her raised teacup.

Pierre bowed his head in acknowledgement. Kai'-ah-mee, he sounded the name to himself. "An enchanting name. I have never heard it before, Kyame. I am André to my friends.

"But as to your suggestion, if successful, I have no doubt that Captain Wörmann would be most pleased. But, I am not an expert in card cheating, though I know magician's sleights."

Kyame replaced her teacup and turned toward him. "I can show you what I observed, and then we can go into the card room together." She continued to explain what she had in mind.

André eyes widened. *Formidable*! Nothing in his training had prepared him for Kyame Piddington.

***

"A magical presence," said Kyame as she finished her tea, "would not use the funny looking boxes and such that all magicians seem to need. The conjurors I've seen from backstage as well as out front, seem to be satisfied if they give their audiences some difficult puzzles to solve; and so long as the audience cannot divine how the illusion was done, the magician has created what he thinks is mystery ... and everyone leaves, more or less smiling."

The Frenchman nodded, then frowned. "But what else can you expect?"

Kyame turned in her chair for emphasis; also she wouldn't have to squint with his shoulder blocking the wind. "If a magician can pull gold coins from the air, as many do, why not pull coins all the time? Why work at all?"

André threw up both hands. "But, Kyame, the magician is only pretending to be a magician, like an actor on stage ... as the great Robert-Houdin himself suggested. The conjuror isn't the real thing."

"What's wrong," she responded, leaning forward. "What's wrong with leaving the impression with the audience that *he is*? The real thing surrounded by fakery so that the magician isn't called upon to produce miracles all the time, but only at times of his own choosing.

"That allows the conjuror to introduce an underlying level of fear along with the laughter ... and fear is always remembered. Is it not, André?

"What are the two greatest miracles?" Without waiting for his response, Kyame said, "Flying like the birds; and raising the dead. N'est-ce pas?"

"So which one, Kyame, are you working on first?" Laughing, they rose and started for the card room.

André grinned as he held the door for Kyame to pass. C'est extraordinaire!

***

The Hamburg-America Line (Hamburg Amerikanische Packetfahrt), or HAP, had been actively supporting the Imperial Navy's expanding intelligence network since 1891. Agnes Herwig had already received two confidential commendations from Admiral Mischke in Berlin which acknowledged her skilled recruitment of two agents, who worked on the New York docks, both Irish-Americans who hated the British and would support the Kaiser in case of war; and a female agent in British Customs in Southampton. With HAP's regular contacts throughout the major seaports of North and South America, the Imperial Navy was gaining eyes in critical areas. Agnes had heard rumors, quiet rumors naturally, that suggested the establishment of a new Imperial intelligence organization in the next year.

HAP was not the only German commercial operation drawn into the Imperial Navy's intelligence development, but had been the most productive thus far.

After a moment of thought, Agnes Herwig added a short note on the young American woman, Kyame Piddington, and her "interest" in naval strategy, to the last page of her report, along with a brief physical description of her. She filed her enciphered report on her observations of passengers twice during each crossing, which included observations from her visiting the lower decks once or twice as well. The report would be transferred during the early morning via the ship's telegraph to a German cargo vessel. What happened after that Agnes didn't know, and didn't want to know. 'Never know too much' was her personal motto.

15

E. S. Andrews was uneasy -- no, he was disgusted and uneasy. Catching the gold chain with his third finger of his left hand, he pulled his watch from his vest pocket, snapped it open. He nodded -- get back to the card room in about twenty minutes. He slipped the watch back and sipped the whiskey slowly. He preferred Kentucky bourbon, but whatever, as long as the suckers were paying. Jellicoe, the starched Purser, had informed him that the expected storm had shifted course so the landing at Southampton would now be only a half-day later than scheduled. .The ship would dock the 19th.

So, as Andrews had explained to Sanders, this afternoon, they would let the marks get back some of their cash; then tomorrow go for their throats before the landing the following morning at 11. Andrews smiled, placing the empty shot glass on his dresser. Ocean or iron rails, the advantage strategy was the same: coddle them early, drain them slowly, then, as the train pulls into the station, strip them clean and get off quick.

But, Sanders had not been carrying his role as a partner should. Sanders had been pitched to him as a solid advantage man, a knowledgeable pair of hands to help work the HAP crossings; but almost immediately Andrews had had to firmly tell the man to leave his damnfool mechanical hold-out hidden in his room for the whole voyage. Andrews wouldn't touch a mechanical aid to card handling at any card table; no professional who valued his reputation -- and his hide -- would touch the things.

At the table, yes, Sanders had been performing reasonably well; but the man was careless to leave cards in various stages of marking on the table in his room where the maids and who knows who else could see them. He had even been leaving the ship's card boxes, opened at the bottom to preserve the original seal at the top, lying on the table as well. The design of the HAP cards was almost made for marking. A rendering of the Auguste Victoria at full speed running left to right across the center of the card, with that row of lighted portholes along the side of the ship. The ship made the deck one-way, easily visible across the table, so that high cards could be casually arranged one way and the low cards the other, to be easily read. And those port holes. He couldn't have designed the deck for marking cleaner than HAP had done for him.

They were only skinning the deck this crossing, not doctoring every card. So, just block out the appropriate porthole with black ink and they could read all the high cards in the deck in an instant. Take fifteen, maybe twenty minutes for each deck, then another ten or so to replace the deck in the ship's special card-box and reseal the box on the bottom. Switch the boxed skinned deck into the game at the right moment, which was always Andrews' call, and then on with the play. Some crossfiring at the right times, where he and Sanders would raise each other until the others dropped out, play it as two-pluck-two. Sanders had seemed to understand, but, damn, he was still careless.

As he settled his coat on his shoulders, Andrews reviewed their moves given the playing habits of the two Irish suckers who would be there, then stopped.

Maybe no one would recognize what was in Sanders' room -- but the image of that Piddington woman -- damn, Andrews would wager better than even money she knows cards to some degree. And she did not look like any man's fool.

And with her moves, and those eyes, she did look really good.

***

André shuffled the deck again, and sprung the cards in a smooth waterfall from hand to hand, which produced a sound like peeling cabbage. He began to show Kyame another trick, as she watched Andrews from the corner of her eye. Andrews' quick glance at them as they came into the card room had not been friendly. Her plan, to which Andre had nodded agreement, was to have Andre apparently show her tricks to which she would react with quiet wonderment, until she caught Andrews ringing in a new deck. Then ...

"Now, André, now," she whispered. "The rigged deck will be in play."

153

André smiled and rose, slipping his deck into his pocket. Taking Kyame by the arm, they walked toward the door but walked near the Andrews table as the players were taking a moment to relax and sip the whiskies a waiter had just brought them.

Kyame told André that he would be asked to do a trick for them. When he responded, "Yes, I can ... but, but what if they don't?"

Kyame replied firmly, "Then we will manage", just as she and Papa had managed so many times.

***

As they had walked to the card room, Kyame had observed to Andre that, "We can't go to the Captain with just observations and demonstrations of blind cheating moves, we need a definitive piece of physical evidence … like a holdout, a marked deck, shaved cards … something like that." Andre had agreed, but how to get such evidence? He smiled as Kyame explained. He raised his eyebrows.

Truly formidable this remarkable woman.

One of the men, one of the suckers as Kyame thought of them, hailed them as they passed. "Monsieur, do you have time for a trick for us? I saw you over there doing some impressive shuffles for the lady."

Kyame stepped to one side as André moved closer to the table. Sanders and Andrews both had assumed carefully neutral expressions as the other two men grinned, sipped and sat back.

"It would be my honor, gentlemen," André answered, "but perhaps, if you will, I will use your deck and not my own to ensure that all things are on, ah, the American expression, on the up and up."

"My name is Brennan", one of suckers said with a rich Irish accent, as he immediately scooped up the cards on the table and handed them to André.

Kyame noted that Sanders flinched as André took the cards. He looked with some brief concern at Andrews who barely moved his head when he shook it.

André shuffled, fanned the deck as he extended it to the Irishman. "Let's begin with a simple play of the cards. Please take one when I ... and Miss Piddington turn away ... show it to your associates then replace it somewhere in the deck. Merci. Now shuffle and cut the deck, or have someone else do it. Again merci." André smiled. "Your card, it is now lost in the deck is it not, Monsieur Brennan?"

Brennan nodded.

"Then as a skilled gambling man, as you are, how much would you wager that this" -- André withdrew a card from the deck and placed it face down on the green surface of the table – "this is the card you removed from the deck when I could not see you do it, and we are using your deck?

I am speaking hypothetically, of course, as I am not a wagering man."

Brennan shook his head. "No, let's make it a real stake. Here's an English five pound note I just won from the last pot. I'll wager £5 you're wrong. No way that you could know, or could find the card even if you did know what card it was."

Cocking her head to one side, Kyame smiled as if the whole affair was strange to her, while she cautiously observed Andrews, who had leaned forward in interest once money was involved.

André hesitated, then nodded. "A money wager, sir? Then so shall it be." He placed a card face down on the table.

Kyame immediately caught Sanders start to grin, then he stopped and leaned back. Andrews didn't move. Either the card selected had been marked or this one was. Either way, apparently, Sanders knew the card was not the one that Brennan had selected. She had no idea what André was going to do.

André placed the deck on the table as he drew his wallet from inside his jacket. "I have only French francs, will that be sufficient, Monsieur?"

Brennan nodded as André dropped the banknote on the table.

The magician reached for the card, then withdrew his hand. Sanders eyebrows suddenly went up.

"Sir, it is your wager, it is your card to discover."

Brennan grinned, then turned the card over. The two of Spades. He slammed it back down. "By God, man, how did you do that?" Then he leaned back, laughing with the other sucker as André picked up the banknotes. "Damn good, Reymond, damn good! I hope you don't play poker."

"Non, Monsieur. I cannot play. I am known as a magician so if I win, everyone is suspicious; and if I lose, then I am an incompetent conjuror. I cannot win, you see."

Brennan laughed. "Understood, sir, but still damn good."

Kyame noted André dropped the gamblers' deck into his pocket, then quickly withdrew it and dropped it back on the table.

"Ah, my mistake, this is your deck not mine." He nodded to each of the four men, then took Kyame's arm. "Mademoiselle and I are meeting others. I enjoyed our moment, and sir, that you may know, your wager will used to purchase the lovely lady's refreshment."

"Best thing for it," said Brennan, rising from his chair to bow to Kyame, who nodded her head in acknowledgement. As the door closed behind Kyame and Andre, he resumed his chair. Reaching out, Brennan

157

shuffled the deck. "Good looking woman there. But on to more serious considerations, gentlemen. I understand we have only one more day before docking at Southampton, so our time of hazard is short."

As the Irishman shuffled again, Andrews expression hardened. He touched three fingers to his cheek as if brushing away something. A warning to Sanders. The deck is queered! He would have to ring in his other skinned deck at the right moment. He bit off the curses that came immediately to his lips.

***

"Amazing!" said Kyame. "Just smooth as glass, André. I have no understanding of how you did that. And, your deck switch was inspired."

"Inspired. Ah, *le mot juste,* the perfect word." André laughed. "But ... not quite one of the miracles you spoke of, but it will do for our purpose, n'est-ce pas, Mademoiselle?"

Kyame's smile was quick and warm.

They walked to the small café near the Ladies Saloon. Andre ordered as Kyame began to riffle through the deck. She nodded as she looked first on one side of a card then on the other. "The deck is skinned, not fully marked. Only the values of the high cards are noted, not the suit, which for an experienced advantage player would be more than enough information. Here," she placed her finger, "the port holes have been filled in. The first filled-in porthole is an ace, two portholes blanked out is a king. Just face cards and the aces. Not very imaginative, but very quick. The Hamburg-America card design is perfect for concealing the markings."

André examined one card than another. He nodded in agreement. "As you suspected, which is why I wanted to set it up with their deck. It made my trick seem more honest, even if my motives were not." He grinned. "I am curious, Kyame, what would you have done if no one had asked me to do a trick."

He leaned back as the coffee was delivered. André laid the £5 note on the table and, to the waiter's astonishment as he picked it up, waved the waiter away. Five English pounds -- more than a week's wages!

Kyame sipped, reflected, "It could have been several things. I would have asked you to repeat one of your tricks and then asked the men to watch and tell me how it was done as I just couldn't imagine how." She mimicked feminine helplessness. Kyame smiled, "Or a couple of other things. Last resort would be that I would do a trick, as they could not have refused a woman … but that would have been the very last resort."

"You would?"

"It would not have impressed you at all, I assure you." Her smile faded. "You have your evidence and

159

observations. I suspect other skinned decks are in Sanders' room, on his desk."

André raised an eyebrow in question.

"The maid in my corridor works for me, part-time."

"I should have known, Kyame. I will see the Captain immediately."

"I will be waiting in the library."

***

"I will be waiting in my room, Sanders," growled Andrews after the two marks had happily left the card room with fatter wallets. "Who the hell is that woman? A ship's detective?

"If we are going to rack up a big score tomorrow, we will have to ring in a fully doctored deck along with a few other things, and, by God, we can't have her or that magician walking by. Understood?

16

New Palace,

Berlin

Monday, February 17, 1896

Admiral, the Graf Von Drascher was becoming impatient. The time for his regular weekly appointment with the Kaiser had come and gone almost -- according to the great clock with its Roman numerals high in the wall across from him -- thirty-five minutes ago. The All Highest had never left him waiting before. He shifted in the uncomfortable carved mahogany chair, the Kaiser's personal seal digging ever deeper into his back, or so it seemed.

The door to the Kaiser's private inner office opened, a jumble of voices erupted, one of which was very much the Kaiser's. An admiral stepped out, closing the door behind him. When he turned, von Drascher could see his profile -- yes, and his forked beard, a style no other naval officer had adapted.

Von Tirpitz! The young ambitious and recently promoted rear admiral was supposed to be en route to Hong

Kong, to take command of the German East Asia Squadron! What?

Alfred von Tirpitz nodded perfunctorily toward him, and strode rapidly to the private door hastily opened for him by one of the Imperial staff of elegantly liveried servants.

A few moments later the door opened again. A Captain's arm, the four heavy gold stripes glistening in the gas light, extended out with a message at its fingertips to another servant. When the servant apparently asked a question, the Captain stepped out, glanced over at von Drascher, nodded to the servant, returned to the office, and closed the door behind him.

The servant walked primly toward him as von Drascher rose from the painful chair, his knees grown stiff from waiting. The servant stopped, ram-rod straight, snapped his heels together as he bowed at the waist.

"Admiral, sir, I am instructed by His Majesty to inform you that your usual appointment today is canceled. His Majesty will see you next week at the usual time." The servant bowed again, snapped a precision about-face and returned to his small desk.

Next week! What about the launch of the first Predator? What about the funds...?

Von Drascher stood, paralyzed for a moment. There were issues that only the Kaiser could resolve, expenditures that only he could authorize, scheduling that had slipped. Never before had the Kaiser dismissed the Predator program out of hand. And the Captain, he knew the name, the name, he had seen him about the headquarters of the AMR, but couldn't recall it -- or the man's duties.

The frustrated Graf von Drascher replaced his handful of documents in his black leather valise, snapped it shut and started walking toward the private door through which Admiral von Tirpitz had just disappeared, but the servant immediately rose and moved to block his path. "Sir, His Highest requests you leave by the public door."

His face flushed with anger and embarrassment, von Drascher turned and after three steps, he stopped. Karl Gustav Hahn, Captain, in the *Nachtrichtenbüro*, called by everyone simply N, the new office of Imperial Naval Intelligence.

Von Drascher resumed walking, his jaw set in anger, the seal of the Kaiser still embedded into his back, chills of fear rushing through him. Hahn had a reputation for unrelenting ruthlessness, even toward his own people.

What course was the Kaiser on now? And for, mein Gott -- for how long? The metaphor for the Kaiser suggested by one of the more junior captains at a friendly regular late night gathering over beer, weisswurst, white mustard, and hot bread two nights ago became more urgent in his memory.

The young officer, promoted to Korvetten-Kapitän only four months in the past and already noted for his contempt for the many new naval regulations being issued and the piles of associated paperwork, had said: "Gentlemen, the Kaiser has become like a battleship under full steam but without a rudder. One day," he had emphasized with a jabbing finger, "one day the All Highest may strike something we will all regret."

There had been a moment of silence, a moment of each of the men in gold braid glancing around the table at the others, then the group had disbanded silently, their beers unfinished, and had not reassembled since.

All of the officers present were known as competent, reliable, loyal...

His pride still burning, Von Drascher wanted to slam the great arched door behind him, but, instead, closed it quietly, professionally, behind him. A young woman walked slowly by as though searching for a particular door. Von Drascher ignored her as he turned away.

She turned, returning to her contact in the Kaiser's office.

***

The Kaiser listened intently as Captain Hahn completed his presentation of the new organization of N. His Highest had smiled at the abbreviation. "The Hamburg American steamship line, Your Majesty, has been most

164

supportive in cooperating with our expanding need for ... selective information. I deeply appreciate your personal touch in this matter."

Wilhelm nodded. One of the major owners of HAP, Karl Heinz Bolten, was a personal friend, who had immediately agreed to encourage the ships' officers and other crew members to recruit, was the word Bolten had used, recruit reliable sources of information within important world ports including most recently Mediterranean ports as Algiers, Naples and Genoa. A thought -- but Hahn was continuing.

"I will take no more of your valuable time, Your Majesty. We are watching for British agents, naturally, as we want to see exactly what they see, when they see it. With your permission, sir, I will place added ... emphasis on learning of their interests and then limiting their access … as we have in southern France."

His jaw set tight, the Kaiser slammed his right fist down on his desk. "Jawohl, Kapitän Hahn!" His lips twisted into a thin line, the Kaiser leaned forward in emphasis. "Ja...!" with added emphasis.

Hahn stood, clicked his heels as he bowed from the waist, picked up his valise and strode to the door.

"One further thing, Kapitän," said the Kaiser as he stood. "No detail is too small for my attention."

Hahn bowed in acknowledgement and gently closed the door after him. His smile was restrained, his arrogance was not. His Highest had just granted him *Immediatbericht:* Immediate and individual access to the Kaiser. That put him personally equal to the highest ranking officers in the Kaiserliche Marine, and designated N as the dominant intelligence operation.

*   *   *

Wilhelm settled onto his saddle-shaped stool at his desk in his book-lined private office. His heavily worn copy of Mahan was immediately at hand, his right hand. His left ear was mildly painful, which was an early forewarning that it could explode in agony in minutes. As he swallowed the second spoonful of the brown liquid, Wilhelm could almost immediately feel the pains recede... but now, in the past month, it had come to require two spoons, not just one, in order to blockade the pain.

He could only drink unsweetened black coffee after the brown liquid; otherwise the taste of the oily liquor would foul his mouth for hours -- though the Herr Doktor had recommended only water, as well as only one spoonful; together with a quiet warning to His Majesty about becoming dependent on the liquid.

Wilhelm had been surprised by Von Tirpitz's emphatic abrupt dismissal of the Predator strategy when His Highest had casually suggested it in the course of their

166

discussion before Hahn's arrival; preparatory to his revealing to the young fork-bearded admiral, with some pride, that the first Predator would sail within sixty days or less.

"A commerce raiding strategy against the British, Your Majesty, could be suicidal without the greatest care in its tactical implementation," the aggressive Rear Admiral had stated, very nearly crossing over the line of Imperial respect. "I fully agree with your first statement. Without sea power, sir, Germany's position in the world would resemble a mollusk without a shell."

The metaphor was emblazoned in the Kaiser's mind. He needed to -- to rethink, to recalibrate, yes, that was the word! To recalibrate the Predators! He would have it resolved by next week's meeting with Von Drascher. And, perhaps, von Tirpitz should be present at that meeting?

Wilhelm smiled. Admiral von Tirpitz had been notably impressed when he had quoted so authoritatively from Mahan.

The Kaiser reached again for the book

17

Captain Joachim Wörmann replaced the gold-rimmed magnifying glass on his desk and tossed the three cards he had been examining toward the rest of the deck that the French magician had given him which was spread on the desk. Quite clever, and, if true, a threat to his ship's reputation. And certainly to his own as well. But there was no direct evidence that the two Americans had actually marked these cards. It could be just as easily a publicity trick by the Frenchman.

"If, Herr Reymond," Wörmann said in English, he disliked using the French language, "if what you have explained and shown me is proven to be a fact, then the ship has two detention cells and I will have the two men in irons within the hour." He jabbed his finger at the magician. "But, Herr Reymond, if it is not proven, then it will be you who will be in irons. Understand? Verstehen Sie?"

"Yes, sir, I do," said André. "May I suggest, sir, two ways that we can proceed." He and Kyame had anticipated Wörmann's response, and had discussed options to confirm that Andrews and Sanders were cheaters. Walk into the

168

card room when the two would be playing, trying to make their big score as Kyame thought would be their objective, or, go into Sanders' room and find the cards spread out on his table. The first, however, would be conclusive.

"May I suggest, sir," said Reymond, "as Andrews and Sanders will undoubtedly be playing now, that we go to the card room under the pretense that you are making a casual visit to ensure the enjoyment of the passengers on their last evening before docking tomorrow. Then, when I see the marked, or as it is called, the skinned deck is introduced into their game, I will alert you, and you can seize the cards from their hands. If I am wrong, sir, I expect irons. If I am proved correct I would expect some evidence of ... of acknowledgement of my service."

Wörmann set his jaw, his lips tightened, then stood. "If," he growled, "you are correct, Frenchman, in what form would you want your 'acknowledgement?"

"A letter, sir, from you that would avail me of the opportunity to entertain on other Hamburg-America crossings."

The German was silent for a moment, then nodded. "Ja, it will be done."

***

André noted Kyame sitting reading a newspaper in the black velvet couch well away from the Andrews table.

169

She glanced up, touched her cheek, then turned the page. A marked deck was not yet in play.

His hands joined behind his back, Captain Wörmann nodded toward the Andrews table, the four players bowed their heads in acknowledgement then resumed play. The Captain continued on, walking slowly across the card room toward two other occupied tables. André walked alongside.

Wörmann stopped to speak with the two couples playing bridge. When one of the women asked André if he could do a trick for them, he agreed, positioning himself so that he could catch Kyame's signal, if the marked deck was in play.

At the edge of her vision, Kyame caught André as he brought out some coins from his pocket, and begin to cause them to vanish, multiply, then disappear to the delight of the four elderly players. The Captain himself appeared to be impressed.

Andrews threw his cards angrily onto the table as one of the marks, the man named Brennan, scooped up the bulging pot. Andrews' glance at Sanders was murderous. Kyame smiled. Andrews had given her a clear warning look when she had come into the card room, but she had ignored it and taken her seat on the couch away from the Andrews table.

Sanders leaned back to light a cigar, broke his match and asked if anyone had matches. When both marks reached into their jackets, Andrews let his left hand idly drop to his side. From the motion of his fingers, Kyame knew he had gotten the reader deck, the fully marked deck, which he then transferred to his lap. Another few seconds, Kyame waited for the cards scattered across the table to be collected in preparation for a new deal. Andre was replacing the coins in his pocket, bowing to the polite light applause. Even the Captain was smiling.

They continued on to the furthest table.

Sanders squared the cards and passed them on to the mark seated to Andrews' right, who then shuffled twice and placed the cards before Andrews to cut.

J.W. had shown her a deck switch in which a reader deck had been transferred from the lap of the advantage player to be hidden in the sleeve who then, as he reached out to cut, flipped the clean deck off the table onto his lap with a quick snap of his fingers, while allowing the marked deck to slide down into his hand. To succeed, the cheat's partner had to deflect the attention of the other mark at the key point. J.W. had said that not many advantage players would take the risk of discovery, unless they were in a tight money-losing situation.

Sanders leaned forward to ask the mark on Andrews left a question, which caused the man to turn. Andrews completed his cut.

Kyame folded her paper, rose and started for the door. The signal. She did not look in Andrews' direction.

"Now, sir, the marked deck is in play," whispered André.

Shaking hands with one of the players in the last table, and touching the bill of his gold encrusted cap to salute the women, the Captain turned back toward the door, Andre walking a step behind.

As the Captain neared the table, Sanders frowned and coughed. Andrews who had just dealt the hands, cleared his throat and started to turn to call a waiter. André saw him start to move his hand down ...

"Gentlemen, may I examine your cards for just a moment?" Without hesitation, Wörmann picked up the deck that Andrews had placed on the table while he picked up his hand and began sorting the cards. "What is the meaning of this intrusion, Captain?" snapped Andrews.

The Captain spread the face down deck into a rough fan, then separated the cards slowly. "Ah, Herr Andrews, I will do a trick for you gentlemen, as Herr Reymond has just done at the other tables." He withdrew one, then two and finally two more. "How much, gentlemen, would you wager that I have placed four queens on the table?"

"Is this a joke, sir?" asked Brennan. "I don't understand ..."

Sanders hand went inside his jacket.

The Captain slowly turned over the cards one queen at a time, until all four ladies were smiling up at him. "Marvelous, is it not gentlemen?" he smiled. "Marvelous, how lucky one can be ... when," he snarled angrily, "the backs are cleverly marked to identify the values!"

Sanders pushed back from the table as if to rise, when at the Captain's signal, three ship's men and the Purser quickly pushed through the doors to the card room. "Place Mr. Sanders and Mr. Andrews in irons for the balance of the crossing and notify British authorities at Southampton." He reached under Sanders jacket and withdrew a knife. He turned to André. "The affair, Herr Reymond, is now in my hands."

Andrews face was red with anger as the Purser and one of the ship's men took his arms to lead him to the door. He glanced back. "I'll get you, Reymond! I'll get both of you!"

Brennan grinned as he stood. "The Captain seems to have a few tricks of his own.

18

Southampton Harbor

Tuesday, February 18, 1896

Wrapped deep into her green wool coat and her hat tied with the silver scarf under her chin, Kyame leaned out from the railing into the stiff chill late morning breeze coming across the deck to scan the great harbor. She saw a tender with a black hull with white superstructure and the name Traffic painted on its bow approaching. Thick gray smoke rose from its single stack, roiling in the chill winds. The Auguste Victoria with its deep draft had anchored about a half-mile off the Southampton pier about breakfast time.

"The tender will get us promptly ashore," said the man standing next to her, in a black double-breasted leather overcoat, his face framed with dark gray mutton-chop whiskers, which, with his thick black mustache, gave him the appearance, Kyame thought, of wearing a mask. He would be fun to draw -- maybe later, if there would be any time. "The tender captains in Southampton well understand their business. They'll get us on land in quick time ... at least a quarter of an hour better than New York." Tipping his hat to her, he suddenly turned and walked away to join a carefully bundled up elderly woman who had just stepped gingerly out onto the deck. Her face lit up with a wide smile at the man's approach, who tipped his black silk topper. Others from First Class were gathering near the railings on both sides of the ship.

Kyame had expected to see André at breakfast, as he had promised, but the magician had never appeared -- and there had not been any message. She felt uneasy.

After the marked deck triumph of the previous day, they had talked excitedly of many things over wine and cheeses in the small café near the Ladies Saloon. On leaving the card room, the captain had nodded agreement to André's suggestion that they arbitrarily change ship's cards using different back designs so that no cheat would know which deck would be used in a particular day.

The captain's letter was delivered to André by the Purser as Kyame and André had enjoyed their wine. After reading it, with a great smile André gave it to Kyame to read. Written in English, the captain credited Mr. Reymond with identifying and aiding the ship's company in capturing two American card cheats, which ensured preservation of the unblemished reputation of the Auguste Victoria. She noted that a copy in German was being sent to HAP headquarters in Bremen. They had toasted the letter and fell to discussing his proposed magic routines, André describing what he had in mind for his next crossing on HAP, to which Kyame had made suggestions that had made André raise his eyebrows in surprise. Formidable!

175

Kyame had to catch herself, more than once she had to admit, from revealing too much of herself and her voyage to Europe.

They had separated when André received a message from a ship's clerk, with the promise to meet the following morning at breakfast.

But no André -- but there was still time before the tender arrived, she hoped.

As big as her ship was, Kyame saw three other ships, one with three smoke stacks, as large, or larger than the Auguste Victoria anchored near other piers within the frenetic harbor as smaller ships, some towing barges piled with crates of various kinds, churned through the short chop of the wind-blown waters with wisps of low hanging dark smoke tossed in the wind.

Their transition from the turbulent English Channel through the quieter waters of the Solent between the Isle of Wight and the mainland, to the slow advance up the Test River to its confluence ten miles upstream with the Itchen River where the Auguste Victoria entered the outer reaches of Southampton harbor had taken almost two hours. Dark clouds overhead became darker as the ship progressed. Kyame had watched each mile with intense interest -- her first European landfall.

***

At dinner the previous evening, Dr. von Müller had been very taken by her sketch of Lora. *"Ausgezeichnet! Excellent!"* he had exclaimed when he unrolled the paper scroll. Kyame was ashamed of the quality of the paper, but that was all the ship could produce. Von Müller had ordered another bottle of champagne to celebrate.

Lora had blushed with pleasure. "Kyame, I have not looked like that for years. *Vielen dank,* my dear. Many, many thanks."

***

But, Kyame frowned, where was André?

Glancing back toward the stern of the ship, the harbor's chop slapping up against docks and the shore, Kyame suddenly went cold inside. The body of a -- of a woman, it seemed, face down with her arms out stretched, was floating along the shoreline. Kyame now could see that the dark blotchy water around her head was her hair spread across water's surface. The woman twisted in the on-shore currents and bounced off the stone pillars supporting some commercial docks.

No one on shore seemed to notice.

"An ill omen for our arrival," said the ship's officer, J. Eichel his brass name tag said, who had stopped for a moment to stand by her. "Such violence so common in England is never tolerated in Imperial Germany." He tipped his white peaked cap and walked away.

Kyame did not believe in omens. She had seen, traveling with Papa, how such beliefs made some people softer marks for traveling spirit mediums and fortune tellers -- and, Kyame had to admit, for their second sight act.

She saw a workman on a dock suddenly freeze when he sighted the body now nudging gently against one of the small boats tied at his dock. He turned, shouting something, then ran to a ladder on the dock. Other men nearby dropped the boxes they were working on to run toward him. In her last glance, the tender coming alongside, she observed three of the men lifting the body into a small boat.

***

G. E. W. Jellicoe, standing at the foot of the gangway, carefully handed her onto the rolling deck of the tender. He had been very solicitous of her following the marked deck episode, as though he connected her with the incident.

"Miss Piddington?"

Kyame turned. A tall clean-shaven man wearing a brown bowler hat, in a somewhat worn but well-tailored tan colored sack suit stepped toward her. Kyame had walked several steps away from the gangway, to get free of the gentle chaos of the debarkation of the other First Class passengers. Second and steerage class passengers were coming down another gangway near the stern of the tender.

"Yes?"

Smiling, he pulled a set of credentials from inside his jacket, pressed the leather folder open and extended it toward her. "I am Sergeant Henry Mullins of Scotland Yard. I am assigned to escort you to your meeting in London. I was given your description by the Foreign Office and that you very probably would be wearing a green coat."

Kyame extended her hand in greeting, which Mullins took in a gentle grip. "A green coat." She smiled. "Yes, I told our authorities that I would be." She cocked her head slightly. "No badge, Sergeant?"

His smile went wider. Kyame noted his friendly blue eyes. "In England the police do not carry badges, as your police do in America. Our warrant cards carry all the authority we need."

"My British education starts early, it seems," she said, raising an eyebrow. "My luggage?"

"Both pieces will be stowed on my carriage. Once ashore we will be at the train station within a few minutes and then on a special train to London." As they turned together, he asked, "Are you hungry at all? There will be grub on the train."

She shook her head. "The ship fed me very well this morning. Thank you, I am fine." Still no sign of André as the tender began to pull back from the black hull that towered over them. Where?

179

As they stepped inside the main cabin of the tender, Mullins apologized for the light drizzle that had begun to fall in earnest, then smiled. "Part of your British education, Miss Piddington. England can often be a very wet and chilly country."

Kyame smiled in return, but the smile was forced. No sign of her French magician.

Within twenty minutes the tender was tied at a pier. Luggage was being handed up near the stern while the passengers disembarked amidships. Mullins held Kyame's elbow as they climbed the short gangway steps to the pier.

"Steady, Miss Piddington. It is normal to feel a little dizzy reaching dry land after a week at sea. Your first crossing?"

Kyame nodded.

André!

There, walking with the Von Müllers with three uniformed police and a stern looking man in a black suit. They were walking rapidly down the pier fifty or so feet away.

"May I ask, Sergeant," said Kyame, anxiously, "what that group with the police is all about? The older man and woman were my tablemates for dinner each night." She didn't ask about André -- almost fearing now what the answer might be.

"That is a group of very clever diamond smugglers, Miss Piddington. In the past five, perhaps even six months, they have moved several thousand pounds ... English pounds ... worth of diamonds from New York through Southampton to fences in England and on the Continent. Very clever, I must say ... but we have them now, and we will learn more of their dealings, and their techniques, before they go to trial. Germany and America have each requested jurisdiction, but we have them, and here they will stay for a number of years, I daresay."

Her heart froze. André -- a smuggler! She bit down on her lip.

No! No!

"You look quite pale, Miss Piddington. Are you feeling well? Getting off a rolling ship to dry land can be a bit disconcerting."

Taking a deep breath, she shook her head. "No, Sergeant, I am fine. I am just shocked that the people I came to know ... know so well ... they were so kind. I ... I guess it will take some time to get used to their being ... criminals." If ever -- she felt queasy -- if ever. She brushed a few tears away. Everything seemed a betrayal. She felt defeated -- and stupidly foolish.

Mullins nodded. "Our carriage is over there. My men are just loading your luggage."

***

181

"Miss Piddington is now in England," said Richard Olney as he handed President Cleveland the cablegram which said only:

abdicate

kp

Cleveland frowned, then looked up for his friend's explanation.

Olney smiled. "Hamburg-America provides a code in their passenger memorandum book for routine messages to reduce costs of cabling. Abdicate means 'Arrived today'. The date and time are given on the cable."

Cleveland nodded, then reached down into a drawer on the left of his desk, removed a sheet of yellow paper, and slid it across to Olney.

"That was hand-delivered to me barely half-an-hour ago from the British Embassy. It is an intercept of a German diplomatic message the British forwarded to us from London.

"The Germans know Kyame Piddington is there, Olney. They know already!" Cleveland lips were tight. "How, man?" He slammed his hand on the desk. "How?"

Olney read: american woman met by scotland yard at sh 1134 today stop appearance matches report stop under surveillance

There was no addressee or signature.

"The message was sent from Southampton to the German Embassy in London," said Cleveland.

"Yes, Mr. President," said Olney, his eyes narrowed, his face pale. "How? ... And who?" It was the identity that Olney wanted before anything. The British would alert Kyame. A bad -- a damnably bad omen on which to start an operation.

19

Hohenzollern II

En route

Admiral, the Graf von Drascher stood at the railing, the gold railing of the Kaiser's yacht, Hohenzollern II. His fingers wrapped around the most gold he had ever held since he had left his father's now impoverished castle. The ship, which in his view could not be called a yacht, slipped smoothly through the coastal waters of the Baltic Sea with clumps of small white clouds scudding across their bow, the light cruiser SMS Seeadler holding station about a mile back. Looking back at the cruiser, Von Drascher frowned, brought his fists down hard on the golden railing.

The waste -- the utter waste!

But the politicians liked to see the All Highest disappear on his "large toy" as von Drascher had once overheard the yacht described. Who was in charge of the nation? The babbling idiots of the Reichstag -- or the unstable Kaiser? And when? And where should his own loyalty lie when the hard test came, whatever that might be? What choices were there for him and the Kaiserliche

Marine, but to follow their Emperor who -- who was a compass without a needle?

At the last minute, von Drascher had received orders to join the Kaiser on the Imperial Yacht where their regular Predator meeting would be held. The Admiral, His All Highest had hoped, would not be unduly inconvenienced by the change in venue. Von Drascher would be dropped off to return to Berlin at a suitable port. Except, von Drascher owed several immediate decisions on the Predators to the management at the Ebing ship yards; but perhaps he could discretely contact them from the yacht -- very discretely. The Kaiser had only just returned from a yacht cruise five days ago with some piece of royalty from Italy, now another? And, after the formalities with Prince Albert of Monaco, the honored guest on this cruise, when will their more business-like meeting take place?

Tall, smartly bearded, well dressed in a double-breasted dark blue suit, dark hair and dark eyes, Albert had been a comfortable, more a professorial than a royal presence at lunch. The Prince had been most knowledgeable about the sea itself, but not of naval matters. But over coffee he began to drone on about some article on ocean current drifts in some scientific journal that only the Kaiser responded to, which blocked any other conversation. The other officers, including von Drascher, struggled to stay politely attentive. Albert and His Highest finally had excused themselves to a more private conversation, and von Drascher returned to waiting on deck.

He slapped his right hand against the railing. When? When? Driften, immer Trieben! Drifting, always drifting!

Von Drascher turned at his name. His Highest beckoned. His face cold, his jaw set, clearly the Kaiser was angry about something.

.***

"We will be meeting the Prime Minister at his home in London on Arlington Street rather than his country home at Hatfield, Miss Piddington. I understand that time is of the essence in this matter, so London was the most central place." Mullins smiled. "I will be leaving you at the gates at Arlington ... and turning you over to the chappies in the Foreign Office. You will take this carriage with your luggage on to the boat train to continue your journey to the Continent."

"Not 10 Downing Street?" Kyame grinned. "I believe I detect some friction, Sergeant Mullins."

"The Prime Minister prefers to work at his Arlington Street home rather than Downing, Miss Piddington. However, His Lordship often meets foreign dignitaries at Downing." He laughed. "Yes, but a friendly friction, if I may say so. We work together as needed." His face grew grim. "I don't know the details of what you may

186

face on the Continent, Miss Piddington, but you have my card. If I can be of any help ... at any time."

She nodded. "Thank you, sir. I hope that will not be necessary." She turned toward him. "What is the Prime Minister like?"

"His Lordship is physically a very large man, quite tall, and somewhat nearsighted. However, I have only seen him, but have never met him personally. I have been told that he is direct, honest, a good listener, a hard worker who often works harder than the people around him ... and a great lover of books. I have personally never supported his government's policies, but that, for today, is of no importance. Of necessity, the police can have no public opinions on the politics of the ruling party. Though His Lordship is faced, as I read in the papers, with the daily problems of guiding a somewhat rowdy coalition government that diminishes, even neutralizes his personal powers." Mullins shrugged, and then grinned. "But politics is not my strong suit."

Kyame smiled and nodded. "Thank you for your guidance." She wasn't sure what she would encounter, but Salisbury sounded like a workable subject. A hard worker, a driven man, perhaps some physical limitations, and just perhaps he is over confident in his own abilities. Papa had always shown her that such men, women as well, could be controlled without their realizing it. She took a deep breath and sank back into the leather cushions to reflect. Kyame's heart was settled, fragile, but settled. André -- well, André--

she would try to get him out of her mind for the time. Later. Later for that. But they had discussed so many marvelous plans. Kyame frowned and pushed the memories away.

She clinched her fists. Later!

Kyame looked out the window of the unmarked black four-wheeled closedcoach, which had been waiting for them at Waterloo Station, as it rolled rapidly, jolting, jerking in every direction over the uneven streets though the bewildering chaotic traffic of London. The streets were in worse repair than New York City, and infinitely worse than Boston. The mingled stench that penetrated the closed carriage, of pungent horse manure, putrefying garbage, decaying dead animals with the limitless mud that would occasionally splatter against her window, that the rain would then wash off, and the unceasing clamor, all that was somewhat familiar -- but in London it all seemed piled on one another in a particularly odious combination. Kyame smiled. But it was London, a special place she had always wanted to see since reading Papa's battered copies of Charles Dickens on the trains, stage coaches and in the hotels from town to town.

Her education in their travels had relied on books they found and a few books that Papa would buy for her. Kyame would sometime go to the lobby of the best hotel in the town or city in which they were performing to read in the libraries that were sometimes available. Often just paper novels falling apart, but she had found Poe, Kipling, the poetry of Whitman, and Shakespeare, the Sonnets that had so enraptured Mama. But now she absorbed as many of the books at the Boston Public Library and at the Boston Athenaeum that she could manage.

Along with her Chinese studies.

The rolling countryside that she had seen from the train in their seventy-minute breakneck journey from Southampton, she wanted to see it all again, when there was more time, to breathe the country air, to walk the lanes, to hear the people, to eat their food -- to absorb England.

There had been only two cars on the special train taking her to London from Southampton. All the tracks, Mullins had explained, had been cleared of normal traffic as she swept through one station after another, scarcely able to fully grasp their appearances and the blurred people waiting on the platforms. When she had asked, Mullins had said that the train had been designated a special Royal train, which was why the Queen's arms had been emblazoned on the side of her car. With Her Majesty's permission, he carefully added. No other explanations were necessary. Without the Royal arms, the train would have drawn unnecessary attention.

***

Lord Salisbury frowned as he walked across his vast cluttered library to open the door. He coughed and wiped a handkerchief across his face as he walked. He could feel a mild fever coming on, like the one two days ago that had slowed him down, then faded away after an uncharacteristic afternoon hour-long nap.

The Prime Minister was still a giant of a man at 65, dressed in a well-worn unfashionable gray suit, well over six feet tall with a large head, a rounded bald dome, a heavy bushy gray beard, massive broad shoulders, and a wide girth. He had easily held his own when, as a young man, he had labored in the gold fields of South Africa. Even without his many titles, Robert Cecil physically dominated any room he entered. His eyes, tightly squinted into slits, were hardly visible. He carried thick glasses in a large calloused hand.

Three other, younger men, fashionably dressed, who were discussing the maps of South Africa laid out on a large table running down the center of the room, stepped aside to clear his wide path.

Kaiser Wilhelm's telegram to Paul Kruger barely four weeks earlier had created a sudden severe stress in the Anglo-German relationship that had undermined the Prime Minister's communications suggesting an Anglo-German alliance, a workable peace. Sent on January 3, 1896, the Kaiser had congratulated Kruger, President of the Transvaal Republic, on his successful defeat of the Jameson Raid on the Transvaal by 650 British irregular troops from the Cape Colony. The objective of the Raid had been to ignite a rebellion against Kruger's government in the Transvaal by expatriate British miners, but the Raid had failed ignominiously. The telegram, written by the

Reich Foreign Office, seemed to promise German assistance if Kruger needed it then or perhaps in the future. Publication of the telegram enhanced the public popularity of the Kaiser in Germany, but kindled anger in the streets of England which led to German shop windows being broken and German sailors being attacked on the streets of London and in port cities. The Salisbury government considered South Africa a British sphere of influence and deeply resented the Kaiser's intrusion. Only a personal letter from the Kaiser to his grandmother, Queen Victoria, had begun to quiet the turmoil.

"Where is the American woman?" Salisbury asked, at the door, his voice, firm with a low resonant timbre, was unmistakable. Everyone knew when Robert Cecil, the third Marquess of Salisbury, Prime Minister and Foreign Secretary, spoke. Though with his severe shortsightedness, he approached near blindness at times when lights were dim, which, coupled with a poor memory, would lead to some awkward moments as at times when on social occasions Salisbury sometimes could not recognize his own family of ten children; or at times members of his own party in Parliament. But even then he loved to read and had, over several years, virtually memorized all of the novels of Jane Austen, while always carrying in a polished wooden traveling case small leather-bound editions of the works of Shakespeare, Virgil, Horace, Euripides and Tacitus, and whatever new works or articles that might appear on the French Revolution, a passionate interest since his youth.

Standing in the vast arched entry hall, Scotland Yard Inspector Alec McGinnis, himself a large man, turned to the familiar voice. "Shortly, My Lord. They left Waterloo only minutes ago."

Salisbury nodded, turning back to the library. God in Heaven! With the still unexplained loss of human resources in Southern Europe, the killing -- for the British government to have to rely on a single young woman to discover what might be threatening British interests in the South of France. He was -- embarrassed. Salisbury grasped his glasses more tightly.

But a single young *American* woman! Only two months ago on December 17, 1895, in a speech to Congress, President Cleveland had implied that America would consider war with Great Britain over the boundary dispute between Venezuela and British Guinea, a dispute in which Venezuela was making extravagant territorial claims, and in which America had no iron in the fire. In private letters, Secretary of State Richard Olney had vigorously pressed the British Foreign Office on Venezuela's behalf, and now, now an American woman! He shook his head and returned to the maps with their many implications in South Africa -- and, on other maps, Turkey with Russian moves and motives becoming an unsettled issue. Should Christian England support Muslim Turkey against Christian Russia? Salisbury had a clear resolution on that issue.

It was called the Suez Canal.

Not even a woman from an outpost of Empire, but America! But was Cleveland sending the American woman as, Salisbury pursed his lips, as he re-entered his library, as a subtle insult? His own request had been genuine. He needed to know, what with the Kaiser's meddling and Russia's indeterminate policies. The deaths of so many agents in a relatively short time had strongly suggested betrayal within his own government, so he could not send any more English agents until he knew what was happening; thus his appeal to Cleveland. He refused to believe that America and Great Britain could ever come to war, and certainly not over a boundary line running through humid swamps hundreds of miles from the American border.

Perhaps using even the French might have been better; but then, he shrugged, the French police had had no explanation for the killings either, let alone be able to explain why, or for him to be able to actually believe whatever the French gendarmes might say.

To send a young woman into a potentially lethal situation -- Salisbury began again with the three men at the maps. To identify the why? He listened as his senior aide, recently returned from the Cape, begin again, first waiting for the Prime Minister to finish adjusting his glasses.

***

Kyame felt the momentum of the carriage slowly begin to diminish. Her heart picked up its beat, like it did each time before she would step out on a stage with Papa. Not nervous -- just prepared and ready, even eager. "Are we there?" Her fingers automatically brushed over the crystal *bi* disc beneath her blouse.

Mullins nodded. "One or two minutes. It will be on your right." He smiled. "May I say you don't appear to be at all nervous, Miss Piddington. Do you meet Prime Ministers often?"

She flashed a quick smile and shook her head. "No, Sergeant, I've never met a Prime Minister ... but I have faced difficult situations before."

***

At the knock, Salisbury looked up as the door to the library opened. A figure in a long green coat entered with Inspector McGinnis beside her. He stepped back from the map table as the other three men went silent and turned toward their visitor.

"Your Lordship, may I have the honor to introduce Miss Kyame Piddington from America," said McGinnis.

Stepping toward her, Salisbury extended his hand in greeting. As she came into focus, he smiled. Cleveland had sent, at least, a beautiful woman. "Welcome to the Queen's Realm, Miss Piddington," he said, gently.

"Thank you, Your Lordship. I am instructed as well to bring you the warmest regards of President Cleveland."

At the Prime Minister's motion, she seated herself in a well-worn, deep brown leather chair near his cluttered desk. She declined tea.

As Sergeant Mullins had described, Salisbury was very large, his shoulders seemed to reach from one end of the desk to the other. But what she could see of his smile behind his gray brush of beard seemed friendly.

"Mr. Joseph, please lay out the map of the killings," said Salisbury. "Miss Piddington, our time is short. I have had a map made which displays the location of each of the seven killings of British observers in the south of France, which you may take with you."

Kyame nodded. "I need as well, Prime Minister, the details of who they were, or pretended to be, what they were there to observe … and the mode of the murders. Had they filed any reports or observations?"

An aide laid a thick file on the desk near the Prime Minister. "This contains the individual files, as Miss Piddington has just suggested, sir."

Kyame caught Salisbury's sharp flinch and momentary deep frown, his left hand went to his jaw only to drop back to his lap. Clearly there had been a flash of pain. A toothache, possibly. Salisbury wiped his forehead with a handkerchief and rose from the desk. "The map is ready, Miss Piddington."

The map covered southern France, Monaco and ended with San Remo, Italy. There were seven numbered red dots, and one black one at San Remo. Edward Joseph, who had laid out the map, explained, "The red dots are the locations where the British bodies were found, the numbers refer to the files on each agent in the dossier you will take. There is no consistency in terms of the mode or timing of the killings. They were done, obviously, to appear random, except for their general focus in the south. As a new agent would be transferred from another post to replace the agent lost, the replacement was killed with 6-10 days, which suggests some urgency in the situation on the part of whomever is responsible." Joseph glanced at Salisbury who nodded. "Which also suggests a ... confidential knowledge of British intelligence resources in the area." Joseph moved back a step to give Kyame more room at the table. A medium sized man of impeccable dress, Joseph had volunteered to go the south of France himself to ferret out "the blacklegs" responsible. But his knowledge of South Africa was too valuable for Salisbury to risk.

"Any apparent motives? Robbery, or ..."

"Yes," said Joseph, as Salisbury's left hand went to his jaw again. "Robbery in each case, though none of the men carried anything of any unique value, perhaps about a few hundred francs, a watch. Nothing more."

"How long had they been dead when the bodies were found?"

Joseph's eyebrow went up. Impressive. She may yet be a huntress, a predator behind the beauty and the brilliant green eyes. "A good question, Miss Piddington. As best we have determined with the help of the French authorities, the bodies had been dead for between six hours and two days before they were found. Those details are in the dossiers."

Kyame nodded. "Were the finders, if I may call them that, already known to the local police in every case?"

Joseph looked up at Salisbury. "We don't know, sir. Your implication, Miss Piddington, is most insightful ... and most disturbing."

"And the weapons used, knives, guns, hatchets, whatever, Mr. Joseph, were they found?"

"No."

Seven killings which someone, or some organization had tried to make look random. She would have to dig for the connections; and quickly.

***

"Fraulein Kyame Piddington is at the Arlington Street home of Prime Minister Lord Salisbury, sir. She was taken to London from Southampton on a special two car royal train that had all traffic cleared for it. Salisbury is clearly serious about sending her here."

197

Johannes Friederich Wagner nodded. "We will be waiting for her, Bäcker. Should Fraulein Piddington even come close to us, she is to be killed. There is no time for any chances." Then he frowned, looking out the window toward the sparkling Mediterranean. On the horizon, a magnificent yacht was heeling over in the winds. Guy, Count de Dampierre's two-masted Cassiopée, most likely. A beautifully designed vessel which, he smiled, so resembled the Count's beautiful wife, smooth and easily guided. He turned back to the Ritter Heinz Bäcker. "But why a woman, and an American woman at that, when the American President has been talking of war with England? There is something else here, Bäcker. Piddington is to be closely watched. The American Navy is pathetic, but ..." He tossed his hand in dismissal. "No complications."

As his senior aide closed the door, Wagner allowed himself a moment for the warm luxury of recalling his last engaging encounter with the lovely Angelique, the Countess de Dampierre.

***

Salisbury gave the telegraph intercept to Kyame. She raised an eyebrow. "Do you know how German intelligence could know you were coming ... even to the color of your coat?" he asked.

"I crossed on a German liner, the Auguste Victoria." She clenched her fist. It was that librarian -- and

Mahan. It had to be her, somehow. Yes, it was her own fault, that stupid arrogant mistake.

"You seem to recall something, Miss Piddington," said Joseph.

She looked up and nodded. "There was a ship's librarian ... Agnes Herwig. Tall, blonde, overly curious. She seemed very interested in everyone. I saw her twice even coming up the stairs from second class, though her cabin is in first. I wondered at the time, why the librarian for the first class library would be in second class, when, as I discovered later, there was no library in second class. She must be it ... and she has some means for communicating."

Salisbury beckoned to one of the men. "Mr. Edesonn, alert Scotland Yard and the Naval Office of Agnes Herwig. Have her followed, note all, I mean *all*, of her contacts." He shook his head. "The Kaiser is as unpredictable as the flight of a swallow. I wonder if even the German government knows where he will turn next?" He flinched again, touching his jaw.

"Prime Minister, you are in pain," said Kyame. "May I be of some assistance to assuage your discomfort?"

Salisbury shook his head. "Thank you, Miss Piddington, but I have enough powders of various colors to numb a horse."

"I don't mean with drugs, sir. Would you allow me to place you in a mesmeric trance for a few moments? I can

199

lift your pain away … for a few days." Which might be true. J.W. had warned her more than once of the uncertainty of mesmeric suggestion. A suggestion made under trance might last five minutes, might last a week. It was totally in the mind of the subject.

"Your Lordship!" Edward Joseph protested.

Salisbury removed his glasses, squinted his eyes to focus on Kyame Piddington's intense green eyes. For a moment the vast library went silent as all eyes fastened on the Prime Minister.

When he nodded, Kyame rose. "Please remain sitting, Your Lordship." She rounded the edge of the desk, and when their eyes met, she smiled. "Thank you for trusting me, sir." Kyame glanced back. "I will need quiet, gentlemen." She began to move her hands and fingers as though gently stroking the air. "Please relax," she said, her voice dropping a note, taking on a rhythm, "You will be in control at all times. There is nothing to fear. We are going on a short trip to a special place. Relax. A special place." Her voice was low, soothing. Her fingers touched and lightly stroked Salisbury's wide forehead as she continued to murmur. "A special place. I'll place these aside to give you more comfort." She gently removed his glasses. "You will see the special place without effort." Kyame brought her fingers lightly down each side of the Prime Minister's head, then brushed her thumbs softly across his heavy eyebrows. His eyes began to lose focus, his breathing was becoming slow and regular as though on the edge of sleep.

Kyame repeated her stroking from the forehead to the jaw on each side. "There will be a light wind in our special place, the sky will be bright blue with large clouds like muffins hanging in the air. The large green leaves will shift and move as though floating on the breeze." His eyes went closed. She heard a gasp behind her, but didn't turn. She continued to stroke his temples, whispering more descriptions of the special place. Salisbury was clearly going deeper into the trance. He was letting go. The pain must be greater than what he chose to reveal.

"There is a cool moist breeze blowing across your face, cooling your fever, flowing through your entire body, wafting away concerns. A light cooling rain is beginning to fall, just enough to wash through you, to relax completely ... to remove all pain for hours, even days. A special place of no worries, no decisions, just quiet music, cool water washing through you completely cleansing, cooling you." His face was relaxed with no apparent stress, no muscle tension. Salisbury was in the special place.

Kyame stepped back, her eyes on his facial muscles. There was no movement -- a moment, then another in the silent library. Kyame said softly, "Now, it is time to begin our journey back to your library. But you will bring the peace you have with you, a peace without pain, a gift from the special place. I will begin to count back from ten, when I reach one I will snap my fingers." She bent down close to his right ear. "When you awake, I will become invisible to you whenever I clap my hands twice. Do you understand?" Salisbury nodded slowly.

Kyame began her count. "Three ... two ... one." She snapped her fingers. Salisbury's eyes opened wide.

"Your Lordship, are ...?" Joseph asked.

"I feel fine." He shook his head. "Truly fine." He looked up at Kyame who had backed some steps from him to ensure he didn't feel crowded. "And, Miss Piddington." He hesitated. "I feel no pain. I feel more relaxed and at peace than anytime that I can recall. No pain at all." He stood, retrieving his glasses from the desk.

"Thank you again, Your Lordship, for trusting me."

"It is I who must thank you, Miss Piddington." He extended his hand which Kyame gripped. He noted the time on the clock on his desk. "But time is now short. Mr. Joseph, please collect the materials for Miss Piddington."

"I will not need the map, sir. I have memorized it."

Salisbury's eyebrows went up as the other men expressed disbelief.

"But you hardly -- you had hardly looked at the map! How?" Joseph exclaimed.

"When we have time, sir, I will be happy to teach you how." Kyame grinned. "It is not that hard. But I do have a question. What does the black dot on the map signify?"

Salisbury laughed. "I could use some help in memory as well, Miss Piddington." He had never felt so free inside -- and the miserable toothache was gone. "But the time has come for you to continue your journey."

As they began to walk toward the door, Joseph said, "That is the place where the body of the Count von Trotha was discovered on February 2, on the beach at San Remo. There has been no resolution of his murder. It is on the map because it occurred during the period of the other killings. It may have nothing whatever to do with our other problems."

As she walked, Kyame immediately recalled James Dixey's mention of the killing of the Count von Trotha and the marvelous jade sword.

Randolph Edesonn stood near the door with the black leather pouch holding the files. As Kyame walked toward the door, she turned at the Prime Minister's cough. "You will be out-numbered everywhere you go, Miss Piddington," said Salisbury slowly, his jaw jutting out. "And the Kaiser's minions know you are coming."

The other three men watched her closely.

"I don't wish to appear foolish, Your Lordship, but I have been out-numbered before and have prevailed. But I do not take anything for granted. If I feel truly threatened I will immediately seek out the nearest escape route. Or, I will just disappear." She clapped her hands twice.

Salisbury stopped, his eyes went wide, his jaw dropped.

"Sir?"

"The woman just disappeared! Before my eyes!" He squinted his eyes, searching across the library.

Edesonn shook his head. "But, Your Lordship, Miss Piddington is standing by the door," he said quietly. "By the door," he repeated.

Kyame clapped her hands a second time. Salisbury shook his great head in wonderment. Suddenly there she was -- by the door. How?

"If it should be necessary, sir, instead of vanishing behind a mesmeric trance," her voice went cold, as Kyame squeezed her right hand into a tight fist, "I will use mesmeric power to stop the beating of a heart." She nodded toward the Prime Minister. Gathering her coat, Kyame walked through the door being held for her.

Well, anyway, Kyame thought, passing the smiling gentleman, she could try. But there was something she had to do as quickly as possible.

20

Inspector McGinnis flashed a quick smile at Kyame's request, nodded, then directed the driver accordingly. The closed coach pulled out into the active traffic of Arlington Street, turned right at the first block, onto an almost empty side street of quiet elegant homes. The only traffic was two housemaids carrying packages walking slowly together along the sidewalk in deep conversation. They hardly glanced up as the carriage rattled by. The carriage continued for three blocks then turned into a narrow lane of neatly kept shops and as the carriage drew to a halt, McGinnis swore softly when a young man suddenly ran in front of the horses causing them to stumble in shying away, then the man disappeared into an alley. McGinnis quickly turned to Kyame. "My apologies, Miss Piddington, but that brash cutpurse should be taught a strong lesson," he said, his jaw tight. "But for another time. I will await you here. The shop you want is there with the black and yellow sign over its door."

Stepping down, Kyame had seen the purse snatcher yank his trick, one of a team of two young men, the second "accidentally" blocking the man accompanying the targeted woman from immediately pursuing his partner. The two were dressed to blend with the modish crowds. The snatcher escaped with the purse while the blocker had skillfully blended away into the jostling throng. She well understood McGinnis' anger, as Kyame had fought off a purse snatcher in Boston just the previous week.

A bell tinkled somewhere when Kyame opened the door. The shop was for, in large stylized black letters, "High Quality Clothing for the Cultured Woman". "Previously Worn" was in smaller plain letters in the lower right side of the sign.

"Yes?" a well-dressed older woman in blue silk asked quietly, appearing from a doorway in the rear of the shop.

"I would like to exchange this coat for one of similar size but different color. Can we manage that?"

The woman smiled. "An American?" She judged the quality of Kyame's coat by running her fingers under its wide collar. She nodded. "A very good piece of goods. I may have something over there ... next to the window."

Kyame pushed along the coats hung from a thick wooden beam jutting out from the wall. Her coat was far better quality than any hanging there, but that didn't matter. She wanted something dark that couldn't attract attention. The German telegraph intercept had mentioned her green coat, so that had to go, if she were to be able to gain some steps on those who may be following her. She chose a black coat with dark red trim that appeared to be about her size.

The woman, Mrs. Whitehead, held her green coat as Kyame tried on the red and black. The shoulders were all right, the waist a bit loose, but the length was just right. It carried a slight musty odor, but it didn't matter. She would change again when she arrived in France at her first opportunity.

"Yes, this will do," said Kyame, turning to Mrs. Whitehead, and smiling. "We have a deal ... do we not?"

"Well ..."

"Do we not?" Kyame repeated firmly, her narrow smile cold.

Mrs. Whitehead pursed her lips, then nodded. "Let's clean your pockets. I don't want you coming back claiming something that ain't here." She dipped her hand into each inside pocket, then the deep outside pockets. "What have we here, Miss?" She handed Kyame a small black cardboard box. "That appears all."

Kyame took the box. She had never seen it before, but put into the pocket of her new coat and walked quickly toward the door.

"You will mention to your friends how well you've been treated here, won't you, Miss?"

Kyame turned as she closed the door behind her. "Yes, of course."

Regaining her seat in the carriage which began to move immediately, Kyame removed the box from the coat pocket. As the horses began to pull more rapidly ahead, McGinnis glanced over, as Kyame lifted the lid -- as she gasped!

In the box between two soft cotton pads were three brilliant square-cut diamonds. Kyame heard the Scotland Yard Inspector whistle. "A carat each, at least," he said. "Don't want to display those rocks anywhere on the street, Miss."

"Are they real, Inspector?" She held the box carefully closer to him, as the carriage jolted over a pothole. Her hand shook, but the diamonds stayed safely in the box.

"Careful, Miss." McGinnis pulled a magnifying glass from his vest pocket, held it close to the diamonds in the box. "I won't touch them, Miss, as they would be too easy to lose." After a moment, he nodded. "As best as I can make out, those stones are genuine. Only a jeweler could confirm that, of course, but I have no doubt you have at least three, maybe more, carats of very fine diamonds there." He looked closely at Kyame who was grinning as she read a small note tucked in the lid of the box. "Kyame, for my Lora's wonderful drawing. My deepest thanks." It was signed Marcus with Canineanalyst in large letters across the bottom. But now, so sadly, the von Müllers were headed to jail -- with André. She took a deep breath to settle her suddenly troubled heart.

Kyame looked up at McGinnis. "Payment from a client from the ship for whom I drew a portrait. An unexpected payment, Inspector. I told him there was no fee, not for friends, but, obviously, he insisted." She shook her head, replaced the lid on the box and pushed the box down deep into her coat pocket.

Cash or keep when she reached Monaco? She would sell them. The diamonds would remind her of too much -- sadness.

Monaco, where she would meet Muffin, the code name of the last British agent in the south of France. As Lord Salisbury had walked with her to his great arched entryway, he had quietly explained that she would meet the manager of Smith's Bank in Monaco, as all visitors banked with Smith's. V.B., as the Prime Minister called the bank manager, would make the appropriate introductions. His Lordship's final whispered assurance, "Victor Bethell can be trusted implicitly. He can contact me directly if necessary." He took her extended hand in both of his, then smiled. "My thanks, Miss Piddington, for the remarkable peace you placed within me."

Another turn, a few blocks, then another, the carriage entered through the waiting open double doors of an empty warehouse. The doors were rapidly pulled closed just as the carriage cleared them by two uniformed policemen.

"We change carriages here, Miss Piddington," said Inspector McGinnis. He grinned. "Your coat change says we are thinking the same things in the same way."

Within less than five minutes, Kyame and McGinnis were driving down a wide street in a lacquered dark brown brougham that bore no resemblance to the black closedcoach she had taken from Waterloo Station. A waiting man with a woman dressed in a green coat had gotten into their former coach which left the warehouse turning right. The brougham turned left and moved at a more leisurely pace, slowly gaining speed as the crowds thinned.

"Now to connect to the Train de Luxe at Charing Cross Station and then, Miss Piddington, you are on your way to the Continent and to Monaco."

***

"Where?" he snarled. "I lost them!"

"There, Markham, there's the coach pulling out from that market garden. Must have stopped for a bite."

Markham jabbed his cane hard twice up against the trap-door. The driver above opened the trap and looked down. "Faster, damnit, Belcase, faster before we lose them again." When the trap closed, he looked over at the scarred face of Charley Foster. "Our esteemed Imperial paymasters won't like it if we lose that American woman. Won't bloody like it at all."

Kyame settled into her first class seat only two cars back from the engine. She had counted six cars in the train as she walked the platform. The compartment with two facing brown leather couches was empty, but penetrated by the noise and cries of the horde of animated travelers rushing past her window up and down the platform. The late afternoon sun threw sharp stripes of shadow and light through the ridge-and-furrowed ceiling of the station across the surging throng. Blue uniformed porters pushed their rattling carts teetering with piled luggage and boxes through the chaos, while some liveried footmen marched through the crowds carrying polished leather portmanteaus with valises wedged under each arm.

A marvelously dressed older woman strolled confidently behind an overloaded silver and blue liveried servant. She shimmered in a luxurious coat of white and silver silk with the fur of some animal draped over her shoulders. She wore a hat of silver satin, with a very large bow and a bigger hat brim than Kyame had ever seen. Kyame grinned. The woman could probably fly like a bird in a good wind.

With the shriek of its whistle, the train on the adjacent parallel track began to move sending expanding clouds of grayish-white smoke roiling about the platform traffic with the engine's loud chuffing gaining in frequency as the power of the steam overcame the drag of the string of several passenger cars.

Kyame had not detected anyone following her through the crowds at Charing Cross Station. Occasionally, as in Boston, a man would politely tip his hat to her in passing, to which she nodded, but nothing suspicious. British train stations were laid out differently from what she was used to at home. The number of trains arriving and departing from Charing Cross was astonishing, but the boat train to the Gare Maritime in Calais and the Train de Luxe was waiting on Platform 29. Kyame stopped at a newsstand to buy a copy of the *Pall Mall Gazette*, the English newspaper she had most enjoyed reading on the Auguste Victoria. Glancing up from the paper allowed her to scan the moving hordes without, hopefully, being too obvious. There was no one, no recurring faces, no one displaying covert interest -- but the Germans could just be handing-off, with different trackers taking her trail as followers dropped off to avoid being "eye-balled". Judson Rowland had explained basic surveillance techniques to her when he had visited her in Boston three months ago. There had been a situation, as Rowland had called it, in Boston that Kyame had helped with, which resulted in the capture of a jewel thief from Ireland. Her role had been to be the bait, convincing bait around which Rowland's observers could position themselves to cover all approaches. Boston police were available but not in the final setup; the thief had developed too many friends on the local force, friends who talked too much.

Kyame felt her car begin to move, the couplings jerking her car as the thrust of the engine worked its way down the six cars of the train. In a few moments the train was rolling smoothly out of the station into the sprawling array of tracks running in every direction as other trains were moving into the station. A conductor walked rapidly by her compartment. Kyame kept the curtains open on the two windows of the compartment so that she could observe passers-by in the aisle.

Kyame was still alone.

She went back to reading the article in the PMG about a thought reader named Stuart C. Cumberland. Kyame resolved she would watch Mr. Cumberland her first chance, after the current situation was resolved. Cumberland was a one-man act, not the two person act of the Impossible Piddingtons. Papa had commented on one-man thought reading, but he felt it was too limited in effect, and an observant spectator might be able to duplicate some of the effects, not as smoothly as the professional, but still enough to queer the public interest.

But maybe, maybe this Stuart Cumberland had something else to offer.

***

"So where did she go? What platform?" Markham was red-faced with fury. By the time they figured they had been neatly hornswoggled and recovered, they had lost at least fifteen to twenty minutes. Markham had decided to wager on Charing Cross as the woman's destination, but that had cost them another ten minutes cutting through the London traffic. Foster had jumped from their cabriolet to run into Charing Cross Station in the hope of glimpsing the green-coated American woman, but returned with nothing.

"Blast! Those Germans don't take kindly to failure." Markham took a breath as Foster settled back into his seat. "I'll tell'm that we lost her in Charing Cross." He had an idea. "What boat trains leave this hour?"

Foster pulled out his Bradshaw, flipped through a few pages. "Boat train connection to the Train de Luxe at Gare Maritime left" -- he thumbed down the column – "twenty-five minutes ago from Charing Cross," he said. "Another to Paris leaves in about an hour."

"So that's what we tell'm, Foster, and nothing else! We never lost her, never fell for their tricks, their setup. She took the de Luxe boat train." Markham snorted again. "Nothing else, hear? We take their fifty quid and smile like the gentlemen we are."

Foster laughed. Bad luck for her if that American woman really was on that de Luxe boat train

21

Plan about ninety minutes to two hours for the crossing from Dover to Calais, McGinnis had explained, depending on the Channel conditions. Gare Maritime, the station for the Train de Luxe, would be a fifteen minute shuttle ride from the docks. Convert her English pounds to francs at Dover for convenience. Exchange rate is running about twenty-five francs to the pound, so a thousand francs would be forty pounds, or, she calculated, $200 US, so remember five francs to the dollar. The Train de Luxe was the only non-stop train from Calais to the French Riviera and beyond to the Italian border, all the cars were sleeping cars with a restaurant car for meals. It would arrive in Monaco tomorrow at about 9am. There would be a lift at the Monaco station that would bring her up the cliff-side to an area adjacent to the Casino. First stop in Monaco for her then would probably be lunch at the Hotel de Paris. Her room was there, her luggage would be waiting.

McGinnis smiled. "The hotel is right across the street from the Monte Carlo Casino. Easy to find … and a beautiful place." He grinned. "My wife and I did our honeymoon week at the Hotel de Paris some years ago. I think I lost only about twenty quid on the wheels at the Casino, but it really wasn't the money for us ... it was the people there. People like you have never seen before." He shook his head. "My wife said that it would take all of my salary from the Yard for at least two years to buy just one of the simpler dresses the ladies wore there... so they lost their money in the height of style.

"The fare for the Train de Luxe," he continued, "is 4£ 19s more than first class, but His Lordship felt that would be the fastest and most secure travel for you, and would best fit your cover story. Normally a passenger would need about fortnight in advance notice to get a reservation, but for you, it was obtained in four days. You will also have a sleeping compartment to yourself the entire trip."

About twenty minutes out of Charing Cross, Kyame purchased a pot of tea with a plate of small sandwiches from the vendor working the first class car. Her armrest was wide enough to allow the pot and plate to fit conveniently at her elbow. While the car swayed gently, Kyame leaned back to study the first of the dead agent files that she carried in the black leather satchel given her by Lord Salisbury. Once through the seven files to get a general understanding, then a second time to memorize them, and finally, once clear in her mind, to destroy them. As she read and sipped, the file was concealed behind her copy of the *Pall Mall Gazette* whose pages she would turn as she changed files to ensure anyone casually watching, as a young bearded man passing her windows had just done, would see her reading through the paper and not spending an inordinate time on one page. Papa had trained her to "think natural" at all times, even when working one of their scams.

* * *

"When she arrives at Dover, sir, what is our protocol?"

"Follow her onto the Calais boat, then ensure she falls overboard. N ordered that no chances were to be taken."

The young bearded man nodded. There had been a very attractive black-haired young woman reading a newspaper alone in a first class compartment, but her coat was black and red, not the green described in the Berlin communiqué. He hoped she was not the one targeted. She was someone he would like to know, to know much better.

* * *

Wilhelm was restless. Von Drascher had been restless at their Predator meeting on the Imperial yacht. Von Tirpitz had cautiously, but emphatically questioned Germany's use of commercial raiders against the British anywhere, whatever the raiders' technology and speed. A false step, he had suggested, could trigger a Copenhagen type of British response; an underlying apprehension at the highest levels of German military and diplomatic thinking that had come to be called "die Kopenhagener Complex". *Die Englische Gefahr,* the English Peril, seemed an ever

217

present menace to German planning and the Kaiser's aspirations.

In twenty days in 1807, the British Royal Navy landed 25,000 Army troops, bombarded Copenhagen and captured the entire Danish fleet without warning; even though Denmark, at the time, was neutral and posed no military threat to Great Britain, though it had turned down a British offer of a Naval alliance. Over 5,000 people had been killed by the British cannons and troops. But with Napoleon's forces moving steadily toward Denmark, however, it was clear that the French Emperor would seize the Danish fleet, neutral or not, which would allow him to seal off the Baltic Sea. Britain could not allow that to happen.

The clear demonstration that Great Britain had no scruples about the use of force regardless of its arrogant humanitarian mask could not be ignored. Now, some Ministers had begun to argue with some passion in Council meetings, that a rapid buildup of German Naval strength, particularly battleships, might trigger the same response from Britain before Germany was ready. A misguided raider attack could provoke the sinking of the Imperial High Seas Fleet while it was still tied up at Wilhelmshaven or at Kiel.

Wilhelm rose and began to stride about his office. His left ear had been painless for two days which cleared his mind for serious thinking. What was the answer? He had begun to admit, only to himself, that his proposed action in the Mediterranean might be -- he fumbled for an acceptable word. Might be -- premature -- yes, that was the word. Not wrong, just premature. He relaxed a little, to recalibrate. So what movements, what distractions could he use? He continued to walk about the spacious office, glancing at the many books arrayed on shelves to the ceiling, most of which he had read, and many, like Mahan, had reread.

For some reason Wilhelm could not explain, the Countess Natalia and her gambling system came to mind. He smiled at the thought of the beautiful and naïve Russian woman, and yes, he intended to try the system with real money and not playing cards. But that roulette system that she had so carefully described, to strive to win consistently, not all at once, win with discipline, not spectacle. No *coup de main,* but a gradual aggression. But that would need time to reach a strong strategic position. Not a victory of sinking British ships, but, rather, *a victory of will.* Wilhelm smiled, brushing his elaborate mustaches upward with his right forefinger. He would still need the Predators and...

Wilhelm returned to his desk, slipped onto the saddle-shaped stool, and began to sketch out his preliminary thoughts. Crossing out some, he wrote more, then paused. He reached down to the lowest drawer in his desk, withdrew and placed the rubber stamp and special ink on the desk. With a single hard stamp, he put *Very Secret, Hand to Hand Only* in Imperial red ink across the top,

219

N had reported that the British Prime Minister was becoming increasingly suspicious of the Kaiser's future plans, most particularly after the Kruger telegram only last month. And, it appeared, there may be an American agent of some kind, a young woman coming to the south of France -- ostensibly to paint portraits of aristocracy. Perhaps that really was all she was doing, but a sudden American presence in the midst of the elimination of British agents, even after the American President had implied in December that war with Britain over Venezuela was possible, was suspicious in itself. And the Russian traffic toward Constantinople. Might Britain have too much to consider responding at once to *his* "traffic"?

The Kaiser started to smile, then grimaced as a sharp pain laced through his ear.

22

Kyame had the seven agent names/identities set in her mind, their cover occupations, the locations of their dead bodies, the rooms where the men had stayed, and was deeply troubled. They had all, in turn, been killed within only a few days. Obviously, the agents had been watched even as they had been watching. There was no apparent consistency, other than they were all British agents. Their various cover identities were all quite different; they moved among different levels of French and Monégasque society; their movements along the coast of the Mediterranean would appear, to any potential observers, completely unconnected. Yet there was something that had marked them all for murder. *Marked them all,* and in a relatively brief time. And, remarkably, had almost immediately marked their replacements. Four were active initially, Peter Pieneer, Walter Bullivant, Sir Cornelius Brand, and Archie Roylance, all who, based on their files, were experienced on the Continent from previous assignments. They had all been active in their new assignments in Southern France for between one to three months, Brand for the one month, then, as though a death warrant had been issued, they were all dead within nine days. The four were replaced within four days to eight days by three others: Dr. Thomas Greenslade, Alastair Buchan, and Sir John Blenkiron. Each had been assigned as each original agent had been killed with the new agents identified almost immediately. How?

What was the giveaway, the gimmick, as Papa would call it? And why? It was the why that she had come for, that was her objective, but the how had to be the first step.

And who was Muffin? Kyame would know that answer by tomorrow afternoon at least.

She planned to ditch the black satchel overboard once she was far enough off shore to ensure no chance of anyone discovering anything. Kyame had already loaded the satchel with the china plates from her tea and sandwiches along with two thick books on English history that she had purchased from a news vendor working the first class car. They would help ensure the satchel would sink successful. The books did look like interesting reads, but for later. A young bearded man had assisted the vendor in handing her the books. He had been the man who had looked in at her in passing her compartment earlier while the train was still at Charing Cross. His face was clear in her mind. Handsome, but troubled, his mouth was too tight. She could easily feel the additional three or four pounds the books added to the Scotland Yard files. Kyame would throw in anything else she might find not nailed down on the boat that might help ensure the files quickly sank -- and stayed sunk.

**

"Watch your step, Miss," cautioned the conductor. "Just to your right there, and up that short stairway. The gangplank to the Calais boat will be to your left. Your luggage will follow you to the Gare Maritime for the Train de Luxe." He tipped his cap. "Have a smooth crossing, Miss." Which he knew was a vacant wish. The Channel had been in a god-awful uproar out there during his previous trip earlier in the morning.

Kyame smiled her thanks, gripped her now heavy satchel and started for the stairs, her musty black and red coat wrapped tightly around her in the strengthening chill winds. The young bearded man had looked at her too closely as he had handed her the two books; had tried too hard to catch her eyes, to initiate a conversation. But it was not the tactic which she had experienced a number of times with amorous young men in Boston. The bearded man had been too intent, almost anxious. Kyame started for the stairs. She would stay clear of the bearded man, amorous or not.

**

Within minutes the short sharp chop of the Channel waves began to buffet and twist the boat making any walking on deck perilous. Thrusting winds blew cold curtains of spray across the windows blocking out the light from a weak sun as a scurry of wild clouds overhead leapt past toward the French coast. It was, Kyame felt glancing up at the windows, like a roller-coaster gone off its tracks.

She pushed herself deeper into her chair. Another ten, maybe fifteen minutes then she would pitch the satchel. Forward as though going to the lady's privy, ensure no one was watching, then open the forward deck door and heave the satchel over the railing and return. Simple and safe.

**

"How do we get her outside without an obvious struggle that will draw too much attention?" frowned the young bearded man glancing at the woman in red and black on the other side of the first class passenger compartment. Apparently the green coast had disappeared somewhere. There was no one else on the boat that resembled the physical description they had been given: tall, black-haired, beautiful, with. green eyes. He had looked closely in the awkward light of the aisle in handing her the books. Large and brilliant green.

Inside the passenger compartment, individual chairs were secured to the deck in rows broken by two aisles fore and aft for access forward to private facilities and backward toward a café. Some people had already rushed forward, their hands over their mouths, their faces pale. The odor of vomit was strengthening with each minute of the boat's wild gyrations. No one was going toward the stern.

After a moment, his partner seated next to him said, "We help her forward after you stun her with your life preserver. We are just gentlemen doing our social duty for a strickened lady."

"But …?"

"You walk over to apparently take the empty chair behind her, you stumble in the boat's bouncing about, slug her at the base of her skull and I immediately come to your aid.

"It will be a simple maneuver, Bart. Once forward, away from the compartment, we go through the portside forward door to the deck, drag her 2-3 steps to the railing, lift and throw … then back inside as quickly as possible. A bit damp and coldish granted, but in thirty or forty-five minutes, we get off at Calais, have a comfortable dinner with our German friends, collect our funds, and return on the night boat."

Bart pursed his lips, then nodded. "When, Peter?"

Peter, wearing a black derby pressed down near his ears against the winds, and fashionably dressed in a dark green sack suit, with a brown raincoat, a fleeting writhen smile, his eyes cold. He saw the red-and-black woman get up, her hand to her mouth. "Now!" he whispered. "Follow her forward, I'll be right behind."

Bart gripped his life preserver in his right hand as he staggered forward up against the back of a chair, straightened up and started up the aisle.

***

It was time. Kyame grabbed the chair in front of her for balance, then the boat's shifting seemed to slow, making short cautious steps possible. The satchel in her right hand, Kyame gripped the back of each chair as she worked her way to the nearest aisle. She brought her left hand up quickly to her mouth to feign approaching sea-sickness, then moved on a little quicker. To her right at the corner of her eye, she noted the bearded man also rise and start for the aisle -- and the man beside him in green was preparing to rise. Why now?

Within a few steps she was in the central corridor with the ladies facilities to the left and the gentlemen to the right, the door to the port side of the boat deck was just beyond the toilets. A crewman in a damp blue uniform suddenly appeared coming up a stairway. Kyame leaned against the wall as though steadying herself.

"Are you all right Miss? May I be of some assistance?" The crewman's smile was friendly and full of understanding to yet another seasick passenger.

"I'm fine, thank you. Just … just catching my breath."

The crewman moved on, but her quick glance back caught the young bearded man, grim faced and -- and he had a blackjack in his hand! With his friend pressing from behind. Like a team of purse snatchers in Boston.

Kyame moved quickly forward toward the port door, the satchel gripped tighter, pushed hard to get the door open and stepped out into the icy Channel spray, then twisted to press her face up against the wet wall. A sharp gust had almost caught her and blown her against the railing.

Both men pushed through the door, it slammed shut immediately. The howl of the wind blocked all sound. The bearded man turned, strode two steps toward her, bringing his life preserver up …

Kyame suddenly twisted, swinging the satchel up hard against the man's head, which sent him staggering, eyes wide with surprise, stumbling toward the railing the life preserver rolling across the deck and over the side.. In one quick step, Kyame turned and swung the satchel again into the face of the surprised man in green, knocking him away from the wall. She felt her hat blow away. The green man tripped, falling, sliding across the wet deck as the port side of the boat suddenly pitched downward into a sharp depression in the waves, which flipped the bearded man over the railing, while it sent the man in green sliding against the railing. He struggled to regain his feet in the cold spray spreading across the deck. He reached out to grasp frantically at a pillar of the railing to right himself, only to be jerked back onto the deck as though someone had suddenly reached out and pulled hard on his shoulder. With the seconds that gave her, Kyame, her jaw set, quickly brought the satchel down hard on his hand, which gave way, then threw herself at him with her shoulder which sent him sliding over the railing and out into the air. He may have cried out, but Kyame couldn't be sure in the wild churning chaos of the Channel. He was gone into the arms of the maelstrom.

Kyame tossed the satchel over the railing. Turning carefully, bowed low, her shoulders against the wind, she struggled the three steps back to reach the door; but she couldn't pull it open! The heavy winds held it closed. Her face was going numb from the freezing spray, her coat soaked, with her hair flying in the winds which had picked up. With both hands, her hair matted across her face, Kyame put all her strength to twist and pull at the handle, but the door wouldn't budge -- when suddenly, as though someone had reached around her to help, it moved! The crewman she had talked to reached out, grasped her wrist, his back braced against the winds and the door, and drew her back inside the boat.

For a moment, Kyame stood struggling for balance against the rolling, wallowing boat, the crewman holding her arm.

"Easy, Miss. Crazy to be out there," he said softly, his grin cocked to one side.

Kyame pushed her wet hair from her face. "My thanks, sir, for rescuing me. It was," she took a breath, "getting … getting quite difficult out there." She grinned. "Isn't there an easier way to get to France?"

The crewman laughed. "I don't think you would want to be up in a balloon in this stuff. That just leaves the boat ... or a long swim." He handed her a large dry red rag from a bag at his hip.

Kyame wiped her face and hands dry with the rag. "Didn't think I would make it to the ladies ... so I thought."

"Outside?" He shook his head. "Not a good idea."

"You are so right," Kyame smiled. "I'll get back to my seat. How much longer?"

"About three-quarters of an hour. This storm is a bad one, but they will hold the train for you." He turned. "Keep the rag. I have a hundred of'm." He nodded, touched his forelock and started down the stairway.

Kyame regained her seat and took a deep breath. Two to kill her, before she even set foot on French soil!

How many more are waiting ahead? These two had seen the German cable. They knew she was their target. But why the urgency to get rid of her out in the Channel?

And, Kyame felt chilled, not from the Channel winds. Something out there, out there in the winds. What had happened? What had caused the second man to suddenly jerk around, giving her the extra seconds needed to swing her satchel a second time? It had been almost like someone had grabbed his shoulder and pulled him off balance, or maybe just a freak twist of the boat in the

229

Channel waves. Dr. Haroon Kahn's parting remark about Kali walking with her -- but no Hindu goddess, even the daughter of stone, could be anywhere near the English Channel. Or?

The *Ku* hexagram, No. 18, returned to her mind. Strike cleanly as with a scalpel. Her smile was faint. The satchel didn't look too lean and sharp, but it did the job. Maybe she should drop the coins again when she arrived in Monaco. Kyame braced herself as the boat suddenly rolled and twisted.

23

The Calais boat had emptied rapidly of passengers as harsh winds swept across the barren docks, but no young woman in a green coat appeared, and the two British men they were to contact did not come off either. Die Engländer were to confirm the woman's death before returning to their country.

Whispering again in German, the older man in black leather cap, white goatee, frameless glasses, heavy black leather coat, said, "No one, Herr Bäcker, no one. Where is *she*, and where are *they*?"

The Ritter Heinz Bäcker shook his head. He frowned, anticipating Herr Wagner's angry response when he received the necessary telegram. "I don't know, Baron Hanau, I don't know." He thought, hopefully, maybe all of them had been swept off the boat, but said nothing.

***

The Kaiser had been the very soul of royal courtesy in wishing the Prince de Monaco a most joyous and comfortable return to his principality on the warm coast of the Mediterranean. He continued to stand at the head of the gangplank, his right hand raised in farewell, until Prince Albert's gilded four-horse barouche disappeared from view. His right hand fell sharply to slap against his thigh.

231

His Majesty turned abruptly, his face twisting in anger, to snap an order for an immediate return to Kiel, then turned back to his library, where once the door was closed, the All Highest unleashed his frustration in a volley of curses. Taking a deep breath, gritting his teeth against short stabs of pain in his left ear, he cursed again, this time slower and with specific targets. Albert, with a casual toss of his hand, had dismissed Wilhelm's *firm* suggestion of a German-Monégasque alliance, as if he were declining the offer of a cup of coffee -- *from a waiter*! To hell with the von Tirpitz strategies! Wilhelm knew he had been right when he had earlier in the day ordered von Drascher to push the Predators forward -- at flank speed!

Wilhelm would see His Serene Highness, the Prince de Monaco again. There would be no offers of alliance then, or of coffee.

***

Kyame settled back into the elegant red leather wing chair in the small sitting room of her gently swaying sleeping compartment. There was nothing like this in America, even in first class. She laughed as she sipped the champagne, 1851 the label said, that the blue-uniformed Train de Luxe car attendant had poured on introducing her to her sleeping compartment.

Kyame felt absolutely -- regal!

The telegram from V.B. had been waiting for her as she stepped up into her car. A blue uniformed gray-haired porter, his blue matched the blue paint on the sleeper cars, handed her the sealed yellow envelope when she gave her name and compartment number, 6B.

V.B. would meet her at the Ascenseur at the Monte Carlo station. There had been another incident, but he gave no details. Time, he had written, seemed to be growing shorter for someone. He would be wearing a red tie.

Kyame fingered the silver coins in her pocket. Placing the crystal flute to one side, she took out the coins, cupped them in her hands, and began to assemble a hexagram from the bottom up. When completed it was *K'an*, No. 29: You are currently in jeopardy, be aware of hidden problems that may suddenly present themselves.

She grinned and shook her head. How helpful! The clean-cutting scalpel suggested from her last hexagram turned out to be a five-pound black satchel. She leaned back and silently emptied the crystal flute.

She felt no need to refill it.

But, she mused, uneasily, the earlier hexagram had been correct -- which sent an edgy chill through her. Was there more with the three silver coins she held in her hand? But how could the dropping of three coins six times have any connection with reality? Not divination, not the future, but just with reality, any reality?

And, she fingered the yellow ruhmal wrapped around the coins, and the incident on the boat, when something, something specific seemed to stop her attacker, even hold him, for a few desperate seconds. Kyame shook her head. Dangerous, even careless, to think something mystic is out there protecting you; when your only actual protection can be only with your own wits.

***

Johannes Friederich Wagner shook his head. His first wave of frustrated anger after reading Bäcker's telegram had passed. Who is this American woman in green who seems to flit about like a ghost? The Train de Luxe was, but for one or two brief stops, non-stop, so there was no chance of reaching her en route. He stood to look out at the dark brooding stillness of the Mediterranean. Welcome, Miss Piddington, welcome to Monaco, to Monte Carlo, he whispered. He turned, walked to the door of his office. He could not be late for his rendezvous at the tables at the Casino with the most cooperative English woman. But first he beckoned to Bäcker's assistant, a young plain faced and plain dressed woman of lethal disposition and bitter blue eyes, with a uniquely developed talent for -- for practical invisibility. Wagner smiled. Yes, her skills had been useful so far against the British.

Now to match them against the American in green.

***

Kyame nodded her agreement to the restaurant car host's request for permission to seat Monsieur Poisson at her table. All the tables in the car were filled. He was an older man, but she could not guess his age. His eyes were a soft worn brown, his face haggard. As he seated himself, he bowed forward.

"Merci, Mademoiselle. You are most kind to a tired traveler."

He spoke very little, occasionally glancing out at the dark night passing their window. He ate slowly, and gratefully, as though unsure of his next meal.

Kyame enjoyed an amazing roast goose, each bite a burst of flavor she had never encountered before. Poisson chuckled gently. "You so clearly enjoy your food, Mademoiselle. It is a joy to watch you ... if I may without intruding."

"I have never eaten goose before. Duck many times, but never goose." Kyame smiled which caused Poisson to smile as well, for the first time.

With that, they began to converse, Poisson slowly shedding his reticence. "Ah, as you have not engaged a goose before; I have not met an American lady before."

Kyame grinned. "I got the better of the deal."

The gentle rhythm of the Train de Luxe's movements felt more as a large ship in quiet waters. Their discussion continued through the meal to the serving of brandy as the dishes were cleared, brandy which Kyame noted was from 1852. "To experience a beautiful young lady who understands elegant brandy," Poisson smiled broadly for the second time. "Ah, Mademoiselle Piddington, you warm my soul as the Napoleon liquor warms my heart."

Kyame raised her crystal balloon glass in acknowledgement of his compliment.

The brandy began to warm Poisson's words as he began to express concern for the future of Europe. His jaw went slack. He nodded to himself. "Yes, I have seen war. I was trapped in the Prussian siege of Paris in 1871. I was a young man with a very young family from a village about forty miles northwest of Paris. I was leaving the city to return to my home, my wife and one small son. To get away from the unprincipled horrors of men killing each other for ... for no ... for no rational purpose." His eyes half-closed, his head swayed in time with the movement of the train. The restaurant car was emptying. His jaw and lips went tight. He looked up at Kyame over the glittering rim of his empty glass. "The Prussians had sealed off everything. There was no way out of the city and no food inside, except for foul smelling chunks of horsemeat and *café au lait*. The *au lait* was chalk and water. The thought of my family kept me alive and sane. But ... but I never saw my family again. The Prussians" – he physically restrained himself, his fists clenched into dense knobs –

236

"the Prussians violated my wife, then murdered her. I don't know, even now, if my son survived."

Kyame went cold, paralyzed inside. She gripped her glass like the ball that Papa had once given her that she would hold tightly sometimes until he returned to their room when she had first become part of the Impossible Piddingtons. Squeezing Papa's ball seemed to bring him quicker. She waited, the blackness outside the window modulating with occasional flashes of light from houses along the tracks.

Finally Poisson pushed back from the table, replacing his empty glass. "There is no war now, Mademoiselle Piddington, but war is their only binding ambition, the only rationale for the titled royals. So there will be war again. And for no rational human purpose, zealously triggered by the most inane or banal incident. And," he emphasized, his fist gently tapping the table, "and it will be started by that pompous hollow Prussian fool in Berlin ... with the other spoiled titled brats in France and Britain, with Russia eagerly joining in." He paused for a moment, catching his breath as if he had been running hard. "But Europe is filled now with spoiled bored royal children serving as monarchs who have been taught that glory comes only from spilling the blood of others." Poisson whispered something Kyame could not hear, then, "May Kaiser Wilhelm II burn in eternal flames."

Apologizing for his unsociable anger and thanking Kyame for her patience and kind understanding, he rose and left the restaurant car. When he reached the door, Poisson turned back toward her and bowed, then vanished through the door.

First taking a deep breath, Kyame remained sitting for several minutes, to let the miasma of deep hatred dissipate from the air. Finally, gathering her skirts, she started back for 6B. That regal feeling would never come back now, she knew.

She would miss it.

***

In stylish evening attire, of medium height, wearing banker's gold-rimmed glasses, his dark hair beginning to recede, the Honorable Albert Victor Bethell, fourth son of the second Baron Westbury, and V.B. to certain friends, smiled as he watched the German banker, Johannes Wagner, throw away his money on a roulette table. The German had been obviously perturbed about something when he entered the *Cercle Privé,* but Wagner was trying to execute a roulette system that assured his eventual defeat, sooner than later. That system was a familiar one, called the Martingale, and was offered under various names, for 10 to 20 francs, to anyone stepping off the train from Nice and riding the Ascenseur up the cliff to the Casino Garden and Entrance.

The Martingale was a system that Camille Blanc, son of François Blanc the founder and first Director-

General of the Monte Carlo Casino, did not want you to know, the well-dressed touts, men and women, would pitch so sincerely, and whisper so conspiratorially. Bethell shook his head. There were about fifteen popular systems that appeared each Season, December through May, under various names, but none of which could ensure success, and all of which could ensure ruin without strong discipline and sufficient capital. Bethell had had to arrange second and third class passage back to England for a number of broken subjects of Queen Victoria, and erstwhile customers of Smith's.

However, Camille Blanc and the Casino Board readily encouraged system players, freely providing indexed cards and pencils on which to clock the wheel, and even to the point of providing adding machines for their use in system calculations, along with a small table to put it on to allow others free access to the wheel itself. If a system player ever seemed to be getting too far ahead of the Bank, some croupiers would begin to spin their wheel more quickly between plays, so that the time between coups would not allow adequate time for the system player to properly calculate his next wager, which would eventually even the stacks of chips up again, and the player would plunge ever more deeply.

A certain Monégasque axiom had become well known over the years since the founding of the Casino in 1861, for good reason: "*Rouge gagne quelquefois, Noir souvent, mais Blanc toujours.*" [Red wins sometimes, black often, but Blanc always.]

Bethell did not recognize the Englishwoman sitting at the table with Wagner hovering over her bare shoulders. Second class gamblers played the public rooms of the Casino (referred to as 'the kitchen' by employees) downstairs; while first class played upstairs in the Cercle Privé.

This was the first time Bethell had seen the woman in the Cercle Privé. The Cercle, located in an upstairs hall, to exclude the patrons of the kitchen, held one roulette table and three tables of Trente-et-quarante. Originally, the Cercle did not admit women to allow for a more "business-like" and competitive atmosphere. Military uniforms were not allowed as well. But when a French Princess complained, the rule was changed to admit women, but only those not wearing hats, as the elaborate hats in fashion could obscure the men's view of the wheel.

Bethell would know her name within the hour. Muffin and the American woman may need the information. Just what sort the American woman might be Bethell would begin to know tomorrow morning.

Bethell turned away from the fashionably dressed enthusiastic crowd at the wheel.

"Victor, old man, not leaving while the wheel is hot are you?"

Bethell stopped to grin at the tall, very handsome James St. Claire-Erskine Rosslyn, the fifth Earl of Rosslyn, in impeccable evening dress wearing a gold-rimmed monacle, rapidly approaching, his heels clicking rhythmically against the polished parquet floor. A thick gold chain hung across his white waistcoat. "Ah, your Lordship, for some the wheel is hot, for others it runs cold. How is your system rewarding you tonight?"

Rosslyn held up a handful of thousand and five thousand franc notes. "My first serious play of the evening, sir. I am nineteen thousand to the good, dear chap. Come, join me for whiskey and sodas at the bar before I plunge back into the battle." He laughed as he hooked Bethell's arm into his. "I have also," he bent down to whisper, "been offered twenty-five thousand francs for the secret of my system by that German over there with the very, ah, winsome Lady 'Smith', she calls herself. It seems I am to win tonight no matter in what pocket the little ivory ball decides to rest."

As Rosslyn, in addition to being a delightful evening companion, also had £6,600 on deposit at Smith's Bank, Bethell readily agreed to retreat from the Cercle Privé. Customers, even the temporarily rich as were many of the titled British, needed nurturing. And he would have the very winsome lady's name shortly. Rosslyn insisted on paying as they approached the arched doorway to the gilded, mirrored and tapestried bar filled with laughter and excited conversations.

241

Accepting his crystal glass from the barkeep, Bethell observed that the gallant Lord Rosslyn knew nothing of the Greek concept of *aidos*, which was to walk humbly and carefully so as to propitiate the fates. It was, after all, Fate who spun the wheel.

24

The very winsome lady was Lady Isabel Ellen Norfolk, the eldest of the three daughters of the recently impoverished gambler, the fourth Baron Norfolk. With the Baron's financial status a quiet topic of some titillating conversation at the Smith & Co. office .-- Bethell nodded and turned away from his informant, a long-term Casino employee who provided certain information to Smith's when necessary. Smith & Co. was the only English bank licensed in the principality. Their ability to move money rapidly anywhere in Europe, and, recently, also to North America, as clients might require, often drew clients from other European locations as well. After two whiskeys and soda, Rosslyn had happily returned to the tables, now to try his luck at Trente-et-quarante, a house card game of even odds, a game of treacherous simplicity, but with potentially much higher stakes than roulette -- a game of some skill and less Fate – and with the ability to consume cash faster than roulette.

Isabel Ellen Norfolk was apparently, in a word, for sale; and was someone who could not be trusted, as Bethell would inform Muffin. A somewhat titled English woman in severe financial need, who could be easily manipulated as an interesting conduit of information could become a serious risk. Bethell stopped at the gilded arched doorway, the excited conversations of the raucous bar fading behind him. Norfolk's close association with the Count Baldur von Trotha had been noted by a few inquiring eyes until his brutal murder a few weeks back in San Remo. Some of Trotha's mysterious money had ebbed and flowed through Smith's, to anonymous accounts in Zurich and Stockholm, and yes, he recalled, once or twice also to and from Rome. There had been no suspects ever identified in that now largely forgotten crime, though as the body had been discovered in Italian territory, that was an Italian problem, not Monaco's, legally, conveniently.

But, his eyes following the animated colorful crowds around the tables, Bethell mused, who *was* Trotha? The Count had first appeared at the bank's office in the arcade of the Galerie Charles III about nine or ten months ago for help in purchasing his villa. Trotha needed a local banking relationship to close the deal on the villa. Not an unusual requirement in the principality. He had easily passed the bank's initial general appraisal, which basically only confirmed balances at various banks. But no one seemed to know him socially, but perhaps pressing a little closer, a little insistently.

When no one had claimed the body, the Italian authorities had returned Trotha's remains to be buried in Monaco. And who was at the burial?

Victor Bethell, who knew everyone of any substance in Monaco, had never encountered anyone who had ever visited Trotha's small villa near Cannes, which was still up for sale. As his eyes met those of a much titled attractive English woman, he pursed his lips. Bethell knew the agent handling the property and would arrange through him to visit the villa to evaluate it for a 'prospective purchaser'. Muffin and their American visitor would certainly be busy with other concerns. Bethell started toward the wheel and the richly gowned, much titled, warmly smiling woman with great anticipation.

His Trotha examination could await the morrow.

***

Her apparel was commonplace, her face plain; the woman did not attract any attention from the men and women waiting for the arrival of the Train de Luxe. But then, she rarely attracted attention, but her skills when the lights were lowered were, in Konstanze Jäger's personal opinion, unmatched.

Konstanze couldn't vanish physically, naturally, but she had learned, with Herr Wagner's insightful assistance, to vanish from their thoughts, which was even better. No one can take any actions against something you cannot remember.

Eleven people, seven men and four women were waiting. The women were Italian, probably heading for the shops at San Remo with three of the men. The other four men, two were clearly French from the cut of their suits, one a flamboyant Spaniard. The always stylish Victor Bethel wore a clashing red tie. His suit was most fashionably cut but the red tie clashed. It was clearly an intended signal for a traveler whom he had never met. The American woman whom Herr Wagner had described?

Konstanze stepped back further. She would join the disembarking passengers to the Ascenseur as if she had also just arrived. No one would notice -- no one ever noticed. She would vanish from their thoughts.

***

Kyame immediately caught the red tie. She liked Victor Bethell's welcoming smile as he strode toward her. Not a banker's cautious smile, just one of pending friendship. She extended her hand as he approached. The passengers moving on and off the train were mixing around them, though one woman didn't move. A habit of reading an audience that remained even after she had stopped performing. Kyame automatically noted the woman's emotionless face of strange intent character.

"Welcome to Monaco, Miss Piddington. I am Victor Bethell." Tall, beautiful, black hair, with startling green eyes. The musty red and black coat did not match her -- her sense of presence, of style. Bethell smiled wider. A remarkable young woman.

He offered her his card.

"Thank you, Mr. Bethell. The coastal scenery of the last hours has been breathtaking. I've seen nothing like it in

America." She frowned as she read his card. "How should I properly address someone who is ... the Honorable?"

Bethell grinned. "I am the fourth son of a Baron, so I am, just barely, Honorable, so Mister will do, but for my special friends I am just V.B." Bethell began to guide her toward the Ascenseur.

Kyame nodded, smiling. "I am Kyame to my friends."

. "We will take the Ascenseur up to the Casino entrance and gardens. I'll introduce you to the Hotel de Paris for a bit of coffee. You will have about two hours to relax in your rooms, then I will call for you at 11:30. We will be having lunch with the Duchess Clanroyden at her villa."

Kyame asked, as they waited for the car to return from the top of the cliff, "How does one address a Duchess? I've never met one before."

Bethell laughed as the attendant pulled the door open. "This Duchess is my favorite person in the principality. I suspect she will prefer that you call her Muffin."

When Kyame raised an eyebrow in question, Bethell explained as they entered the car. "The Duchess Angelica was a Gaiety Girl in London who married very skillfully, intelligently, and very happily. And who has never changed even with her titles, wealth, and estates. Her

247

husband, the Duke, died from a tragic riding accident about two years ago. They have no children."

As the car rose, Bethell asked, "Your green coat, Kyame, I was looking for it. Did something happen?"

"Others were also looking for it, I believe." With her eyes on the attendant whose back was to them, and noting the others were lost in their own conversations, except for the plain woman who was looking down at her hands, Kyame quietly summarized her trip from the Prime Minister's residence and her encounter on the Calais boat.

As the door was drawn open to the gentle bustle and fragrances of the glorious Casino Gardens, Victor Bethell saw the beautiful young American as someone other than the young woman who had entered the Ascenseur only moments ago. She was someone possibly very deadly.

25

After introducing the vivacious Angelica, the Duchess of Clanroyden, to Kyame Piddington, Victor Bethell excused himself from lunch to pursue a 'situation possibly of mutual interest'. Muffin's quick nod acknowledged his meaning. At the request of the Duchess, her coquettish smile irresistible, he would return for afternoon drinks ... not tea.

***

Bethell opened the door of Trotha's Villa von Freude. A place of joy, the dead man had called it. The agent, Bruno Durand, said that nothing had been changed in the villa as there was no family to give it to. There had been no interest thus far in the villa as it was too small and too isolated for most purchasers. The new owner could keep what he pleased of the contents and trash the rest. The sale proceeds would go to pay off Trotha's few remaining debts, and then the remainder to charity -- net of a suitable commission, naturally.

As he walked into the large well-furnished open living area with broad mahogany stained glass French doors leading out to a wide balcony stretching across the entire front of the structure with a glorious view of Cannes below and the sea beyond, Victor Bethell reflected that Trotha, though good looking, strongly made, still youngish with a solid bankable capital base, had not socialized as other titled men did through the seasonal society of bored wealthy women. There had been one or two rumored romances, but then all aristocrats in Monaco, men and women, had rumored romances. Even he had had a rumored romance or two, but still no wife.

Of the few times Bethell had seen him at the Casino, and once in the company of the Norfolk woman, Trotha had played cautiously in the Cercle Privé, not playing any system at roulette that Bethell could recognize. As though the man played only to be seen playing -- to appear -- local -- normal -- to blend in. He reminded Bethell of something a colleague in London had said about some people occupying queer worlds and half-worlds. The colleague had been later convicted of embezzling £3,000 from Lloyd's Bank on St. James Street.

Trotha seemed to have been living in some kind of a half-world.

His bedroom was barren. Unlike the more public richly furnished front living area, with its well filled pseudo-Chippendale liquor cabinet of crystal decanters and ewers, there was nothing in the bedroom that was evidence of a life style, no pictures on the walls or on any of the tables -- simply a place to sleep. Only the top three drawers of the dresser, the only bedroom furniture other than one straight-back cane chair, contained any clothing, stockings, underclothes, collars and shirts. All the other drawers were empty. Perhaps the closet -- then Bethell abruptly turned back. He began to pull out the dresser drawers and turn them over. About three weeks ago, a notorious jewel thief had taped two £10,000 diamond necklaces under a dresser drawer in his hotel room in Nice just before the police arrived. Bethell couldn't recall the details of the story, but the quick hiding place seemed an inspired one -- except to an imaginative inspector of the Nice Sùreté.

There! One of the bottom drawers. A piece of paper taped to the bottom with a number – a bank account number it appeared. It was not a Smith's account number. With another number under it that Bethell could not identify. He removed and stuffed the paper into his pocket and replaced the drawers. He would have his assistant do some trawling through Trotha's slim account to determine if either number matched with any account that Smith's has interacted with on Trotha's behalf.

Seven suits of good, though not the highest quality, hung in the closet with nothing in any of their pockets. Three sets of the highest quality evening wear, again with empty pockets. Several casual Swiss knit sweaters hung at one end. Two pair of very good quality hiking boots, and -- odd -- two and a half pair of black patent dress shoes. One shoe of one pair was missing. So why keep the one shoe?

A large black leather satchel was concealed in the back corner behind the boots. In it was a black sweater that smelled of stale sweat, tightly tapered black trousers, soft black rubber shoes, and a black wool full-face mask that carried the fading odor of expensive hair oils. Much like what Bethel used himself. The belt in the trousers had a black leather pouch attached that held -- a set of lock picks, a file, a small oil lamp with a box of self-striking matches, a small wrench, and a pair of needle-like pliers. A cracksman outfit! The Count von Trotha had been a thief of some sort -- and was most probably not named Trotha. Bethell disengaged the pouch from the belt and slipped it into his jacket pocket.

The kitchen was a minimal kitchen, a bachelor's kitchen at that. The ice box was empty. Few spices. Laughing, Muffin had once told him that that was the mark of a bachelor, just salt and pepper. He smiled at the remembrance. Muffin's laugh was infectious.

The dining room was also bare. Trotha had a small smoking room with one wall of books of popular French and German novels along with a few volumes of German poetry. Some Goethe and Schiller interspersed with minor poets. Some musical interest, records of Beethoven, Mozart and Wagner were piled near his Victrola standing in the corner. An expensive record player -- one personal area at least. Trotha clearly liked his music.

His writing desk was plain with only a few pens and pencils held in a beer mug from a Munich Biergarten. In the one wide central desk drawer there was a blank pad of paper and assorted scraps that accumulate in any desk.

His shoulder pressed against the window frame, Bethell angled the pad to the sun at one of the windows.

253

Taking one of the pencils, he lightly scraped the pencil across the pad. A list of three names became roughly apparent. The Norfolk woman's name was first, then another English name he couldn't quite decipher, and finally, Konstanze Jäger, whoever she was. Obviously German – an earlier acquaintance, perhaps. Her name was underlined twice for some reason. He tore off the page and stuffed it into his pocket.

Victor Bethell locked the front door behind him. A desolate place of joy for a moneyed fraudulent Count, as though -- the banker stopped for a moment -- as though the man was packed, ready to run on short notice. As he descended the steps back to his carriage, Bethell had some work to do before drinks with the Duchess and -- Kyame. He grinned. He liked the way that name slid off his tongue.

***

Konstanze Jäger had been nonplussed. Herr Wagner had instructed her to follow and carefully observe the American woman, to eliminate her if there was a clear opportunity, but the American had met the banker, Victor Bethell, who had escorted her to the Hotel de Paris, then, Konstanze had waited, unnoticed, in the opulent hotel lobby among the wealthy fools passing through on their way to the Rooms at the Casino. At 11:30, the banker returned to appear again with the Piddington woman, dressed now most stylishly in vivid black and white. Kyame Piddington, now Konstanze had her full name. Only to observe them drive off. Konstanze had followed in a hired gig she had waiting outside -- she was pleased at how well she had prepared; to follow them to the impressive villa of the celebrated Duchess Clanroyden. Then, anticipating a luncheon meeting, Konstanze had moved down the road to a small café a short distance away for a coffee and croissants, only to observe the banker suddenly leaving! Follow him or wait for the American? Bethell may only be returning to his office at Smith's -- her gig was waiting -- waiting.

Konstanze followed the banker

26

Centuries ago the demi-god Hercules had built a temple in honor of himself on the great rock cliff where *Le Palais Princier* now stood, it had been explained in response to her question by Yves LeGard, a smiling concierge who accompanied Kyame to her room at the Hotel de Paris. Only one monk, whose name was Monachus, was charged with the safeguarding and rituals of the temple. Thus Monaco. There were other, less romantic stories about the source of the name, Yves had laughed, but the temple story was the preferred one for visitors. And the main harbor of Monaco was called the Port d'Hercule.

And, Yves added, as they arrived at her door, Monte Carlo is named after Prince Charles III who, sadly, died only seven years ago, in 1889. Then he opened the door to the most amazing bedroom Kyame had ever entered. In the high central bow window, the two white sculptured cupola towers of the Monte Carlo Casino were to the left with the enticing blue Mediterranean Sea stretching across the horizon with white yachts bending to the wind. Kyame shook her head. Boston will never be the same after this.

Rested and dressed in a high-collared black jacket with swirling black and white skirts, no hat, and her brushed black hair fixed with a silver comb embedded with green stones to flow over one shoulder, Kyame absorbed the wordless lobby of the Hotel de Paris. Wordless because Kyame could not think of any word adequate to describe the stylish, yet restrained opulence. None of the grand hotels that so flaunted money that she had visited in New York City could match the appointments, the soft glowing woods, the remarkably inventive use of just enough gold detailing to set the mood -- set, well, set the style. As an artist, Kyame shook her head. Wordless. After a moment, confident wealth was the only combination that seemed to ring true. As she walked briskly toward the main entrance, her black and white skirts rustling about her, Kyame politely declined the offer of chairs from fashionable young gentlemen who immediately rose at her unescorted approach.

A woman could get used to this very quickly, she grinned to herself.

Seeing Victor Bethell enter, his clashing red tie replaced with a re-stated and restrained blue and black, Kyame walked quickly toward him. She liked his smile on seeing her. Not at all like some bankers that she had experienced in America. Monaco was clearly a unique experience that could grow on you very rapidly, if -- if you weren't careful.

"You look well and most beautiful, Kyame," he said, bowing his head, and gently touching her elbow, turned back toward the entrance, allowing her to precede him.

"You're most kind, V.B," she said, walking a pace ahead of him – and taking quick note of the unmoving woman from the train station platform sitting in a corner chair of deep blue velvet, wearing a different but still plain brown dress, who, as discretely as she could manage, watched her and Bethell over the top of a tea cup with hidden eyes.

Stepping out into the brilliant noon sun of Monaco, Kyame first squinted then glanced up at the hills rising beyond the Casino Gardens. Like a giant amphitheater, tier after tier of pastel colored villas rose up into the rocky green hills. Still too early for the explosion of color to come when flowers of every description began to bloom in May. May 10, Yves had explained, was the date most years for the gods to ignite Monaco's colors.

V.B. pointed as he explained. "The *Tête de Chien*: The Dog's Head, is there, that promontory. It stands about 550 meters above the sea. And over there, that is Mt. Agel. Those are the two highest points in Monaco -- though they are actually in France. The French border is only about half-a-mile that way." He laughed. "The French border is never more than half-a-mile away so matter where you are in Monaco. The whole principality is less than one square mile, about the size of a city common in your country. But Monaco's sovereignty and independence has been guaranteed by France since about 1884."

***

Kyame discovered that the wondrously dressed Duchess Clanroyden was a one-legged, one-eyed woman with a wickedly quick sense of humor and engaging smile whom Kyame immediately enjoyed. Dressed in silken multiple hues of blue with a necklace, bracelet and ear-rings of diamonds and sapphires, Muffin as she had insisted she be called, had a lyrical voice that simply commanded the conversation.

As Kyame responded to her questions, Muffin relaxed; a mischievous smile began to cross her face. Here was a fellow theater girl who knew the world of the stage! Her world! Muffin's missing eye, covered by a sapphire blue patch, had been lost in a riding accident while the one leg was lost from a gunshot inflicted in a dual that had gone very badly. Muffin had stood at what she had thought was a safe distance from her lover of the time, Roland, who had defaulted on substantial gambling debts, owed to the wrong kind of gentlemen, and had been challenged to a duel as a result. An illegal duel, but the law could not touch Roland's adversaries. There had been, Muffin recalled, a light rain in the forest where the dualists met making the fallen leaves slippery. The site was most captivating, she smiled sadly, almost poetic in its beauty -- but, Roland was killed by a shot to the head -- however his opponent had also been wounded. In his twisting, he slipped on the leaves, and falling from Roland's shot, the challenger had squeezed his trigger again, sending the lead ball through Muffin's leg above the knee, severing an artery. By the time a surgeon arrived (the doctor presiding at the dual had been a friend of Roland's, but not experienced in gunshot wounds, the Duchess explained) Muffin had passed-out from loss of blood and the wound had started to fester with infection, leading finally after the ball had been painfully extracted, about three days later, to an amputation just below the knee, which had ended her theater career – so, Muffin shrugged, she had married a Duke.

When Kyame gently laughed, Muffin joined her. "Well, Kyame, a woman has to do *something* with her life." Muffin shifted her foot and peg leg preparing to rise. Then raised a finger, as though to lecture. "Kyame, you must always ensure that your lovers are good shots." They had both laughed.

With V.B.'s quick departure, Muffin became quiet. "After our lunch, we go to work. My contacts coupled with your legs, energy and …?" she raised an eyebrow.

In answer, Kyame slipped her derringer from her skirt pocket. "I reloaded at the hotel to ensure dry powder. I have already used it, more than once. It is more powerful than any small gun you would have seen, Muffin.

"Also, I would like to sketch the face of a woman who showed unusual interest in V.B. and me when we left the hotel. She was also at the train platform, but didn't meet anyone. She seemed to very much want to blend into the background for some reason."

Kyame chose not to mention the yellow ruhmal in her other pocket.

***

Konstanze Jäger was uncertain of her next step. The banker had left the Trotha villa. Waiting a moment, Konstanze urged her gig forward to stay at a workable distance, her target in view but allowing others to come between them. But when Bethell, crossing back into Monaco from France, made a sharp left turn to start up the hill, he could only be returning to the Villa de Poésie, the villa of the one-legged Duchess. She needed to tell Herr Wagner of Bethell's visit to Trotha's place, but needed as well to watch for where the American went next.

Her lips tight, Konstanze made her decision.

***

Kyame finished her drawing and gave it to Muffin.

The Duchess noted the almost physical presence of the woman as Kyame had drawn her. "You draw, paint from memory, Kyame? That is most remarkable."

"Yes, it is easier that way. My clients are not tied down to long dull sittings … and neither am I."

"Could you then do my portrait now?"

"Yes, and it would be fun to do, though my paints, brushes and other materials are in my trunk at the hotel.

My problem would be to get your *joie de vivre* onto the canvas."

Muffin flashed a smile, then frowned. "I think I have seen this woman, but I cannot recall where. Couldn't have been recently, I haven't been socially active for the last week or two." She glanced up from the drawing. "Some pains in my short leg." She pursed her lips. "V.B. may recognize her. Everyone needs a bank." She looked up at Kyame. "She looks … dangerous. What do you think?" She placed the drawing back on the table next to her stemmed glass of fino sherry.

Recalling the woman at the train station and then dressed in the same muted manner in the Hotel de Paris lobby even two hours later, Kyame nodded. "There was a lethal set to her eyes similar to what I have seen in some of the places that Papa and I performed in, and in some of the men I came to know in our travels. Some were good men, but clearly deadly if necessary. Yes, I think you are right, Muffin.

"And, of course, why her interest in V.B. and myself?"

Her cane in place, Muffin stood. "Let me show you around my villa of poetry, Kyame, and know, my friend, that you are welcome here at any time in the future… even after the present affair is settled.

"And," she said as she took Kyame's arm to direct her toward an arched doorway, "tonight we will challenge the wheel at the Casino, using V. B's roulette system. Do you know the wheel?"

Kyame nodded. "How many zeroes in Monte Carlo roulette? There are two in American roulette."

Muffin's eyes went wide. "Zeroes! You have played! There is only one zero on our wheels. It is sometimes called the *refait*."

"Yes, I've played a few times with Papa or a friend at my elbow, but only very cautiously with very strict limits on my losses. I would be very interested in V.B.'s system, as I have never won anything. I can see though, how the wheel could subtlety seduce a player, if it is a fair wheel. I've seen some systems reduce even hardened gamblers to tears and self-destruction."

"Self-destruction. Yes, Kyame, Monte Carlo knows well of self-destruction."

They walked through the doorway, arm in arm as two theater comrades.

***

V.B. put the drawing back on the table next to his whiskey and soda. "She is an assistant of the Ritter Heinz Bäcker, a senior aide with Herr Wagner's investment office a few doors away from Smith's in the Galerie Charles III."

He pursed his lips. "I believe her name is Jäger, or something like that. I don't know her Christian name. I was speaking not 5-6 days ago to Bäcker regarding one of his clients, a titled gentleman of some stature in Prussia, who was having some serious gambling problems. We were only standing in the Galerie's arcade walkway with people around us, so a more detailed discussion was not possible at the time. However, that woman" – he tapped the drawing – "came up to Bäcker with an envelope. He referred to her in passing as Fraulein Jäger or Häger after she had left. He did not introduce her to me. And for the life of me, later I couldn't really recall anything about her, as though she had never been there.

"But now," he looked across the table at Kyame and Muffin. He dropped the Trotha notepaper on the table with the just visible names. He had already given the paper with the apparent account numbers to his assistant at the bank for investigation. "Now I know her with certainty. Her name is Konstanze Jäger. Trotha knew her. Her name, which he underlined, is on that notepaper that I took from Trotha's desk. The Norfolk woman is also on his list, as we already knew. There is one other British name, but I can't make it out. And, we now know with some certainty, that the mysterious Count Baldur von Trotha was a thief." He placed the black pouch on the table.

At Kyame's raised eyebrow, Bethell nodded.

Kyame opened and emptied the contents on the table: a file, spirit lamp, matches, lock-picks, and pliers.

She ran her fingers over the five different shaped pieces of bare steel. "These picks have been used several times. The edges have been worn and then refinished. They are virtually useless now as they have almost lost their shape. I would throw them away. Trying to use them in this condition would not be worth the risk." She reached into her skirt pocket and withdrew a small brown leather pouch. Kyame opened it and placed it on the table. There were six black differently shaped pieces of steel held in position with straps in the pouch. She pointed at one angular shaped piece. "This pick will open many of the doors in the hotels of western America," she said with a small mischievous smile. "I know because I have used it." She grinned. "And for the lock on my room at the Hotel de Paris, I have used this one." Kyame small smile was pure mock innocence. "I always experiment. Just for practice … naturally."

Muffin looked toward Bethell, her mischievous smile lighting the room. "It would seem that America has sent us the knight-errant we need, V.B."

***

"Trotha! Bethell was in his villa. Why?" Wagner demanded. That damn fool thief again. When will I finally be rid of him? But more important what did the English banker find – and what was he looking for?

Konstanze pressed deeper into the wing chair as in defense. "I don't know," she said evenly. "He went to the Duchess's villa with the American, Kyame Piddington, then left after only a very few minutes. I chose to follow him, as the American clearly would be with the Duchess for some time." Konstanze breathed a little easier when Wagner nodded. "The banker stopped first at the agent handling the property in Cannes. Then he was in the Trotha villa for almost half-an-hour, but I did not see him leave with anything in his hands. According to the newspapers, the price for the villa is as-furnished, but the agent has mentioned to people whom I know that there has been no interest in purchasing or leasing the villa, as it is too small and too inconvenient to the Casino.

"*No one*, Herr Wagner, knows of my interest," Konstanze emphasized. "In following Bethell back, he stopped first at Smith's for a short time, perhaps five minutes, before returning the Duchess' villa."

Wagner drew on his cigar, then nodded again. "Trotha again. I thought I was finished with the man, until he washed up in San Remo. But a 'retired' thief is still a thief, and still thinks like one. The Norfolk woman has proven to be an excellent source of British indiscretions." He sniffed and sniggered. "We know that the 'Baron Renfrew' will be paying his regular call to the Casino in two days. A British plan that is, naturally, highly confidential.

"Unfortunately, the brief incognito visit of the All Highest a few days ago was not as ... successful as his Russian system was supposed to assure, nor as 'confidential'." He smirked. "He lost 390,000 francs in two days. Two! As though no one would notice!" Wagner whispered to himself, "The fool."

But Konstanze read his lips, as she could read lips in German and English.

She enjoyed recalling, at Herr Wagner's order, how easily she had drawn Trotha into physical indiscretions. She would have preferred a knife, but being naked, she was left to use the sharp edges of a broken wine bottle on the drunken 'master thief'. And then the fool Bäcker had failed to properly dispose of the body! Left to her, Trotha would never have been seen again. Perhaps she will be asked to assure that that will be the fate of the American woman.

Konstanze hoped so.

***

Muffin held up her glass. *"Deo Juvante"*, she said. "With God's Help, Kyame. That is the motto of Monaco. Hopefully, He will be listening when we call on Him, as I suspect we may have to."

V.B. and Kyame raised their glasses in response.

27

Headquarters

Imperial German General Staff

February 19, 1896

Count Alfred von Schlieffen pushed several well marked maps of Belgium and western Russia aside as a middle-aged woman in the black and white uniform of a maidservant sat demurely in the straight-backed chair at his desk. She removed her glasses, smiled and became fifteen years younger. Von Schlieffen's brief smile was uncharacteristically welcoming in return. Few people ever saw the Count smile or had heard him laugh.

"So, Fräulein Böhn, what are your observations?"

Katrin Böhn waited until the silent sergeant placed her filled tea cup before her and, rounding the desk, placed a filled coffee cup before von Schlieffen, then quickly withdrew. The cups of gold-rimmed ivory bone-china were adorned with the colorful von Schlieffen family coat of arms. The cups were rarely used for routine visitors.

Böhn sipped her tea, replaced the cup and said, "You will not like anything I am about to say, sir. And ...

His Highest could make my life either very miserable or very short, depending on his mood at the moment."

"You will *not* be touched, Fräulein." Von Schlieffen's lean face was cold. For all his known isolation from social amenities, the Count relentlessly protected his people from higher harassment. "Continue."

"As you are aware, sir, the Kaiser and the Admiral of interest have a weekly private meeting, though that meeting was canceled by His Highest a few days ago to allow Admiral von Tirpitz and Captain Hahn to meet privately with him. Admiral von Drascher had not been informed of the cancellation and was forced to sit with office underlings without explanation for almost forty-five minutes after his regular time before he was informed that there would be no meeting that day.

"Needless to say, the Admiral was incensed.

"However, sir, there was a meeting two days later on the Imperial yacht that caused von Drascher to immediately travel to the shipyards at Ebing." She sipped, then said, "It was difficult to keep up with him without my following becoming obvious."

"Ebing? There are no Kaiserliche Marine activities there."

Böhn smiled and sipped again. She began to speak of Predators and accelerated building schedules.

269

Stunned, von Schlieffen went pale.

"The Kaiser has ordered the killing of any Britons who showed any interest in the shipyards. According to my contacts in the area, three Englishmen were murdered near Ebing with their bodies dumped elsewhere. I don't know where.

"Six British agents have been killed by various means on the French coast near Cannes and Nice. The agents have not, so far as I have been able to determine, been replaced by the British government. Though there seems to be" -- she paused -- "some question, a rumor of some kind of American aid in that regard. I am unaware of what the reaction in London has been." She leaned back in her chair, emptying and replacing her cup on its saucer.

Von Schlieffen was speechless. He could not doubt the work or word of Katrin Böhn. He had relied on her insights too many times, at sometimes serious professional risk.

Like all senior officers and ministers, von Schlieffen was accustomed to the Kaiser's sometimes erratic enthusiasms and wildly changing interests; but this killing of British agents, along with the unexplained ships being built. He had never heard the designation Prädator before. Four of them. For what?

An *American* response! What in God's name could that mean?

He had had no objection to the Kaiser's creation of the Kaiserliche Marine to protect the coastline, to cut off British resupply in the war that was certain to come. But what was this? He could well imagine what the British reaction might be; it took no imagination for that.

Lord Salisbury has now been alerted to something urgent and threatening. The British Prime Minister is now obligated to find out what form of activity may be menacing his nation. But not even the Imperial German Army knows what that might be.

In spite of the coffee, the Count was cold inside. What was that -- that creature in Berlin planning now?

Noting the Count's reaction, after a moment, Böhn asked. "Should I continue to observe, Count von Schlieffen?"

He shook his head. "No, Fräulein Böhn, your work is finished for the time … and it never happened. I have kept no records." He opened a drawer and withdrew a sealed manila envelope. "This is yours. You have done very well, as always. My thanks." He slid the envelope across the desk.

Without opening it, Katrin Böhn slipped the envelope into a side pocket of her coat, replaced her glasses, and frowning, regained fifteen years, turned and left the office, closing the door gently behind her, as would any well trained servant.

For a few moments, the Count von Schlieffen sat quietly. The Ebing situation was, or would become a Kaiserliche Marine problem for the nonce, but he had to understand its potential impact on the Army, and specifically on the Belgian question. He pushed the Russian maps to one side and slid the Belgian maps back onto his desk in order to complete the initial details for the Imperial invasion of Belgium.

He needed to re-evaluate the problem and timing of moving critical munitions a long distance from two, perhaps three railpoints. It was the timing that could prove decisive for the success of his planned massive flanking move through Flanders and into the very bowels of France.

His next step regarding the Prädators was not clear, as yet. He hoped he, the Army, would not have to act. There was, literally, enough on the table for the Army to work on.

He needed to activate his contact within N -- to begin to understand the Kaiser's intentions. N would have to know. Von Schlieffen shook his head. He now had to spy on his own Navy as though it were a foreign enemy. Another gift from the All Highest, he sneered, and began again on the Belgian problem.

28

"Normally a thief is murdered because he becomes inconvenient for some reason," said Kyame. She stood by the tall mullioned windows that filled a wall of Muffin's library with the Dog's Head seemingly within reach. She turned back to the large well-used library. Books were piled on shelves, across two tables, even stacked in several places on the floor. Her kind of library; the library Kyame hoped to have one day.

Sitting in a dark red leather chair, holding a whiskey and soda in his hands, V.B. slowly nodded agreement. "Trotha, assuming that is his name, had been living in his villa for almost ten months before he was killed, so his killing most likely was not a delayed payoff from some earlier job going bad. Something more recent. But there have not been any major thefts on the Cote d'Azur for several months. A few small ones here and there, but no robbery over a few thousand francs of jewelry, and mostly due, according to what I have learned, to carelessness, not to some romantic master thief. Nothing that required Trotha's apparent skills. And," Bethell emphasized, "nothing within the boundaries of Monaco."

Kyame resumed her straight-backed chair near one of the two marble fireplaces that warmed the library, declining V.B.'s offer of his chair. "The description of the killing, the messy cuts to the throat, would suggest that it may not have been planned ... a sort of sudden angry reaction. A broken bottle was probably used," said Kyame. Muffin's eyes widened at Kyame's almost casual description of the brutal killing. "Why some people think of thievery as romantic, I can't imagine," said Kyame. "I've met a few thieves, reformed and otherwise, and none of them were romantic. More they seemed just lost and broke."

V.B. said, "That is an unusual attitude, Kyame. Novelists have been using romantic thieves for decades. There are a few of those books up on those shelves, not so, Muffin?"

Muffin nodded, then shifted on the couch, rubbing her short leg. "There was the Count de Dagoneti affair two weeks ago, or maybe three," said Muffin. "Remember V.B.? When the Count went to the Casino to cash in some chips he had mistakenly taken away with him the previous night, but the Casino refused to pay, saying the chips were counterfeit ... and remarkably well done counterfeits, a fact which has caused the management to reexamine all the chips currently in use. "

"Yes, you're right. The Count was astonished since he insisted the chips were some of those he had used the previous night at roulette. They came directly from the croupier," said V.B. "He claimed he put them into his coat pocket, to separate out his profits from his current play. I do the same actually. There were ten of them, the new one thousand franc chips made from mother of pearl. He forgot about them, then brought them in to be cashed the next morning when the Rooms opened for play.

"If the Casino has quality counterfeits floating about," Bethell said with some urgency, "some of the credibility of the management is certain to be damaged, and some titled players may not want to play, not knowing if their assets are genuine or not. This is not the first time for something like this. Recall, Muffin, the Grant affair?"

Muffin looked up from rubbing her short leg again. "Ah, yes, V.B., I had forgotten, but that was before Trotha appeared." She leaned back in her chair, sipped, and nodded. "Yes, there were other small incidents that were carried about on rumors and such. But some of that is inevitable around a Casino as prominent as Monte Carlo. Croupiers giving aide to pretty young ladies, or such things, that suggest that things at the Casino are 'flexible' as my experienced husband used to say." She paused. "But yes. There appears to be an increase in their occurrence as though someone had begun to actively push a wave, a campaign of rumors. Then, this Dagoneti affair with the chips, which directly threatened a well-known personage."

"When did the increase start to happen? Is the Count trustworthy, solid?" asked Kyame. "If he is telling the truth, then there may have been a switch in order to throw more suspicion on the Casino itself. According to a certain source, virtually all of the money, all the income for the principality comes via the Casino. Crippling the Casino would cripple Monaco, cripple Prince Albert ... would it not?"

"I have dealt several times with Dagoneti. He is honest." V.B. grinned. "You are coming to a quick understanding of our little world on the blue sea. Your source, Kyame?"

"My concierge at the hotel, Yves. He has been working at the Hotel de Paris for twelve years and misses the presence of Prince Charles III. He dismisses Albert as only a college professor in the wrong job. When Papa and I were performing, I would always talk to the workers who see everything; that was as important as anything else I did in the act."

Both V.B. and Muffin laughed.

"Yves is not alone in his insight, Kyame," observed Muffin. Continuing, she said, "According to Dagoneti's story in the daily *Riveria Times*, he and his wife returned from the Casino directly to their rooms at the Hermitage, to their room on the third floor. There had been no indication of anyone being in their room when they arose in the morning."

Kyame hesitated for a moment, then asked, "May I see their room, V.B.? I have scaled a wall or two." She grinned. "Second sight does have its physical side."

V.B. laughed gently. She was an astonishing young woman. "The answer to your other question about when the rumors picked up, Kyame, is" – he raised his eyebrows, glancing at Muffin – "is about three, maybe four months ago, when Trotha had become an established member of Cercle society." He looked at Muffin who nodded.

"A little less than three months," Muffin said, standing, "as though some urgency were in play. That matches almost with the beginning of the killings." She looked over at the servant who had entered the room. "Yes, Angelo?"

"Pardon, your Grace, but a message has been left for Mr. Bethell." He held out a Smith & Co. envelope to V.B., then turned, closing the door silently behind him.

"Those two numbers I found under Trotha's dresser drawers. One is a bank account in Rome, the other is the password to that account. My assistant took it on himself to request the account balance, which he very promptly received." He looked up at the two women. "A deposit was made on January 6 of 150,000 Imperial Gold Marks. That was five days before the Dagoneti affair. The deposit came directly from Berlin, from the Berliner Handelgesellschaft bank. Three days later, the 9th, Trotha ordered the deposit converted into £7,500 which is where it stands now. Trotha's account balance at the present time is £9,000. A very healthy sum."

"I am no expert on banks and such," said Kyame, leaning forward, her elbows on her knees, "but it would seem, living in France, unusual for him to keep that account in English pounds, would it not? Which may suggest that he had other accounts for his French living. All the reasonably successful thieves that I came in contact with always had multiple money accounts for different purposes. They all had a running-away money account of some sort."

V.B. was silent for a short moment, then said, "Given what we now know of Trotha, Kyame, I think you may be correct. That was his payment account for services rendered, very possibly. Perhaps as well, he kept that account in pounds, planning to escape to England if getaway became necessary." His friendly smile twisted slightly, as he said, "Apparently he could not run to Germany for some reason."

"He would certainly run if something went wrong," said Muffin. "So, if his paymaster was the Kaiser's government, he could not run to them."

***

Kyame looked down from the third floor balcony of the Dagoneti room. The Count and his wife stood to one side of the balcony, the Count intent, the Countess nervously squeezing her hands. Dagoneti had readily agreed to Kyame's investigation. V.B. stood quietly in the background.

There were ledges, indentations in the wall for toe-holds. Yes, she was confident she could scale the three floors -- and in the dark. Leaning further out, she smiled as she felt V. B.'s restraining hand on her shoulder. There was something down there, behind the bushes.

Stepping back from the railing, Kyame said, "There is something down there. I need to see what it is."

***

Kyame pushed the tightly trimmed bushes aside as V.B. and the Count held them back for her. The manager of the Hermitage, Gregory Fouralt, stood to one side to watch. The Countess, her eyes wide, held her hands over her mouth, clearly anxious.

Yes. The clear marks of a ladder in the black soil. Deep into the soil. Someone had placed and mounted a ladder against the wall. She looked up. It would take only a -- four-foot ladder to enable a man to reach the lowest ledge. She would need a five-foot to reach it herself. Kyame turned to the manager. "Mr. Fouralt, have any gardening people been working here in the past eight or nine days, who could have put a ladder up against the wall?"

After a moment, Fouralt shook his head. "No, Mademoiselle, the gardeners have been too busy putting in new plantings on the other side of the hotel. They will not be trimming these bushes for another four to five days."

Kyame stepped back from the wall and through the bushes. Turning to the Dagoneti's she said, "A thief put a ladder there which enabled him to reach that first ledge ... up there. From there he climbed up the wall to the third floor. It would take perhaps three to five minutes, with practice or experience, to reach your balcony. It would take about two minutes to come down. With perhaps no more than five or six minutes in your room, the whole operation would require not more than, say, twelve to thirteen minutes." The Count had explained that they always left the French doors on their balcony ajar before retiring to allow the night breezes in to cool their bedroom.

The Dagoneti's looked at each other, then at Fouralt whose jaw tightened. The Count looked back at Kyame. "Mademoiselle, you speak with ... with a certain authority, as if you could do this ... this operation as you call it ...yourself."

Kyame shook some black soil from her skirt. She looked up at the troubled hazel eyes of the Count, whose reputation was under serious threat. "Oh, yes. This wall would be relatively easy to scale in the dark. If there was a moon, it could be done even faster, while carrying a bag for the swag."

"But ..." The Count started. "But why us?" finished his wife.

Kyame looked at V.B. An idea was forming in her mind. A conversation of about three years ago came to mind. It had been in Laramie, Wyoming, with two elderly former robbers recently released from the state prison. Kyame had come across them behind their hotel. Papa was at the Famers Hall finalizing the billing of The Impossible Piddingtons. Kyame was doing her job of listening to the town, as she had called it.

The robbers, one of whom must have been quite handsome in his younger days, a romantic thief perhaps, responded even eagerly to Kyame's questions about setting up a job, a nicking, a grab. Until the other finally asked, "You planning on nicking someone, Miss Piddington?"

"There were one or two observers at the Casino that night," Kyame said, "perhaps even every night, looking for a specific opportunity that could create suitable problems, or to discredit the Casino in some highly public way. When they saw you, Count, drop the chips into your coat pocket, then when you left without cashing those chips, you became their target." A sudden thought came to mind. "Did you happen to see, by chance, the Count von Trotha at the tables that night?"

For a moment both of the Dagoneti's faces went blank, then the Countess responded. "Why ... why yes, I spoke with him that night. I had first met him several evenings earlier. A most interesting gentleman ... with some marvelous tales to tell." She lowered her voice. "You know he was an agent in the French Deuxième Bureau. Retired now, of course, but so interesting."

Bethell's jaw dropped. "But, Kyame, what if the Count Dagoneti …"

"If the Count had cashed in his chips before leaving," said Kyame, "then he would not have been targeted. Von Trotha would have targeted someone else. And, if not that night … then another night. I learned from some experienced thieves in our West not to be impatient. Play for the right score, not for just any score. If you are going down, go down for the right thing. Only a fool risks prison-time for settling for the wrong nick, for grabbing the wrong bag." Then a thought. Kyame pulled her drawing from her pocket.

"Have you seen this woman?' She showed the drawing first to the Dagoneti's and then to Fouralt. "She would be dressed very plainly and has bitter blue eyes."

There was momentary silence, then Fouralt nodded. "Yes, I have seen her. And it was *that* night." He paused to collect his thoughts. "Her name is Konstanze Jäger, she told me. She was rushing out to catch a train, she said, and tripped on a rug in the lobby. I helped her up. She had the most chilling blue eyes."

"What was she doing at the hotel?" asked V.B.

Fouralt said, "I believe she was checking a room reservation for a friend."

"That's how Trotha learned your room number," said V.B., "from Jäger. Somehow he had learned of your hotel, but needed your room. She was hurrying to give him the room number."

There was silence as each looked at the other, while Kyame looked back up the wall at the balcony above.

Yes, about three minutes would do it.

29

As Kyame and Bethell mounted the carriage first to the Hotel de Paris, and then return to Muffin's villa, Kyame suddenly smiled, then asked, as the carriage began to move down the l'Hermitage driveway toward the Rue des Lilas, the white and gold spires and cupolas of the Monte Carlo Casino just visible above the palm trees, "V.B., would it be possible to arrange with the Casino management to publicly say they had made a mistake and that the chips of Count Dagoneti were in fact genuine ... and issue a public apology to him?

"It could prove very disconcerting to the people behind all this. The failure of their carefully planned assault, one of many I would presume, that they may plan on the credibility of the Casino. That could sort of get their tails twisted into knots ... maybe ... maybe force them to take some unwise action of some kind. That might make it easier to identify the who. I think we may be starting to get the outline of the why. Someone wants to cripple the principality."

Kyame pursed her lips. The increase in rumors, the Dagoneti grab, maybe other nicks that have been kept quiet but rumored anyway, and then the killings. She had reviewed the timing of the agent killings against the timing of the rumors as V.B. and Muffin had recalled them in her mind as they had traveled to the Hotel de Paris. Something was there.

So, darn it, what was it?

In returning to the lobby of the Hermitage, Gregory Fouralt and the Dagoneti's had been smiling. Even the Countess was no longer nervously squeezing and twisting her hands. But now even with some questions still unanswered, there was less uncertainty. As they walked, Kyame had outlined her understanding of the specific night: clearly a thief had switched the chips, a somewhat daring thief – even if not romantic – who apparently had been paid a great deal to take the risk, on short notice, when he apparently had stolen nothing while in the Dagoneti rooms. He thus could not gain his reward from fencing his swag. Why, Kyame had further suggested, why would an experienced thief, as this one must have been, even if paid £7,500, take such a chance unless something more than money was included in his payoff?

Or, Kyame had hurriedly added, multiple thoughts running through her mind, what if the thief had been given no choice? A respectable fee perhaps being offered; but with the implied threat of something else if he had declined -- or had failed. Like getting his throat slashed?

Her four listeners had been silent as Kyame had offered her thoughts. Fouralt was the first to speak. "Mademoiselle, your mind runs in *manières éstranges*, ah, strange ways, forgive me; but you may be headed in the right direction of a solution." He grinned. "My experience with Americans thus far has been very limited, but from what I have seen in the past few minutes, I am glad it is not you, Mademoiselle, who is climbing my walls."

The group laughed as Kyame and V.B. said their goodbyes after declining the offer from Count Dagoneti for cocktails at his expense. The Countess added dinner when convenient.

***

"Kyame, may I present Sir Septimus Browne, a senior aide to the Prime Minister."

V.B. had dropped off Kyame at the Hotel de Paris to change into something more formal, as Muffin had suggested, for dinner at Ciro's Restaurant, then on to the wheel at Monte Carlo. He returned in evening dress an hour later.

Now dressed in brilliant green tiered satin skirts with billowing silver and green sleeves to her wrists and a modest décolletage, Kyame extended her hand. "Sir Septimus, I am honored." Bearded and bent, but with intimidating eyes that exhibited an equally formidable intelligence.

Browne held her hand for a moment, then squeezed gently and released it. "Thank you for coming to our aid, Miss Piddington."

Kyame flashed a quick roguish smile that brought an awkward smile to the bearded man leaning on his black cane. "I am trying to be of help, as President Cleveland directed."

They seated themselves in Muffin's drawing room whose great windows showed the darkening of the skies, the Dog's Head blending, gradually vanishing into a widening thick mist. Gas lights and candles were lit about the room. Muffin had a crowded cart positioned next to V.B of multi-colored bottles which, standing amongst them, were a few still with fingers of dust across their painted labels.

An aperitif or something more -- serious, Muffin had smiled, as she closed the door behind her. She would rejoin them within a half hour. She had to attach a more stylish leg, she laughed.

The smiling men bowed, then turned back to their chairs. Attach a stylish leg? Kyame kept, just barely, from laughing. Muffin was gloriously unpredictable.

A silver tray of rich seafood collations, several specialties of Muffin's Danish chef, were spread on a large low oval mahogany table in the center of the circle of chairs. Spiced crab balls; smoked trout with crème Fraiche and pickled onion Crostini; scallops wrapped in bacon and awash in a green sauce; coconut shrimp breaded in something she couldn't recognize, and -- Kyame couldn't begin to recognize the rest. She had once seen a spread something like this during a Sunday at the Palace Hotel in San Francisco, but she hadn't learned the names of the dishes -- they had all disappeared so quickly.

"Miss Piddington," said Browne, as he poured himself a balloon glass of rich brandy from a dusty bottle, "V.B. has provided me with a report that I will be taking with me to the Prime Minister when I return to London tonight on the Train de Luxe. Your role has been central to giving these difficult circumstances more form … with some preliminary understanding."

"Thank you, sir, but we have much still to do ... and it seems … less and less time in which to accomplish our task." Kyame chewed and swallowed a scallop wrapped in bacon covered with a unique tarty sauce. She could eat several of these for dinner, but held back, to not appear too hungry. She sipped the chilled Sémillion that V.B. had poured for her.

Muffin reappeared with a practiced flourish in a glorious deep metallic antique copper gown with a daring neckline had immediately raised the eyebrows of the men as both stood and bowed. She smiled broadly. "Sir Septimus, it is so enjoyable to be with you again. You have been away for some months … in South Africa?"

"Your sources are spot on, as usual, dear woman," Browne nodded, settling back into his deep leather chair. "Yes, the Cape Territory. There are situations developing that will require His Lordship's close attention. Along with

288

the situation you have here." He frowned as though a thought had just struck him. "May I suggest Duchess, Miss Piddington, V.B., that you might consider ... that your problem in Monaco may be connected in some way with the Cape, given the Kaiser's very unwise telegram to President Kruger on the Transvaal situation on January 3rd of this year. I can't begin to conceive how that may be, but, please keep your thoughts open to the possibility of such a connection."

Kyame felt a cold chill as her thoughts from earlier, before their visit to the Hermitage Hotel, returned. There was something she was missing.

"Kyame, something?" quickly asked V.B., "I am beginning to respect your frowns."

She nodded. "Something, but I don't know what just yet." It was there. Just beyond her reach. "But something."

"May I suggest dinner at Ciro's and then, Sir Septimus," said Muffin, "if you could join us at the Casino?"

As Muffin took his proffered arm, Browne smiled, then shook his head. "I fear, dear Muffin, the pleasant portion of the evening for me must only be Ciro's, then to the train. There are reports from Berlin and recent comments made by the Kaiser at court, careless I trust, but one cannot be certain of anything relative to Wilhelm. I must convey all this as quickly as possible to the Prime Minister. Some of those Imperial comments I have mentioned to V.B. who is free to share them with you ... with you both," he emphasized with a nod to Kyame.

CIRO'S BAR

AND

HIGH-CLASS RESTAURANT,

GALERIE CHARLES III,

MONTE CARLO.

LUNCHEONS, DINNERS,

TEAS, SUPPERS,

'THE VERY BEST.'

***

Villa de la Mirage

Nice, France

Just finishing his personal preparation for Ciro's and the Casino, carefully examining his image in the mirror, ensuring his waxed upswept Imperial mustaches, as the Kaiser's, rising up at each end of his mouth were perfect, Johannes Friederich Wagner stopped, astonished.

He threw the late-hour issue of the *Menton and Monte Carlo News* left by a servant back on the dressing table. The Casino, the newspaper headlined, had apologized to the Count Dagoneti! The chips the Count had wanted to cash had been proven upon closer examination to be not counterfeit, but genuine. A terrible mistake by a junior accountant, who has been dismissed, had led to the Count's embarrassment for which the Director General, Camille Blanc, personally, together with the Directors of the *Société Anonyme des Bains de Mer,* the owner of the Casino, most deeply regretted. There was more, but Wagner had seen enough.

The whole Trotha business was now rendered a complete waste of time and money. With the result that the impact of the other carefully placed rumored indiscretions was now greatly diminished.

Wagner had noted the growing absence of several high spending titled regulars from previous years, most likely dissuaded by his group's carefully placed negative press stories regarding the Casino, its operation, together the apparent decline in security on the streets of Monaco. All titled European aristocracy felt, at one time or another, as though they were wearing an inviting target on their backs for anarchists, protesters, and assorted political fanatics to strike at, so the implication of lowered security would keep many such clients of the wheel away, with the result of diminished cash flow into the Casino and thus into Prince Albert's pockets.

But now this!

A case of 2,000 fake Monte Carlo chips of the just introduced new design of various values, up to 5,000 francs, had arrived that afternoon in the diplomatic mail from Prussia -- two weeks late. Each handmade by Prussian craftsmen, the chips were flawless copies, but with an intentional mistake that would become obvious, requiring only moderate care in examination. The counterfeits had to be assimilated into the Casino secure inventory within the next two days in order to regain and expand the effect of the Dagoneti affair in order to further undermine the Casino operations.

The compromised *Chef de Partie*, whom Jäger had identified and on whom Bäcker had very skillfully, Wagner had to admit, dug up confirmed data on his personal perilous financial condition and other awkward situations, had not yet been completely turned.

Alphonse Beaupariant was one of several very visible men, dressed in black frock coats present on both of the gaming floors, who were ultimately responsible to the Administration as well as to the clientele for the integrity of the play, whether roulette or Trente-et-quarante. But, there was also the *Brigade de Ju*, the Casino's plain-clothed private detectives who were also present throughout the Casino and whose identities were known only to the Director-General, Camille Blanc. Rumor had it that Blanc had recently added two or three women to the Brigade, which demanded now even greater caution. Beaupariant

292

could not risk a member of the Brigade seeing or hearing the wrong thing.

But, he had waivered when Konstanze had whispered a rendezvous with colorful elaboration.

The man must be turned -- tonight without fail.

Wagner cursed, then cursed again. Mein Gott! They would have to redouble their plans for destabilizing the Casino. Timing according to the Kaiser's schedule was getting uncomfortably tight. An act that could shut down the Casino while emptying the Prince de Monaco's vault almost immediately -- a moment -- a moment. Wagner hesitated.

Baron Renfrew in two days?

He smiled. The risk was, assuredly -- exceptional. Flooding the tables with counterfeit chips could certainly help achieve the purpose, but Wagner could not have full control of the timing. Another week, possibly, would allow the tainted chips to do their job, but there just wasn't the time.

Albert had to be brought to his knees within the Kaiser's timeframe.

Wagner turned back to his private desk. In a few moments he had the telegram enciphered. He had to have the direct approval of the Kaiser before moving.

Wagner started down the stairs. The telegram would be sent from a very private facility that had been installed in a corner of his wine cellar three floors below. His Highest would see it within 2-3 hours. Wagner should have the Kaiser's answer in the morning. The English woman would have Renfrew's latest schedule tomorrow morning.

Wagner now smiled, breathing a bit more rapidly from his taking the steps two at a time, he would have the English woman for himself well before morning when he would have time to refresh her mesmeric instructions and, he paused, and adding one or two more. He issued orders for his carriage and started to return to his room to complete his preparations. Then stopped.

There was, he smiled, an additional highly visible Imperial action that would not require the Kaiser's personal attention. The means was already in place. It would require only his signal. A smirk spread across his face as he stepped rapidly up the stairs, an expression that his servants had learned to evade instantly.

His breathing returning to normal, Wagner recalled a firm warning he had once received from his demanding and violent tempered father: Be careful about doing something irreversible.

***

The discrete sign said Ciro's in gold on black on white over the mahogany and stained glass of the large arched door of the main entrance of the two-story building. With the Metropole Hotel at the left of the arcade, Charles III Galerie, Kyame noted Smith & Co. to the right of the restaurant, and other shop-fronts beyond to the right into the darkness. She caught the reflections off the brass *Wagner Finanzdienstleistungen* sign swinging in the strengthening chill breezes about two doors beyond Smith's. An immense glass window was centered to the right of Ciro's door which displayed a large table of active men and women at which a strongly built quite handsome man seemed to be presiding, with the pulsing vibrant activity of the other tables in the background. When he glanced out the window at the growing winds, she saw he wore a stylish black mustache.

A threatening northwest wind had begun to build, a wind that V.B. had called the Mistral, an uncomfortable wind which often continued erratically for several days. It was the price of being in Monaco in February, he had said. Muffin had dressed for it with a heavy cloak over her antique copper gown, while Kyame's Boston cloak only created the illusion of comfort.

Once inside, the restaurant was warm and alive with light, the jumbled joyous cacophony for which Chiro's was renowned. All of the tables on the covered terrace had been abandoned with the developing chill. Kyame could not see any open tables in the room. Everyone appeared pressed tightly together.

"*Buonasera*, Duchess! Ah, my friend, V.B.! And Sir Septemus, and ..." The diminutive very well dressed man, his smile wide, his arms open, his eyes laughing, nodded his head toward Kyame. He bowed over Muffin's extended hand to gently brush his lips to her skin, then turned and bowed to Kyame. "*La mia bella signorina*, my beautiful young lady, welcome to Ciro's!"

"Ciro," said Muffin, "may I have the pleasure of introducing a very close friend from America, Miss Kyame Piddington, who is here to paint my portrait."

Ciro's eyebrows went up. "An artist with the beauty of her subject! Magnifico! Would that I could master the paints for such an occasion." He shrugged. "But I am but a hard working cook." He beckoned. "Please ladies to follow me. Gentlemen, you may find your own way."

With everyone laughing, Ciro leaned back toward Kyame. "Miss Piddingdon ... have I said that right?"

"Piddington," Kyame gently corrected.

"*Le mie scuse*, my apologies. My ear is but tin, Miss Piddington. I worked in your New York a few years ago, in the kitchen of your famous restaurant, Delmonico's. Have you eaten there?"

"Yes, I have Mr. Ciro. It was a glorious evening."

He stopped, sweeping his hand toward a circular table covered by an ivory-colored lace tablecloth with a

296

glistening crystal centerpiece supporting two expansive bouquets of large yellow and blue flowers that Kyame had never seen before. He very lightly touched Kyame's arm and whispered, "I am Ciro to my friends. No mister."

Two waiters materialized to hold the chairs for Muffin and Kyame while the two men settled onto their chairs on their own.

"So, my *stregone* of food, my sorcerer, what have you for us tonight?" Muffin's warm smile ignited an even wider smile from Ciro.

Upon Ciro's nod, the waiters flourished a square of parchment before each of his guests, as Muffin, Bethell, and Sir Septemus were nodding to nearby friends. Two of the women were pointing at Kyame, clearly inquiring who she was.

Kyame had seen tables filled with remarkable dishes as they had made their way to other tables, but the entire dining room was beyond anything she had ever seen, including Delmonico's. She couldn't begin to guess at the exalted identities of Ciro's clientele, but clearly a great deal of wealth was on display. The extraordinary gowns of the women made her feel --underdressed, almost impoverished. Seeing the vast array of diamonds along with other stones of every color, awash in gold, reminded her of her box of three diamonds hidden in her hotel room that she had not yet dealt with. There would be time later -- for that.

Kyame turned back to the parchment with the menu in voguish hand-lettered black ink:

Hors d'Œuvres varies

Œufs pochés Grand Duc

Mostèle à l'Anglaise

Volaille on Casserole à la Fermière.

Pàtisserie.

Fromage Brie.

Café

Vins et Liqueurs.

Château Carbonnieux, 1891

Fine Champágne, 1846.

Ciro leaned forward. "Also," he confided, "because of the skill of Sir Augustus McAvoy with his guns this morning, I have also this night *a canard à la presse*." He turned to Kyame. "That, *la mia bella amica americana*, my beautiful American friend, is a delicacy of slices of roast-duck served with a sauce made from juices pressed from the duck, and cooked with cognac and butter." He bowed to the table. "I leave you for a short moment, then return." At Ciro's withdrawal, the waiters began placing a variety of hors d'Œuvres around the table.

Just inhaling the ambiance of Ciro's was intoxicating. "Amazing, Muffin, just amazing," said Kyame. "Where did Ciro come from?"

The Duchess replaced her crystal flute of 1846 champagne. "He is rumored to be Egyptian-Italian from the Naples area. He is a master of creating culinary miracles. The mostéle on the menu is the most prized Mediterranean white fish. It is better than any fish I ever ate in England. Wouldn't you agree, gentlemen?"

Both V.B. and Sir Septemus nodded as they sipped their aperitifs. "Have you decided, Kyame?" asked V.B.

"Yes, I am going to enjoy the duck that Sir Augustus has provided. A duck juice that includes butter and cognac sounds too good to miss. This way I can more directly compare Ciro's to Delmonico's where I also had roast duck."

***

As Kyame took her first bite of the duck, it hit her. She chewed and swallowed too quickly, but the flavor was like nothing she had ever tasted before. She leaned toward V.B.

"Something has occurred to me regarding our ... joint problem. May I ask a question ... safely?"

V.B. glanced quickly about him, then nodded. The attention of Ciro's had been drawn to the door as the

German banker, Johannes Wagner, with the Lady Norfolk entered. She removed her cloak, revealing an exceptionally low neckline which triggered a disapproving tittering that spread across the restaurant, growing in volume, but only from the women.

"The third agent murdered," said Kyame, softly, as Sir Septemus and Muffin leaned toward her, "was Sir Cornelius Brand, but he was also the first agent to be replaced, by Sir John Blenkiron, who was then the first to be murdered of the replacements. They both had their throats cut, while the other agents were shot, strangled or bludgeoned which suggests in their case that it was likely the same killer. The first killing was in La Turbie which seems to be a village nearby, while the second killing, of Blenkiron, however, was at a small harbor port near Cap Martin. Only two days separated them. That is the issue. The other killings of agents and their replacements were separated by five to eight days, with less urgency, it seems. Why were these two agents, of the group, killed with such dispatch? I want to learn why. They may have been killed elsewhere and then their bodies dumped, but it is the timing. What had they seen, or were about to see that required their quick deaths?" She looked up as a waiter passed their table, then continued, "The files indicated that Brand had traveled to the north coast of Prussia, to follow-up a rumor he had encountered in La Turbie, only to return to his death *at* La Turbie apparently before he could file any report. Also according to the files, Blenkiron had already been in the north on another assignment under another name, when he was redirected to replace Brand in the south and was killed, apparently on his arrival, in Cap Martin. Both had been to the north; but none of the other agents had been. But where in the north of Prussia had they been, it isn't clear in the files." Kyame looked up at V.B. "Could it have been to the same place?" As V.B. started to respond, Kyame added, "And is the north, whatever it is, connected to what is happening here in Monaco? I think that is a vital question we must answer very quickly."

With both Muffin and Sir Septemus nodding agreement, V.B. said, "I believe you may be right, Kyame. Did the files say anything about where in La Turbie Brand found the rumor? We can have an early breakfast in La Turbie tomorrow. It is a twenty minute train ride away. And then lunch at Cap Martin Hotel. I know the manager there."

Kyame reviewed the files of the two men in her mind. She saw Ciro enthusiastically greeting someone at the door. "Is there a Roman monument in La Turbie? Brand mentioned a small café almost within the shadow of the monument."

Muffin said, "I know the place, *Le Café d'Auguste*. My Duke so loved to go there." Her voice softened. "It is a most romantic place. There is a marvelous inn about two centuries old a short distance from the café with a view from Monaco to Mentone and the sea that is unsurpassed. Auguste is truly in the shadow, only about fifty yards from the base of the ruins of the monument.

301

"If I remember," she said, "the café was originally owned by a retired Dutch sea captain who sold it two years ago to a German friend who has maintained the northern coastal touch in the kitchen. The menu is small but worth the climb up the mountain." She shook her head. "I wish I could still manage the *La Crémaillère*, but the slope of the first half-mile is just too steep for me."

V.B. grinned. "Then, Kyame, we will have a Dutch breakfast."

"Wonderful," said Kyame. "And something that was not clear in the files. How did the two men plan to transmit messages to Lord Salisbury? By enciphered telegrams, carrier pigeons, or some other way?"

"I suspect," said Sir Septemus, leaning toward Kyame, "based on other situations, that a neutral drop point was used that was serviced by Foreign Service messengers whom neither of them would know. But I don't know what the drop point in Monaco would be. It would have to be something that they both could approach without suspicion. My apologies. I should have ascertained that fact before leaving England." He sipped more of his 1846.

Kyame tapped lightly on the table. "Further, we know that Trotha, Jäger and Wagner are all connected in some way, along with the Norfolk woman." She turned to V.B. "I think I should visit the Norfolk hotel rooms tonight for a quick look around. Do you know where she stays?"

Clearly disturbed by her proposal, V.B. nodded. "Smith's has been of some limited assistance to her father, so yes. However, Kyame, that may well put you at some serious risk."

Kyame shook her head. "That is why Mr. Cleveland sent me, V.B. To take those risks on behalf of honored friends." Smiling, she leaned back in her chair to sip her 1846 as Sir Septemus reached over to gently touch her arm. "My thanks, Miss Piddington," he whispered. "His Lordship will be made aware."

Kyame saw the handsome man at the window table get up. He was quite tall. Broad shoulders, strongly built, he was a dominant presence even within Ciro's. And he was coming their way. At his approach, both Bethell and Sir Septemus immediately stood.

When he arrived at their table, the man bowed first to Muffin, Kyame noted that his smile was reflected in his eyes and was almost regal. Muffin bowed her head in acknowledgement then turned to Kyame. "Your Imperial Highness, may I have the honor of presenting Miss Kyame Piddington of America. Kyame, this is the Grand Duke Cyril of Russia. He is the nephew of Czar Nicholas II."

When Kyame extended her hand, Cyril bowed as he raised her hand to his lips, holding only the tips of her fingers. She tightened her jaw -- his thick mustache tickled.

The Grand Duke then nodded his head to the two men who resumed their chairs. "My dear friend, Muffin, Miss Piddington of America, and gentlemen, a very great pleasure. I wanted to ask if I will have the enjoyment of your company tonight at the Cercle. My success a few evenings ago, V.B., was solely due to your inspired guidance." He added quickly, awkwardly, "It is your presence that I enjoy, not just the growing piles of chips and gold."

Muffin answered, "Yes, sir, we will be there. It will be Kyame's first visit to the Casino."

"Excellent. And," he turned to focus on Kyame, "I would greatly enjoy observing how you address the wheel, Miss Piddington. You are only the second American woman I have met in my travels outside my uncle's empire ... but I must say, Mademoiselle, that your beauty is more than equal to any I have seen in any country."

Kyame blushed, feeling the heat on her cheeks. "Sir, I hope both our encounters with Fate at the wheel tonight will be victorious."

The Grand Duke's quick smile was more than friendly. "Until later then, Muffin, Miss Piddington ... gentlemen."

As all eyes in Ciro's followed the Grand Duke back to his table. Muffin laughed. "You handled Cyril very well,

Kyame, as though you meet a Grand Duke every day in Boston."

V.B. quickly added his agreement, as Sir Septemus looked carefully at her from behind his crystal glass of 1846.

Kyame could still feel the heat in her cheeks.

30

Outside Ciro's, in the dark quiet of the Casino Gardens the tall palms clicked faintly in the chill breezes with a sound like distant castanets. Sir Septemus Browne paused before he stepped up into the carriage to carry him to the Train de Luxe. He beckoned them all closer. Browne whispered, "Be aware ... A change of plans. The Baron Renfrew is arriving tomorrow evening on the yacht Syrnix of Sir Abdy of Moores, Baronet. Given the very recent irresponsible comments of the Kaiser at court, along with what appears to be happening here, the safety of the Baron becomes paramount." Leaning heavily on the carriage steps with V.B's assistance, Browne gained his seat. "Something, I fear, may be focusing on the ... Baron." He closed the door as the carriage began to move ahead.

Kyame stepped nearer to V.B. "Who is the Baron Renfrew?" she murmured.

V.B.'s jaw was tight. Glancing at Muffin, whose expression had become filled with concern, he said softly, "He is the one person we really don't want here at the moment. Baron Renfrew is the title which Albert Edward, the Prince of Wales, the next King of England always uses when he travels ... incognito. I understood that he was not coming to Monte Carlo for his annual visit for at least another three to four weeks. He has never before come in

February." He looked at Muffin. "We have unexpected complications."

Turning to Kyame's quick whispered question, he said, "If the Prince insists on the Renfrew title, then the reigning royalty of whatever country he is in is not then obligated to formally acknowledge his presence. It can simplify a situation, but unfortunately not ours."

***

"*Faites vos jeux, messieurs, faites vos jeux*. Place your bets, gentlemen, place your bets." The chief croupier swiftly examined the players jostling about the roulette table, probing, recalling, first to one side of the wheel then to the other, the fateful white ivory ball held at his fingertips.

He stood in the center at the wheel itself with the table extending to each side to accommodate the players. Of his five assistant croupiers, like their chief wearing tight blue and white Casino livery with high starched collars and without pockets, two were at each end of the table holding their long rakes at the ready to assist in positioning the wagers of the punters on the correct bet on the table while the fifth croupier standing opposite the chief acted as banker with stacks of chips, banknotes, and five-franc gold coins arrayed before him.

As he did regularly throughout his four hour shift, the chief croupier glanced upward at the oil lights over the table to gauge their brilliance. Above the tables were suspended huge lamps with green shades – much like the lights over a billiard table. There were two lights over each end of the table, along with one light centered over the wheel itself; all of which were burning with a full brilliance. Though all the chandeliers in the Casino had recently been converted to electrical lights, with all due publicity, the lights over all the gambling tables remained oil, so that in the case of an electrical failure, or a criminal gang cutting the cables, the tables and the wealth spread over them would remain fully visible.

Kyame stood behind Muffin who was seated at the table, the wheel itself only a foot or two to her right. All but two of the twenty chairs around the one roulette table in the Cercle Privé were taken by women, who had removed their hats as required by Cercle rules. A few of the men standing beyond the group of players were smoking. As several men approached the table, each extinguished their smokes on arrival.

The German banker, Johannes Wagner, sat in one chair, ignoring the play for a time. His eyes met momentarily with those of the American, yet dressed in green as if mocking him, who had evaded every Imperial effort -- thus far, he reminded himself, only thus far -- to remove her as a factor. Her ability to seemingly vanish at difficult times. He shook his head. After a moment, the American looked away to speak with the Duchess, who would also receive close Imperial attention, at a suitable time. Wagner admitted, now seeing the Piddington woman's black-haired beauty and startling green eyes only a few feet away, that he would like to arrange a conversation with this Fraulein Piddington, to explore her mind under mesmeric trance, then to further explore what was behind that modest, yet bewitching lace bodice. He glanced over his shoulder, catching the contemptuous pride of the Norfolk woman in her approach amid the glares of the women and the stares of the men.

A well-dressed and clean-shaven young man with protruding beaver-teeth sat in the other chair on the same side of the table as Kyame. The young man immediately stood when a heavily jeweled overdressed elderly lady appeared, her white hair elaborately coiffed. With no change of expression or glance at the young man, she seized the chair, assembled four stacks of thousand franc chips before her, glanced up at the chief croupier, as though measuring him; then she placed a stack of seven chips on the color red.

She sat back to evaluate the others around "her" table, her judicious eyes stopping for a moment when she encountered the intriguing green eyes of the young black-haired woman behind the impossible Duchess Clanroyden; then she continued her assessment of the evening's players. She frowned. It appeared that only the Grand Duke Cyril would provide any excitement this evening.

Wagner relinquished his chair to Lady Norfolk when she appeared behind him in her gown of laurel green with its astonishing neckline.

At Norfolk's arrival, even the chief croupier froze for a moment then repeated his call for bets. When he shook his head once, Kyame could only speculate on the man's thoughts.

The Grand Duke Cyril stood opposite Kyame, intent on making his first decision of the evening. He had smiled a greeting when Muffin seated herself and smiled again when Kyame stood behind. But now he was intent on the business of the evening. Kyame watched the Duke place 5,000 francs on 9 red. Betting *en plein*, i.e., on a single number, would return a 35 to 1 payoff. The Duke could realize 175,000 francs on his first coup! That would be, she quickly calculated, $35,000 in less than a minute! She could recall Papa's brief lecture on the seductive qualities of the wheel, "That were greater", he had warned, "than most human beings could resist."

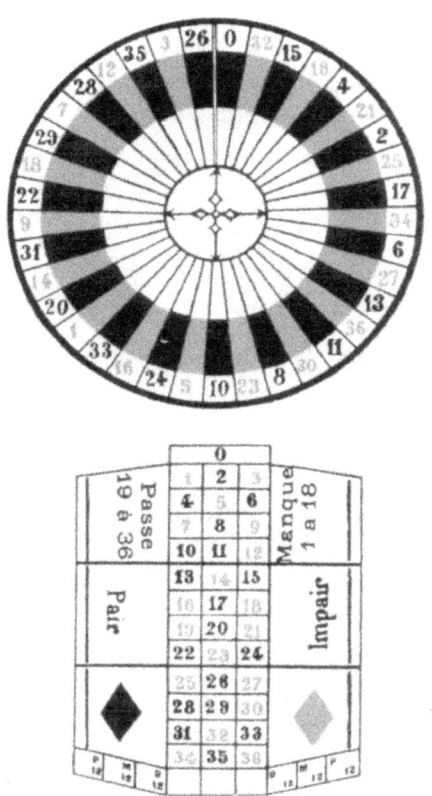

Roulette Table

Even the disheartened and disillusioned former pastor, Solomon Royale, had once quoted Shakespeare to her on the lure of the tables. "It was in *King Lear* in the third act, I recall," he had said as their train had swayed and bounced over the uneven tracks, "that Shakespeare had his character, Falconbridge, say:

Bell, book and candle shall not drive me back

When gold and silver becks me to come on.

"Bell, book and candle, Kyame, was the ultimate *final* condemnation of the soul of a sinner by the church at the time, the 17th century; consequently, even the firm promise of eternal damnation could not overcome the temptation of the tables."

***

Seizing an arm of the capstan of the wheel, the chief croupier started the wheel rotating to the left; then spun the ball to the right. A quick glance, Kyame saw the Duke do a strange thing. He turned his back to the wheel -- while everyone else, herself included, had eyes only for the little white ball. Kyame felt pressure against both her arms and her back as observers and players behind the chairs pressed forward to catch the brief flight of the white ball.

Just as the ball almost touched one of the brass diamond-shaped obstacles above the spinning wheel, she heard the croupier call out, "*Rein ne va plus*. No more bets. No more bets." All the players, but one, watching the ball seemed to breathe in at once. Striking an obstacle, the ball bounced into the air perhaps a quarter-of-an-inch, then rolled at an angle toward the passing brass frets that marked each number. As the wheel slowed its rotation, the ball rattled against a fret, then bounced across to another, then another, the ball rolled finally to rest at 14 red, two pockets away from the Duke Cyril's 9 red. With the chief croupier's call of the number and color, the Grand Duke turned around.

The long rakes of the four croupiers shot out from every corner of the table, threading their way deftly in and out of the masses of gold, notes and chips with extraordinary and most delicate manipulation. The losses were collected and transferred to the banker who separated out the different forms of currency and stuffed them into slots in the table. Once the table was cleared of losses; the winnings were then swiftly distributed by the same rakes. Instantly there was a stir about the table as arms appeared from all angles to claim their successes.

The elderly woman did not touch her winnings on red. She let the 14,000 francs ride.

The entire process required less than two minutes to settle all the wagers.

With the table settled, the Duke placed 5,000 francs on 18 red, two pockets away from his first play, then again turned his back.

The almost instant loss of $1,000 seemed nothing to the Grand Duke. Kyame had never bet more than $20, it was on red, once, and lost. She never bet more than $5 on even odds after that, the four or five times she had ever been at a roulette wheel.

Kyame marveled. There had to be over $100,000 scattered over the table. Yet the money seemed to ebb and flow in almost complete silence. Even at the three Trente-et-quarante tables that were near the far wall of the Cercle, there was little vocal reaction from the players; only a low sighing sound, like the fluttering of leaves in the wind -- the whispering of the people around the tables.

At the gambling saloons she and Papa had experienced, the cursing, laughing and taunting never stopped; but then the wheels were not always straight, the croupiers often wore guns at their hips -- and the dragging fragrance of raw rye whiskey floated over everything. Of the few times she had played the wheel, Kyame had been the only woman at the table.

But, now -- this strange restrained silence of Monte Carlo.

Kyame noted that a few of the twenty players nearest the table were trying to hide their anxiety at whatever they had just lost. The wide-eyed joy of a few of the winners was fun to watch. Then there were the others, almost expressionless, frowning as they made notes on a card, then cautiously began to place different sized stacks of chips at various places on the table. Once they lifted their hand away, they seemed to freeze in place.

The Lady Norfolk simply leaned over and pushed another stack of four chips on a number and sat back, always smiling; the German banker scarcely took his eyes from her plunging display.

Wagner felt his hands itch looking down at the Norfolk breasts almost spilling out of her gown. Baron Renfrew always wanted only large breasts on his women, the face was unimportant, as it was rumored the Baron had once stated, "It is only what you can enjoy in the dark that is of importance." He would know in the morning his direction: whether the Kaiser would authorize the disgracing, even perhaps the death of his own cousin. He would prepare Norfolk accordingly.

Muffin had not yet played. Her arsenal, as she had laughingly called it, of two stacks of thousand franc chips with a shorter stack of five thousand franc chips stood like a miniature wall in front of her. She was playing a system that V.B. had called *Avant Dernier*. This was the system that he had recommended to Kyame. After the next coup, Muffin would then play red because it would be two plays in the past. The system, with even odds of 50-50 and which paid one for one, was based on playing the color two plays in the past with flat stakes. Most other systems required quick and sometimes complex calculations of the next wager, which added to the stress of the play.

Kyame liked the flat stakes. It left more time to enjoy the experience and watch the other people. But Avant Dernier[2] could fail if you weren't careful as V.B. had

---

[2] See Appendix: Avant Dernier.

explained the procedure when you hit a certain combination of colors, or if you lost ten times in a row. V.B., just to her right behind her, seemed preoccupied with concerns other than the landing place of the white ball. She saw him glance about the room, hesitate for a moment looking at the Trente-et-quarante tables, then return to the roulette table.

The brilliantly lighted décor of the Casino was overwhelming, its soaring ceilings with gilded murals, the vast walls with the large gild-framed paintings, all of which were classical landscapes, three huge crystal chandeliers, even in the *Salle de Jeux*, the public rooms with its four roulette tables and two Trente-et-quarante tables.

They had entered through the Atrium, a huge hall with its galleries, eight black onyx columns (only one of which, V.B. had whispered, was genuine onyx) and tessellated floors, its gleaming lights in the roof, and its little groups of extravagantly dressed people dotted here and there. Locals were not allowed entrance to the gambling halls, thus each player had to have their names recorded, then received their entrance tickets at the vestiaire.

Kyame had seen to the right as they approached the great hall that lay ahead, a billiards room, a reading room, and a large concert room. Only two or three men were seated in the reading room with newspapers, drinks at their elbows; while four were aggressively playing billiards throwing banknotes on the table after each shot.

Then, the Casino itself; an enormous salon of great height with a polished parquet floor. It resembled an immense ballroom of some royal palace. Even the word 'regal' wasn't adequate. Beyond this huge salon she saw, under an immense archway, there was another even larger hall crossing it at right angles, and beyond that still another. It was beyond imagination.

Kyame followed as V.B and Muffin, who, frequently nodding to acquaintances, walked toward the white carpeted stairs up to the Cercle Privé, to experience there even more elaborate chandeliers and with only four tables, there was a circulating crowd of women in dazzling gowns and sharply dressed men. Away from the tables there was more animation. Kyame heard the muffled mélange of active conversations from the arched entrance to the Cercle's bar.

But there were no windows, anywhere. No ready reference to time. No outside distractions from the tables.

***

"Now, Kyame, said Muffin, "your chance to play."

Kyame reached around Muffin to place two one thousand franc chips on red, next to the Duchess's four one thousand franc chips.

With her money in play, Kyame watched the white ball with enhanced interest. She felt a sharp thrill with the croupier's announcement.

317

"Seize rouge … sixteen red."

V.B.'s system worked the first time! She turned to share her joy to see V.B. accept a slip of paper from one of the many servants in blue plush knee-breeches and white silk stockings that circulated through the hall. When he looked up at her, after whispering to Muffin to leave her wager in place, Kyame stepped away from the table.

"Norfolk is in room 414 at the Grand Hotel St. James," whispered V.B., "The hotel was opened only three months ago. She has had lodgings there for two months. It is to the East of the Casino, about a ten to fifteen minute walk away. Almost opposite the Hotel de Paris, behind the Café de Paris."

"I'll stay at the wheel for a few minutes more," said Kyame softly, "then Muffin and I will retire to the ladies room, at which point I will leave. Is there a back stairs or must I exit out front?"

"I will have a reliable guide waiting near in the hall leading to the ladies room. His name is Cecil … and there he is near the bar entrance."

Kyame saw a uniformed servant in blue and white with reddish hair, then looked away. She raised her voice. "My first play using your system, V.B. It was a winner!"

He smiled. "I'm always glad to hear that, but you must still be very disciplined in your decisions." He escorted her back to Muffin, then stepped back.

She had won again while away, so following V. B.'s system, Kyame moved her stack of four chips to black, beside Muffin's eight. Kyame smiled as she recalled the extraordinary glazed porcelain portrait hanging in Dr. Mar-Tan's elegant home in New York of Chi Kung, the Chinese god of gambling; who, she reflected, must have had a few good systems of his own. Mar-Tan had assured her that Chi Kung was a reliable presence to know.

Kyame wished she had time for a reconnaissance of Room 414, but she would deal with whatever she found. After winning again, the thrill was muted compared to what now lay ahead of her. She bent over to move her chips back to red, whispering her plan to Muffin as she did. They both had won again.

Muffin removed her chips and Kyame's, signaled that she wanted them cashed in, then putting her cane in place, Muffin stood. She smiled when the Grand Duke tossed a finger toward their winnings, smiled and bowed his head.

Muffin affected a painful limp as she moved with Kyame at her shoulder away from the table, as V.B. moved closer to the table to begin his play.

***

Wagner watched the two women leave the table, the Countess apparently having some difficulty with her bad leg. He caught the eye of one of the servants hovering near

319

the table. He brushed his up-swept mustaches and turned back to Norfolk and her steady losses. The Imperial time had arrived.

***

Another man, young, dark-haired and well-dressed at one of the Trente-et-quarante tables also watched the two women walk toward the arched hallway. Looking up from his newspaper in the reading room, he had just caught sight of the three of them pass. He had immediately dropped the paper to follow them.

The older appeared *malade imaginaire* – that she was faking distress. When he had observed the Duchess, whom he now recognized, climb the stairs and enter the Cercle, she had walked with graceful purpose, her cane scarcely necessary.

His face was tight, but not with indecision. He turned back to cash in his chips. Pausing to give the women more distance, he started after them, maintaining a cautious separation. He couldn't help that his heart had started to pound.

31

Nearing the end of his ten hour watch moving about on the parquet floor, jumping to respond to any request of Cercle clientele, Josef Schmidt had reached his customary state of numb boredom. Yes, he knew and understood his real role, but boredom nevertheless. Handsome, with a carefully trimmed brown mustache, but dressed like a French Christmas doll, he had to cautiously vent his frustration standing about the Cercle Privé watching overdressed *Zocker*, punters, throw more money away in five minutes on the tables than he could earn in a year.

He needed more, cash, stature, *and* freedom. The thoughts always came again at the end of each shift. Ten hours of subservience that only allowed him to eat regularly -- and dream.

Schmidt shifted and moved again. He had to keep moving or draw uncomfortable attention from one of the Chef de Partie in their black frock coats. There were many, usually unspoken, graphic names for the watchers in black frock coats. Schmidt pressed back a laugh. One of the other French Christmas dolls had referred to them this morning as *chèvres noires et blanches*, black and white goats. All they needed, the man had smirked, were bells around their necks; they already had the horns.

A bare thirty minutes to go until he could try to be himself. But, he reflected looking attentively about the glamorous hall as a well-trained French Christmas doll should, there had been the seductive promises from the banker, Herr Wagner. There was the one way, what his role really was, that had paid off very well, three times in fact for him over the past two months. Fifteen thousand francs to implement, he smirked, an Imperial action. He moved away from the Trente-et-quarante tables back toward the roulette wheel, as other French dolls moved about in other areas of the hall -- ignoring as he went, the attempts of two bulky money-spinners to attract his attention to run some utterly foolish, degrading errand for ...

Mein Gott! Herr Wagner's signal. Here? In the Casino?

His juices surging, Josef Schmidt walked primly toward the end of the roulette table where Herr Wagner stood. As he approached, Schmidt passed a stylish man cursing his losses vehemently in the soft slurring patois of southern France. Johannes Wagner stepped back to shift clear of the elbowing yet silent crowd who immediately moved to absorb his absence -- instantly ignoring the two men as one began to speak.

***

As Muffin continued to the ladies lounge, Cecil led Kyame away to a -- blank wall. Golden pilasters ran down each side of a large gild-framed portrait of a nymph peeking around a rock with a group of centaurs galloping in the distance. Cecil put his fingers against a large golden swirl on the frame and pushed. The painting swung back, he stepped in beckoning Kyame to follow.

Quickly gathering her skirts close about her, Kyame stepped sideways into the darkness while Cecil quickly pushed the frame back in place.

"There are panels and concealed corridors all over the Casino, Miss Piddington, for security. A moment while I light a lamp."

She heard a scraping; a small flame appeared then a larger one inside a square lamp that lit Cecil's smiling face.

"Please follow me. Be very careful with your skirts as they may catch on the rough walls. We will be outside the Casino in about five minutes. The Hotel de Paris will be about thirty yards to your left."

Tightening her grip on her flowing skirts as she lifted them, Kyame followed as closely as she could manage. She struggled to avoid sneezing as their shuffling shoes began to raise dust.

"If you need to sneeze, it is all right. The walls are quite thick along this corridor."

She sneezed once, then twice. "I'm all right now."

"Watch the steps here. There are three of them." Cecil held the lamp down to allow her to see them.

A few more feet, Kyame began to feel the air start to become cooler. A moment then Cecil said, "We must stop here. I need to look through a peekhole just ahead to check if I can open the outside door. Once you move through the door you will be outside the building. Don't look back; just keep moving down the walkway to the light at the bottom. You will see the hotel."

"My thanks, Cecil," she murmured. "For all your help."

"Helping a beautiful lady is never trouble, Miss Piddington. Get ready, please." He stepped away, holding the lamp up. Kyame could see a small wooden block in the wall. Cecil opened it, shifting to look out first to one side then to the other, then stepped back.

"Clear." He looked back at her. "Good luck," as he pulled the door open.

***

Stepping from the hidden dark corridor, Josef Schmidt dropped the black scarf over her head and down around her throat, jammed his knee in her back and jerked back hard. The one-legged Duchess went over easily as he looped his garrote once again around her throat then pulled the two ends apart as hard as he could before she could gasp. No sound, Wagner had commanded; leave the body

324

where it can be easily found. Twenty thousand francs for this action, tomorrow morning at his office.

Struggling on the floor, Muffin's eye bulged out as she tore frantically at the silken noose. Black and odd colored forms floated before her as the walls faded...

Josef Schmidt never heard or saw the young man who appeared suddenly behind him. A hard fist smashed into his jaw then another straight into his face breaking his nose and jaw. Schmidt dropped silently to the parquet. With the garrote quickly unwrapped, after ensuring the Duchess was breathing, the young man drove the metal point of a black patent leather shoe hard into Schmidt's throat to crush his windpipe and his life. Schmidt was only a tool who carried no information worth saving. The young man kicked into his throat again.

He carried the still barely conscious Duchess around the corner to the velvet couches along the entrance to the ladies lounge. He signaled to one of the maids who ran toward him to help.

"Madame has fainted. She needs the attention of a doctor immediately," he said in fluent Parisian French. The maid ran to a wall panel, threw it open and pressed the red button inside.

***

Wagner, back in his position behind Lady Norfolk, could not feel any of the electricity of the gambling crowd.

His own gamble was more interesting. Then, two men, one with a medical bag appeared from one arched doorway walking rapidly through another toward the ladies lounge. Gut! An attack on a Duchess within the Casino itself would drive many of the money-spinners away from Monte Carlo.

Even better! Wagner saw the head of Casino Security with two of his men also appear and stride rapidly toward the ladies lounge. He turned back to the table with the seductive movements of the white ball. A successful evening was assured.

***

The physician quietly assured her that her throat did not appear to have any permanent damage but speaking would be difficult for a day or two. At the beckoning of someone Muffin could not see, the doctor withdrew.

V.B. knelt beside the couch where Muffin lay, her coloring and breathing returning to normal, though his throat was marked with deep red blotches. "I could not see the man, V.B. I was alone in the hallway just passing that corridor over there, when the assassin struck, and the young man, thank God, appeared out of thin air as I lost consciousness. Where is he? I need to thank him. He saved my life."

With V.B.'s help, she pulled herself to a sitting position in the couch, then plucked at the sleeves of her gown to straighten them. A maid quickly rearranged the cushions.

Muffin shook her head as she just recovered a lost thought. "Kyame, V.B., my God!" Muffin's strained voice shook. "Is she all right? Where is she?"

"Cecil sent her on her way. She should be leaving the hotel in her 'prowler' outfit, as she called it, about now."

Her hands clinched into fists, Muffin leaned back into the cushions with tears appearing in her eyes. "Kyame must be all right, V.B. She ... *just has to be*."

"I am sure Kyame is a cautious young woman, but I share your concern just the same. But an interesting thing, Muffin, that Monsieur Pariseau revealed to me a few moments ago. He could not give me your protector's name, but he said that he was puzzled when the young man asked about Kyame ... *by name*."

As V.B. stood, Lucien Pariseau, Director of Security, stepped to his side. "Duchess, you appear to be recovering. *Louange à Dieu*! Praise God. I deeply regret that, for certain reasons, I am unable to reveal to you the name of your guardian. But perhaps sometime in the future." He frowned. "But I can give you the name of your attacker, who was killed. He is, to our shame, an employee of the Casino. Josef Schmidt, who has been working as one of the liveried servants in the Cercle for two years, who has caused no trouble at all, until this moment. We will investigate vigorously with the cooperation of the police, naturally, but I have no inkling as yet as to his motive for such an attack… and in the Casino itself!"

Muffin acknowledged Pariseau, then, "By name, V.B.? But Kyame knows no one in Monaco."

V.B. shrugged, shook his head. "I hesitate, even knowing your courage, Muffin, to suggest this. Do you feel well enough to return to the tables as if nothing has happened for perhaps twenty minutes or so, then we leave to return you home?" Turning to Pariseau, he continued. "And, Monsieur le Director, can you hold off your investigation of Schmidt for a few days to avoid any chance of news of this crime becoming public? I am aware that bodies can be removed from the Casino without being seen, and Monsieur Blanc has influence with all the local newspapers; but I am concerned about a visitor sending the story to London or Paris." He turned back to Muffin. "Your attack fits their pattern. Not publicizing it will frustrate them further until we understand more clearly what the stakes are. Kyame may be able to help us tonight."

In answer, Muffin swung her legs around, pointed at her cane leaning against the other end of the couch, which the maid immediately handed to her. Using both hands, Muffin leaned heavily on the cane and stood, with Pariseau reaching out to her shoulder to steady her. She took a deep breath then grinned, her voice breaking, "I could always do a half-hour for the right audience. But," she added after a moment, "not for much longer … at least not tonight."

The Duchess smiled at Pariseau. "Your cooperation would be a great help, sir. Should His Serene Highness express any concern, please ask Prince Albert call on me directly."

At the invocation of Albert's name, Pariseau immediately bowed his head. "As you request Duchess. I will so inform the Director-General."

***

With growing impatience, Wagner glanced up from the latest losses by Norfolk. His jaw dropped. Mein Gott! The Duchess Clanroyden was walking toward the roulette table on the arm of Bethell! Where was Schmidt?

32

Kyame looked up at the fourth floor, three rows of windows above her. It was the top floor. The Grand Hotel St. James had a "Parisian roof garden", according to its advertising, crowning its "avant-garde establishment". Standing, invisible, blending with the trunk of a tree, she could just see the elaborate white wrought-iron fencing about the edge of the roof between the branches. The St. James was surrounded by dark gardens and palm trees silhouetted against the slim moon, with meandering silvery walkways.

Moving with quick careful steps, in a moment Kyame came up against the hotel wall. The lower wall was smoother than the Hermitage and, she estimated, would require a six-foot ladder for her to reach the lowest usable ridge.

She must do the work inside.

Changed into her prowling outfit with her maid's small hat, Kyame had left through the workmen's entrance at the rear of the Hotel de Paris. No one noticed her as she walked down the back stairs, unbolted the door and, using her lock picks silently relocked from the outside. Walking with her head down as though deferring to the greater social status of the few people she passed, and staying just outside the great circle of light from the Casino and Ciro's, and other smaller cafés, it took fifteen minutes to walk to the St. James gardens, much as V.B. had estimated. She smiled at recalling V.B.'s swift reminder of how Europe counted floors as against the American count. The ground floor was floor 1 in Europe, while floor 1 American would be floor 2 European. Kyame had assured him that she was aware of the difference.

The small empty lobby of the St. James, though attractive in polished woods and gold trim, could not compare with even a corner of that of the Hotel de Paris. Dressed plainly in black and carrying a worn black cloth satchel, she resembled a private maid of one of the titled guests at the hotel returning from her late supper. Her head bowed with her searching green eyes concealed behind heavy-rimmed glasses, Kyame, observing no one at the registration or at the concierge desks, immediately diverted to walk rapidly to the main stairway. The St. James had no lifting rooms, or elevators as some people now called them, only the stairs. Grasping her coat, she took the stairs two at time. Reaching the second floor, she walked toward the end of the dimly lit corridor to continue up to the top floor using the servant's side stairs. Within another five minutes Kyame was walking the corridor looking for 414. How long Norfolk and Wagner would remain at the Casino she couldn't guess, and so gave herself a maximum of twenty minutes to search and get out of the room. She did not want a confrontation now, there was too much yet to understand.

Kyame knocked on the door preparing to spin a humble story of a maid at the wrong door, but no answer. She knocked again, took a breath, then quickly extracted her leather case from the coat pocket, selected the picks and went to work. After three minutes, Kyame muttered a curse as her lock picks failed again. A new German make of lock that she had not encountered before. V.B. had explained that the hotel was new. If there had been time, she could have tried the locks earlier in the day before actually having to open any doors. The locks at the Hotel de Paris were older and easy.

Though J. W. Cadwell had warned, with some emphasis, that if she ever needed to touch up her picks with a file while working at a lock -- *don't*. Stop and find another way in. But Kyame began to file one of the picks to narrow the probe. Another minute -- another. Now try it. Kyame bit her lip. There was something blocking her picks.

Pocketing her leather case of picks, Kyame realized she had to go outside, try to enter the room from the wide balcony that every room on that floor had. The outside lock was unlikely to be as tough as the inside. And, if she had a quick moment, she would look at the door lock from the inside. Picking up her skirts, Kyame ran to the French doors at the end of the hallway and to the balcony beyond.

Standing on the balcony, Kyame shook her head. The memory of the empty house dream on the ship suddenly hit her mind. No, she shook her head again, then quickly dropped her coat on the tiled floor and her black skirt, immediately feeling the chill Mistral winds as they grew in strength. The narrow black trousers she wore under the skirt were always a part of her prowler outfit. Her pouch of tools was belted on one hip, with a throwing knife on the other. The yellow ruhmal was tucked behind her belt. She slipped the derringer into one pocket. Thin coarse-finished black canvas gloves would protect her hands and aid her grip. Kyame climbed up, balancing on the edge of the balcony railing, reached up to a ledge above and began to pull herself to the roof.

The empty dusty house would never return.

It was enough. Tonight at the wheel was to be a major coup, a major step forward to match the Kaiser's schedule, but instead it had proven to be a miserable failure. The Duchess was effervescent upon her return to the table with Bethell at her side. She began to win immediately. The Piddington woman was somewhere else and would rejoin them within a few minutes, he overheard.

Johannes Wagner had had enough. He whispered a mesmeric command in Norfolk's ear. The woman stopped as she was mechanically pushing yet another pile of chips toward the numbers. Wagner reached out, scooped up all of the remaining chips and dropped them in his pocket. A moment, then the two of them began to walk back toward the cloak room in the Atrium. There was work to do in the Norfolk room, and then other work.

***

In five minutes, lowering herself from the edge of the roof, her fingers and toes pressed into the rows of bricks, Kyame was at the lock of the French doors at the balcony of 414. A moment, a satisfying click, she was in. The whole change in plan had cost her possibly fifteen minutes which cut her time in the room to no more than fifteen, though ten would be safer.

Nothing in the papers on the desk, and the drawers of the desk were empty. The undersides of the drawers were also a blank. The dresser was full, as though Norfolk had bought out a dress shop. Nothing. Nothing on the undersides of the dresser drawers either. The dressing table had the usual lotions and makeup, nothing underneath. The closets were overwhelming. Nothing among the twelve pairs of shoes, nor in the two shoe boxes. No time to search each gown, but unlikely to have anything. Closing the closet doors behind her, Kyame took a deep breath, searching the darkened room with her eyes. Where else would she ...?

Nothing between the mattresses.

Nothing in the row of books on the shelf near the bed.

Kyame stopped. Steps approaching. She moved back to the French doors -- the steps receding. Norfolk was arrogant about her beauty and displaying her bust. Kyame turned back to the dressing table and looked behind the mirror. An unmarked envelope. Kyame lit the small candle from her pouch. Inside were four yellow telegraph sheets:

renfrew arrival feb 21 Signed W

gottrau in place. contacted albert. Dated January 28

A scrawled note with no date: k requires earlier date for predator – need... A portion of the note was torn away.

A marked up enciphered telegram dated Feb 4: n – ebing visit two days. confirm

Steps again. A key into the lock!

The telegrams memorized, Kyame stuffed the envelope behind the mirror, and was behind the curtains at the French doors in two quick steps. A quick glance back at the French doors. One was ajar! The doors had been locked. Definite evidence that someone had been in the room. Kyame bit her lip. Could cause some kind of trouble.

She heard the door firmly closed, the bolt thrown. Still no light. A man grunted, there was ripping of cloth, a woman's sudden cry of alarm that was instantly muffled. Some jumbled sounds, some kind of struggle, steps and then a firm thud on the bed. The man snapped: "Shut up!" The sound of a hard slap. When the bed began to rock rhythmically Kyame, kneeling down, cautiously peeked around the base of the curtain to see Wagner's face pressed hard against the Norfolk neck.

Her lips parted in a half-smile as Kyame recalled Papa's red face trying to explain the sounds and poundings on the wall from the building that shared a wall with their boarding house in Kansas City. The building next door was a brothel, he had explained. Though just thirteen at the time, Kyame had already learned what a brothel was. She had just never directly observed one in action before.

335

Kyame stood, reached out, pushed the French door closed -- gently allowed the lock to slide silently home, then withdrew back into the darkness behind the curtain.

And waited.

33

New Palace

Berlin

February 19, 1896

Wrapped in a fur-lined red leather robe embossed with the Imperial insignia, Wilhelm looked up from reading Mahan by the fire as the liveried servant approached. There was a standing Imperial order that any communications from the south were to be delivered directly to him without delay.

"My pardon, Your Majesty. An urgent telegram from the south." He held out a yellow envelope with two red stripes across it. Once the Kaiser had the envelope, the servant bowed and backed away, then turned to retreat smartly to a position about ten feet away to await an answer if there was to be one.

The cipher required three minutes work. Wilhelm read:

Renfrew in two nights. His humiliation or death would bring death of the Casino.

His cousin, Albert Edward, on his annual whoring and money throwing trip to the South of France -- though it was very early for him this year. His boredom waiting to be king must have gotten the best of him. Wilhelm was still smarting from the humiliation of his losses from that Russian woman's stupid roulette system. He would burn the Casino to the ground today if he had the option.

Tod odor Beschämung. Death or degradation/shame. But the Casino must be shut down to force Albert to accept without condition Germany's Imperial offer of financial support, in return for control of all Monaco harbors while building a large coaling station on-shore with access to the railroad. The coaling station would allow the permanent presence of the steam-driven Kaiserliche Marine in the Mediterranean within one day's sail at flank speed of the Suez Canal. Each Predator could be anchored at Monaco, once launched and equipped, within fifteen days or less from the Ebing shipyard.

Sea power is not just ships, as Mahan taught so plainly again and again. A well-positioned naval presence, even without battleships, would cause hesitation in any British strategic decision. Von Tirpitz's warning against needlessly provoking the Royal Navy, possibly even creating another Copenhagen situation, had been dismissed from

Wilhelm's mind since Albert's intolerable rejection of his offer, his *personal* offer, of an alliance during Albert's last visit on the Hohenzollern II.

A senior member of the Kaiser's staff, posing as a French-speaking Swiss financier from Geneva, Henry Gottrau, had been in Monaco for a month, and had already met Prince Albert socially. By affecting a convincing interest in ocean currents, a position which had required several days careful study before departure, Gottrau had readily become a welcome guest at the Prince's table.

Gottrau, actually the Count Karl Leopold von Wolf, had full authority to sign on the Kaiser's behalf the secret documents he carried that were ready for Albert's signature, and to transfer any funds necessary from Wagner's bank for Albert's immediate use.

According to Wilhelm's marine engineers, it would require a month to complete dredging out the Harbor of Hercules to accommodate the draft of two fully equipped heavy cruisers. The Predators could dock in the Harbor now. The Harbor, however, could never accommodate a battleship, but could still act as a coaling station for one. Wilhelm had a dredge positioned off-shore near Tangier while a German engineering group discussed harbor expansion there. The dredge could be in the Harbor of Hercules within three days and at work on the fourth.

But for royal cousin Albert Edward, the Prince of Wales, who had had so little time and regard for him at the last Royal Navy Regatta?

It took only a moment to encipher. Wilhelm beckoned the servant, returned the red-striped yellow envelope with its security warning. "Immediate dispatch," ordered the Kaiser. The message was simple: 'tod renfrew' with the Kaiser's very private mark: 'dergrosse'.

***

"Kyame has been gone now for over an hour, V.B. ... an hour. My God, what can we do?" Upon their return to the Villa de Poésie, Muffin's personal maid had gently applied a lotion to her bruised throat, then wrapped a thin white cotton cloth around it to protect the application and withdrew.

He turned from his pacing. "We wait, dear Muffin, we can only wait." Victor Bethell was still disturbed by Muffin's nameless rescuer, who somehow knew Kyame's name. They didn't need any more mysteries. "Kyame is a most impressive young woman who would not be here did not the American president have confidence in her. But I do share your concern. She is alone and … for now … beyond our aid."

***

Wagner's deep rumbling slumber continued, but Kyame heard the springs of the bed. Norfolk was moving. Kyame knelt down to pull the edge of the curtain back an inch. Norfolk lit a small oil lamp on her dressing table. She was naked, with red marks on her breasts and throat. She took a dressing gown from the closet, wrapped it tightly about her, then, with a quick glance at Wagner's form lost in the blankets, she went to his suit coat across the back of a chair. Norfolk quickly rummaged through all of the pockets, then pulled out his wallet, removed some currency, then a slip of paper. The money she shoved into a pocket in her dressing gown, as she then reached behind the dressing table mirror to extract the envelope. A few seconds, the slip of paper she pushed into the envelope and the envelope replaced. She sat at the dressing table to begin to brush her hair.

A deep cough, another and Wagner sat up. For a moment he looked around as if remembering something, then eased himself off the bed to disappear into the bathroom without closing the door. The sound of urination and a flush, he returned and began dressing as Norfolk continued to brush her hair, over and over again.

341

Kyame recognized the mechanical action. Norfolk was in a complex mesmeric trance of some sort. She had moved normally in leaving the bed, but once Wagner was up and awake, the trance gripped her mind.

Once dressed, he lit a large lamp. Wagner stood behind Norfolk and spoke in a soft quiet voice, "Stop and listen carefully, my dear woman." His tone was gentle. She instantly dropped the brush on the table, placed her hands in her lap, and sat very straight. "We are going to take another of those trips you love so much. To the land where you rule as a queen should rule." He reached around placing his fingers gently on Norfolk's forehead, as Kyame watched in the mirror, stroking lightly across her eyebrows. He lifted his fingers, and pressed his thumbs across her eyebrows, "Sleep, my dear, there is nothing to fear. No one can touch or harm you."

Kyame watched her eyes close. Norfolk had been in earlier trances -- that was obvious. Wagner's induction was very quick.

"Now, upon meeting the Baron Renfrew tomorrow night, you will eagerly beguile him as you know so well and will do whatever he wishes. Is that understood? Anything."

Norfolk nodded. "Yes, my lord." Her voice was quietly happy, accepting her direction.

"You will see Konstanze, your close friend, who will always be near you. You will treat her as your personal maid who must accompany you. Konstanze will be carrying a valise of very becoming lingerie in the Baron's favorite colors that you will change into as the Baron prepares himself.

"Now," Wagner emphasized, "these commands come to you by my voice only, but you *will obey* Konstanze's voice when you hear it. Understood?"

"Yes, my lord. Konstanze ... Konstanze's voice. I will obey."

Kyame blinked and shook her head. Wagner was very good. She had caught herself drifting toward a trance condition.

Wagner put on his suit coat, finally adjusting his black cloak over his shoulders, as Norfolk continued to sit motionless at the mirror. "You will awake from your marvelous trip, eager to serve your lord whose name you do not know. You will awake when you hear this door close, you will return to bed to sleep, to sleep deeply, to be fresh for the coming of the Baron. Understood?"

"I understand, my lord."

343

"You will obey the orders you have received when you hear me clap my hands twice, like this." The two claps were rhythmic, one, then the second. "Now I leave you. Your slumber will be untroubled as though floating on the clouds of the sky." His voice had changed, lighter, even joyous.

"Yes, my lord."

Kyame heard the door open, then close. She pulled the curtain back, Norfolk was now in the mesmeric suggestion and would not see her.

Norfolk rose to return to bed.

How would Konstanze address Norfolk?

Kyame walked to stand behind the woman. "Lady Norfolk, you will pause at my voice," said Kyame, gently and plainly. She would not attempt a German accent.

Norfolk took another step, another, then hesitated as if not being sure.

"Good, Lady Norfolk, you are correct. Listen to my voice as you have listened to the words of your lord. Will you do that?"

Norfolk still hesitated.

Kyame needed something to connect, to provide reassurance. "I need to know where to place my valise."

"Yes, I will listen."

"Good. When you hear my voice, you will obey me as you would obey your lord. When I clap my hands like this" – two quick claps – "you will be released from all your lord's commands as he wished. Understood."

"Yes, Konstanze, I understand."

"Turn and look at me."

Norfolk turned. There was no reaction on her face.

"You will not recall ever seeing me before. If I clap my hands three quick times, like this ... I will disappear from your vision. Understood?"

"Yes, Konstanze, I understand."

"Now go to your slumbers as your lord directed; slumbers as though floating on the clouds."

Norfolk turned back to the bed, lifted the silken comforters and slid under them. Her eyes closed immediately.

Kyame extinguished the one lamp, then memorized Wagner's small paper that Norfolk had stuffed into the envelope behind the mirror. It was coded in some way, signed W. She blew out the small oil lamp on the dressing table. Kyame was on the balcony and climbing back to the roof in only seconds.

Next time she would understand the locks.

34

"Your Grace, Miss Piddington has arrived." The servant stepped back as Kyame entered the room still dressed in prowling black with the maid's cap. She had walked the few minutes to the cab stand near the Metropole Hotel to get completely clear of the St. James. The cabby, seeing only a maid, would not take her without payment in advance.

As Muffin struggled with her cane and V.B.'s help to stand quickly, Kyame rushed forward. "Muffin, you've been hurt!" She embraced the happily sobbing Duchess. Her own eyes were becoming moist. She felt V.B.'s hand rest gently on her shoulder. Only Papa had ever made her feel this wanted before -- and --

"Welcome home, Kyame. You've been missed ... in case you hadn't noticed," he laughed.

Once Muffin settled back on the couch, she insisted Kyame sit close beside her, then said to the servant who was smiling, "Please bring the best champagne in the cellar. I want to celebrate properly."

V.B. explained the white cloth around Muffin's throat and her nameless protector. "And Kyame, that nameless young man asked about you *by name*," said V.B.

"By name?" Kyame was astonished and instantly uneasy. "But I know no one in Monaco, except this room, or all of Europe for that matter … well, except for the Prime Minister of England. How could he be in the Casino without having given Security his name?"

"That is a clear point," said Bethell. "I will make some inquiries tomorrow, but I doubt anything will come of it. He seems to occupy some unnamed official capacity. Perhaps, we will meet him again.

"But come, Kyame, tell us of your adventure."

"I will need a piece of paper," she said. Muffin drew a small pad and pencil from a drawer in the end-table beside her. Before Kyame could write, the liveried servant returned with a dusty bottle and three crystal flutes on a silver tray. He held the tray before Muffin for her approval. When she nodded, he poured into the flutes. Bowing again, he served Muffin, then Kyame and finally V.B. Placing the tray and bottle on the end-table he quietly withdrew.

The painted white date on the dusty black bottle was 1829. "My heavens, Muffin, it says 1829! It is real?" Kyame had never heard of any wine from 1829.

The Duchess laughed, raising her glass. "It is very real, dear Kyame. It is the only wine worthy of celebrating your safe return to this, your home on the sea." Their glasses rang with a clear rich tone. "Please always be safe."

The flavor and aroma was indescribable, like nothing Kyame had ever encountered before. A unique richness -- an essence that just floated over her tongue. She smiled. Here was something else that would be too easy to get used to. "My deepest thanks, Muffin... and V.B., for caring so" – Kyame pursed her lips, to hold back tears – "for caring so." Then the tears ran down her cheeks anyway. She felt Muffin's arm around her shoulders.

"I apologize for my messy response to such a wonderful toast." Kyame sniffed and wiped her eyes with V.B.'s proffered handkerchief. "Only Papa has ever made me feel this special before."

"Now," Bethell said, settling back into his chair, "tell us of your adventure."

Taking another deep swallow of 1829, Kyame quickly wrote out the lines she had memorized from Norfolk's envelope. "The last one is clearly coded and may be in German. But I think that at least one word is English. Renfrew."

The lines were:

renfrew arrival feb 21 Signed W

gottrau in place. contacted albert. Dated January 28

A scrawled note with no date: k requires earlier date for predator – need...   A portion of the note was torn away.

A marked up deciphered telegram dated Feb 4: n – ebing visit two days. Confirm

An enciphered telegram of only two words.

Kyame described her experiences, mentioning in passing her trouble with the locks. "I will figure out that miserable lock for all the trouble it caused me."

"Lady Norfolk is mesmerized, like Trilby? Wagner is that skillful, a virtual Svengali?" Bethell shook his head. "He becomes more lethal with each discovery."

"Yes" said Kyame. "I even found myself slipping a bit listening to him. It appears that he has entranced Norfolk several times. His induction of her was so brief that she had to have been under some earlier suggestion.

"I have modified some of his commands. I could not do more without possibly triggering some challenging reaction from the woman … but I can, for at least a day or two, take control of Norfolk if need be. It is difficult to estimate how long a mesmeric suggestion will continue to hold a subject. An hour, a day or even only a few minutes. Clearly, Wagner would know Norfolk's limitations.

"Konstanze Jäger will be acting as Norfolk's maid and carrying a valise." Kyame's jaw tightened, then she said, "The valise may be carrying killing tools. Lady Norfolk is now conditioned to take direction directly from Jäger if Wagner is not present."

Muffin frowned. "You *modified* Wagner's mesmeric commands? That suggests that you are a mesmerist yourself, Kyame." Her sidelong glance was questioning.

Kyame nodded. "I was taught by the greatest mesmerist in America, and the closest friend of Papa and me, J.W. Cadwell. J.W. was a strict mentor who very clearly helped me establish my boundaries. I have had reasonably good success in a number of situations, but enough failures to always be careful. Lord Salisbury, by the way, was an excellent subject."

V.B.'s flute was halfway to his lips when his mouth dropped open. "You've mesmerized the Prime Minister?" Dumbfounded, he looked at Muffin who began to laugh softly.

"Yes," Kyame said, with a small smile. "It was apparent in our brief meeting that His Lordship had a terrible toothache, so I offered to help. His associates were a bit apprehensive, as they should have been, but he trusted me … and I was able to remove his pain. For how long I don't know, but possibly even a day." She sipped the champagne again. "Have you encountered a man named Gottrau, V.B.? According to one of the notes, he is a part of all this, in some way. And, he apparently has had direct contact with Prince Albert."

V.B. felt the eyes of the two women on him as he searched his memory. Gottrau. Yes, Henry Gottrau, a Swiss

351

financier, as he was called, but actually he seemed to know too little of finance according to Lord Rosslyn, who had met him at a reception at the Palace. Rosslyn actually thought him a fake. Bethell had found that Rosslyn's judgments regarding people were generally sound -- unlike his roulette systems.

"Yes, yes. Henry Gottrau first appeared in Monaco about a month ago. His money is being held in Wagner's hands, according to what I heard. He has had one or two routine funds transfers through Smith's but nothing of any notice. I have never met him, but in just the last couple of weeks he has had three or four invitations to the Princier Palace. Apparently he shares Albert's passion for the ocean. But now, from this message, we know he is a concealed member of the German Imperial presence, and very likely not who or what he seems to be." He explained Rosslyn's reservations regarding the man.

"And Ebing. What might that be?" asked Kyame.

"A shipyard in northern Germany. A friend bought a yacht that had been built there," said Muffin. "He was most impressed with the workmanship."

"The agents Blenkiron and Brand were in the north. Maybe it was at Ebing?" said -Kyame. "What else do they build, other than yachts? And," she paused. "And I wonder what N is … and predator. What could that be?"

V.B. twisted his empty flute at his fingers. "I will telegraph London tonight for more information on Ebing, and give His Lordship a brief update of how we see things developing." He stood and placed his flute on the silver tray. "Unfortunately, we cannot warn Baron Renfrew prior to his arrival, but I will make some contacts to ensure that you, Kyame, and I will be included in the reception tomorrow evening.

"We do know now with some certainty that Johannes Wagner is the leader of a group of Imperial agents or whatever, including Josef Schmidt, Muffin's attacker, and very likely Henry Gottrau." He noted the time on the stately tall clock in the corner. "I believe, after tonight's experiences, some good rest is needed.

"I will pick you up at eight o'clock tomorrow, Kyame, for our breakfast and investigation at La Turbie." As the two women stood, Kyame helping Muffin, Bethell said, "I would also recommend that you keep your derringer within easy reach, Kyame. If they will strike at Muffin in the very heart of the Casino, they may try again at you at the Paris. I will be armed for our trip tomorrow."

***

Konstanze Jäger nodded as Johannes Wagner carefully explained the arrangements for the reception for the Baron Renfrew. Though her features remained plain and unmoving, her heart began to beat more rapidly, even eagerly. To cut the throat of the future king of England --

how satisfying. And also the new promises to her from Herr Wagner to acknowledge her success in bending the Chef de Parte. All of the 2,000 fake chips would be in the Casino secure inventory within two day. A most satisfying result.

But there still remained the American -- the American bitch in green -- the nuisance, she sneered. "Ein Belästigung!" she snapped out loud. A pest!

-

35

Standing under the peaked green roof of the diminutive Gare La Turbie which provided some shade from the morning sun, Kyame reflected on the hexagrams she had assembled with her silver coins before leaving her room at the Hotel de Paris. It had been No. 15, *Ch'ien*. There is value in humility, if you try applying a less aggressive attitude you are far more likely to advance.

She shook her head as she replaced the coins. Whatever that might mean -- if anything. Divination systems, the I Ching or any other, Kyame had finally concluded had only a hollow, unreal timbre to them, regardless of their exotic trappings; even if they might prove to be occasionally accurate. She looked forward to resuming that discussion with Dr. Mar-Tan on her return home. She touched the crystal *bi* disc that lay beneath her blouse. It suggested assurance, of safety.

At the first sound, she turned to find that *Le Crémaillère*, the Rack, was a small steam-driven locomotive pushing one open-sided green-roofed passenger wagon up an extraordinarily steep track. It was much like a small cog train she had once seen in Colorado, but here the cogged rails curved up the mountainside over graceful stone bridges to disappear from view. The wagon appeared to hold about twenty-four people on five straight-backed benches with little room for baggage. The small first class bench that held four people at the front end had cushions as opposed to the hard wood seats that she and V.B. occupied in second class which had cost 2.30 francs each. He had apologized for the coming rough ride, but it would be only twenty minutes to the main square of La Turbie with one brief stop at Bordina.

"Far better than riding a mule for almost an hour that was virtually the only way up to La Turbie until two years ago," said Bethell as they settled on the bare board, then sliding over to allow a mother and her young son on board. "It required twelve years of planning and engineering before Le Crémaillère opened. La Turbie has prospered some as a result, but it has remained a charming village with a striking view of Monaco and Monte Carlo below it, and, sighting from the right position, all the way east to Mentone.

"We will be at table in Le Café d'Auguste within about 25 minutes, Kyame, and," he laughed, "the chairs there will have cushions."

As the train puffed its way up the steep mountainside, overcoming, just barely it seemed, the alarming very steep first half-mile, Bethell leaned closer to Kyame. "I heard from London, Kyame. Ebing is a very busy shipyard that Brand had observed before his assignment to Monaco. Even with all the activity, four keels had been laid for unusually fast cargo ships that stood out to him. Brand ... he spent his youth in the merchant marine ... had noted that the ships did not appear to have either the cargo or the coaling capacity to be competitive against other merchant ships, even with their apparent planned speed. He made a comment about coaling stations, but never ..." He glanced over at the mother next to them who was completely involved with her fussing little boy. "But was never able to follow up. Interestingly, however, the nick-name that the yard workers gave the four ships was predator ... which matches with one of those notes you found from Wagner's pocket."

Kyame took a breath. "Brand had seen too much, it seems. Ebing and Monaco are connected then ... in some ... some maybe terrible way."

Bethell leaned back against the hard backrest and nodded.

***

V.B. was right on all counts. The view from the square of La Turbie down on the coast of Monaco was breathtaking with the Dog's Head promontory seemingly only a short walk away. And the cushions at the café were very comfortable.

But it was the huge cylindrical fluted stone monument, *Tour d'Auguste*, the tower of Augustus built in 6 B.C., that dominated Kyame's thoughts. According to the waiter who appeared immediately to take their orders, the original tower, a lofty monument to the triumph of Roman arms and the arrogance of the Emperor Augustus, had stood almost a hundred feet taller than the still commanding remains.

"You will find, Mademoiselle, that most buildings in La Turbie contain stones from the monument." He laughed. "You could also say that it is La Turbie that is now the monument."

As had been described in the Brand file, the café was almost within the shadow of the tower. The ancient inn that Muffin had described was only about fifty feet away up a cobbled alleyway with a catwalk on its roof that…

A tall man, his black beard and mustache carefully trimmed, in a gold-buttoned naval jacket appeared at their table, momentarily blocking out the sun. Kyame noted his brown eyes flash briefly with suspicion. "Sir, Mademoiselle, I have not seen you in my café before. May I?" he said, motioning to the empty chair at their table. "New faces fascinate me. I am Captain, former Captain, I should correct, Alex von Holdern, of the Imperial German Merchant Marine."

Bethell introduced Kyame and himself. "We come at the recommendation of a good friend, the late Sir Cornelius Brand, who described your menu with great enthusiasm."

A grimace swept across Von Holdern's face immediately replaced with a broad smile. "Ah, Sir

Cornelius." He cocked his head slightly. "I was surprised to discover after two or three of his visits that he was quite fluent in my language ... and a most appreciative client. For an Englishman, he was well-traveled in my country, mainly in the north. It was a tragedy to learn of his terrible death.

"So ... excellent, Herr Bethell. And Fraulein Piddington, you are the first American of my experience. A very good start, if I may boldly say."

The sharp chill breezes of the Mistral that tossed dust and leaves about the square caused Kyame to brush her hair from her eyes. Her new khaki-colored coat with its thick lining blocked out most of the Mistral chill. "May I ask, Captain," she said softly, brushing her hair back into place again, "what part of the German Empire you are from? This is my first experience in Europe, thus I want to learn a great deal before returning home."

"Let me check on your order and ensure your coffee is delivered, Fraulein, then I shall return with my life's story." Laughing, he went around a young couple, clearly mountain climbers, at an adjacent table, stopped a waiter with a towel over his shoulder, glanced quickly around the seven tables of his café, four of which were occupied, then disappeared into a shaded doorway.

Kyame noted he was not smiling as he closed the door behind him.

"The file said nothing about Brand being fluent in German," said Kyame. A thought that had been pestering her through the night returned. "I've been troubled by the slips of paper I found in Norfolk's room. And with her taking money from Wagner's wallet. Wagner seemed not to notice, nor to care. How could that be … unless he is aware of her actions and allows her to do these things as part of giving her a sense of well-being … even of security? She would know nothing of what the slips might mean, of course, but might be led to think that they would give her some, well, protection, if ever needed."

V.B. pursed his lips, waiting for the waiter to leave their coffees, a bowl of small brown sugar-coated rolls, and almost an after-thought, white jars of sugar and cream. Once the waiter had moved to another table, Bethell murmured, "Brand may have been pressing too hard for information and chose to use his fluency to …"

Captain von Holdern reappeared, carrying a heavy mug of coffee. "If I may rejoin you? Your breakfast will be ready in only a few moments." As he settled himself, he reached for one of the rolls. "A specialty of my Dutch cook, Aleida. She was the key reason I bought the café," he laughed, swallowing the last piece.

Kyame enjoyed the crisp crust that broke apart to reveal a rich center of white marzipan imbedded with chopped hazelnuts, surrounded by a rich dense white cake. Two bites were all it took. She smiled as she reached for another. "I would agree, Captain. That roll is sufficient

360

reason to come back. And, may I say, how good your English is … almost no accent at all … almost American."

Grinning, Von Holdern nodded his head in acknowledgement. "I will provide a bag of the rolls on your departure, Fraulein, with my compliments. I am from Hamburg, a great city in the north of Germany. I was a merchant captain for twelve years for the Norddeusche Reederei with our home port at Bremerhaven. We sailed largely about the Baltic and North Sea, the Scandinavian countries, *natürlich*, along with the Netherlands and occasional landings in France, Spain, and Portugal, but only twice to England … Southampton. I was injured during a vicious storm off the coast of Denmark, and thus became involved in ship building rather sailing."

"What kind of ships did you build, Captain? Big ones?" Kyame grinned, her eyes meeting his, that were filling with lust. "I can't see you building small ones."

Von Holdern laughed as he leaned back to allow the waiter to deliver the breakfasts. "We built fast ships at the Ebing shipyards, Fraulein, some big, some smaller … before I became a café owner." Hearing his name called, he rose, bowed to Kyame, and walked to another table.

Her first bite of her three-egg omelet of sour cream and goat cheese mixed with grains of golden Osetra caviar was unique, but Kyame questioned V.B. with her eyes. He nodded. "Yes, the Ebing reference. Brand may have pressed on Ebing and thought to follow up his earlier

361

observations … and became a marked man as a result." He replaced his fork. "Why would a ship builder from Northern Germany become the owner of a small café in a small village with a superb view of the harbors and surrounding sea of Monaco …if not," he continued his thought as he picked up his fork, "if not to …?"

Yes," agreed Kyame, "if not to keep watch. If Von Holdern paid an unusual price for this café then that would seem to answer that question."

"We will know later today," promised Bethell, returning to his pork -sausages and eggs.

***

As promised, Captain von Holdern handed Kyame a bag of the brown rolls as V.B. laid payment for their breakfasts on the table.

"My thanks, Captain. Marvelous view … and memorable food. I look forward to returning." A sudden insight, like she had sometimes flashed into her mind while sitting blindfolded on the stage interpreting Papa's silent signaling. Kyame turned slightly. She glanced back over her shoulder to speak to von Holdern. "Oh, Captain, were there any ships called predators constructed at your shipyard. I saw that name somewhere."

Von Holdern's wide grin vanished instantly, then in a moment reappeared, though muted. "Ah, no, not in the years I was there. Where, may I ask, did you see the name?"

Concerned, V.B. turned about, his head cocked to one side, his right hand went deep into his jacket pocket.

Kyame laughed. "Oh, I think it may have been, yes, it was a review in a newspaper of a fanciful British novel regarding some future invasion of England that I saw on my crossing to Calais. The reviewer thought the novel too far-fetched and poorly written to be of commercial interest. My thanks again, Captain."

***

Konstanze stepped back into the doorway to watch the Englishman and the American walk away from von Holdern. She watched as they re-entered La Turbie square apparently on their way toward the one-car train whose name she could never pronounce. She had complete freedom of action from Herr Wagner to eliminate both of them. They were, in his words, "… becoming too close, too familiar. They were an obstruction to remove, before Renfrew or after, no matter."

Konstanze would speak first with the Captain, and sample those rolls again before leaving.

36

"About 6:20 o'clock tonight, Lady Norfolk. Sir Abdy's yacht will berth in the Harbor of Hercules. There will be a small welcoming reception at 7:15 o'clock on board the vessel … to be followed with a visit of His Roy … His Lordship to the Cercle Privé at about 9 o'clock until the Baron tires of play. At which time, the Baron will adjourn to his suite of rooms at the Hermitage. The Baron has taken, I believe, the entire fourth floor."

Isabel Ellen Norfolk smiled her thanks, enjoying the intent blue eyes of the young aide to the British consul that swarmed all over her. A strange satisfaction surged through her as she walked through the door he held open. The arrival of the Baron Renfrew seemed to fulfill an unspoken need within her. Stepping carefully down the three stone steps and back into her landau carriage, the feeling reassured her that she had accomplished one of the commands that her lord had given her, though she could not recall his exact wording.

Isobel Norfolk would be ready for the Baron.

The plan was now set when Baron Renfrew would arrive tonight on the celebrated twin-screw steam yacht, Syrnix, of Sir Abdy of Moores, Baronet. Norfolk had even been able to learn where it would berth in the Harbor. An hour later at the welcoming reception on the yacht, she would be formally presented to the Baron by the British Counsel himself, the Viscount Fretwell, a school friend of Albert Edward. Yes, she would certainly be -- available for the Baron. Somehow Konstanze Jäger had already visited his suite of rooms on the fourth floor at the Hotel l'Hermitage, in spite of the additional security, four house detectives, added by the hotel management.

Prince Albert could not officially provide Monégasque security personnel as the Prince of Wales was not on a state visit, and the Prince had declined his offer anyway. It would, Albert Edward had responded, draw too much unnecessary attention. After all the King of Sweden walked the streets of Monaco without protection and without incident.

Why not a mere Baron?

* * *

Roquebrune. The village was spread over the top of a high hill with all of the peninsula of Cap Martin spread before your feet, as V.B. had described. The view was stunning as they stood at a wall looking down. Were there no bad views in Southern France? Kyame turned as V.B. said, "There," he pointed, "the fourth villa down on your right is the justly renowned Villa Cyrnos of the Empress Eugénie. A good friend, Captain Gerald Wentworth, has his villa just to the right below us concealed behind those trees. Gerald and I misspent our youth together at various points of the Queen's Empire."

To the right was a clear view of Monte Carlo and the Tête de Chien, while to the left all of Mentone and some of the Italian coastline were on display. Kyame shook her head. She had to return some day to Monaco just to be able to have the chance to absorb the insistent beauty – and maybe, she reflected, begin to learn the art of the landscape. At a special exhibition at the Boston Athenaeum a few weeks before her departure to Europe, Kyame had been attracted to a 17th century illusory landscape by Claude Gellée, which had suggestions of -- Kyame turned as Bethell took her elbow down the narrow stone street.

The Cap Martin Hotel had opened in 1890 with its first guests the Prince and Princess of Wales, explained Richard Ulrich, the hotel manager. V.B. had whispered as they had approached the wide roofed veranda of the hotel with its unobstructed view of the Mediterranean, that Edward Smith of Smith & Co. bank was one of the co-owners of the hotel. With the immediate English royal stamp of approval, the hotel always had a royal presence of some kind in its fifty rooms, though the Prince himself had not returned in a formal royal visit. He hoped very much to see the Baron Renfrew when he next visited Monte Carlo, whenever that might be. The Baron was always a most pleasant experience.

Lunch, served *table d'hôte*, proved to be a delicious dish of eggs, which Kyame could not begin to describe, together with a sparkling dry wine from Italy called prosecco which she had never encountered before.

Ulrich, who at V.B.'s invitation had joined them at their table, said that his chef knew more ways of serving eggs than anyone in Europe. But when V.B. asked of the visit of Sir John Blenkiron, Ulrich shook his head.

"I read of Sir John's killing near here in one of the papers, but he has never been a guest at the hotel. I know of no one who knew the man. I suspect that his killing was the work of roving bandits with his body dropped here … though the newspapers said he had not been robbed." Ulrich shrugged. "I know nothing further." He glanced at a beckoning waiter. "Ah, please excuse me. A guest appears to have a problem."

Laying her fork aside, Kyame frowned. Something had just occurred to her.

"That delightful frown, Kyame …you're seeing something." V.B. smiled.

"I think I just connected something. None of the dead agents were robbed, according to their files, but there was little detail about what the agents were, in fact, carrying on them. But with Brand and Blenkiron, a specific note was made of them each carrying a packet of Norwegian stamps. I wonder, V.B., if the drop point for the agents' communications was a stamp shop here in Monaco. Are there many?"

Bethell wiped his lips, folded his napkin and pushed back from the table. "There were at one time three stamp shops actually. Stamp collecting had become of great interest in the principality because some foreign royalty, neither Prince Charles III nor Prince Albert, a royal whose name I have forgotten, had become infatuated with the hobby. But, after the royal's death, interest faded. There has been only one now for the past year or so. Two or three months ago, a minister suggested to Albert that he authorize new designs of Monaco stamps to sell to collectors as an additional source of revenue. No decision has been made yet that I know of."

"So at the time of our interest," said Kyame, "there would have been only one shop. Have we time?"

***

The stamp-shop name, Monaco Timbrophily! was carved into a wide piece of rich walnut over the door. It was wedged in between a dress store and shoe shop. The shop's one window displayed sheets of stamps of marvelous colors with three stamps, separately framed, hanging from the back wall. Entering to a riff of bells, there was a glass counter with a number of stamps, sheets of stamps and special envelopes spread out. Along the walls were notices of upcoming European stamp issues, and Kyame noted, notices of meetings of stamp collectors in the south of France. A set of wooden pigeon-holes was on the back wall opposite the door. Thirty-six slots Kyame quickly calculated.

A tall well-dressed gray-haired gentleman behind the counter turned to greet them.

"An American, how remarkable," he said. "We have little interest in American issues here, naturally, but I suspect the American hobby will gain in interest in the years ahead. I am John French ... and no I don't speak it."

V.B. gave French his card. "I have an interest in Norwegian stamps. Do you encounter many who share my passion?"

"Ah," said French, "Smith & Co. I am most pleased to meet you sir. Your people have been most helpful to me on a number of occasions." He slid the card into his vest pocket. Then shook his head. "There were a few men who regularly enquired about Norwegian issues and past issues, but there has been no interest at all over the past ... oh, month or so.

"They would usually leave a note of enquiry in one of the slots over there on the wall. The slots are arranged by country with a breakdown of France and England into more specific interests. But all European countries have a slot. It facilitates contacts between collectors of similar interests."

"I have a friend, Sir Cornelius Brand," said Bethell, "who first got me interested in Norwegian stamps. Has he been one of your customers?"

French nodded. "Sir Cornelius was a regular customer. I would see him almost each week. He purchased

369

a number of truly fine issues … and usually left a note or two in the Norway slot for other collectors with a shared interest. Even a businessman, a Mr. Baring-Gould, traveling through France from England would sometimes come by looking for Norwegian issues. I believe he and Sir Cornelius struck up sort of a correspondence through the slots. Unfortunately, they never met. At least, not here in the shop."

V.B. glanced at Kyame who nodded once. This was the drop-point for the agents. Other agents probably used other country slots. Following one agent to the shop could then lead to setting up surveillance. Once the drop procedure was detected, the agents could be identified and murdered as necessary

V.B purchased a Norwegian plate-block of vivid blue for 100 francs. As they turned to leave, Kyame asked, "What is Timbrophily, Mr. French? I have never seen that word before."

John French laughed gently. "Every new visitor asks me that question. It is the original French name for stamp collecting. It fell out of use in favor of philately. It seemed a very natural name for my shop."

Kyame laughed, smiled and stepped quickly through the door held by V.B.

***

At Smith & Co., both Kyame and Bethell were stunned at the price paid by Captain von Holdern for the Le Café d'Auguste Café two years ago.

"Victor, it was at least 18,000 francs beyond what would have been a solid market price for a café that size in that location," said Eric Houstoun, Smith's commercial real estate manager, whose eyes had lit up at Kyame's approach. "The owner, from Nice, who had run the café for almost seven years, naturally accepted the offer immediately. The total amount of money was paid in full within twenty-four hours with a bank check drawn on the Rothschild bank in Paris. The owner would not accept a check from any but a French bank. Von Holdern had originally offered a check on a German bank, the Berliner Handelgesellschaft. To switch banks that quickly certainly suggested ample funds were available." Houstoun frowned as he replaced the documents on his desk. "But Captain von Holdern, who was the owner by title deed, did not actually taken charge of the café until about three months ago. Another German, a Baron Ralf-Friederich Hanau from Bremen, had been the active operator until the reappearance of von Holdern."

"Did you ever meet the Baron?" Kyame asked.

Eric Houstoun nodded. "Yes, on three occasions, Miss Piddington. He was an older gentleman with a white goatee and mustache, always dressed in black leathers. A pleasant enough man" -- Houstoun smiled – "for an arrogant Prussian nobleman.

371

"The Baron lives in the hills behind Nice in a large rented villa near the also large rented villa of the German banker, Johannes Wagner. The Baron mentioned Wagner in a couple of our conversations with the utmost respect. Almost … almost too much respect, with, perhaps … with a bit of fear."

Bethell glanced at Kyame, who nodded. The café was clearly intended as a lookout, and what else? And why the initial urgency so long ago; and then the timing of the sudden reappearance of Von Holdern?

"Each step has seemed to create more questions, but," Kyame said, "there seems no doubt of how critical the timing seems to be."

Bethell, frowning, agreed as he assisted her into their carriage.

37

In its vast expanse of white, polished teak-wood decks, brilliant brass, and painted wrought iron, the Syrnix resembled a civilized battleship with its cannons hidden. Kyame was dressed in her last special gown that she had packed of silver and blue, but dressed as well for prowling, wearing her narrow black trousers beneath the petticoats, and a thin black silk sweater folded tightly in one pocket with the ruhmal. Her loaded derringer was in the other pocket.

She observed Isobel Norfolk, humbly followed by Jäger dressed as a maid, promenade confidently across the outsized parquet dance floor of the main deck reception area. Stopping, Jäger nodded deferentially to Norfolk, then retreated away from the gathering crowds of the higher-class to a corner of the extensive expanse of polished woods, gold-flecked wrought-iron window frames supporting large windows along three walls, to join the plain black and liveried maids and gentlemen's servants awaiting their master's and mistress's directions.

Kyame noted that Jäger was carrying a black canvas valise.

Sir Abdy of Moores, Baronet, was a small swarthy-skinned man with penetrating blue eyes in immaculate evening dress with colorful decorations of some kind on his chest. He remained within a few steps of the Baron as the royal presence moved across the dance floor to the center of the room. The reception line formed seemed to include every British subject in the little principality of Monaco who wanted, first bowing, of course, to grip the hand of the future king of England, or to curtsy ever lower to his friendly enwrapping eyes.

The Baron Renfrew had an enormous girth, wide shoulders, and large hands. He wore a closely trimmed brown beard, as with his closely trimmed and oiled brown hair. The Baron also was in immaculate evening dress, but without decorations, or any symbol that could resemble or suggest royalty. His eyes, Kyame couldn't determine their color, appeared friendly and his gracious smiles seemed genuine; as if Renfrew actually enjoyed meeting all these people. Or, more likely, the Baron had become an excellent actor from all his practice. V.B., standing at Kyame's side, half smiled as he softly suggested actor to her whispered comment. The line continued to move slowly, pausing at various moments as the Baron greeted an old acquaintance or two.

Kyame suddenly had to twist away and hold her breath. Someone had released a sudden blunt burst of sour aristocratic flatulence. It sharply reminded her of the less stately environments and men of the saloons of her early experience. With her eyes closed, she could have been smelling the American West once again. But here, the fragrance hung alone in the air. She noted that those nearest the source struggled not to notice. When she turned back, V.B. was smiling.

"A title doesn't change humanity, does it?" he grinned.

The Viscount Fretwell stood to the Baron's right, introducing the richly dressed column as they positioned themselves before His Lordship who then, having received the royal blessing, retreated to the tables of drinks and hors d'oeuvres at the far end of the room. A polite circle of about three to four feet around the Baron ensured some privacy to the conversations, however brief.

Kyame noted that Fretwell lingered at length in his introduction of Lady Norfolk, as the eyes of the Baron lit up as Norfolk had curtsied very low in her very low cut but elegant pink satin gown. She saw the Baron nod briefly as the Lady Norfolk swept away toward the drinks, as Jäger began to walk to rejoin her mistress.

"May I have the honor, sir, of presenting The Honorable Victor Bethell, with a good friend whose acquaintance I have not yet made."

A wide grin ignited Albert Edward's expansive face. "Victor, old man, how damned good to see you!" His eager handshake following Bethell's bow was clearly genuine. "You will be at the wheel with me tonight, I pray. I trust only you when the wheel is at issue." He turned toward Kyame.

"Your Lordship, may I have the marked honor of presenting Miss Kyame Piddington of America, a most treasured friend of the Duchess Angelica and of myself."

As Kyame extended her hand to allow the Baron shake it, he instead bowed over it to kiss her fingers. There was an immediate murmur about the room. His voice lowered, he said, "We are enchanted, Miss Piddington. Salisbury has briefed me on your mission and its promising results. You have our personal thanks for coming to our aid. The Queen has also been made aware." He stood back, then grinned. "I find colonists, even former colonists of great interest."

Kyame could not but flash a quick smile. The Prince was truly charming. "We colonists do labor to ensure the old country feels proud of us," she grinned, her head cocked mischievously to one side. "And may I say, Your Lordship, how skillfully you project sincerity with each person. I have not seen your equal on our side of the Atlantic."

Albert Edward exploded in laughter as V.B. joined in. Kyame let a half-smile appear on her lips. "I hope I have not offended, Your Lordship," she said, bowing her head slightly.

He leaned toward her. "Were there not the people still waiting behind you, dear lady, you, Victor and myself would immediately retire to my library for some enjoyable conversation … and refreshments."

As they started to turn, V.B. leaned back. "I also bring you the warmest greetings of the Duchess Angelica, Your Lordship."

"Muffin! She is well? She is one of my most prized friends."

"Muffin has been having some troubles with her short leg, as she calls it, and could not manage tonight. She carefully instructed me to extend an invitation to Your Lordship for dinner or lunch at her villa, at your convenience, of course."

"Please tell that marvelous woman that I look forward to that, and more than once in my stay, and to her joining me in my rooms for dinner as well. I have always found that the world looks more … approachable, after an evening with her."

Bethell bowed. "I will so inform the Duchess, sir." Taking Kyame's arm they backed two steps then moved away as another couple approached.

"Along with Grand Dukes, Kyame, you handle crown princes with a certain élan."

"He is a most likeable man, V.B. He must lead a most frustrating life in some ways."

V.B. nodded. "That's true, but that is the weight of royalty. Let us explore Sir Abdy's riches."

Clapping her hands together softly, Konstanze whispered, "Position yourself by that door with the crossed anchors, Norfolk. That is the door by which the Baron will exit when the reception is finished in about another fifteen minutes. You will be available to him, and I will follow. Understood?"

Isobel Norfolk's eyes blinked once, then twice, her expression softened as the mesmeric command took hold. "Yes, my lord, I understand."

"When the Baron leaves the room where will he go?" asked Kyame.

"He entered by that door with the crossed anchors, so I assume he will exit the same way. I have only been on this yacht once before two years ago, but I believe there is a short stairway down to a corridor that runs along the entire length of the ship on the starboard side." He raised an eyebrow.

Kyame smiled behind her raised still-full flute of champagne. "Yes, my friend, I know starboard from port." She suddenly started. One of the many silver and black liveried servants moving through the crowd of people had turned away, his profile -- she shook her head and moved her shoulder to catch Norfolk's movement -- toward the crossed anchors.

"Is there another way to that corridor … a back way?"

Bethell frowned then took her arm.

"Please remain visible as I do the opposite, V.B. I need to be there to blunt Jäger's blade however I can." She gripped his arm. "There, V.B., there by that tall plant in the green glass bowl. That man. It's Wagner. He is made-up, but I know it is. His ears are unmistakable."

Bethell saw a servant in livery standing as though in waiting for his orders. At first, V.B. shook his head, then, "By god, Kyame, I think you are right. But we cannot take any action against him here … and now."

"If you move toward him, in that general direction, it will force him away from me to avoid your possibly recognizing him."

A quick nod, a whispered direction, and Bethell turned to move toward Wagner as Kyame in turn moved toward the kitchen doors at the far starboard side of the room.

***

Johannes Wagner had decided not to incorporate Von Holdern, Bäcker, or the Baron Hanau tonight. Gottrau could not be considered. Within the confines of the ship he and Jäger would be sufficient for the task, and would be able to escape the ship more easily. The American, he admitted was a beautiful woman, even elegant in her gown of silver and blue. She will be even more beautiful in a casket. He glimpsed Bethell moving in his general direction as the American walked away. Wagner stopped one of Abdy's servants to inquire the location of a servant's lavatory.

***

Kyame waited as a servant shouldered his way through the kitchen doors, then, after a moment, pushed through herself, turning left to the stairs there. It had been a glimpse of a profile, but no ... she knew no one in Monaco and certainly not on a British nobleman's yacht. Gathering her skirts about her, to the rapt attention of the cooks and helpers, she stepped rapidly down the stairs. Kyame paused to carefully open the door. It was the starboard corridor. Now to find a place to change. To become an apparent servant herself. There, two or three feet away. Kyame pulled the narrow door open. Cleaning equipment. She lit the oil lamp hanging on the wall as she pulled the door closed behind her. There was room, barely. She carefully pushed a pile of empty pails toward the back, then shoved a box of soaps to one side with her foot. Enough. In a moment, her belt loosened, she dropped her skirts to the floor, gathering, folding then pushed them into an empty box that stood on top of the soaps. She unbuttoned the covered buttons down the front of the top of her gown, slipped it off her shoulders and placed that on top of the skirt. She had already placed the black pouch of tools, the derringer and the ruhmal on a shelf. The black silk high-necked shirt slid over her head smoothly and quickly, the crystal *bi* disc slipped into its familiar place. She strapped the leather belt around her waist then loaded the pouch, the ruhmal and the derringer in their required places. Kyame wrapped a black cloth loosely about her neck to help conceal her face.

Now to move.

***

At the instruction of the Baron's valet, Lady Norfolk, with Jäger a step or two behind her carrying her valise, passed through the door of the crossed anchors, down the six steps and into the long corridor. Toward the stern, the corridor was dark, but ahead, oil lamps in brass holders were lit along both walls. Norfolk fell her heart begin to beat more rapidly, Wagner's mesmeric suggestions becoming stronger with each step. Ahead, perhaps twenty feet or so, was an elaborately carved teak-wood door. The Prince of Wales awaited her behind that door. She could hear her lord's voice giving her direction.

***

Kyame stretched her legs, moving more rapidly toward the light at the far end of the corridor. A glance behind her as she came out of the storage area had revealed an empty corridor with what appeared to be an area from which to dump the ship's garbage into the sea. But now to track Norfolk. She stopped to press against the dark wall. The door at the far end opened with brilliant light bursting out into the corridor. A man dressed clearly as some sort of senior servant closed the door and stepped quickly toward a stairway.

The stairway to the crossed anchors!

Kyame waited until the man had disappeared up the stairs, then moved quickly, half-running, to a marble column a few feet beyond the stairs that projected a foot or so out into the corridor. There was a small cylindrical opening around the column from the floor to the ceiling apparently to allow polishing and cleaning. Kyame wedged herself into the opening -- and waited.

Clearly some kind of rendezvous had been arranged between Norfolk and Renfrew, so the woman had to come in this direction. First, disarm Norfolk – then, as necessary, disarm Jäger. She heard a door open -- then soft steps on the staircase. Kyame's heart beat increased even as her eyes grew cold, calm and focused.

The rustle of the Norfolk skirts on the floor grew closer. Kyame edged around the column, ready.

As Norfolk drew abreast, Kyame clapped twice quickly. Norfolk suddenly stopped, her eyes went wide. "Yes, my lord," she whispered. Kyame heard Jäger grunt in surprise.

"You will faint," ordered Kyame, "faint immediately. Fall to the floor. You no longer can hear my voice, ever."

Norfolk collapsed into a heap of pink satin.

As Kyame reached out to check Norfolk, she heard Jäger curse, and whirled to face her.

A dagger with a curved blade raised in her hand, Jäger, her plain face grotesque in the oil lights in its fury, leaped forward. Kyame twisted to one side throwing up her left arm to block the stroke as she launched her stiff right-hand fingers extended as if a spear point, driving her thrust from her legs through her hips, hard up under Jäger's ribcage – just as Mar-tan had instructed her in her training months ago. The woman's loud gasp of pain and surprise proved Kyame had struck home. Jäger slumped to her knees clawing for air as Kyame raised her fist to strike ...

An explosion in Kyame's mind, then blackness.

***

At the splash, the young man turned to lean over the railing. A large bag had been thrown from below through the garbage door. But it wasn't a bag. Against the moon's silvery glimmering across the tossing waters, he caught the glimpse of a human body, long hair blown by the winds. Damn his orders! His heart thundering in his chest, he ran down the deck, threw off his shoes, and launched himself out into the air toward the spot where the body had hit, floated for a moment, then disappeared.

38

Even well concealed among the liveried servants of several wealthy Englishmen, Johannes Wagner was uneasy. He had altered his appearance with stage makeup, even to combing out his Imperial mustache, altered the manner of his movements, hidden his pride; but the feeling remained, it even growing in intensity. He had always had a feel for situations, *ein Gefühl von Gefahr*, a sense for danger that had always sustained him. With only Jäger and himself to cover, the killing of the Prince of Wales would not be easy, but would be direct and effective, then out. With both of them on stage as servants they would be largely ignored by the elitist upper class, unless something stupid happened. Jäger's razor-like knife needed only a few seconds near the fat walrus to end the British royal line, stop the Casino, and to turn Monaco into a German province on the south coast of France.

Wagner had expected Victor Bethell to be present; the banker had been a friend of the Prince for some years and had, according to rumors, extricated the undisciplined royal fool more than once from financial ruin, to rescue Albert Edward from having to force Queen Victoria to publicly bail her son out with public money. Wagner had no fear of Bethell interfering. Bankers by nature did not seek risk – which was why Wagner, he laughed to himself, was not an adept banker.

But the American woman, Kyame Piddington, was an unknown with the frustrating ability to vanish from under the hands of his agents. He had learned that morning of the bodies of the two English killers whom he had hired to prevent Piddington reaching Calais, had washed up near Dover. The woman was lethal as well.

Bethell and the woman had just stepped back from their conversation with the Baron Renfrew. He saw that Norfolk and Jäger were positioned correctly. A few more minutes of bland acknowledgements and, finally, the Baron, followed by Fretwell, started to withdraw to his stateroom on the second deck below. He saw Renfrew's small nod toward Norfolk as he went through … Piddington! She was walking away as Bethell started walking toward the gathering of servants and maids. Where? He enquired the location of the servants' lavatory but to go that way would take him directly across the track of Bethell. Wagner stepped back, moving behind two wide-bodied chauffeurs, still keeping a limited view of the American. She was going into the kitchen doors even as Norfolk and Jäger were still waiting to give the Baron suitable time to reach his rooms before following him.

His lips tight with suppressed anger, Johannes Wagner had to abort their original plan in order to start for the kitchen himself after Piddington, just as Bethell neared the servants, apparently searching for someone. An older maid stepped out to engage the banker in some kind of obviously friendly conversation.

386

Wagner walked faster.

Bethell noted the well-dressed liveried valet start across the room, dodging hastily through the shifting crowds, drawing scowls and sharp-tongued reproaches as he brushed shoulders with his betters. Wagner? Closer, V.B. wasn't as sure as Kyame had been. He saw another, younger servant disengage from a gentleman with a nod of confirmation, and start for the kitchen doors carefully avoiding as he did any contact with the reception crowds.

Kyame was not in sight.

Reaching the kitchens, Wagner looked quickly about. The American was not around. The cooks, helpers and the chef stopped to stare at him, then a moment, they returned to their labors. A mere retainer of no interest. Wagner pushed through the door to the left and started down the stairs to the darkened starboard ship-length corridor. Upon reaching the deck, he glanced first toward the stern, noted the garbage disposal door, then back toward the forward lighted portion of the passageway. A dark form was running in the light then suddenly disappeared behind a marble column to the left. Piddington! She had left her gown somewhere to become black as a burglar.

Another minute, he saw Norfolk and Jäger appear, coming down the stairway. Wagner held back. If Jäger handles the American quickly, they can reassemble most of their original plan. He moved to edge of the darkness, pressed against the wall to wait.

What? Norfolk collapsed to the floor! Wagner started walking rapidly. When he saw Jäger raise her knife he started a fast walk in long silent strides. Jäger lunged forward as Wagner saw the American in the light, her face strangely calm, her eyes cold, whirl beneath the blade and fell her attacker with a single blow. When Piddington turned back toward Norfolk, Wagner leaped forward, bringing his lead-filled life-preserver down to crack across the American's head. She dropped silently to the floor.

Jäger was gasping for breath as she struggled to gain her feet.

"Get out! Now!" snapped Wagner. "Meet at Hanau's villa. Neither of us can be found here. I will take care of the American." His sharp-edged German was swift, emphatic and immediately answered as Konstanze Jäger propping herself against the wall, staggered back toward the stairs, then turned back to retrieve the valise.

Wagner lifted the lifeless body of the American, tossing her easily over his shoulder and began to walk as rapidly as he could back toward the darkness and the garbage door. As he passed the stairs Jäger was just starting to open the door back out to the reception crowds.

He strode faster.

A quick twist of the two brass latches holding the door. A push, the doors swung open into the darkening Monégasque twilight. As he lifted the lifeless black-clothed body of the woman, Wagner realized that for all the trouble she had caused him, he had never heard her voice. He lifted the body to the edge, there was a ripping sound as he heaved the body out into the gathering mists, a moment, then heard the satisfying splash into the harbor waters. He pulled the doors closed and returned to the stairway to the kitchen, mounted the stairs two at a time, and disappeared through the door. Silence was all he wanted from the American.

***

The Baron Renfrew's frown melted away into a wide smile when Kyame opened her eyes. "Thank god. Kennedy, she will be all right?" It was clearly a royal command not a question.

Dr. Erastus Meredith Kennedy, the Baron's personal physician, nodded. "Shaken, with a headache for a day or two, but Miss Piddington will fully recover, Your Royal Highness."

Kyame blinked her eyes. For a moment she couldn't understand why the future king of England was looking down at her. Then the pieces began to fit once again. Then the dizziness hit her. She closed her eyes for a moment, then opened again.

"Kyame, how do you feel?" asked V.B. whose concerned face, a bit blurred, appeared over her.

"I ... I think I am still in one piece. Where am I? How did I get here?"

"You are in my rooms, Miss Piddington ... oh, damn it all ... Kyame, I owe you my life." Renfrew clinched his jaw. He breathed hard, then relaxed and grinned. "You colonists are a tough lot."

Kyame had to grin, though it hurt some. "We colonists had to beat some very tough people ourselves." She rolled to her right, to try to push herself up to a sitting position. The doctor quickly reached out to support her back. "Not too quickly, Miss Piddington. It will make your head ache more."

Finally sitting, her dizziness beginning to fade, she pressed her hands against her face. A bandage was across her right cheek, and one on her neck. She looked up at the doctor, but V.B. answered her.

"When Wagner threw you out off of the yacht, your face and neck scraped against a railing. You were pretty bloody, but the doctor has cleaned everything up with the help of three stiches."

Her black clothes were still damp. "How long have I ...?"

"Almost a half hour. You were hit hard, I would guess, with a lead-weighted life-preserver, to raise that impressive lump that is on the back of your head." The doctor gently wiped a cool cloth across her face. Kyame was beginning to feel alive again.

"I was thrown off the yacht? But how did I get back on board?" She brushed her fingers against where the crystal bi disc would hang. Her touch of reassurance ... but it was gone!

At Kyame's sudden expression of concern, V. B. asked, "Kyame ... something?"

Kyame glanced around her. "My *bi* disc that has always hung from my neck. It's gone."

The doctor shook his head. "There was no necklace of any kind found, Miss Piddington. You must have lost it when you hit the water."

Kyame pursed her lips, the long ago gift from J.W. gone. She would explain when -- she took a short breath -- when they met again. She looked about her at the concerned expressions of the men, and smiled. "A loss, but I still have the friend who gave it to me."

First glancing at the doctor who nodded, the Baron Renfrew offered her a flute of cold champagne. "To celebrate your return to the living, Kyame. Your rescuer must remain nameless for several reasons, but it seems he may know you in some way. He left this note."

Kyame sipped, seeing the men, including Viscount Fretwell, raise their glasses to her. It tasted cold, refreshing and restorative. She opened the note, gasped, tears instantly appearing in her eyes.

Kyame, it said, I could not let you go. It would empty my life. You fill my thoughts of happy times on the deck of the Auguste Victoria planning miracles. I cannot stay, my duties carry me away. But know that no other woman walks my mind as you do. This time the miracle is mine.

A

Kyame pressed the note to her lips as the tears flowed -- unrestrained.

39

"At least the American is dead." Johannes Wagner, his mustaches back in place, his eyes blazing, paced across the thick rug of the Baron Hanau's library. "Even though the Prince was completely untouched and now amply warned." He stopped by the great bow window that looked down on the city of Nice. "But the Prince must be killed, quickly before the situation collapses into a farce that we will all deeply regret." He turned. "It has been two days. They will think we have fled to somewhere. The Baron returns to the wheels tonight." He turned to Konstanze Jäger. "Norfolk?"

The plain woman said, empty of expression, "She apparently committed suicide this morning, before fully recovering from her sad fall of yesterday. She cut her wrists and bled to death. Very messy."

Wagner nodded in satisfaction. He started to say something, then stopped. "Norfolk is no longer of any importance." He clenched his fists. "We kill Renfrew tonight at the Casino. Here is the plan." He walked to long central table of polished carved mahogany which had been in the villa when the Baron Hanau had rented it. A plan of the Casino was one of two charts that lay spread out on it.

The Ritter Heinz Bäcker had fled Monaco on learning of the Syrnix fiasco. Once this situation was closed, then Wagner would turn the resources of N on bringing Bäcker to him. What little money that was left in the accounts of the Wagner Finanzdienstleistungen had been seized by Monégasque security under direct order of Prince Albert, but he had been able, once he evaded any followers to return to his office, to transfer almost all the funds into a private N account in Munich, leaving only an empty rented office. Though, Wagner had mused, he would miss Ciro's being so close at hand.

The Baron Hanau, dressed in black leather, was sitting quietly near the low fire sipping schnapps. Nothing yet tied him directly to Jäger and only a little to Wagner, he was confident of that. Tonight, he too would flee beyond the reach of the Kaiser.

***

André. Even after two days, Kyame could scarcely believe it. Not a diamond smuggler as she had so long, it seemed, believed. What he actually was, she didn't know, but miracles, she laughed softly, their favorite topic, miracles do happen, it seemed.

She was dressed in the ruffled green gown with its modest lace décolletage, the first gown she had worn in Monaco. The blue and silver, her favorite of those she had brought, had not survived a bottle of drain cleanser falling on it in that cleaning closet. But she still wore the narrow black trousers beneath the petticoats along with the other weapons. Once her mind had cleared and the headaches subsided on the second day, Kyame had cleaned the derringer and reloaded.

Kyame watched as V.B. guided Baron Renfrew in his bets and placements on the Cercle roulette table. At first undisciplined, losing 22,000 francs within the first half-hour, the Baron retreated to following the Avant Dernier system with V.B. ensuring adherence to the system. Not the exhilarating excitement of risking and losing great sums, but winning was always more fun in the end.

Lord Rosslyn had joined them. A clever and enjoyable man, but too impressed with his own cleverness, though very handsome and most gallant. Muffin clearly enjoyed his attentions, but Kyame's heart was settled. With André back in her life, somewhere anyway, her heart was settled. They would meet again – that was their next miracle. She looked up, suddenly realizing that Lord Rosslyn had been speaking to her.

"My apologies, Your Lordship, I was eagerly gathering wool I'm afraid."

Rosslyn smiled his much described smile. "Would that I could be that man," he said. "Are you ready to attack the table itself? We have all weakened the wheel's resistance on your behalf."

Muffin laughed. "Yes, Kyame, come sit beside me and let's break the bank."

***

It was to be only Jäger and himself again this final time. Quick, with minimum cleverness but with clear escapes. With Bäcker disappeared, Johannes Wagner couldn't trust Hanau's aged resourcefulness, so before they had left the Baron's glorious villa, at his whispered direction, Jäger had cut the Baron Hanau's old throat. The villa was left as though burglars had killed him in the course of trashing the villa looking for loot of any kind. He and Jäger would be on a fast boat later tonight for Cairo, there to await the further orders of N -- and to celebrate the personal congratulations of the All Highest that were sure to come.

Dressed modestly, upon arrival Konstanze had moved near the back wall of the Cercle Privé to the Trente-Quarante tables where she was to play conservatively until the agreed time. Her heart stopped when she looked up to see the American alive! Alive! Was there no way ...? Piddington walked with her arm entwined with that of the Baron Renfrew to the roulette table, followed by the Duchess, Bethell and Lord Rosslyn. For an instant her will faltered -- can nothing stop the American? Then, finding she had just won four thousand francs, Konstanze felt her blood rising, eager to resume their previous meeting.

Even if it meant to attack that green whore here in the Cercle itself.

Wagner was dressed modestly in a nondescript Italian-styled suit, a fake beard and pince-nez glasses. At first, he was dumbfounded. He had not planned on the

396

presence of the American, in green yet again, as if to mock him one final time. No matter. He glanced across the tables to where Jäger was playing. She looked up, saw him, nodded and returned to her play.

***

With the piles of chips growing steadily in front of her, Muffin leaned back to sip a demitasse of coffee with cognac. "I have a need, Kyame," she whispered. "Would you accompany me?"

40

As the two women stood, the Baron, who had been winning steadily, Lord Rosslyn who had been losing the most rapidly of the group, and V.B. who had not yet played, stood back bowing as the women passed.

At their movement, two others in the Cercle also moved. Their first target was in motion. Wagner had assumed that the Duchess would bring one of her serving ladies with her, who would have not presented any issue. But with the American here, both of them would attack. As agreed, if anything didn't match their assumptions then they would both strike and escape through the nearest Casino secret passage which had been marked out on the charts of the Casino.

Hopefully the Baron would be the first to move, but then …

Wagner raised two fingers as though ordering a drink, but the young man in breeches understood another order and moved immediately as the two women walked, their arms joined, in deep conversation.

"As attractive as Lord Rosslyn is, Muffin, my mind is settled. He does not have a title that I know of, but he does have my heart."

Muffin squeezed Kyame's arm. "I want to meet your André. He seems fascinating … and if he has captured you, my beautiful one, then he is something special."

Kyame's joy subsided as she saw one of the uniformed orderlies suddenly change direction and begin to move toward them. The story of the attack on Muffin was very fresh in her mind. She glanced around but saw no hostile approach that she could identify.

Konstanze saw the orderly move. She began to walk faster, but not so fast as to draw attention. Kill the Duchess virtually in the presence of the Prince of Wales, to humiliate him and to humble the Casino, then in the crowded melee certain to follow, shoot the Prince himself and run to the secret door marked on her Casino map that she had memorized. Wagner would take another secret door. His promises for Cairo were all she had ever wanted.

As Muffin reappeared and they started to return to the table, a uniformed orderly in blue breeches came walking directly toward them. His eyes were cold, unsettling. She looked quickly around but saw no one else, as Muffin continued to talk of André. Kyame pulled the yellow ruhmal from her pocket letting the corner with the silver coins hang down. As she glanced around, Kyame noted with the scarf hanging down, her shadow on the wall appeared as though she had four arms.

As Kyame saw him suddenly pull a knife from his waistband, she pushed Muffin up against the wall. "Stay behind me, Muffin!" Kyame stepped quickly in front of the surprised orderly who shifted his attack to her.

"First you, pretty one, then the old hag," he snarled as he lunged.

Kyame whirled, his knife slashing across her skirt, as she snapped her wrist just as Buhram had taught her so carefully again and again and again in their room in Portland. The scarf whipped around the man's throat, once, twice, Kyame jerked it toward her, to pull him off balance. She kicked at his leg to trip him as she sidestepped his fall. Without a sound, Kyame twisted around to his back as he fell, driving her knee hard into his back as she snapped the yellow scarf around his neck a third time -- then jerked upward with all her strength. The sharp snap was strangely satisfying, as Buhram had said it would be, if she ever had to kill for Kali.

"Kyame, my god, my god! What ... ?" Muffin saw Rosslyn and V. B. coming around the corner with the Baron a few steps behind.

Kyame was still, the scarf still pulled tight, her jaw set, her eyes deadly cold. The man stopped quivering. Another moment, she felt a hand on her shoulder. She instantly looked up,, but into V.B.'s gentle smile. "You have saved her, Kyame. You have saved our Muffin. Just as André must have saved her."

Kyame relaxed her hand and began to unwind the scarf as Casino security men began to appear from every direction. With V.B.'s hand at her elbow she stood to see the odd expression on the Baron's face. He was breathing hard from his run.

"Kyame, the yellow scarf," gasped the Baron. "That is Thuggee. I witnessed a demonstration on my last trip in India near Calcutta." He struggled to get a breath. "How can you know the yellow scarf?"

Kyame saw Jäger suddenly appear around the corner of the wall, a gun in her hand. "There! There! She has a gun!" Kyame's derringer was immediately in her hand as she pushed the Baron to one side. Seeing the woman's gun, Rosslyn quickly stepped between the Baron and Jäger spreading his arms. Kyame fired once, then again, and, dropping the derringer, she grabbed up her skirts to run toward Jäger, who staggered back, then slumped to the floor.

Oh, how she hated that green-eyed American whore, as everything went dark.

Once he had seen the American, Wagner went straight to his secret door, abandoning Jäger to her fate. He could explain to N when the time came in Cairo.

41

Princier Palace

Monaco

February 23, 1896

Once the Baron Renfrew, Lord Rosslyn, the Duchess Angelica and Victor Bethell explained what had happened at the Casino and the explicit threat to his Principality, Prince Albert immediately agreed that Kyame Piddington, though an American, must formally receive the proper recognition. He also agreed that all friendliness toward Imperial Germany would cease – at least for a season. Albert needed the German gamblers.

Prince Albert stepped away from her to confer with a court official as the shifting bejeweled crowd blocked the way between them. Of her friends, among the titled personages of Monaco and other countries, only V.B was present in the back row with other commoners. His broad grin of satisfaction seemed to warm the ornate throne room. Kyame glanced down at the large gold medal as she turned toward a large window with the white-capped blue Mediterranean rippling across the horizon. A half smile crept across her lips. Now she had yet another private name; she was now *Commandeur de Ordre de Saint-*

Charles – Chevalier de Monaco. Blue bow on her left shoulder.

But it was the name given her eight months ago by Dr. Mar-Tan that went deepest into her soul: *Shadow of the Tiger.*

Standing at the window, Kyame saw strong wind gusts suddenly strike, bending over a two-masted yacht in the distance, digging deep into the sea to toss white spray across the waves closer into shore. The now surging sea brought back brief memories of her first days on the Auguste Victoria racked for two days with agonizing sea-sickness. Kyame tightened her lips. She would be ready for her next sea voyage.

Kyame glanced down again at the glistening gold medal in her palm -- but for the first time it wasn't Papa who came to mind. It was the face of a young Frenchman, his small smile seeming to beckon, to challenge, who had once gently asked:

"So, Kyame, which miracle are you working on first?"

✳✳✳

Headquarters

Imperial German General Staff

February 23, 1896

Count Alfred von Schlieffen pushed aside the now familiar heavily marked-up maps of Belgium and France with red security warnings stamped front and back. Most of the principal invasion issues had been reasonably resolved, but several still remained. The key concern was to retain the critical element of surprise; consequently, all the necessary troops, support and supplies could not be pre-positioned for immediate movement into Belgium.

The Count set his jaw as he signed his name to the package to be presented to the All Highest tomorrow. Once triggered by some suitable 'incident' that could be taken as a deliberate affront to the Kaiser and the German Empire, von Schlieffen confidently assured in his letter to the Kaiser that the Imperial Army would be in Paris before the French could mobilize any defense. Seven days maximum with poor weather; with the operating objective of four days. The quick surrender of France would stop any British mobilization as there would be no undefended French ports or beach areas capable of handling the disembarkation of the thousands of British troops that would be necessary. Von Schlieffen included an explicit role for the Kaiserliche Marine to sweep the seas clear off the coasts of Belgium and France in coordination with on-shore coastal defensive positions.

To minimize the time for German mobilization and to provide diversion from observation, von Schlieffen's staff had worked out a schedule of apparent training maneuvers that would ensure that at least one-third of the necessary invasion force would always be in proper position and the remaining two-thirds within one to two days march. The beauty of the revolving invasion forces approach, *Operation Karussell*, would be that whichever of the thirds was in place, they would spearhead the invasion. There would be no delay, no waiting for a specialized group of regiments. He smiled. A merry-go-round the French would never forget. And neither would the British.

He looked up as one of his senior aides, Captain Franz Biermann, knocked lightly at his door.

"My pardon, Count von Schlieffen, there is an urgent action message from the south."

Von Schlieffen put out his hand for the double-red-striped yellow envelope. A moment to rip it open -- a quick glance across the five lines of deciphered message. His jaw dropped. The Chief of the Imperial Army turned pale. He read it again, slowly.

"Gott im Himmel!" he breathed. What insanity was this? He glanced up at Captain Biermann waiting for his instructions. "Arrange an immediate appointment for me with the All Highest. Of the utmost urgency."

The message revealed that agents of that arrogant fool, Captain Karl Gustav Hahn, of the *Nachtrichtenbüro*, or N, had actually attempted to assassinate the British Prince of Wales in Monaco yesterday! Their attempt had

405

been thwarted by an American woman, an Englishman, and, apparently, an agent of the French Deuxième Bureau. It was signed by a trusted Army observer the Count had personally assigned to the area. The leader of the local N group, Johannes Wagner, who had posed as a banker, had disappeared, apparently, only a best judgment his writer cautioned, on a yacht bound for Cairo.

To kill, or even wound the next king of England would bring untold dangerous complications before the Imperial forces were ready and render all of his planning useless. Who ordered such insanity? In an instant of reflection, the Count von Schlieffen knew.

***

The All Highest nodded with satisfaction as the senior Imperial railway engineer, Maxim von Pressel, explained the planned routing of the rail line. Pressel noted that the line would be beyond the range of any Royal Navy cannons throughout its length, which would require some extensive tunneling through the Amanus Mountains in Southern Turkey. Estimates of the cost and timing were included in a folder stamped *MOST SECRET, Hand to Hand Only* in Imperial red across it. A German owned and operated rail line from Berlin, through Constantinople, to Baghdad would expand Imperial trading opportunities -- and which would include gaining a seaport on the Persian Gulf. That port would elevate the presence of Imperial Germany in the Indian Ocean, the highway to India. The railway would provide as well a means of moving, as necessary, a fully equipped Imperial army to seize the Suez Canal without any possibility of Royal Navy interference. The Kaiser had already initiated friendly contact with the Sublime Porte in Constantinople with initial discussions that included inciting Islamic jihad against British and French interests in the Middle East and North Africa that would tie down large quantities of troops in the next war.

Wilhelm sat back as von Pressel slid another map across the desk. Even the normally suspicious Chief of the Imperial War Staff had been supportive of German aid and finance, as necessary, for the proposed Muslim revolt across North Africa that would include seizure of the Suez Canal.

Wilhelm had abruptly abandoned the Predator program as a result of the failed assassination attempt on Cousin Albert Edward. There could not be a second attempt in Wilhelm's view without his direct involvement becoming exposed. With the Casino now alerted and protected which ensured that Albert's income was also protected, the coaling stations planned for the harbors of Monaco could not be put in place; thus there was no need for the Predators. He had peremptorily terminated the building program at Ebing. The Berlin to Baghdad railway promised a more reliable answer to Germany's long term strategic needs.

***

The All Highest received with due expression of regret the news of the suicide of the Admiral Hans Hugo, the Graf von Drascher from a self-inflicted gunshot wound. Wilhelm had sent copious flowers in the Imperial colors bound with his personal seal, but did not attend the funeral at the old Drascher-Lippe castle on the Weser River as he would be away, cruising the Baltic Sea on the Imperial yacht, Hohenzollern II.

RMS Lucania

Southampton, England

Wednesday, February 26, 1896

Kyame Piddington stood at the starboard railing of the first class deck of the liner Lucania wrapped in a double-breasted green overcoat. Her matching green hat was held in place against the wandering winds by a silver scarf wrapped around the hat and tied in a bow under her chin. The Lucania would sail from Southampton for New York within the hour. Dr. Mar-Tan would meet her at the New York docks in seven, perhaps as bad as ten days. The weather forecast promised cold wet winds and hard challenging seas. But this time, she reflected, no sea sickness and no copies of Mahan.

The cablegram from V.B. had arrived just as she was checking out of the Charing Cross Hotel in London to start for the train to Southampton. The money from the sale of the three diamonds given her by Dr. von Müller that Muffin had insisted on handling through her favorite jeweler in Nice, had been confirmed received by her bank in Boston. $7,000. Kyame swallowed hard. That was enough to allow her to live comfortably, *without even working,* for -- she quickly estimated her rent and food -- almost four years. Four years! Only three colorless stones? Diamond smuggling was more lucrative than she could ever have dreamed.

The past three days in London as the guest of the Prince of Wales still seemed so unreal, like a *Wizard of Oz* story come alive. During her brief audience, Queen Victoria had been gracious in her praise, really too generous as Kyame had become increasingly embarrassed. She found that she could not envy the constrained and tightly ordered life of the British royal family.

Her meeting with Lord Salisbury at his London home had proven delightful. He had enjoyed almost three days of relief from his toothache pain. Laughing, he had said that she had been responsible for at least two of his best decisions. His invitation to return had been warm and genuine.

Muffin had insisted she come back to Monaco to spend a month at her villa of poetry and paint landscapes. V.B., laughing, had enthusiastically endorsed the firm order of the Duchess who then made it two months.

Konstanze Jäger survived with two bullet wounds: one in her right shoulder that forced her to drop her gun; and the second in her right knee to prevent her getting away. But Konstanze refused to answer any questions about Wagner, or her own lethal activities. With Prince

Albert's approval, Jäger was being transferred to a location outside of Paris for closer interrogation by a select group at the Deuxième Bureau with Scotland Yard observers. Agents of the French Bureau were pursuing Wagner en route to Cairo. The young Khedive Abbas II of Egypt was firmly, even violently anti-British, thus the situation had to be very carefully handled.

There was ample evidence to charge Jäger with the attempted assassination of the Prince of Wales, a trial that, V.B. had assured her, would bring out the anarchists and other protesters who wanted to eliminate royalty entirely, using any method that worked. Their issue would be that Konstanze Jäger had failed.

Bethell doubted that a trial would ever happen.

She looked up from observing the last minute scurrying activity below her on the pier as a white-jacketed steward approached.

"Miss Piddington? I have a cablegram for you. It arrived about an hour ago, but you were not in your stateroom. If there is a reply, please come to the telegraph office. We will be able to send it for at least another three hours if the present weather holds." He touched the stiff black bill of his cap and left.

Kyame tore the envelope open. Tears began to flow. She couldn't stop. There could be no answer.

Kyame:

Our dear friend J.W. died of pneumonia three days ago. He looked forward to your return. Let us celebrate the joy of his humanity when you arrive. Mar-Tan

Momentarily touching her blouse where the crystal *bi* disc would have been, that amazing gift from J. W., Kyame realized she was now alone, that there was no one left from her early years still alive who could truly understand her life and experiences, who knew who she really was, sometimes better than she had known herself.

As she was finally able to wipe away her tears, Kyame understood that now there would be only the promises of the future. As she turned away from the strengthening blasts of cold wind to return her stateroom, Kyame found she could smile, at least a little, as she thought of where she and André might next meet.

Maybe, Kyame hoped, pulling the door open with both hands against the cold winds, maybe -- maybe without anyone shooting at them.

The End

Appendix

Roulette Systems

"Perseverance, strong nerve, and the constitution of a dray-horse are absolutely necessary to success."

Lord James Rosslyn, on playing roulette systems.

1896

"There are no infallible roulette systems."

V.B.

1898

In 1909, the *Anglo-American Gazette* in Nice, France, ran a worldwide competition to identify the best roulette system. Each entrant was to commence with an imaginary capital of £100 and then was to play 7,500 coups, or spins of the wheel, using his/her system consistently. Though the capital was imaginary, the spins were on a real roulette wheel spun by a trained Monte Carlo croupier. Most entrants went broke long before 7,500 coups were spun.

THE CHAMPION SYSTEM
OF THE WORLD

.. In 1909 ..

THE ANGLO-AMERICAN
GAZETTE

Organized a Competition for the

BEST ROULETTE
SYSTEM

The Contest was Open to the whole World and
secured a large Entry

The FIRST PRIZE was won by "V. B."
with a System showing a Profit of £592
on 7,500 Coups, commencing with a
Capital of only £100

THIS PRIZE SYSTEM CAN NOW BE OBTAINED FROM

THE ANGLO-AMERICAN
GAZETTE

15, AVENUE DE LA GARE, NICE

Send Fcs. 20, or Postal Order for 16s.

The winner was Victor Bethell, whose system after 7,500 coups led to a £592 profit from the original £100. Bethell's system was available for 20 Francs from the newspaper.

V.B. published two systems some years before the contest, one in 1898 and one in 1901, however, which specific system he used in the contest is no longer known. Either could have done the job. One system, the simplest, is

414

described below, where *Avant Dernier* is the system V.B. explained to Kyame Piddington.

Almost all operational roulette systems are based on even chance wagers, i.e., red-black, high-low, odd-even. Most are progressive, in that they attempt to recover lost capital by increasing subsequent stakes following a loss. The longer the sequence of losses continue, then progressively higher stakes are required to continue to play most of the systems, until, under the most negative conditions, the gambler's capital is exhausted. All systems are focused on defending the player's capital and moderating his losses.

No system, in itself, can guarantee success.

Most writers on roulette systems, including Victor Bethell, emphasize that gambling at roulette without a system ensures disaster, much sooner than later. With a system and with the discipline and capital to persevere, the gambler is always aware of his financial status and is not tempted to recklessly attempt to quickly recover losses.

However, different systems require different levels of starting capital, and some, to be absolutely avoided, ensure more rapid losses than others. And, the one somewhat banal element that undermines many systems is that they are tedious, given their repeated requirement for detailed calculations, even though, in the end, they may be safer.

But, regardless, no system can guarantee success.

Many roulette systems are also based on a myth. In 1903, in his incisive book, *Facts and Fallacies of Monte Carlo,* Sir Hiram Maxim, inventor of the machine gun, pointed out that the concept of "evening up", (assuming that the frequency of one color appearing must eventually equal the frequency of the other, the basic assumption of many systems), was a manifest fallacy. Regardless of the number of consecutive coups of, say red, the odds of black coming up on the next spin always remains the same, i.e., 50-50. The wheel has no memory of what came before, a point emphasized by Fyodor Dostoevsky in his 1867 novel of obsession, *The Gambler*: "The roulette wheel has no conscience and no memory."

Avant Dernier

In the basic system, the gambler backs the color that came up the coup previous to the last, betting one unit each coup. When four units have been won, i.e., four units net of any losses, the gambler quits for the day, whether he has won his objective in one hour or in eight hours.

For example, assume R, B, R had come up. The player would play B with his first stake, and then no matter what turned up; he would play R next. Always the second color prior, which ensured success if there was a long run of a single color (if for example there was a run of one color eight times, the gambler would win 6 of the 8 coups), or shorter runs of two or three in the right sequence. There

416

are two combinations of R/B that could undermine the system, which could occur in any day's play, and the player needs to quickly recognize them.

They are: runs of two consecutive colors in sequence, e.g., R, R, then B,B, then R,R, etc. where the system loses every bet made; and where the wheel runs three colors in sequence, e.g., R,R,R, B,B,B, etc. where the Bank would win two out of every three coups.

With the procedure set, a daily goal should be established which, when achieved, the gambler pockets his winnings and leaves the table, e.g., the gambler may set his goal to win four units a day, with the unit being, e.g., twenty euros; but he would always quit when those four units had been won. The gambler uses "flat stakes", which means he plays the same number of units each coup, thus eliminating tedious progressive calculations required by most systems.

If, however, the Bank wins ten coups from him before he has won one coup, the gambler would then increase the flat stakes to two units at each spin until all losses were recovered, then revert to one unit and continue. But, regardless of the run, the gambler *would always quit when his goal of four units were won*, whether in an hour or in a day. To make "exceptions" because it seemed the wheel was playing his way would be to invite ultimate disaster, a mistake that most system players make at some point.

V.B.'s first book, *Ten Days at Monte Carlo at the Bank's Expense,* 1898, is devoted to the experience of V.B. and a barrister friend using only the Avant Dernier system for ten days. Every day's play is recorded along with the decisions made at each key point. When not at the wheel, the two men bicycled around Monaco and Southern France describing the routes taken and the restaurants visited. The book has an onion skin map of all their biking trails. At the end of ten days all their expenses for the trip including travel expenses to and from Monaco had been covered leaving a profit of 1,350 francs to be divided between them. A very pleasant read about a world now long gone, and never to return.

One day, Victor Bethell asked an older lady he had seen regularly at the tables, if she had been winning. He was impressed with her answer. "No," she said; "I find that I never *win*; I only *borrow* from the Bank, and a precious high rate of interest they make me pay as a rule!"

For a brief overview of several roulette systems see, "Monte Carlo Systems: Myths and Promises", Barry H. Wiley, *History Magazine,* December/January, 2010.

For a more detailed examination of all the popular roulette systems, and certainly one of the most pleasant reads on the subject, V.B., *Monte Carlo Anecdotes and Systems,* 1901. The book is available on the internet. You will find his second system, "The Author's System", on page 78.

And, if you add up the numbers on a roulette table, they do add up to the ominous 666, a point used in many anti-gambling sermons in the late 19th century, especially those preached in Monaco.

***

Interest in roulette systems continued unabated even when in September, 1908, His Lordship, James St. Claire-Erskine Rosslyn, accepted the challenge of Sir Hiram Maxim, he of the machine gun, to prove the validity of Rosslyn's celebrated roulette system, a system that Rosslyn had recently publicly offered to sell for £25,000, but with no takers. When asked about Rosslyn's offer, Maxim had declared that no system including Rosslyn's could ensure success.

The contest was inaugurated in London at a Piccadilly club on September 20, 1908. The capital would be an imaginary $50,000 for each side, Maxim acting as the bank against Rosslyn's system. The wheel was spun by an experienced croupier. Rosslyn at one point was $16,000 ahead, but after ten days Rosslyn's capital had been reduced to zero. "Lord Rosslyn's system has been proved to be utterly fallacious," declared the New York *Times* on September 30, 1908.

A Note

On March 27, 1911, Ciro's in Galerie Charles III, Monaco, was sold to a British syndicate which promised to

419

open branches in London and New York. Ciro himself retired from business on May 1.

A final note:

The Honorable (Albert) Victor Bethell, the fourth son of Richard Augustus, 2nd Baron of Westbury, died at the age of 64 on July 20, 1927. His London *Times* obituary listed his interests as cycling, shooting, traveling, and bridge. In addition to his two popular books on roulette systems, V.B. wrote *Bridge Reflections, Containing Problems and Solutions and 'Maxims to be_remembered'*, published in 1908, 165 pages.

V.B. never married.

Writing in the *Times* three days following V.B.'s death, a friend, G.R., said, "He had his favorites in people as well as vintages, but he was a good judge of character and was tireless in his attempts to help those whom he liked … he was no believer in the discovery of an infallible roulette system, and would do his best to help the broken gambler who had experimented with too much faith."

Pi Ying Xi

The Shadow Play

Adventures in Second Sight

Volume 3

The third volume in the *Adventures in Second Sight* series will be set in 1897 with Kyame Piddington now 18. It continues the story of Kyame's remarkable life to San Francisco, Honolulu, Cairo, and finally to Tahiti, where Kyame must learn to walk on fire in order to confront 'Oro, the war god -- and a certain Frenchman re-enters her life.

Other Books by Barry H. Wiley

The Thought Reading Craze, McFarland, 2012. A non-fiction study of the intense search by scientists, academics and others to establish telepathy as a fact of human nature and perhaps the first scientific proof of life-after-death. The book also tells the story of the men, woman and, occasionally, children who so successfully hoaxed the scientists; as well as the parallel story of the creation of the one-man minding act one Monday morning in 1873 in a Chicago saloon. The stage performers used the scientists to gain public credit, while the scientists used the performers to maintain public interest. In the end, the performers gained and lost fortunes, while the scientists gained and lost reputations. Winner of the 2013 Christopher Literary Award.

The Thought Reader Craze is available on Amazon, Barnes & Noble and the McFarland website in both print and e-book formats.

The Indescribable Phenomenon: the life and mysteries of Anna Eva Fay, Hermetic Press, 2005. The biography of the woman whom, in 1909, magician Harry Houdini called, "the greatest female mystifier". In 1875 Annie was publicly acclaimed by scientists and psychical researchers in Great Britain as a genuine psychic, capable of exerting a "non-human force at a distance"; while in 1877, detective Allan Pinkerton called her, "… a woman possessing a terribly fascinating power and capable of any devilish human accomplishment."

Raised in conditions of near slavery in northeastern Ohio, five feet tall, blonde, blue-eyed, Annie Fay was the quintessential con woman. Though a fake, she became celebrated as one of the premier spirit mediums of her day; when the profits from her spirits began to fade, in 1894 Annie went on the vaudeville stage doing what she had been doing in the séance room. She stole the mindreading act of magician Samri S. Baldwin to fill out her act, and became celebrated as a greater showman than Houdini himself. Baldwin himself said publicly that she performed the act better than he did. When Anna Eva Fay died in 1927, she was eulogized in the New York *Times*. The biography was considered for a film by Walden Media, but the project never moved ahead. Available on Amazon, and from the publisher, Hermetic Press in Seattle, WA www.penquinmagic.com

A Spirit of Fraud. Set in 1876. A British occult Brotherhood under the apparent direction of the Archangel Uriel plans to seize defenseless America in the waning months of the Grant administration. Only the celebrated spirit medium, Annie Eva Fay, detects the threatening presence of Uriel's minions. Gaining the help of the Pinkertons, Annie moves to stop the Brotherhood. But Annie's spirits are all fake. Is the Archangel a fake as well? And will there be time enough for Annie to learn the truth? The novel was reviewed October, 2014, on *Kings River Life Magazine* (www.kingsriverlife.com) with a comparison to *The DaVinci Code*.

A Spirit of Fraud is available on Amazon, Kobo, Barnes & Noble, and Apple iBookstore.

Beyond The Tempest, a sorcerous tale of Bermuda. Bermuda. Pink sand, exotic beauty, mysterious history, a three billion dollar national debt, and a per capita murder rate twice that of New York even with the most draconian gun control law in the Western world: Ten years in prison without parole for possession of any gun, or any part of a gun. In *Beyond The Tempest,* the real Bermuda is a principal character in the novel, not simply a tourist backdrop.

Set in contemporary times, the novel tells the story of mentalist and former physicist, Kaarin Larsson, who is booked at the last minute into a venture capital conference in Bermuda to replace Tony DiMarco, celebrated memory expert who has been murdered twice, shot with a .32 and a .41 magnum at the same time in a deserted Bermuda cemetery. DiMarco's killers thus were risking hard time just holding the guns. But why two killers?

Kaarin is attacked by two killers her first night in Bermuda, one with the .41 and one with a knife. She knows no one in Bermuda – why her?

Together with Inspector Keith Haggard of the Bermuda Police Service, she searches for answers. Why are her friends Serreta and Sugar Alberts, magicians currently performing at the Pink Sands in Bermuda, also targeted?

But the constant underlying question that torments her nights, and her unguarded moments: is she human?

Note: Research for *Beyond The Tempest* included interviewing the Bermuda Commissioner of Police, which resulted in his assigning an officer to show Bermuda as the police see it -- a remarkably fascinating afternoon in paradise.

Beyond The Tempest is available on Amazon, Barnes & Noble, Kobo, and Apple iBookstore.

For more information on the stories and books of Barry H. Wiley visit his website at www.creatorofmysteriousstories.com. Follow his Author's Page and his blog "Plotting the Impossible" on Goodreads.

SHADOW OF THE TIGER

ADVENTURES IN SECOND SIGHT

www.ingramcontent.com/pod-product-compliance
Lightning Source LLC
Chambersburg PA
CBHW060806030726
47503CB00002B/362